Books by Jack McDevitt

Deepsix
Infinity Beach
Moonfall
Eternity Road
Ancient Shores

JACK McDEVITT

MOONFALL

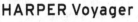

HARPER Voyager
An Imprint of HarperCollins*Publishers*

This is a work of fiction. Names, characters, places, and incidents are products of the author's imagination or are used fictitiously and are not to be construed as real. Any resemblance to actual events, locales, organizations, or persons, living or dead, is entirely coincidental.

HARPER Voyager

An Imprint of HarperCollins*Publishers*
10 East 53rd Street
New York, New York 10022-5299

First Harper Voyager mass market printing: September 2011
First Eos mass market printing: September 2000
First HarperPrism mass market printing: January 1999
First HarperPrism hardcover printing: April 1998

Harper Voyager and) are trademarks of HCP LLC.

Printed in the U.S.A.

22 23 24 25 26 LBC 15 14 13 12 11

For Fran and Brian Cole,
the Clearwater Desperadoes

ACKNOWLEDGMENTS

I am indebted for assistance, advice, and encouragement to: Franklin R. Chang-Díaz of the Lyndon B. Johnson Space Center; Ted Dunham and Bruce Koehn of the Lowell Observatory; Terry Gipson, St. Louis Science Center; Sergei Pershman, University of Pennsylvania; Eileen Ryan, Kitt Peak National Observatory; Jim Sharp, formerly of the Smithsonian Air & Space Museum; George Tindle, U.S. Customs Service; and Judith A. Tyner, California State University, Long Beach.

The manuscript also profited from the guidance of Fred Espenak of NASA Goddard, both directly and from his excellent book, *Fifty Year Canon of Solar Eclipses: 1986–2035* (Sky Publishing Corp., Cambridge, MA, 1988). Thanks to Ben Bova for permission to use his version of Moonbase, the details of which were derived particularly from *Welcome to Moonbase* (Ballantine Books, 1987).

Geoff Chester of the U.S. Naval Observatory and science fiction writer Walt Cuirle of the Isaac Asimov Seminar were subjected to constant harassment during the production of this book. They bore up patiently and both are, I believe, still talking to me.

Maureen McDevitt helped the manuscript through several incarnations, and Caitlin Blasdell provided her usual good judgment at HarperPrism. Thanks also to Dolores Dwyer for editorial assistance.

Ron Peiffer assisted with the Coast Guard segments, and Lewis Shiner brought the duct tape.

MOONFALL

Far better is it to dare mighty things, to win glorious triumphs, even though checkered by failure, than to take rank with those poor spirits who neither enjoy much nor suffer much, because they live in the gray twilight that knows not victory nor defeat.

—Theodore Roosevelt

Chapter One

TOTALITY
Monday, April 8, 2024

1.

Cruise Liner *Merrivale*, eastern Pacific.
5:21 A.M. Zone (9:21 A.M. EDT)

The *Merrivale* was bound for Honolulu, four days out of Los Angeles, when the eclipse began. Few of the passengers got up to watch the event. But Horace Brickmann, who'd paid a lot of money for this cruise, wanted Amy to understand he was a man with broad scientific and artistic interests. *Yes,* he'd told her last night while they stood near the lifeboats and listened to the steady thrum of the ship's engines and watched the bow wave roll out into the dark, *total solar eclipse. Wouldn't miss it. To be honest, it's why I came.* And when she'd pointed out that the eclipse would also be visible across much of the United States, he'd added smoothly that it wasn't quite the same.

She'd hinted she'd also like to see the event. Amy had been beautiful in the starlight, and his heart had pumped ferociously, bringing back memories of his twenties, which he recalled as a time of romance and passion. It was Horace's impression *he'd* terminated the various relationships of his youth, much to the despair of the women; that in those early days he had not been ready for serious commitment. But still there were times he woke in the night regretting one or another of his lost paramours. He wondered occasionally where they were now and how they were doing.

It was an odd sort of dawn, Sun and Moon clasped together in a cold gray embrace. The ocean had grown rough and Horace sat in his chair sipping hot coffee, wondering what was keeping Amy. He tugged his woolen sweater down over his belly and reminded himself that it was dangerous to look directly at the spectacle. Most of the other early risers had brought blankets, but Horace wanted to cut a dashing figure and the blanket just didn't fit the image.

To his consternation, a voluble banker whom he'd met the previous day appeared before him, greeted him with the kind of cheeriness that's always irritating early in the morning, and sat down in an adjoining deck chair. "Marvelous experience, this," said the banker, lifting his eyes in the general direction of the eclipse while extracting a folded copy of the *Wall Street Journal* from a pocket of his nautical blue blazer. He tried to read the paper in the gray light but gave up and dropped it on his lap.

He began to chatter about commodities and convertibles and price-earnings ratios. Horace's eyes swept the near-empty decks. A middle-aged man at the rail was watching the eclipse through sunglasses. A steward strolled casually over and offered him one of the viewing devices the ship had been distributing. Horace was too far away to hear the conversation, but he saw the man's annoyed expression. Nevertheless, he accepted the viewer, waited until the steward had turned away, dropped it into a pocket, and went back to gazing at the Sun. The banker babbled on, fearful that the Fed would raise the prime rate again.

The wind was beginning to pick up.

The steward approached Horace and the banker, holding out the devices. "You don't want to look directly at it, gentlemen," he said. Horace took one. It consisted of a blue plastic tube about six inches wide, with a tinfoil disk attached to one end. "Point it toward the eclipse, sir," said the steward, "and it'll project the Sun's image onto the disk. You'll be able to watch in perfect safety." The tube was decorated with the ship's profile and name. Horace thanked him.

She was now twenty minutes late. But Amy had an eight-year-old daughter to take care of, so there was a degree of unpredictability in any rendezvous.

He became aware suddenly that the banker had asked a question. "I'm sorry," Horace said. "My mind was elsewhere."

"No problem, partner." The man was finishing up with middle age. He was oversized and prosperous-looking. His hair was shoe-polish black, and the deck chair complained whenever he shifted weight. "I know just what you mean."

A deep dusk had settled over the ship. The banker cleared his throat and essayed a quick look at his watch. He had to raise his arm, so that the face of the instrument caught a reflection from a porthole. It seemed almost as if by consulting the time he was exercising control over the event. The last of the gray light drained from the sky and the corona blazed out, pale and somber. Horace heard awed conversation and drawing in of breath.

The stars emerged, and the ocean was swallowed up in the dark.

"Wonderful thing, nature," said the banker. "Beautiful."

Horace mumbled an appropriate response.

Over the course of an hour or so, the event concluded, the eclipse passed, and the banker went in to breakfast. Amy didn't show up, and the *Merrivale* plowed through a sea that remained gray and unsettled.

Horace stayed in his chair a long time. A damp chill had stolen over him. Later, wandering the decks, he saw Amy and her daughter at a dining table with several others. She was deep in animated conversation with a man Horace had seen going off the high-dive yesterday. He lingered for a moment but she never looked up.

It was as if the shadow that fell across the ship had touched the heart of the world.

●   ●   ●

Space Station L1, *Percival Lowell* Flight Deck. 8:03 A.M.

There was never a time we didn't know that the canals were bunk, that Percival Lowell's network of interconnecting lines, and the areas that darkened in the summer as the water flowed, were just so much self-delusion. Adams and Dunham, in 1933, before I was born, showed that Martian oxygen was less than one-tenth of a percent of the terrestrial level. That should have been enough. But people still hoped, even as late as when I was in high school during the sixties. Until Mariner 4 sent back those godawful pictures just after Thanksgiving 1964 and we knew we were looking at the end.

Rachel Quinn's grandfather had wanted to be an astronomer, but he went to the wrong college because it was local and it didn't cost much. He had to take what they offered and somehow he ended up as an accountant. But he owned a marvelous telescope, one through which Rachel had seen Jupiter's moons and the demon star Algol and the Great Comet of 2011. And she too had thought what a pity it was that Mars had no canals.

The thought was in her mind a lot these days as they prepared for launch. How different this mission might have been, had there been someone at the other end. *Welcome, people of Earth.* Well, Mars has some primitive biological forms, but nothing that would take note of her arrival.

She wondered why the drive to find other beings among the lights in the sky was so strong. It was, in fact, so deeply ingrained that no one ever seemed to make the point that we'd be far safer if we were alone.

Launch was twenty-two days away. Sunlight blazed through the windows and gleamed off *Lowell's* silver prow. They were at the Lagrange One station, popularly known as L1, suspended between Earth and Moon, fifty-eight thousand kilometers above the lunar surface. And they were ready to go. The ship's nuclear power plant had been tested in the Mojave Desert and in lunar orbit; its navigational systems were already locked on Mars; its survey gear was loaded; spare parts were on board; and the video library was in place. One of the technicians had programmed its control circuit to ask Rachel each morning a variant of the question, "Is it time yet?"

NASA had invited schoolchildren around the world to name the nuclear-powered vessel that was going to Mars. The winner would receive a trip out to L1 to get photographed with the six astronauts and to watch the launch. Hundreds of thousands of suggestions had poured in, names in all the languages of Earth. An army of secretaries and junior assistants and interns had culled through the deluge, relaying those that seemed to have originality and flavor to a panel of judges. There'd been rumors of animosity and deadlock, and one judge did in fact resign, but the panel eventually emerged with its choice: the *Percival Lowell.*

There was irony in calling the Mars vessel after a man who had been both monumentally wrong, and persistent in that error until his death. *But he had dreamed,* the winner said, *for all of us. Without him, we would not have had Barsoom or the Chronicles. The irresistible ache that carries us outward was born with* Percival Lowell. That was the phrase that stuck in Rachel's mind. She didn't agree with it, but you could make a plausible argument for it.

The child was Chinese, a high school senior from Canton, who was scheduled to arrive in two weeks with the rest of the crew. So far, other than herself, only geologist/flight engineer Lee Cochran was aboard.

Rachel didn't much care what sort of name they stenciled on the hull as long as the ship was ready to go. And for the first time in her experience with government projects, everything seemed set with time to spare.

The *Lowell* consisted of a long central stem, with flight deck and crew areas forward and the nuclear engine at the rear. Crew areas, but not the flight deck, could be rotated to simulate .07 g. It wasn't enough to make the trip comfortable, but it approached the effect generated on the station itself, and was almost half lunar gravity. A lander was tucked under the belly of the craft. Sensor dishes, telescopes, feeder ports, and antennas projected from the hull.

The engines were powered by a Variable Specific Impulse Plasma drive. The system, electrodeless, electrothermal, radio-frequency heated, and magnetically vectored, had been designed during the late 1990s, but not actively developed until President Culpepper took the decision to push for a Mars mission as the natural second step after the establishment of Moonbase.

Years ago Rachel had flown a prototype moonbus on powdered aluminum and liquid oxygen. Now she sat atop a nuclear monster that would take her across the interplanetary void.

It was a nice feeling.

The hatch to the flight deck opened and Lee poked his head in. "Hello, Rache. What are you doing *here*?"

She was seated in the pilot's chair. The day's simulations were over and she felt almost guilty, as if she'd been caught playing solitaire with the computer. "Smelling the roses," she said. It seemed now that her entire life had been directed toward this moment, had been intended to get her into this seat. And she was making it a point to savor the success. She'd wanted it when she was ten years old, peeking through Grandpop's telescope. It had been in the back of her mind when she went to flight school, when she was flying patrols over Zagreb, and when she'd begun piloting the buses between the lunar installations and L1. When Culpepper announced nine years ago that the nation would go to Mars, Rachel Quinn had fired off an application before the speech ended. "Where should I be?" she asked Lee.

"It's Monday. Director's breakfast."

She'd forgotten. Yesterday she had lunch with the vice president, who'd been passing through to do the honors at the Moonbase ribbon-cutting ceremony this afternoon. Today it was to have been bacon and eggs with the station director. Tomorrow it would be another lunch, this time with a Chinese delegation of diplomats and industrialists. It seemed as if the most time-consuming part of her job was rubbing shoulders with every VIP who arrived on L1. And with the Mars flight imminent, and Moonbase officially opening today, there'd been a horde of heavyweights.

Lee frowned. "Another faux pas for the NASA team."

Rachel shrugged, trying to suggest she had more important things to do. But in fact they were well ahead of schedule.

Most of the *Lowell* jutted outside the station. Only the forward sphere, which contained the flight deck, was enclosed within a pressurized bay. She looked down at a single technician switching umbilicals. "I'm ready to go, Lee," she said.

So was the ship. It was now only a matter of briefings and politics.

Lee sat down in the copilot's seat. An image of Mars, wide and bleak and rust-colored, floated in the overhead display. "It'll come soon enough," he said. "Meantime, I think you ought to get yourself over to the breakfast. You're the star of the show these days, and it wouldn't look real good if you ignored the director."

Rachel frowned. "I hate the politics involved with these things." Actually, she didn't. Not all of it, anyhow. She'd enjoyed meeting the vice president yesterday. But it was part of the astronaut code that all groundhuggers, even vice presidents, were comparative unfortunates. Members of an inferior species.

"What the hell, Rache, grow up." He grinned. Major Lee Cochran was tall and easygoing, with animated good looks and hair that consistently fell into his eyes. "Half the job is politics and public relations. Who do you think pays for this toy?" He was the media darling of the crew. Still in his thirties, he'd shown up last month on somebody-or-other's list of ten most eligible bachelors. Unlike Rachel and the others, he had a talent for delivering quotable lines. He was a twin kill, two for the price of one, an astronaut flight engineer who was also a world-class geologist. Cochran would eventually use the lasers and sample collectors to get at the heart of Mars, to begin putting together, finally, a definitive history of the planet. Still, though no one would admit it, it wasn't his technical skill that had gotten him the assignment, but his ability to relate to the media. *He says the right thing,* the mission director had told her. *Talk to him before you go down the ladder. Get his input. Listen to Lee and there'll be no more of that "giant leap for mankind" crap.*

Yeah. Rachel had pretended her feelings were hurt, but the man was right. As was Lee now. If they didn't want to repeat the Apollo scenario, make a couple of trips to Mars and say good-bye, they needed to take the PR seriously.

Moonbase Spaceport. 8:11 A.M.

When Vice President Charles L. Haskell stepped out of the microbus onto the passenger walkway, he became simultaneously the highest-ranking U.S. government executive ever to set foot on the Moon, and an overgrown ten-year-old kid. His heart hammered and he very deliberately placed his foot on the exit ramp that led directly through a tube into the passenger lounge. He thought, *Yes, this is it, I'm really here.* He took a deep breath, recalling the dinosaurs and model starships that had once filled his life. He passed an innocuous remark to Rick Hailey to hide his feelings, and accepted the handshakes of the Moonbase officials waiting to greet him.

Despite all the travel, he felt fresh. It helped that the two space stations and Moonbase operated on EDT, the eastern

U.S. time zone, corresponding with the time zone in which both the Lunar Transport Authority and Moonbase International maintained their corporate headquarters.

Officially, Moonbase did not yet exist. It had been up and functioning in one form or another for seven years, or maybe eight, depending on where you wanted to begin counting. But today it would be formally declared operational. That was why Charlie Haskell had come to the Moon.

Journalists were waiting as he emerged into the passenger lounge. They recorded his handshakes with Evelyn Hampton, the chief executive officer of Moonbase International; shouted a few election questions; and wondered why the president hadn't come. Was it because the president wasn't running for a second term and wanted to give Charlie a leg up on other potential nominees?

Charlie pointed out that no head of state was present, that Moonbase was a commercial venture, and that he was on hand because it might be his last chance to get free transportation to the Moon. (The latter remark was a reference to the fact that few expected Charlie to get his party's nomination during the summer.) "But," he added, adopting a serious tone, "the United States is the major stockholder in this venture, and space has always been the special preserve of the vice president. Goes all the way back to Lyndon Johnson."

The truth was that the president didn't like Charlie very much, that Charlie had been on the ticket four years before only because he could deliver New England. From Washington, Moonbase looked like an investment boondoggle, and Henry Kolladner had no wish to be associated with it, even if he had taken himself out of the running. "He knew how much this program meant to me," Charlie continued, bending the truth substantially, "so he asked me to represent him. I'm delighted to be here." He turned and beamed at Evelyn Hampton, who nodded modestly.

Behind the gaggle of reporters, a window looked out over the regolith. The land was flat and gray and flowed out to a very close horizon. *TR would have loved it,* he thought.

Teddy Roosevelt was Charlie's role model. Tough. Unbending when he thought he was right. Scrupulously honest. Fascinated by the world around him. What would the old Rough Rider not have given to have been able to gaze across that landscape?

Hampton showed him to his quarters while four Secret Service agents accompanied them. The agents were unhappy that they'd been unable to clear the regular occupants out of the area prior to Charlie's arrival. But there wasn't much space yet at Moonbase, and it simply wasn't possible to move out whole wings of people and put them somewhere else. Furthermore, Charlie had pointed out to the senior agent, they don't allow wackos on the Moon.

Evelyn Hampton was a startlingly attractive Senegalese who spoke precise English with a trace of an Oxford accent. She had luminous dark eyes and an imperious manner that left no doubt among her subordinates that she was in charge. "We're delighted you could come, Mr. Vice President," she told him, standing at the threshold to his quarters. "We hope your stay with us will be satisfactory." Her eyes momentarily seemed to promise something more. "Your people have my number," she said. "Please let me know if I can be of assistance."

"I will," Charlie said. He was a bachelor, and the one real regret he had about his political success was the media attention that made it so difficult to lead anything approaching a normal life.

She wore the formal version of a Moonbase uniform, white blouse, navy jacket, slacks, and neckerchief. A pocket bullion was stitched with her name and the Moonbase logo, the Armstrong Memorial. "We're having a celebratory luncheon after the ceremony," she said. "We hope you can fit it into your schedule."

"Of course," said Charlie. "I wouldn't miss it."

His apartment was located in Grissom Country, the section reserved for senior personnel and visiting VIPs. It was more spacious than Charlie had expected: He had two reasonably large rooms plus bath and kitchenette, with a desk, a compact conference table, a couple of occasional chairs, a bookcase (which someone had thoughtfully filled with current novels and histories), and a coffee table. One wall held a universal window through which he could see the lunar surface. Or, if he preferred, Tequendama Falls in Colombia, Mount Bromo in Indonesia, or the limestone hills of Kweilin. If he was feeling homesick, various views across Cape Cod were available. The push of a button brought a bed out of the wall.

Someone had thoughtfully left two Moonbase uniforms on his sofa, one dress uniform, one jumpsuit, and a jacket. The uniform would look good on camera, so he decided he'd wear it to the dedication.

Despite the fact that there was water ice on the Moon, its extraction was still expensive and difficult. Consequently, water was scarce. It was available, but a large sign invited him to substitute the ultrasonic scrubber for the shower. Moonbase personnel had a meager allotment to use as each one chose. Charlie knew that he could run as much water as he liked and no one would complain. But someone would unquestionably leak it to the media. He smiled at his own pun. He climbed out of his clothes, stepped into the stall, drew the curtain, and selected ULTRASONIC. The sensation was not at all unpleasant. A thousand tiny fingers poked and probed, loosening dirt and dried perspiration. He wiped down with a damp cloth.

Afterward he dressed, and accompanied by a staff assistant and his team of agents, went out sight-seeing. Main Plaza, the heart of Moonbase, would not be officially open until after the ceremony. But some of the shops were already doing business.

Main Plaza consisted of a vast dome approximately fifteen stories high and a half-mile long. A canyon five levels deep cut a zigzag through the center of the plaza, housing living quarters and work areas. The ground level was remarkably green: Lawns and parks and patches of forest rolled out in a slight uphill grade toward the perimeter.

Down the length of the structure, four massive columns supported the overhead. These were regularly spaced, two on either side of the administration building, which anchored the center of the plaza. Shops and restaurants were located in strategic areas, and an orchestral shell dominated one of the parks. Charlie gazed up at the roof, where luminescent panels produced a remarkably good approximation of sunlight.

The air was sweet and clean and smelled of spring. He strolled its walkways, rode the elevators and trams, got his picture taken by half the people at Moonbase, signed autographs, shook hands with everyone, and generally scared the devil out of his agents.

There was a lot more to see: the reservoir, the communication center, the space transportation office, the departments of management and technical services, the solar power assemblies, an automated solar cell factory, the research labs. He wanted to visit everything, but he wanted to do it at leisure.

He had some difficulty adjusting to the one-sixth g, even with the weighted boots supplied by his hosts. But he was pleased to see that his agents also fell over themselves periodically. The lone staff assistant, Rick Hailey, was the only one who seemed to adapt easily, a circumstance that irritated the agents. There was an old joke about a football game between the Secret Service and the White House staff: Ten minutes after the agents left the field, the staff scored.

But Rick, who was his campaign manager, seemed born to low gravity. He'd gotten around L1 as if he'd lived there all his life. Now he was showing the same agility on the Moon. When Charlie commented, Rick laughed it off. "Public relations means never having to touch ground," he said.

Then he recommended they cut the stroll short to sit down in a café and talk about the ribbon-cutting ceremony.

It was an election year, and consequently the political overtones of every act were intensified. Especially when you were behind. Charlie was not yet forty, too young to be taken seriously as presidential timber. His lack of a mate offended the family values people, who'd become a major force in American politics. Furthermore, he'd been given little of substance to do in the Kolladner administration, and the president had not always hidden his own preference for "older, wiser heads."

"After you're finished with your remarks," Rick said earnestly, "the media people are going to want to talk politics. Don't get sucked into it. Moonbase is a special place. Above politics. Talk about the stars, Charlie. Where we're going. Opening up the future. That sort of thing. Everything else is trivial."

There was this about Rick: He was the only purely political appointment Charlie had ever made who was worth a damn. His full name was Richard Daley Hailey and he was the son of a particularly well connected Chicago alderman. He'd started as a speechwriter back in Illinois, had developed a natural talent for orchestrating campaigns, and was credited with the uphill victory of Mike Crest in the last Illinois gubernatorial.

He knew what made Charlie look good, what the voters wanted, what the hot-button issues were. (Voters always assume that politicians simply avoid talking about things that are important. Sometimes that's true. But more often, the pols just don't know themselves. In the rarefied air of the nation's capital, it's often hard to figure out what drives people who have to make trips to supermarkets.)

While they talked, sipping coffee and munching moon-cakes (yeast disguised as chocolate baked goods), Charlie glanced up at a wallscreen. An exotic forest moved beneath the camera eye. A ringed planet floated in the background, and a river sparkled in blue-tinged light as it vanished into thick purple trees. "You're right, Rick," he said. "Absolutely. Place like this, politics just looks ugly."

Rick stared at him across the lip of his cup. "But you have to remember, it's all bullcrap," the campaign manager said. "The action's downstairs, in D.C. Always will be, during our lifetimes, and that's all that counts. But I think if we handle this right we can take a long step toward securing the nomination." He finished off the last of his cake. "This isn't bad," he said.

It wasn't. The cake was very close to real chocolate.

Charlie looked back up at the screen. The camera eye had raced out over open water, and a second world, silver and misty, was rising out of the sea. And it wasn't bullcrap. Of all the places Charlie had visited in an extraordinarily well traveled life, none had ever struck him with the sheer emotional force that had come with looking down out of the shuttle at the cluster of brave lights blinking near the center of Alphonsus Crater, the home of Moonbase. Some had come here and described a religious experience, a sense of the power and majesty of the creator. Charlie had felt instead uncompromising neutrality, timelessness, an infinite indifference to everything human. It was a place for which he was not psychologically designed. The rock-hard void, the absence of living things, the extreme temperatures, drove home the fact that he was an interloper.

This plain had looked the same when the first protozoans began swimming in terrestrial oceans. It was bathed in the soft light of the unmoving home world. There had been a time when one could have stood on the regolith and seen that same world in that same place in the sky, the land masses all crowded together in a single supercontinent. He remembered having read the name of the supercontinent once, but he couldn't remember what it was. *Godwannaland.* Something like that.

He would never have come here on his own initiative. He'd seen all the visuals, artists' impressions, holograms, and the rest of it. He thought he understood how it would be. How it would feel. The ten-year-old Charlie who'd collected dinosaurs and built model starships had gotten lost somewhere. But he'd come back with a vengeance, and now the vice president absorbed the moonscape, took it into his soul, and understood he was living through an experience he would remember all his life.

He'd read extensively about the Moon in preparation for this trip, hoping to find something to insert in the remarks that his campaign manager would prepare. Rick got nervous when Charlie did that. He was heavily armed with examples of well-meaning public servants whose presidential ambitions had foundered on the rocks of an impromptu comment. Still, Rick was only a political advisor. A hired gun. Trained to weigh everything against polls, public reaction, party ramifications. Like most of the other hired guns, he was decent enough, and would be honest with whoever happened to be paying him; but his perspective was limited to thinking about what was needed to win elections. Nothing else mattered.

Teddy Roosevelt would not have liked it.

The decision to establish a permanent presence on the Moon had been championed almost a dozen years ago by President Andrew Y. Culpepper, who convinced the taxpayers, united the industrial nations behind the effort, and sold the idea to a reluctant Congress. *There are those,* he'd said, *who would tell us that we can't afford to establish a permanent presence on the Moon. They are the descendants of Isabella's advisors, who thought Europe could not afford to open up the Atlantic.* Those words were engraved on a plaque mounted in the center of Main Plaza.

Culpepper had not lived to see his dream realized. But today the shadow of a total eclipse was moving across North America. And when the shadow reached Culpepper's small Ohio hometown, at about twelve-thirty eastern daylight time (which was also Moonbase time), Charlie would cut the symbolic ribbon at the front door of Main Plaza and declare Moonbase operational.

Growth had been slow at first. But interest in lunar manufacturing capabilities was on the rise, and the Lunar Transport Authority was up and running. As accommodations became available, people and laboratories were moved out of temporary shelters and installed within the permanent facility. The base consisted of the central complex of administrative and residence areas, several scattered research sites, and mining and industrial operations concentrated for the most part near Alphonsus. An extensive system of electric-powered cable cars, called trolleys, would eventually connect the various units. There were even plans to construct a trolley link with the automated observatory on Farside.

The Moonbase flight terminal, the Spaceport, was located on the floor of Alphonsus just outside Main Plaza, accessible via trams.

Charlie planned to spend two days touring the facility and establishing in the world's eyes the American interest in and support for the lunar enterprise. There'd be a round of luncheons and celebrations. Dignitaries were here from around the world, and on the whole, the vice president looked forward to the experience.

Wednesday afternoon he'd board a bus for L1, catch the ferry to Skyport, the earth-orbiting space station; and then take the SSTO space plane into Reagan. If all went well, he'd arrive home with plenty of momentum going into the late spring primaries.

2.

Mexico. 6:43 A.M. Mountain Daylight Time (8:43 A.M. EDT)

The path of totality, moving generally northeast, glided ashore at Mazatlán. Six minutes later the skies darkened over Durango. Strollers in the *zócalo* paused and glanced up. Lights came on in the shopping district.

At about the same time, the shadow of the Moon reached the continental divide. Birds along the shores of Laguna del Llano grew quiet. It swept over the Sierra Madres and the wide semi-arid plains, and while late risers were having breakfast, crossed into Texas. Traffic was heavy, as always, at the Piedras Negras and Eagle Pass border stations; but even here, among the banging of trunks and the roar of tractor-trailers, there was a brief pause, a momentary stillness.

It passed between San Antonio on the east and Lubbock on the west. Early arrivals for the Rangers' home opener against the A's watched the parking lot darken. It was moving more slowly now than it had been when the passengers of the *Merrivale* first observed it.

Teachers in Fort Smith, Arkansas, took classes outside so their students could experience the gathering dark. In the Batesville Regional School, a visiting astronomer from the Delmor Planetarium in Little Rock explained to an auditorium of third- and fourth-graders how eclipses happen, why people used to be afraid of them, and why they should never look directly at the Sun.

At thirty-seven thousand feet over Springfield, Missouri, the shadow overtook a specially modified Lockheed C-311 cargo jet, which was running northeast on a parallel course. The jet housed a sixty-inch telescope and associated equipment, a team of six astronomers, and a three-person flying crew. The telescope was mounted in a shock-absorbing cradle just forward of the left wing, and was equipped with gyros and sensors to keep it locked on target. It was cold in the plane, and the jet engines were very loud, far too loud to permit casual conversation. The astronomers needed headphones and microphones to talk with one another. They wore heavy woolen sweaters beneath down jackets. The team had begun their work as soon as the lunar disk bit into the Sun. But the period of totality was especially precious. The aircraft, trying to keep up with the racing umbra, would give them an extra minute or so. The mission was sponsored by NASA Goddard. It had a multitude of tasks, collecting data to help explain anomalies of the inner corona, conducting multi-wavelength studies, comparing active features on the solar surface, hoping to establish correlations with coronal gas velocities. And a dozen or so others.

They had almost six minutes of totality. Then the darkness left them behind, passed through the Mark Twain National Forest, and closed on St. Louis.

In Valley Park, a pleasant suburb with picket fences and shady lawns, Tomiko Harrington was using her keyboard to activate the imaging disk in her electronic Magenta 764XX reflector, which was temporarily mounted on the deck outside her observatory over the garage. Tomiko was a systems designer for the Capital Bank and Trust Company of St. Louis. She was also an amateur astronomer and had called in sick that day.

The morning was clear and crisp, perfect for an eclipse. There'd been predictions of storm fronts and overcast skies, but none had materialized. Tomiko's passion for astronomy had been ignited by another Missouri solar eclipse, seven years earlier. That had happened August 21, on her eighteenth birthday, and the event had seemed like a sign, an invitation from the cosmos to get beyond the parties and the frivolity and put some meaning into her life. It was an invitation she'd accepted. Tomiko was now a member of the University Astronomy Club, she had written a couple of scripts for the planetarium in Forest Park, and she was about to collect her master's from SLU. Today she'd get a complete visual record of the period of totality.

When a friend had asked why, she hadn't quite known how to answer. "Just to have," she'd said finally, knowing that at least one of the images would be mounted and framed on her brag wall, taking its place among her stunning color photos of the Pleiades, the Crab Nebula, Mars and Deimos, the gorgeous M31 whirlpool, the 2019 Hercules supernova, and her personal observatory.

She relaxed in the love seat with a Coke, facing four video displays, three of which depicted the dark lunar rim closing over the last of the light. One screen, mounted on her desk, carried the feed coming from her own telescope, a small clock in the lower right-hand corner ticking off the last minutes to totality. The other two were commercial programs. She'd turned off the sound on these, not wishing to allow a newscaster's commentary to spoil the moment. The fourth monitor provided a map of the eclipse's path through the Northern Hemisphere.

She finished her Coke and put it down on a side table. The sky was getting dark, and she shuddered with pleasure. A passing car switched on its headlamps.

When her father was alive, the rooms over the garage had been rented, usually to students at the Bible college. But Tomiko had no real need of funds, and the old apartment was situated far from streetlights, which made it ideal for use as an observatory. In addition, it was surrounded by a wide deck on which she could install mounts for her telescopes. When two students had broken their lease and run off in the middle of the night, owing her two months' rent, she'd been almost grateful. She'd taken it over, renovated it, installed computers and two reflectors and imaging equipment. She'd promised herself that if the big money ever came in, she'd remove the roof and make a real observatory out of the place.

Her lawn sprinkler snapped on.

Tomiko was diminutuve, amiable, self-assured. She wore dark green slacks and a yellow blouse open at the throat. Her black hair was combed forward, almost concealing her left eye, in the fashion of the time. She had her father's penetrating gaze, but lacked the epicanthic fold of the Japanese ancestors on her mother's side. At times like this, when she was deeply engaged in her hobby, she wore a mildly distracted look. An observer would have concluded she was far away from the garage apartment.

A cool wind shook the trees. Somewhere a phone was ringing.

Now night came. The sky filled with stars. She felt utterly alone in the world.

The darkened Sun was in Pisces. She could see the Great Square of Pegasus just above the drugstore, Aldebaran up over Doc Edwards's house, Deneb at the top of the elm, and Betelgeuse down near the intersection. Jupiter, white and brilliant, was east of the Sun; and Venus, west.

Even Mercury was visible, riding its lonely arc.

She went out onto the deck and sat down in one of her wicker chairs, crossed her arms on the guard railing, and rested her chin on the back of her left hand. Lights came on in Conroy's kitchen.

A few degrees south of the Sun, just on the edge of the corona where the glare faded into night, Tomiko noticed a bright star.

What *was* that?

She measured it with her eye against the surrounding constellations, frowned, and hurried inside to her computer. She logged into the USL Celestik program, and brought up a star diagram.

• • •

Moonbase, Grissom Country. 11:10 A.M.

Rick Hailey appraised Charlie's outfit, grinned at the Moonbase patch, and shook his head. "No," he said. "Don't do it."

"Why not?" Charlie thought it would be ideal for the situation.

"Because politicians who try to look like something they aren't inevitably come off looking dumb. You're too young to remember Michael Dukakis and his tank. But how about Bill Worthy?" Worthy had been knocked out of his party's nomination by Andrew Culpepper, then a relative unknown, after he'd tried on an astronaut's uniform for the cameras. He'd succeeded only in convincing the electorate he was frail and near death.

Charlie sighed. "Yeah," he said.

"I mean, I can see the editorial cartoons now. They'll send you to Mars."

It was annoying. He looked so good in this outfit.

"This is your day, Charlie," Rick said. "This afternoon we'll be creating our campaign theme. *The future belongs to Haskell*." He drank off a glass of moon rum, which was nonalcoholic.

"I'm a little uncomfortable about this," said Charlie. "I keep thinking the president should be here. Or maybe it's the low gravity." He grinned uncertainly.

"You'll do fine. Like you always do." Rick's voice dropped an octave. "Don't forget God," he said.

Charlie sighed.

"It's important. Out here, people expect you to notice creation. The blue Earth. The stars. The sense of human insignificance." He stopped and thought about it. "No," he continued, "not *human* insignificance. *Your* insignificance. Right? We don't want the voters to get the idea you think *they're* insignificant."

"I know."

Sometimes Charlie thought of his ascent to the vice presidency as some sort of cosmic joke. He couldn't recall having set out to become a politician. It was something that had just happened to him. He'd been running a small electronics business in Amherst twelve years ago when a dustup began over school prayer, evolution, creation science, and *The Catcher in the Rye*. Charlie, who'd thought those battles fought and won during the last century, had shown up at a school board meeting where he'd intended only to lend visible support to the English and science departments. But he'd been outraged by a tall, dark-haired, brimstone-eyed preacher who'd informed the board what their duties were, and left no doubt he was speaking for a higher power. The preacher had brought his congregation, one of whom was waving a sign with the number 649 on it, supposedly the number of obscenities in *Catcher*. Unable to contain himself, Charlie had taken on the preacher.

In hindsight, he hadn't thought he'd done well. The preacher was louder and more practiced than he, but the small group of school supporters liked what they saw. They asked him to run in the fall election, and as Charlie saw it, next thing he knew he was vice president.

He looked at his watch. "Give me a minute to change," he said. "And then we better get started."

"Yeah. Listen, on second thought, wear the jacket. Okay? It'll help you bond with these people. But the uniform's too much."

Rick's value lay in what Charlie liked to think of as an ability to see around corners. If there was a booby trap ahead, he could be counted on to find it before it exploded.

Wearing only the jacket would be a halfway measure. A sign of weakness. When Charlie came out of the bedroom, he'd pulled on his own custom-made gray suit.

Rick frowned. "I don't know why you keep me on," he said.

•   •   •

Skyport, NASA/Smithsonian Orbital Laboratory. 12:13 P.M.

The Orbital Lab at the Earth satellite Skyport served as a worldwide clearinghouse for astronomical data. New variable pulsar analyses, fresh information on large-structure configurations, the latest findings on extra-solar terrestrial worlds supporting oxygen atmospheres—all were funneled into the Orbital Lab, collated, cross-indexed, relayed to interested consumers, and made available on the Web for the general public.

Tory Clark was watching the progress of the eclipse across North America on the overhead monitor while she looked through incoming reports. Although there was an enormous amount of activity connected with the event, nonrelated routine inputs did not slow down appreciably. She had, for example, a quasar update from Kitt Peak, a new report on R136a in the Large Magellanic, and corrections to the velocity measurements for the runaway star 53 Arietis. She also had something else.

"Windy?" She held up a hand to get the attention of her supervisor, Winfield Cross. "You want to take a look at this?"

Cross was in his fifties, medium size, medium build, medium everything. People tended to have a hard time remembering who he was, or what his name was. He was African-American, had grown up in south Los Angeles, gone to Princeton on a scholarship, and now seemed worried only by the possibility that his age would catch up to him before he achieved his one ambition. The automated observatory at Farside, the hidden side of the Moon, was going to be expanded and provided with a human staff. Windy hoped to get the director's job.

He held up one hand to signal that he understood, finished writing on a clipboard, and turned to his own screen. She heard him inhale. "What is it? You check it yet?"

They were looking at Tomiko's splinter of light.

"Don't know."

"Sun-grazer, you think?"

"I guess. Can't imagine what else."

There was nothing new, of course, about sun-grazing comets. They approached from the far side of the Sun and returned the same way. Consequently, they were virtually impossible to see from Earth, unless they happened to show up during a total eclipse, as this one had.

Windy's fingertips drummed on the computer table. "Who've we got?"

Tory was ready for the question. "Feinberg's at Beaver Meadow for the show." She was referring to the eclipse.

"*Feinberg.* Well, no point monkeying with the small fry. Okay, try to get him and ask him to take a look."

Moonbase, Ranger Auditorium. 12:17 P.M.

The place was named for the only ship lost during the second wave of lunar exploration. The second vessel to go back to the Moon after more than thirty years, the *Ranger* had been less than forty minutes from reentry when a fuel line blew. The explosion damaged the navigational guidance system and forced Frank Bellwether, its skipper, to try an eyeball insertion, a seat-of-the-pants reentry. But the procedure was exceedingly difficult, and he'd misjudged the approach, had come in at too wide an angle. *Ranger* had skimmed off the atmosphere, and without enough fuel to return, had drifted into solar orbit. It had been the most traumatic incident of the age of space exploration, far more painful than the *Challenger* loss, because Bellwether and his crew were able to communicate for several days afterward, until their air supply ran out.

A plaque commemorating the captain was mounted in the auditorium. In addition, the five ferries that carried passengers between L1 and Skyport were named for the individual crewmembers.

When Charlie entered, a wallscreen was keeping track of

the scene in Clifton, Ohio, where the high school band was lined up on the stage of a gymnasium. Concurrently with the lunar ceremony, the institution was being renamed the Andrew Y. Culpepper Memorial High School. The gym was crowded with students, and the band was playing an old tune, "Moon Over Miami." Well, it wasn't Miami, but Charlie imagined nobody cared about details. At Moonbase, some six hundred people, constituting visitors and virtually the entire population of the station not then on duty, had crowded into the auditorium.

Evelyn Hampton's technicians had erected a temporary platform and set out a row of chairs across it. A pair of double doors off to one side led out into Main Plaza, and a wide silver ribbon had been draped across these. The double doors were being treated symbolically on this occasion as the front entrance to Moonbase. The platform was decked with white, green, and blue bunting, the colors of Moonbase International. Flags of all (or almost all) the world's nations were mounted on the walls. A range of VIPs from international commerce, various governments, and the entertainment and academic worlds were seated on the platform. Prominent among these was Slade Elliott, known to millions of TV viewers as Captain Pierce on the immensely popular *Arcturus Run*. A recent poll had shown that Elliott had better name recognition than the president of the United States.

Evelyn saw Charlie and joined him. "Well, Mr. Vice President," she asked congenially. "Are you ready to do the honors? This is an historic moment. What you say here today, people will be quoting a thousand years from now."

"Thanks," said Charlie. "I really needed a little more pressure." He glanced toward the pool of journalists, many of whom he recognized. Rick had insisted that there was no more important skill for a politician than to remember the first names of the reporters. It was a habit Charlie had taken time to acquire. "Where are the TV cameras?" he asked.

She pointed to the far end of the auditorium, where a cluster of black lenses jutted out of the rear wall. Other cameras were concealed on either side of the platform.

Evelyn introduced him to the other guests, and Charlie was surprised when Elliott asked him to autograph a program.

Then it was time to proceed. His seat was located immediately to the right of the lectern, the place of honor secured by the fact that the U.S. government was Moonbase International's biggest shareholder. An attractive young woman in a Moonbase jumpsuit caught Evelyn's eye and held up both hands twice, fingers spread, signifying twenty seconds. Evelyn went to the lectern. The crowd grew quiet.

A display suspended from the ceiling acted as a monitor, and she glanced up to check her appearance. *She looked pretty good for a CEO,* Charlie thought.

A red lamp blinked on at the far end of the auditorium, which meant they were using the rear camera. The young woman did a silent countdown, and when she reached zero, Evelyn leaned forward and welcomed everyone, the entire world, to Moonbase. "Before we go any farther," she said, "I'd like to introduce our nondenominational chaplain, the Reverend Mark Pinnacle."

Pinnacle looked frail and ill at ease. He came forward clutching a sheet of paper, thanked Evelyn, put the paper on the lectern, and in a shaky voice began to read. He asked the blessings of the Almighty on this great effort and thanked him for past favors. One of the VIPs near Charlie whispered that if the chaplain hoped for results, he ought to speak up.

Pinnacle never got away from his monotone, but fortunately, he had the good sense to keep his remarks short. With obvious relief, he turned the program back to Evelyn.

She introduced several of the notables, each of whom spoke for a couple of minutes, with perhaps the most exhilarating moment coming when Slade Elliott strode to the microphone accompanied by the rousing strains of the theme from *Arcturus Run*. Slade contented himself with delivering a tag line from the show: "Borders exist only in the mind."

Charlie, the principal speaker, was of course last. His name was met with polite applause. "Thank you," he said. He glanced back at Elliott and then looked at the cameras. "I want to thank you for inviting me. This is an hour I'll never forget. And I suspect it's one the human race will never forget."

Two Secret Service agents were seated unobtrusively, in Moonbase jumpsuits, in the front row. Sam Anderson, who headed the unit, and his lone female agent, Isabel Heyman, watched the wings. Rick Hailey, on the aisle, studied him intently. He would be keeping score, of course.

"Moonbase is the future," continued Charlie. "We're taking our first tentative steps away from the home world, and you folks are showing the way." Rick nodded, urging him on.

Charlie looked into the cameras, speaking past the gathered "lunies," addressing himself rather to the voters back home, and maybe to the vast audience beyond American shores. "Moonbase is expensive. We've lost people to get here, and we'll lose others before we're done. We've spent a lot of our national treasure. And sometimes we wonder whether the investment is worth it. Why are we here at all?

"The simple truth is that the planet has become too small. Not for our populations, but for our dreams. We have a rendezvous with the stars. The seeds are already sown. They were sown when the first men and women looked up at the constellations. And they will come to flower in the fountains of the Moon.

"Today people still visit the site of the Apollo landing, where they can see Neil Armstrong's footprints." Charlie looked down at his audience and knew he had them. "Our distant descendants will visit Moonbase," he said, "or its equivalent in their age, and they will see the marks that we have made, you and I, and they will know that we too were here." He allowed his emotions to show. "We've come to believe that we have a cosmic heritage. We've come to the Moon. Within a few weeks, we'll launch the *Percival Lowell* for Mars.

"Slade Elliott and his alter ego, Captain Tobias Pierce, are absolutely correct: *Borders exist only in the mind.*"

He lifted his right hand to salute his audience, turned from the lectern, waited for Evelyn to join him, and started across the platform. A small ramp led to ground level. An aide appeared beside the beribboned door with a pair of golden shears.

Charlie reached the ramp but decided instead to leap from the platform, forgetting he was at one-sixth g. Despite the weighted boats, he would have sailed out into space and ended in the front seats had Evelyn not seen it coming. She grabbed his jacket and pulled him back.

"Careful," she whispered.

Charlie, grateful to have been saved from a clumsy fall in front of a couple of billion viewers, thanked her. "I owe you a drink," he said.

"At least," she smiled.

The guests flanked him and the aide gave the shears to Evelyn, who passed them to Charlie. Two others held the ribbon for him. "On this eighth day of April," he said, "in the two-thousand and twenty-fourth year of our era, and the two hundred and forty-eighth of the independence of the United States, in the name of the United Nations, I declare this facility, Moonbase, to be operational."

He cut the ribbon. An electric motor in the wall hummed and the doors opened. Beyond, Main Plaza lay in darkness. But a spotlight mounted atop the administration building blinked on, highlighting a park, a cluster of elms, some benches, and a pool. Then the overhead solar panels brightened, and daylight came to the parks and shops and restaurants and overhead walkways.

Applause began. At first it was restrained and polite. Almost perfunctory. But someone cheered, and it built and became a crescendo and went on and on and on.

NEWSNET. 12:30 P.M. UPDATE.
    (Click for details.)

BUDDHA'S BIRTHDAY CELEBRATED BY ADHERENTS WORLDWIDE

DID NASA CONSIDER ALL-WOMAN CREW FOR MARS?
    Leaked Report: Best Way To Ensure Psychological Stability
    Deny Politics Influenced Current Assignments

TRANSGLOBAL GETS CHICKEN LITTLE PRIZE FOR WHITE PLAGUE COVERAGE
    Falsely Reported That Zambesi Virus Is Airborne
    "Scared Wits Out Of Millions"
    34th Annual Award By National Anxiety Center

Baseball:
AARON BROKE RUTH CAREER HR MARK 50 YEARS AGO TODAY
    Hit 715th Against LA Dodgers In Atlanta
    Aaron's Total of 755 Still Unsurpassed

TOKYO FERRY CAPSIZES
    Hundreds Feared Lost
    Eyewitnesses Say Boat Was Overcrowded

TOTAL SOLAR ECLIPSE TODAY
    Sky Spectacular Visible Across Much of U.S.

VATICAN DENIES POPE SERIOUSLY ILL
    Innocent "Exhausted But Fit"

MOONBASE OPENS TODAY; VP PRESIDES OVER CEREMONIES

Beaver Meadow Observatory, North Java, New York. 12:38 P.M.

Wesley Feinberg had twice won the Nobel Prize for his work in calculating the age of the universe and for establishing the relation between gravity and quantum effects. He was also director of Harvard's AstroLab in central Massachusetts. He was respected by his peers, treated like a minor deity by the graduate students, and granted every perk by the institution, which was delighted to have him. The latest perk: temporary assignment to the Beaver Meadow Observatory in North Java, New York, which was in the path of the eclipse.

Feinberg was happy to go. And not only because of the celestial event. He was a bachelor, a man who'd devoted his life to astronomy and discovered it wasn't quite enough. The trip to Beaver Meadow got him out of the apartment he'd grown to detest, and threw him in with a new group of people. The reality of his existence puzzled him. He'd accomplished everything he'd ever wanted, had gone well beyond what he'd thought possible. Yet he sensed that something round and dark had moved across the essence of his own existence, blocking off the light.

Beaver Meadow wasn't a big facility. It had only three telescopes, the largest being a forty-five-inch Clayton-Braustein reflector, which would relay images onto an eighteen-foot wallscreen. The observatory had reserved a prime-location computer for him, overlooking the wallscreen. The director, Perry Hoxon, asked whether he required anything else.

Hoxon was a busy and innocuous little man. Feinberg explained he was not working on a specific project. In fact, he would have been content to sit quietly outside on one of the benches in the adjoining park, and simply enjoy the eclipse. But yes, he was certainly grateful for the prime location. (He would in fact have been irritated had it not been offered.)

Now, as the event unfolded, he wondered whether he shouldn't have gone outside and watched from the parking lot. Several hundred people had crowded into the facility. Kids were laughing, babies crying, and there was a minimum level of conversation that did not subside even during the final moments before totality. Feinberg had seen the phenomenon before, an utter lack of respect for what was happening, people who had dropped by the observatory on the way to a supermarket. Then the last of the light ran off the screen. Bright spikes and beads flashed into existence, haloing the dark disk. The diamond ring effect. A few people cheered, as if someone were about to score a touchdown. He sighed and concentrated on the event, shutting out the rest of the world. How unlikely, and how fortunate, that Sun and Moon were the same apparent size! No other world in the solar system could experience an event even remotely like this. If *he*, Wesley M. Feinberg, had been designing the system, this was exactly the sort of spectacular effect he would have wanted to create for the one intelligent species among the worlds. And he wasn't sure he'd have thought of it.

A noise in the auditorium recalled him to the present. The voice was male, filled with impatience: *"I'll wait in the car."* How dull and unimaginative the general population was.

"Professor Feinberg?"

He looked away from the screen. One of the observatory's interns, a very young man who seemed intimidated in his presence, held out a piece of paper. "Sorry to disturb you, Professor. This just came for you."

He took it, nodded, pushed it unread into his pocket, and went back to the eclipse. The solar corona was magnificent: Plumes and streamers a million miles long blazed out of the darkened disk. The spectacle rose and fell with mathematical precision, a cosmic symphony in light and power. He watched, hearing now only his own heartbeat, willing himself closer, trying to grasp the enormity of what he was seeing.

"Professor. I think there's some urgency." A new voice this time. Hoxon. At first Feinberg wasn't sure what the man was talking about. Then he remembered the message. He fished it out of his pocket.

It was from the Orbital Lab:

WES,
ANOMALOUS OBJECT REPORTED BY ST. LOUIS AREA
OBSERVER. PLEASE VERIFY.

At the bottom of the page, in a box, there was a set of coordinates. The object was square in the middle of Pisces.

"I'll be back," he told Hoxon. He wanted to be out in the eclipse anyhow, away from the crowd, away from the auditorium. He wanted to wrap himself in the event, taste it, draw it into his soul.

He buttoned his sweater and hurried quickly across the parquet floor and out into the parking lot. It was unseasonably cold, and he pushed his hands into his pockets. The observatory was located in a nature center. The walkways and lawns were deserted. Feinberg picked out Van Maanen's Star, looked to its left, and saw a light that shouldn't be there. He cackled and pumped his right arm in the air with pure pleasure.

3.

Moonbase, Grissom Country. 12:49 P.M.

Sam Anderson had been agent in charge of the vice president's Secret Service detail for six months. He was not happy. The assignment should have been relatively straightforward. They were in a limited-access zone. Residents of Moonbase had all passed psychological screenings to eliminate nut cases, and the visitors were VIPs who, in a less restricted area, would have been traveling with their own security units.

Nevertheless, it was not a comfortable situation. Of course, on assignment, Sam was never comfortable. He always assumed that a potential assassin existed, looking only for the opportunity. And Moonbase put him at several distinct disadvantages.

People here tended to live and work in close proximity to one another. In the corridors and meeting rooms, it was literally impossible to maintain a ring around "Teddy," their codename for Haskell. It was, of course, a reference to the TR sketches and memorabilia that the vice president kept in his office. Sam's favorite was a doctored photo showing Theodore Roosevelt and Charlie Haskell, both in buckskin, standing together outside the Dakota Saloon in the Badlands.

Firearms were prohibited at Moonbase. No exceptions, Sam had been told when he tried to argue the point. Consequently, the agents carried only stun guns. They wouldn't be worth much if someone else had gotten a revolver past the sensors.

Backup was, of course, far away. Moonbase had no security force worthy of the name. The assumption was that its residents would abide by the policies and live by the rules. A person who drank too much and created a problem could be dealt with. But a couple of people with criminal intent, if they were able to smuggle weapons into the facility (which Sam thought would not be all that difficult), could pretty much have their own way. He wondered whether the lunar operation would suffer a minor disaster before they got smart and installed a tough, efficient police detail.

Something else worried him. It took a while to get used to moving around at one-sixth g. If the agents had to respond to an emergency, he wasn't sure how efficient they were going to be. Quick moves tended to cause people to bounce off walls.

Sam was thirty-eight years old, twice divorced, had one

child by each marriage. He was a graduate of Ohio State, where he'd run the two-twenty better than anyone else in the school's history. He'd majored in poli-sci, gotten a commission and served as a naval officer for four years. A fellow officer had convinced him of the many advantages and the glamor of the Secret Service. He'd joined, while the friend changed his mind at the last minute and went to law school, where he'd learned to make big bucks defending the indefensible.

Sam's first assignment had been to the Detroit office.

There was, of course, no glamor to speak of, but the pay was decent and he enjoyed the work. A man couldn't ask for more than that. He'd done well, shown a flair for the intelligence desk, and been twice promoted. Eventually he drew an assignment with the White House unit. This time next year, he expected to be Special Agent in Charge at one of the major stations.

Sam was six-feet even and right out of central casting for agents: spare, chiseled features; alert brown eyes; and conservatively cut black hair. On duty, he fell easily into the polite cool monotone that was almost a parody of Hollywood agent-speak. But nobody seemed to mind, and at retirement parties and award luncheons, his colleagues never missed a chance to mimic him. It always got a laugh.

He was good at his job: tough, dependable, smart. Both his wives had also understood he had a soul that he kept carefully hidden. That might have been the reason they'd eventually given up on him, that they saw only glimpses of the part of him they loved. Unlike the other members of the detail, Sam would have enjoyed being at Moonbase if he could have relaxed for a few hours.

Because of the nature of the assignment, only three agents had been assigned to him for the detail. They all stayed with their charge constantly during the ceremonial functions. At other times Sam split the assignments so they could get some rest. (There was no question here of engaging in sight-seeing.) But four was just not enough to do the job right. They'd been hovering around Teddy since they left the White House and they were getting weary.

Like most other high-level politicians, the vice president didn't care much for all the security, but he was good-natured about it, and freely admitted he wouldn't want to have to go looking for his agents when he needed them. *His* agents. Charlie Haskell was smart enough to let them know he understood what they had to do, and that he appreciated them. This alone ensured that, if Teddy got his party's nomination, he'd also get the votes of his security detail.

The Secret Service had been assigned a double suite to use as combination quarters and operations center. Sam knew that the evening's festivities would run late, and that Teddy liked to party. So it was going to be a long night. Sam was getting one break, at least: Moonbase operated on Washington time, so there was no equivalent to jet lag.

It was a no-sweat mission, the operations chief had insisted. But Sam worried, as he was trained to do. The Secret Service hadn't lost anybody in over sixty years. Sam had no interest in breaking the streak.

Skyport Orbital Lab. 1:00 P.M.

The lunar shadow glided northeast into New England and Canada. It tracked just south of the St. Lawrence River. Toronto and Montreal, on the northern side, saw only a partial eclipse. But buses, cars, and trains had carried thousands of enthusiasts to Granby and Magog and St.-Hyacinthe, and across the U.S. border to Burlington and Plattsburg. The eclipse crossed New Brunswick, passed into the gulf, and began to accelerate as Earth's surface curved away. It moved rapidly across the southern tip of Newfoundland, reached St. John's in the late afternoon, local time. A band struck up and the citizens threw a citywide party, which lasted well into the evening. By then the shadow was long gone, having moved first into the North Atlantic and then off the planet altogether.

Meantime, Wesley Feinberg had confirmed Tomiko Harrington's discovery, that something new had indeed appeared in the sky.

"Recommend action to determine nature of object," his report read.

Probably a sun-grazer, he told Windy Cross on the phone.

Unfortunately, the thing had retreated once again into the solar glare. No local optical telescope was going to be of any immediate use. But Windy had other resources.

Moonbase, Main Plaza. 1:11 P.M.

Tables had been set out along the concourse and heaped with food. Evelyn took the occasion to thank those who, as she said, had come so far to share in this special occasion. She passed out commemorative plaques to the vice president and to many of the other guests. When it was over, the celebrants drifted into the half-dozen or so shops and bistros that had opened their doors for the festivities.

A tram moved through one of the parks. Rick watched it, recalling the summer trolleys he'd ridden as a boy on Lake Michigan, and glanced up at the Moonbase headquarters building. An elevator was descending. A few workmen were putting the finishing touches on a light standard. Another was installing an elevator door, and two more seemed to be inspecting the gridwork across the central canyon.

Rick felt better than he had in thirty years. Lunar gravity induced a sense of general well-being, of sheer effervescence. If there were a way to bottle this, he told the vice president, we'd make a fortune.

Afterward he spent time with the journalists, buying them drinks, talking casually with them about the vice president's plans for the future, why the nation would profit under his leadership, and in short, doing what he could to ensure their support during the coming campaign. It was thoroughly enjoyable duty. Rick was born to socialize. He genuinely liked the journalists, they knew it, and so they naturally tended to shade things for him. Not consciously, of course, but nevertheless, there it was. Rick Hailey was a guy any one of them would have had over for dinner, even if he weren't an administration source. It was this camaraderie with the media that constituted Rick's primary value to a candidate.

He was also careful not to neglect press officers. On this occasion Moonbase's media rep would be giving interviews, and Rick wanted to exert some influence over what was said. He therefore made it a point to stop by the public relations office, introduce himself, and feign interest in the operation. *Would you like to tour our little corner of Moonbase, Mr. Hailey?*

Of course he would. *This is the video production department, and that's the VIP coordination group.* While they were strolling through the training facility (which was directed by the same person who oversaw the press office), Hailey saw an extraordinarily striking young woman. She had green-flecked gray eyes and blond hair, and she looked at him with the curiosity to which vice presidential confidants become accustomed.

"Who is that?" he asked his escort innocently.

"Oh," the escort replied, "just one of the communications technicians."

He let it drop. It would have been unseemly to push.

Then she was gone, out the door, with a sheaf of papers in one hand.

Richard Daley Hailey enjoyed the electricity and dazzle of politics, where the rabbit was power rather than money. So when an uncle running for alderman had asked Rick's help, he took a leave of absence from his public relations job and directed the campaign. He decided which issues they would put up front (garbage collection and street repair), which aspects of their opponent's corruption they would emphasize (nepotism and paybacks), which voting blocs they would pursue and which concede.

He discovered that he had perfect pitch in these matters, and his uncle won easily. Rick never went back to his old job.

A few years later he saw to the election of Avery Foster, the most thoroughly incompetent mayor Chicago had ever seen. It was the victory that made Rick's reputation. When, during later years, journalists tried to corner him about Foster's corruption and incompetence, Rick took the position that it was not his purpose to find truth in a political campaign. "My job," he once told Fox TV, "is to champion one side or the other. Truth emerges from the clash of ideas, not from one person's advocacy."

He'd won a lot of campaigns since Foster, had never lost, and was pleased now to be working for Charlie Haskell, although riding a good candidate to victory struck him as less of a challenge. Charlie was behind at the moment, but that was only because he lacked Kolladner's support. He was an ideal candidate, honest, reasonably intelligent, with Avery Foster's knack for saying the right thing. He was young, physically imposing at six-four, good-looking, the kind of guy most people wanted their daughter to bring home. And he had a great smile. With American voters, a single aw-shucks smile compensates for four years of invisibility.

Rick wished he'd been able to get the name of the woman with the green-flecked eyes.

Skyport Orbital Lab. 1:58 P.M.

Tory glanced at her central display, which provided a live view of boiling Venusian clouds.

The Venus probe of 2016 had contained a Hofleiter 0.8-meter telescope which, after the main package had been injected into that world's atmosphere, had gone into orbit.

The Hofleiter was capable of making ultraviolet, optical, and near-infrared observations over wavelengths from 115 to 1010 nanometers. It carried two spectrographs, a high-speed photometer, a wide-field Advanced Charge-Coupled Device, and a fine guidance sensor. Its primary mission was to map the Venusian atmosphere, to track its turbulence, and thereby to contribute to a better understanding of terrestrial weather patterns.

Now they had permission to retarget. It was a process they did only with reluctance. In planetary atmospheric observations, continuity was everything. Sequence and development mattered. But a second message from Feinberg had forced their hand:

PROBABLE COMET. VERY LARGE HALO.

A comet.

Tory was delighted. It was always exciting to be in on a discovery like this, even if credit would go to Tomiko What's-her-name in St. Louis. But if it was a comet, it would orbit the Sun and go back out the way it had come. Which meant it might not be visible to the naked eye for several months, until Earth had traveled to the other side of its orbit.

But that raised a question: Why had no one noticed it, say, last October, when it was on its way in and Earth was on the far side of the Sun?

"Ready," she told Windy.

"Do it."

She'd already entered the comet's coordinates and had only to activate. This she did with a flourish, and she and her supervisor watched the monitors blank out. The orbiter would need several minutes to shift on its axis, realign, and focus.

"It's probably because it isn't very bright," said Windy. "Happens all the time."

"All the time?"

"Well, occasionally."

Images started to come in. The definition adjusted, and they saw it! "Comet Tomiko," said Tory.

Windy grinned. "Stay with it," he said. "Eventually you'll get one of your own."

She increased magnification. "Not much of a tail." It was gauzy. Barely perceptible.

Windy shook his head. "I wonder if we've seen it before."

Tory called up the register for regularly recurring comets and initiated a search.

"Negative," she said after a time. "We don't know this one."

CHAPTER TWO

MOONBASE
Tuesday, April 9

1.

Moonbase, Director's Dining Room. 7:15 A.M.

Charlie heard about the comet at breakfast. He was with a dozen or so other special guests when Slade Elliott mentioned the subject. The comment was offhanded, of no particular significance. To Charlie, as well as to most of the other VIPs, a comet was a light in the sky that one might take a look at if one happened to be on a dark patch of road. But it struck him as appropriate that the information would come from the man who'd made his fortune playing the swashbuckling captain of a fictitious starship.

Evelyn took advantage of the breakfast to introduce Jack Chandler, who would be the first director of Moonbase. Chandler was stocky, intense, reserved. He did not look entirely comfortable shaking hands with the notables, but he radiated an air of quiet competence. He wouldn't have been worth a damn as a politician, but the vice president sensed he'd do all right as an administrator. What he'd need though, Charlie thought, would be a good public affairs advisor. Somebody like Rick. The director of Moonbase was going to become a political animal whether he wanted to or not.

As they were breaking up, Charlie cornered Evelyn. "I'd like a favor," he said.

"Name it."

"I want to go outside."

Sam Anderson lost most of his color and began to shake

his head vigorously *no*. Charlie put on a bemused expression for the senior agent.

"On the surface?" asked Evelyn.

"Of course. On the surface."

She hesitated. "You have any experience with p-suits?"

Sam looked as if he were going to explode.

"Your people can show me," said Charlie.

"Mr. Vice President, we don't allow anyone to go out who isn't thoroughly familiar with the equipment."

"How long does it take to become thoroughly familiar?"

"Usually a few days. We do some training and administer a written test and a practical. And a physical."

Charlie sighed. "I'm not going to be here that long."

Evelyn smiled sympathetically. "What do you think they'd do to me if I lost a vice president?"

"Give you a medal."

She dazzled him with a brilliant smile. "I don't think so."

An aide had been trying to get her attention. She turned away momentarily, signed a clipboard, and then looked back at him. Her expression had grown very serious. "It is a risk," she said, "that I'd prefer not to take. May I ask why you wish to go out?"

Because it's something I've always wanted to do and this might be my only chance. "I might not get back here again," he said.

She looked at him for a long moment. "When do you want to do this foolish thing?"

Charlie felt like a boy confronting a disapproving teacher. How hard could it be to learn how to walk around in a pressure suit? "At your leisure," he said.

She sighed. "Understand, I do not think this is a good idea." She glanced at Sam, establishing her witness for the future inquest. "However," she added, "if I were you, I would also wish to go outside." She took his hand, and the grip was curiously electric. "We can do it now, if you like."

Yes, Charlie decided, he would like very much. He called

Rick and directed him to cancel his morning's schedule. Rick was, of course, appalled.

Sam wasn't happy either. "I'm sorry, sir. I just can't allow it. It violates procedure."

"Relax, Sam," said Charlie. "I'll be fine."

Moonbase was an underground facility. The surface was nine floors up from the Director's Dining Room. Evelyn, Charlie, Sam, and Isabel took the elevator, which climbed the outside of the headquarters building, providing a panoramic view of Main Plaza. From this perspective, Moonbase resembled nothing so much as a vast park.

At the top level they passed along a winding corridor whose walls were decorated with a series of prints depicting Moonbase at various stages of construction. They stopped before a heavy metal door marked CAUTION—AUTHORIZED PERSONNNEL ONLY. An intercom was mounted on the wall. Evelyn keyed it, said her name, and the door opened.

They entered a long room filled with benches, equipment bins, cabinets, and racks. Pressure suits in various bright colors hung from overhead bars. A technician rose from a desk and stood by.

"We have several ground-level exits," Evelyn explained. "We're quite busy outside. Moonbase is still under construction, as you know. The crews are in and out all the time. And researchers. And our maintenance people. And occasional tourists." Here she brightened and pursed her lips.

The technician provided them with two p-suits. One was gold and the other, vermillion. Evelyn accepted the gold suit and removed her shoes. "You get the loud one," she smiled.

"Wait a minute," Charlie said. "I didn't intend for you to have to go out."

"Nobody goes out alone. We don't allow it."

It made sense. "Okay. But why not send someone else? I don't want to take up your time."

"It's my pleasure," she said.

"I'll need a suit, too," said Sam, looking resentful.

"Why?" said Charlie. "Who's out there to take a shot at me?"

"Sir, I don't see that it matters. It's dangerous and I wish you wouldn't do this."

"It's settled."

"I *have* to go along. It's in the regs."

"How familiar are you with the equipment?"

"Not much."

"Which means, in an emergency, how much good would you be?"

The muscles in Sam's jaws were rippling. "Not much."

"You might even *become* the emergency. Sit tight. Evelyn'll take care of me and we'll be back in a few minutes."

Evelyn gave him a quick course on procedure, which consisted mostly in not jiggling the suit's controls unnecessarily once they'd been set. She showed him how to modulate the air pressure, how to control the temperature, and how to use the radio. "Keep in mind the gravity differential," she said. "That's the real danger. There are lots of fissures, craters, cracks, you name it, for you to fall into. Keep your eyes open. The suit is tough, but it's still possible to punch a hole in it. Red light means you've got a problem and you should come back immediately. If *you* see a red light, they'll see it at the same time back here and they'll tell you to return. Anything like that happens, no argument, okay?"

Charlie was no dummy. "How often do you get red lights?"

She shrugged. "They're not unheard of."

They put on his helmet and air hissed into the suit. Evelyn did a radio check. "You okay?"

"I'm fine."

"Good." She was pulling on her own helmet. "You'll enjoy it, Mr. Vice President."

The technician led them into an adjoining room where an airlock stood open, waiting to receive them. Charlie followed Evelyn inside and the technician closed the door. Colored lights flashed. "You'll feel a tingle as the air pressure changes," Evelyn said.

He couldn't see her face anymore behind the smoked Plexiglas. "How many times have *you* been outside?" he asked.

She laughed. "Once or twice."

Charlie assumed she was tweaking him, but a long silence followed. "You're kidding," he said.

"Yeah. I've been out a few times. Not as often as I'd like."

A green lamp came on and the exit door irised open. Charlie looked out at the lunar surface, a broken plain, etched in silver light. The sky was black, but filled with rivers of stars.

She waited, letting him go first.

"It's magnificent," he said. He stepped through the hatch. Out onto the regolith. The illumination, most of it anyway, was coming from Earth, which hung blue and white and very big almost directly overhead.

"It's about forty times brighter than a full Moon," said Evelyn.

The horizon looked close. Had there been natives on Luna, they would have known without any question they lived on a globe.

There were no words. He'd seen the hologees many times, but they were nothing like this.

Evelyn led him out to a rectangular area that had been cordoned off. It was about one hundred by fifty feet. A walkway had been built across it, a few inches above the surface. Here and there he saw footprints, each marked with a small post and a yellow tag. She showed him the names on the tags. They were all familiar, all well known: Sheila Davidson, who had commanded the first return mission to the Moon; Angela Mikel, the first woman to give birth on Luna; Ed Harper, who'd overseen most of the construction efforts. Evelyn pointed to an unbroken piece of ground. "I'd like you to step down onto the regolith," she said.

"Why?"

"You belong here."

"I don't think so."

"If you win in the fall, people will look at your prints centuries from now and remember the first president to walk on the Moon."

"If I lose?"

She smiled. "We'll take down the rope and run a roller over it."

He looked again at Earth, blue and warm and inviting in the black sky. "I can understand," he said, "why people come out here and get religion." And then with a rush of caution: "Can they hear me back inside?"

"Every word, sir," said the technician's voice.

"It's okay," said Evelyn. "Nobody'll quote you."

"Good." As Rick would have reminded him once again, it wouldn't be the first time a spontaneous remark had sunk a candidacy. George Romney had faded after commenting on his return from Southeast Asia that he'd been brainwashed; Teddy Roosevelt had ruled himself out of a second term without stopping to think; and Mary Emerson was on the verge of becoming the first woman president when she told a reporter there were a lot of deadbeats on Medicaid.

He stepped down onto the marked ground, trying to leave clear prints. It was gratifying to imagine people standing on this spot ages from now, pointing out to one another that Charlie Haskell had walked here. First president of the Space Age. It had a nice ring to it.

It occurred to him that Evelyn was probably wondering whether his moonwalk was a political stunt. Something that would appear later in a campaign biography. But there was nothing he could do about that. And Charlie wondered, not for the first time, whether his political career was worth all the hassle. He enjoyed the cut and thrust of politics, he loved winning, and he enjoyed being in a position to make things happen. But there was a price to be paid. He would never again be able to go out to a restaurant or run over to Wal-Mart without attracting a crowd.

A fan in the back of his helmet changed pitch, adjusting to temperature or humidity.

His one major political drawback was that he was a bachelor. The party believed the voters would not be comfortable without a first lady. That notion did not show up in surveys, but it was the common wisdom in a society that had become increasingly concerned about personal morals while only one marriage in six now stayed the course.

The ground was gray and crumbly. The guidebooks maintained the Moon hadn't changed much in three billion years or so. There was no volcanism on Luna, no climate, no wind to move things around. It was a world where nothing ever happened except occasionally it got plunked by a falling rock.

He climbed back up on the walkway and looked around at the flat plain. "I thought Moonbase was inside a crater," he said.

Evelyn was behind him, allowing him an unbroken view. "It is. But the crater's *big*, and the Moon's small. Alphonsus is a hundred seventeen kilometers across. We're in the center of the crater, and its walls are all below the horizon. But they're there. If you like, we can take a ride over."

"Yes," said Charlie. He studied her for a long moment, wishing he could see her face. "*You'd* like to do that, wouldn't you?"

She chuckled. "I think you caught me," she said. "But yes. With the vice president's permission, we can turn this into a jaunt."

"By all means," said Charlie. He looked at the horizon. "I wonder if we can see the comet from here."

Evelyn was silent, and the voice of the technician came over the radio. "No, sir, it's not visible from Moonbase."

"Pity," he said.

2.

Beaver Meadow Observatory. 9:30 A.M.

Wesley Feinberg canceled his flight home and stayed on at Beaver Meadow. Hoxon gave him an office and a computer and he got on the circuit with Kitt Peak and NASA and Zelenchukskaya and twenty other institutions. The astronomical community, of course, was fully aroused and scrambling to pin the comet down. Could it be identified with anything in the record? How *big* was it? Where was it going?

The quick way to get a handle on the object was to track down where it had been, say, in January or February. Then it would become possible to work out a trajectory. It should have been visible in the early part of the year. So it was just a matter of conducting a thorough search.

But as yet there was insufficient data to make even an intelligent guess where it might have appeared in the winter heavens. Feinberg worked methodically, bringing up sections of sky and comparing them against the database, hoping to find an object that did not belong. The images were produced by ACCDs, Advanced Charge-Coupled Devices, mounted on major telescopes around the world and in orbit. The pictures were far sharper than the photos with which he'd worked when he'd begun his career near the end of the last century.

He knew that an army of professionals and talented amateurs were doing the same thing, but he wasn't interested in waiting for someone else's results. Although he'd have denied it, he was a competitor and wanted very much to get there first. He was, after all, less likely to be led astray by every point of light that didn't fit the catalog. But after working through the night, he had nothing. That was understandable. What he did *not* understand was that no one else had anything either.

Feinberg had stayed with it until almost six A.M., when he began to doze at the keyboard. Finally he'd given up and commandeered a couch in a utility room, where he slept until noon. By then several sites had reported positives. But after a glance Feinberg dismissed their "finds" as the carcasses of junked earth satellites, two known asteroids, and in one case, a nebula.

By late afternoon there was still nothing.

Curious. "It's very hard to understand," he told Hoxon, who had done some nominal searching on his own.

The director agreed. He was a garrulous, beak-nosed man who spent most of his time organizing public tours and who seemed to have remarkably little interest in real astronomy. He persisted in carrying on pointless conversations with people around him who were trying to work.

Feinberg extended his search, on the theory that the comet might be moving substantially faster or slower than the forty kilometers per second that was more or less the ballpark velocity. He worked through the late afternoon, sorting images while the mystery grew.

At six P.M. a postdoc at Cerro La Silla in Chile asked for help. She sent pictures that seemed to indicate she'd found a *second* comet. The pictures revealed an object on the far side of the Sun, out near Jupiter's orbit. The images had been run on successive nights, March 25 and 26. But the same area in another set of images taken six days earlier showed nothing. Nor did the object appear in a third series beginning March 30. The object had apparently been in the sky for ten nights *at most* and then vanished. Where had it gone? The postdoc was asking if anyone else had pictures of the area during the subject period.

Now, *that* was odd. They had *two* elusive comets.

Hoxon appeared and suggested Feinberg join him for dinner. "My treat," he said.

Astronomers do not, as a rule, command large paychecks. Consequently, Feinberg wasn't surprised when Hoxon took him to the local Shoney's. They talked about the Chilean business. In fact, Feinberg knew he was babbling about it. But Hoxon's only significant response was to observe that it was only a postdoc after all, and who knew what she really saw.

We've got the pictures, nit. But Feinberg let it go.

ACCDs functioned by counting photons and converting the results to optical images. Feinberg began thinking about photon counts and fingerprints somewhere between the meat loaf and the ice cream sundae he decided he deserved. Two objects, one near Jupiter, one near the Sun. Both hard to track.

He did a quick calculation to check the idea that had been unconsciously forming, and smiled at the result. He'd been scribbling on a napkin, and when Hoxon asked him what it was about, he shrugged. "Nothing," he said, dismissing his result.

His host did not think it was a good idea to go back to work, announced that he was going home, and suggested that Feinberg also quit for the night. Feinberg wondered what would have happened to the spirit of scientific inquiry if everyone had possessed the director's driving curiosity. "No," he said, "I have one or two things to finish up."

Unfortunately, what Feinberg wanted to finish up couldn't be handled directly from his keyboard. He made two phone calls. The first was to the Skyport Orbital Laboratory, which had used its Venusian probe to make the images of Tomiko's Comet; and the other was to Cerro La Silla. In both cases he asked for the photon count that had produced the comet images. Both sites said they would get back to him.

Cerro La Silla returned his call within the hour. He

recorded the result and waited eagerly for the response from the Orbital Lab. It was a procedure that could take time, especially if they were busy, as he suspected they were. At midnight he was still sitting by his phone.

He didn't recall dozing off, but he remembered coming out of a deep sleep, seeing gray light coming through a window, uncertain at first where he was. The telephone was ringing.

Windy Cross at Skyport apologized for the delay, but gave him the data. "If you don't mind, Professor," asked Windy, "what use is it?"

Feinberg remembered the count from the Jupiter comet. It was almost identical. Not definitive, but damned near. *They were possibly the same object.* "I'll get back to you, Windy," he said. "When I'm sure."

He stared at the numbers, puzzling over the problem. The Cerro La Silla sighting was way the hell out of range. Comets had an upper speed limit of about fifty kps. If this was the same object, it would have to be moving at eight or nine times that velocity. Four hundred–plus kilometers per second!

That meant it did not, *could not*, belong to the solar system.

There was no question that vast numbers of comets drifted through the interstellar void, unattached to any sun. The latest estimates Feinberg had seen placed the number of unattached comets in the neighborhood of the solar system and out to, say, the half-dozen or so nearest stars, somewhere in the range of a *trillion*. He did not personally subscribe to that view. It was true that comets were periodically ejected from the solar system by the Sun, and sometimes even by Jupiter. He could not see that the process happened sufficiently often to support the more wild-eyed theorists. But who really knew?

In any case, this appeared to be a true interstellar. If both sightings *were* the same object, it *had* to be.

No interstellar comet had ever been recorded. If he was

right, Wesley Feinberg was going to take his place with Shapley, Herschel, Eddington, and Galileo.

Assuming the two bodies were the same, he now tried to calculate a trajectory. At the kind of velocity he'd expected, around forty kilometers per second, the comet would curve around the Sun and go back out. But at four hundred kilometers per second, it was going to keep coming.

With any kind of luck, they might get an extraordinary show.

He went out and delivered a cheerful good morning to the security guard, who seemed to be the only other person in the observatory. "I thought about waking you, sir," the guard said. "You didn't look comfortable on that couch. But I thought it best not to disturb you."

Feinberg gave the man his most amiable smile. "Exactly right, sir," he said. "Exactly right." He turned on the coffee machine in the meeting room adjoining Hoxon's office. He was hesitant to move precipitately, but it was only a matter of time before someone else drew the same conclusions he had. If that happened, he'd have to share credit. So he went back to his computer and forwarded his data to the Astronomical Union's Central Bureau in Cambridge, where they would be logged and redistributed.

Please, God, let it be true.

NEWSNET. 12:30 P.M. UPDATE.
(Click for details.)

MAN JAILED FOR CARJACKING WINS $20 MILLION IN LOTTERY
   Alleged Thief Faces Ten Years
   "It's Not Going To Change Me"

HASKELL CUTS RIBBON AT MOONBASE
   Takes Time Off From Primaries For PR Bonanza
   "We Have A Rendezvous With The Stars"

CORMAN WINS IN PENNSYLVANIA
> Leads In Total Delegates By Sixteen
> Haskell A Distant Third

MOSCOW OPENS WORLD'S LARGEST MONORAIL
> System Covers 700 Miles, Will Serve Two Million Passengers Daily

PRESIDENT HANGS CHURCHILL PORTRAIT IN WHITE HOUSE CEREMONY
> World War II Leader Became Honorary U.S. Citizen 64 Years Ago Today

YOUTH DRUG REPORTED CLOSE
> Predict Life Span Will Double For Newborns
> Population Activists Warn Of Disaster

TWO KILLED IN DENVER ELEVATOR CRASH
> Passed Safety Inspection Last Week

WORLD POPULATION PASSES TEN BILLION
> India Announces New Education Effort

ST. LOUIS WOMAN DISCOVERS COMET DURING ECLIPSE
> Sun's Glare Had Hidden Celestial Visitor

Moonbase, on tour. 4:30 P.M.

Isabel Heyman, who usually worked with the special response detail at the White House, had politicked to get the Moonbase assignment. That she'd succeeded was less attributable to her influence than to the fact that the agents usually assigned to the vice president had been working long hours as he plunged into the crucial early primaries. Unlike Isabel, they did not perceive a flight to Luna, with a reduced force that guaranteed round-the-clock hours, as a benefit.

So now Isabel toured the Greenhouse, keeping station on Teddy's left, surveying faces for any telltale suggestion of ill intent, looking for tics or compressed lips, for eyes perhaps a little too narrowly focused, for any sudden movement, for a hand slipped inside a garment.

It was hard, wandering among Moonbase's wonders, to keep her mind on her job. But her training took over, and it was enough just to know where she was.

She would come back, she decided. On her own.

CHAPTER THREE

FORECASTS

Wednesday, April 10

1.

Arecibo, Puerto Rico. 8:03 A.M. Atlantic Time (7:03 A.M. EDT).

The radar returns had been coming in for several hours. Tomiko was a *monster*, 180 kilometers in diameter. But the incredible revelation was its velocity: It was moving at 480 kilometers per second! Yesterday Foster Cardwell would have bet the mortgage that order of velocity wasn't possible.

Cardwell was director of operations at Arecibo. He stood over the display, rubbing the back of his neck. He was wearing a bright yellow shirt stenciled with palm trees and dolphins. "Run it again," he said.

Penny McGruder nodded and keyed in the command. "It's not going to look any different."

A cursor moved unerringly toward a rendezvous with the Earth-Moon system. The comet was passing the Sun now. It would cross the orbit of Mercury later today, and that of Venus early Friday. It would close to within 384,000 kilometers of Earth. Where it would strike the Moon!

"Are we sure?"

They checked everything again.

Saturday night. At ten thirty-five EDT.

"Cardy," she said, "this comet doesn't obey the rules."

He nodded and shrugged.

She highlighted the velocity: 480. What would it do to the Moon?

"It'll be a hell of a show," he said.

•   •   •

Beaver Meadow Observatory. 7:33 A.M. EDT.

Feinberg was ecstatic. Messages of congratulation had already begun pouring in. Tomiko was indeed an interstellar. But even given that, its velocity was difficult to account for. They would have to rethink some of their assumptions.

A variety of emotions washed through him when he saw it would impact on the Moon. There would be a magnificent display, and they'd have an unparalleled opportunity to observe their extrasolar visitor. Why, then, did he feel a sense almost of despair?

He'd have given much to see a mission to the comet. Who knew what they might have learned, given an opportunity to do an inspection. Perhaps they would even have uncovered the secret behind its velocity.

He'd given much thought to the matter. The object was billions of years old. Had to be. It had experienced a series of encounters, each accelerating it until it reached its present rate. It seemed a farfetched explanation. Yet, what other possibility was there?

Hoxon dithered about, worrying that Feinberg's health would suffer if he didn't "get out and get some fresh air."

"In a while," said Feinberg.

"Where's it going to hit? Will we be able to see it?"

"It'll impact on the back side."

"That's a pity."

"Maybe not." Feinberg let his concern show. "Giant comet coming hard." He made a noise deep in his throat, and tapped a key. A single set of numbers appeared on the screen:

$$7 \times 10^{29}$$

Hoxon made a face. "Energy release?"

"Approximately."

"Wes, that can't be right."

Feinberg ignored the familiarity. "I'd like to think not," he said. "It's enough to take the top off the Moon." He stared out at the cool green lawn, still damp in the morning light. "There might be a downside to all this."

White House Dining Room. 8:04 A.M.

"Sorry to disturb you, Mr. President." Al Kerr, Henry Kolladner's chief of staff, loomed in the doorway. He looked unhappy.

The president was seated at his breakfast table with the first lady. Emily Kolladner frowned. She had fought a losing battle for two years to guard the family's privacy, before finally acceding to the reality that a president has no personal life. Henry had tried to find time for her; he usually rose early, worked two hours or so, and then joined her for a casual breakfast. It was supposed to be understood that the meal not be interrupted for any calamity short of nuclear war. Of course, that understanding had been violated almost daily. The first chief of staff, Kerr's predecessor, had lost his job over the issue. Henry smiled at Emily, shrugged, and finished chewing a piece of bacon. "What is it, Al?" he asked.

Kerr stepped into the room and only then did Henry realize he wasn't alone. A middle-aged, officious-looking woman entered behind him. He'd seen her before.

"Mr. President," said Kerr, "you know Dr. Juarez."

Yes. His science advisor. "Of course. Mercedes, how are you?"

Mercedes Juarez wore black slacks and a black jacket with a gold scarf over it. Her hair looked somewhat windblown and her eyes were dark pinpoints. "Quite well, thank you, Mr. President." She opened a leather briefcase. "Sir, we have an emergency." The observation didn't faze Kolladner, who saw two to three dozen emergencies daily. She extracted a picture and held it up for him. It showed a field of stars. One was especially bright. "This is Tomiko," she said.

"Who?"

"The comet, sir."

"Oh. Of course."

"It's very big. It's traveling very fast. And it's coming this way."

Kolladner put his fork down. The room seemed to have gotten cold. "And—?"

"It's going to hit the Moon Saturday night."

"Okay . . ." He paused for a moment, trying to recover his equilibrium. He'd thought, from her tone, the news was going to be a lot worse. "You're telling me Moonbase is in danger?"

She took a deep breath. "That, too."

He glanced up at Kerr, not understanding where this was going. *"Too?"* he asked.

Dr. Juarez's eyebrows drew together. "Mr. President." She made a strange face, like a child being forced to eat asparagus. "It's *big*. We've never seen anything this big before. It's possible it might demolish the Moon altogether."

Kolladner looked at his wife, and at Kerr. Emily's hand touched his wrist. The United States had a multi-trillion-dollar investment in the Moon. He found it hard to consider the ramifications, the idea was so off-the-wall. "There's no mistake?"

"No, sir. There's a fudge factor, but it's not worth discussing."

"How much of a fudge factor?"

"Very little, as far as the actual strike is concerned. Considerably more with regard to energy release."

Henry pushed back from the table. "Okay. I assume they're evacuating Moonbase?"

"We haven't heard anything formally yet, Mr. President," said Kerr. "We've passed them the word, but I don't think they've had time to digest it. But yes, they'll have to move everyone out."

"Yes. I'd think so." He studied the science advisor. "What do you need from me?"

"Mr. President," she said, "it's possible—likely—that fragments will be blown off the Moon. If that happens, we could catch some of the fallout."

"*We?* The United States?"

"The world."

"Pardon me," said Emily, "but why don't you just tell us what you know?" Emily rarely intervened directly. But she looked exasperated. "Are we really worried about falling moonrock?"

"Yes, Mrs. Kolladner. Maybe a lot of it."

"How much?" asked Henry. "How likely?"

"I don't know. I'm not sure anybody does. We've scheduled a meeting so you can talk to the experts firsthand."

Henry glanced at Kerr. Kerr nodded. He looked worried.

The president pushed his plate away. Falling sky was hard to take seriously. But if Juarez had managed to scare Kerr . . . hell, she'd scared *Henry*.

Henry Kolladner was nearing the end of a long and distinguished career. He'd made sacrifices for his country. His lungs had been damaged thirty-three years ago by Iraqi chemical agents, and as a young congressman, he'd walked into a militia hostage situation, been shot twice, but brought the captives out. He'd also taken Culpepper's dream of returning to the Moon and carried it to fulfillment, and he'd bitten the bullet and restructured Social Security and Medicare programs to compensate for the fact that people now lived longer, and the nation could no longer afford a retirement age of eighty. (He'd read only yesterday that the average person who made it to fifty could now expect to become a centenarian. *My God, how were they going to handle that?* He wondered whether they shouldn't bring back tobacco.) He'd presided over a robust economy that had come very close to providing enough jobs for a workforce that was growing at a frightening pace.

He was constitutionally eligible to run again. And he was popular enough to win easily. But he'd contracted a rare form of lymphatic cancer, and the doctors weren't even sure he'd live out his present term. So he'd announced his intention to step aside. It was a pity; there was still a great deal to do. Whoever succeeded him would have to face some tough decisions. He'd been well on the way to establishing a reputation that would have placed him among the outstanding presidents. Now everything would depend on whether his successor finished what Henry had begun. Consequently, while maintaining formal neutrality among the candidates, he was hoping that anyone other than Charlie got the nomination. He liked Charlie, but the man lacked the political savvy and will to get things done.

Henry was the country's second African-American president. (Culpepper had been the first.) He'd been grateful to be second. Everyone had stood around waiting for Culpepper to make a mistake, to get something wrong, to lean too far left or right. The old son of a bitch had walked a tightrope for eight tough years. But he'd pulled it off.

Now it looked as if a major problem had fallen out of the sky. He doubted they really need worry about Moon fragments raining down on the world, but the American investment on Luna was something else. The major world powers were all shareholders in Moonbase International, and the loss of the facility was going to constitute a debacle of major proportions. The glitter would go off his name, and he'd be forever associated with it, as Lyndon Johnson was with Vietnam, and Herbert Hoover with the Depression.

"Is there any chance of a mistake?" he asked hopefully.

"They're still checking the numbers, Mr. President. But I don't think so."

He glared at her. "Wonderful. We spend a couple of trillion dollars to get Moonbase open for, what, a week? And then close it down again."

Juarez said nothing.

The president's mouth was dry. His first thought was that, however he proceeded, there was going to be a lot of finger-pointing.

Moonbase, Director's Office. 8:27 A.M.

Evelyn Hampton was conferring with Jack Chandler, in his first official day on the job, over the remaining senior vacancies. Chandler had worked in executive capacities for years with various corporations with which Evelyn had direct or indirect connections. He'd twice come to her assistance, helping to get new operations up and running. It was his specialty and he was very good at it.

Moreover, he'd become a kind of father figure for her, an advisor in matters both professional and personal, the man she went to when she was in trouble.

He was in his fifties, a widower with three kids who were all off on their own. He was mildly overweight, with that washed-out look that people have who've recently lost fifty or so pounds. Chandler had suffered a severe heart attack the previous Christmas and had been put on a stringent diet.

Evelyn, anxious to help this closest of friends, had gone farther: She'd inquired whether the light lunar gravity wouldn't help Chandler by easing the strain on his damaged heart. There'd been talk all along of providing a sanctum sanctorum on the Moon for heart patients, and this seemed a good way to get the ball rolling. The disadvantage was that his physician didn't think he'd ever be able to return groundside again.

Chandler was more than willing. So Evelyn had gotten the director she wanted, and simultaneously performed an act of kindness for a man to whom she was indebted. Did he feel better? "Twenty years younger," he said. "I'd gotten to a point that it was like having a lump of lead in my chest." He beamed at her. "The weight's gone."

They were debating the merits of the applicants on the short list for his assistant's job when the phone rang. "It's Orly Carpenter, Mr. Chandler," the secretary's voice said. "He wants to speak with Dr. Hampton."

Carpenter was the NASA operations director at Houston. Chandler passed the phone.

"Good morning, Orly," said Evelyn. "How's everything?"

"Not good." Carpenter was an ex-astronaut whose voice tended to flatten when he was reporting trouble. "We've got a situation," he said.

She was seated on the edge of the desk, watching the Boston street scene that played across one wall of the director's office. People with umbrellas were moving through a sudden rain storm. "What is it?" she asked casually. Orly was okay, but she knew from long experience that government types in general tend to overreact to problems.

"You know about the comet," he said.

"Of course."

"We think it's going to hit. It's big, and it's coming fast. My God, Evelyn, we've only got three and a half days."

"Relax, Orly," she said, smothering her own sudden alarm. "I'm putting you on the speaker. Jack Chandler's here."

Chandler shared her view of government alarm. He said hello.

"The thing's going to hit *what*?" asked Evelyn. "The Earth? One of the stations? What?"

"The Moon." He caught his breath. "The Moon. It's going to give you one hell of a whack."

"You're not serious."

"Do I sound as if I'm not serious?"

"When?"

"Saturday night. Late in the evening, looks like."

"How sure are you?"

"About ninety-eight percent."

Evelyn tried to collect her thoughts. "You're talking as if it's something we need to worry about. Is it going to hit near Moonbase?"

"Looks like Mare Muscoviense."

"The observatory," whispered Jack. "Is it going to take out the *observatory*?"

"At the very least. This thing's going to trigger major quakes. Maybe worse."

"What could be worse?" asked Evelyn.

"There's a distinct possibility it could shatter the Moon."

Shatter the Moon. The phrase hung in the still air. Evelyn stared at sheets of rain battering the Prudential Building, trying to understand what he was really saying. "How do you mean," asked Evelyn, "*shatter*?"

"How else do you want me to say it? Think of a bag of loose rock."

Evelyn picked up a pad and began to scribble. They had three moonbuses, which among them could carry forty people out to L1. Round-trip took a little over five hours. Between now and ten thirty Saturday night they could make seventeen round-trips.

"Jack," she said, "how many people do we have at Moonbase now?"

He was already working on it. "Seven hundred thirty-four," he read off his screen. "Plus twelve on their way from L1."

Evelyn stared at him.

"I don't think we can get them all off," he said.

2.

The SSTO *Arlington* was about a half hour from launch. George Culver tried to concentrate on his checkoff sheet. He'd finally scored with Annie last night and his mind was filled with images of her. In back, he could hear the passengers beginning to come on board. He shook himself and tried again to read his instruments.

The Single Stage To Orbit space plane had capacity for two hundred thirty-five passengers, and usually carried a crew of twelve. It was slightly more compact than ordinary jumbo airliners, and baggage restrictions were far tighter. But contrasted with the old shuttles, it constituted a remarkably cheap and efficient means of getting into orbit.

George had started his career as a carrier pilot. He'd flown the A-77 Blackjack jet, had become a squadron commander, gotten married, and made the jump to civilian aviation. In all, he'd married three times—all medical types, one physician, one nurse, one hospital systems analyst. He'd gotten bored with each, and had pulled the plug on all three. His wives didn't seem to be all that upset when it happened, and the marriages had ended more or less amicably. None had lasted two years.

He was just finishing with the preliminary readouts when Mary Casey, his copilot, strolled onto the flight deck and sat down.

"How we doing, Mary?" he asked.

"Guidance wasn't lining up," she said. "I put in another box."

He nodded, reached for his clipboard, and gazed at the manifest. "How's Billy?"

Billy was her son. He was a teenager now, just learning to drive, just beginning to assert his independence. His grades were down, and George knew that Mary was unhappy with his choice of friends. "He's been better," she said.

The plane was only three-quarters full, not unusual for a Wednesday morning. There were some vacationers among the passengers, but not many. Fares to the space station were still high, and despite its obvious attractions, Skyport remained out of range for persons of moderate means. But the Lunar Transport Authority, a semiautonomous corporation, was promising that costs would come down dramatically with the planned arrival next year of the second-generation SSTO.

Mary pulled on her headset and adjusted the mike, still talking about Billy.

The captain listened politely. "All part of growing up," he said. "I bet you weren't easy to handle."

The SSTO flew three times weekly from Reagan to the space station. George's crew also made occasional direct runs from Reagan to Moscow, Rome, and London. But this was the flight they enjoyed, riding the thrusters all the way into orbit.

Mary tapped the mike. "Tower," she said, "this is Flight One-seventeen. Comm check."

"Flight One-seventeen," returned a female voice in their earphones. "Check is five by."

"Where's Curt?" asked George.

"Right here, Captain." The flight engineer poked his head in. "Just getting my coffee."

The flight to Skyport would take one hour, forty-three minutes. They'd unload, refuel, pick up returning passengers and cargo, and be back in time for a late lunch.

Mary finished her procedure. George handed her the passenger list and pointed at a couple of names. Big-time singers. She also recognized a well-known TV critic and an Arab oil dealer. There were some kids back there, too. Headed for the vacation of their lives. And a couple of families were going all the way to Moonbase.

"Flight One-seventeen, Tower." Same female voice.

"Go ahead, Tower."

"Your flight is cancelled. Unload your passengers and stand by."

Mary frowned at the captain, who had not yet put on his earphones. She switched on the speaker. "Say again, Tower."

"One-seventeen, abort the flight."

George took off his cap and pulled on his headset. "What's the problem, Tower? What's the reason for the delay?"

"FAA did not give us a reason, One-seventeen. This is *not* a delay. The flight is *canceled*. Please return your passengers to the gate."

"What am I supposed to tell them? The passengers?"

A baritone replaced the other voice. "Tell them there won't be any flights to Skyport today. Just say it's a mechanical problem."

"What *is* the problem?"

"One-seventeen, can we talk about this later? Tell your passengers that agents will be waiting to assist."

Moonbase. 9:04 A.M.

Charlie was touring the mining and manufacturing section when Al Kerr got through to him on his cell phone. "The place is going to get hammered, Charlie. The president wants you out of there."

Charlie walked away from the small group of VIPs. "Come on, Al, it can't be *that* big."

There was an irritating three-second delay while the radio signals traveled between Earth and Moon.

"All I'm telling you is what the experts are saying. There'll be a general evacuation. *You* are to leave Moonbase posthaste. Hampton knows and is arranging it now."

Suddenly Sam came out of nowhere, huddled with his people, and they all looked over at Charlie. The agents must have gotten a call at about the same time, he figured.

"Okay, Al," he said to Kerr. "I think the word's getting around."

"Good. Henry'll be relieved to know you're on your way back." Kerr switched off, leaving Charlie looking at his phone and wondering whether anybody got less respect around Kolladner's White House than the vice president.

Sam took him aside. "You heard, sir?"

"Yes."

"They've got a bus leaving at noon. We'll be on it."

But Charlie was wondering what the voters would think of an aspiring president who caught the first ride out of town. "No," he said. "They're saying Saturday night. We have plenty of time."

Sam frowned. "Mr. Vice President—"

Charlie shook his head and signaled that the conversation was over.

It had been a shattering few minutes. The space program was probably dead. More important, public opinion would crucify the president and everyone associated with him. Half a trillion dollars in Treasury-held MBI stock would become worthless overnight. And how much had the nation invested over the years in development costs?

He cut his tour short and went up to the administrative offices looking for Evelyn. The secretary was startled to see him, but after a whispered conversation with her boss, she took him to Chandler's office, where Evelyn was still meeting with the director.

"Hello, Charlie," she said, rising as he walked in. "I see you got the news."

"Yeah. A few minutes ago." He nodded a greeting to Chandler, then turned back to Evelyn. "The White House sounds rattled. How bad is it?"

She waved him to a seat. "It isn't good. Everybody I talk to thinks Moonbase won't survive. Some of them think the *Moon* won't survive. I talked to Wes Feinberg a few minutes ago." Charlie didn't know who Feinberg was, but he caught the inflection in Evelyn's voice that implied he was the reigning expert.

"So what did Feinberg say?"

She shook her head in the manner one might use discussing a dying patient. They stared at each other for a long moment. "I can't believe this is happening," she said at last.

"What are you going to do?"

"What *can* I do? We'll evacuate." She asked whether he wanted coffee. He did, and she poured a mug and handed it across the desk.

"Anything I can do to help?"

"Get us more buses." She smiled.

"I don't think we have them in our inventory." And then, seriously: "You're not suggesting you can't get everybody out, are you?"

"Things are a bit tight," said Chandler.

Evelyn nodded in agreement. "We don't have enough buses to take everyone over to L1."

Charlie's stomach tightened. "So," he said, "What do we do? Are there more buses somewhere?"

"Under construction. And one so far down for repairs as to be useless. No. Jack suggested we bring in the SSTOs."

"The space planes?" said Charlie. "But my understanding was they could only fly between Skyport and the ground."

"It's true," said Chandler, "they aren't designed for long-range space flight. Too much mass, inefficient fuel usage. But any port in a storm."

"Can they *land* out here?"

Evelyn shook her head. "But they can go into orbit around the Moon, and we can send the buses to them. They'll be closer than L1, so the bus ride'll be shorter. Not by much, but enough that we can get everybody out. While we're waiting for them, we'll keep moving people over to L1."

"Thank God," said Charlie. He was relieved, not only because no one would be left behind, but because he already foresaw the political impact if people died while he escaped.

BBC WORLDNET. 10:01 A.M.

"A spokesman at Moonbase International headquarters in Boston revealed today that a general evacuation of Moonbase has begun. The spokesman stressed there is no danger to base personnel or to visitors. The evacuation has been prompted by the impending collision with Comet Tomiko early Sunday morning, Greenwich mean time. The collision will not be visible from London.

"In a related development, astronomers at the Royal Observatory are speculating that the object is not strictly a comet, as the term is traditionally understood. "Comets are members of the Sun's family," said Wilfred Hodge, a staff member and well-known science writer. "Tomiko is an interstellar object, probably a cometary body that was expelled from another star system, and has been traveling for millions and perhaps billions of years."

Moonbase, Grissom Country. 10:17 A.M.

Evelyn Hampton found herself, in the supreme operational crisis of her life, with little to do. Jack Chandler was organizing the evacuation, and the last thing Moonbase needed was a second boss. So she'd withdrawn into the role of Visiting Dignitary Who Had To Be Rescued.

This status gave her a perspective similar to Charlie's. Consequently, it seemed almost in the natural order of things that the two of them arranged to meet in the private dining room of the Huntress, a bistro set back in a grove of trees in Main Plaza, where (while the agents watched) they exchanged condolences and words of encouragement. "No blame should attach to either of us," said Evelyn, "but it will. It's Hampton's Law."

"What's Hampton's Law?" asked Charlie. The vice president looked dazed, as if he hadn't quite caught up with events.

"When things go wrong, whatever the circumstances, it's always somebody's fault."

As a rule, Evelyn disapproved of politicians. They tended to break down into two categories: the completely unprincipled, who composed the vast majority; and those who lived by their principles no matter who suffered. Her early impression of Charlie was that he did not fit easily into either category. It was almost as if he'd somehow wandered in off the street and gotten into the wrong profession. He embodied a kind of casual, we're-all-in-this-together approach to business relationships that she wouldn't have believed for a minute coming from the other seekers-after-power whom she had known. And even with Charlie she was mildly skeptical. For one thing, they *weren't* all in it together. Charlie might have to face some political fallout, but Evelyn stood to lose everything—the corporation, her holdings, her career. Her reputation.

"So what will you do now?" Charlie asked. "Do you see a way to salvage any of this?"

She shrugged. "It doesn't look hopeful."

They were having coffee and toast. About half the tables in the main dining area were occupied. People strolled casually along the walkways, and somebody was riding a hang glider down from the top of the dome. "How about the evacuation?" he said. "Any problems?"

"I don't think so. The LTA says they'll cooperate and get the planes out here forthwith. It'll be tight; some of us leaving on the last flight Saturday will have a damned good view of the fireworks. But everybody will be off. Barring glitches." She bit into her toast. "We always assumed the most likely emergency would be an upturn in the solar flare cycle. Something like that. That all we'd have to do would be to get people under cover. I don't think it ever occurred to anybody we'd have to evacuate the entire complex. We're talking about the *Moon*, for God's sake." She was having a hard time keeping her voice steady. "We've already shipped off the first load of people to L1."

Opposite them, a virtual mountain brook ran through a tank. There were rocks in the water, and a broken cupola stood off to one side, half-submerged in the stream. Evelyn glanced at it, watched the image change and dissolve into a *USA Today* headline:

COSMIC BULLET TO STRIKE MOON
Narrow Miss For Earth,
But Other Objects Have Come Closer

The headline was replaced by an image of the comet. All comet heads—at least, all the ones whose pictures she'd seen—looked alike. Below the golden halos they were dark fissured chunks of ice and dirt, occasionally cratered, irregularly shaped. They were singularly uninteresting, and she never quite understood why anyone would care about them. This one was no exception. It had a couple of craters, and some long parallel rifts, as if someone had taken a scraper to it. "It looks pretty ordinary," she said.

Charlie shook his head. "It's wider than New Jersey. We don't want to be here when it shows up."

Evelyn felt thoroughly beaten. Had the comet given her a few years, allowed Moonbase to prove its value and develop a cash flow, the corporation might have survived even this kind of catastrophic hit. But not now. This was the critical moment, and she could not escape the sense that the comet's appearance was somehow deliberate, as if the universe were out to get her. "You know what else?" she said. "When this is over, L1 won't be worth a damn anymore either."

"Why not?"

She looked at Charlie, surprised. "Because it's the mutual attraction of Earth and Moon that keeps it in place. You won't be able to maintain a satellite there if the Moon goes south. There won't *be* a Lagrangian point."

"Oh."

"So we'll be confined to low earth-orbit, and there won't be a convenient short-range target left in the sky. Charlie, we had a window when the technology, the money, and the will were all there. Briefly. But I think the window is closing."

3.

Moonbase, Grissom Country. 10:55 A.M.

The newscasts were now beginning to run simulations and comparisons. There was enough rock and ice in the comet head to fill the Grand Canyon a hundred and fifty times. Or to construct a covering fifty feet high completely around the Earth.

Here's what it'll look like Saturday night. Viewers could watch an animated graphic of the comet crossing the orbit of Venus, arrowing toward the Moon, and finally blending with it. A little cloud appeared at the point of impact.

People were packing. There was what one might describe as a sense of calm urgency. Jack Chandler's staff put together a departure schedule and copies were posted everywhere. Visitors would leave first, followed by all those deemed nonessential: astronomers, mathematicians, chemists, hydroponics experts, entrepreneurs, recreation directors, general maintenance workers, and everyone else not needed to launch spacecraft or keep the power on. They *did* need the life support technicians, the spaceport people, the communicators and systems analysts. And, Chandler decreed, senior managers. Even if they couldn't help directly.

Personnel from outlying stations were recalled. The issue of whether there should be an attempt to salvage equipment was raised and quickly discarded. Whatever we can't put on a disk, Chandler told his people, we'll forget about. A modest luggage allowance was announced and a duty officer was made available to receive suggestions or complaints, and to assist with problems.

Rick Hailey read the document on his wallscreen and noted that the Micro, which was to have carried the vice presidential party off at lunchtime, was preparing to leave momentarily with a different set of passengers. He'd gone to bed last night in a sedate facility that was looking forward to a long period of prosperity and discovery. This morning he'd awakened to chaos. In physics, he realized, as in politics, things can turn around in a hurry. And without warning.

His phone rang. "Hailey," he said quietly.

"Rick." It was the vice president. "Things have been happening. If you've got a few minutes, we need to talk."

Rick watched the news reports while he brushed his teeth. He saw an interview with Tomiko Harrington, saw an animation of the expected collision, noted the noncommittal stance taken by the White House. (*"The president is watching developments."*)

When he reached Charlie Haskell's quarters, the agent stationed outside wished him good morning, knocked, heard a response, and opened up. Haskell was on the phone.

"Yes, Henry," he was saying, "everything's under control. As far as I can see."

That would be the president.

"No, you can tell them we're fine. There's plenty to eat and everybody'll be gone well before the thing gets here." Charlie was stretched out across his sofa with his long legs thrown across a coffee table. He pointed at a chair for Rick. "Henry, I assume we'll be getting back sometime Sunday morning. I'm not sure they have a detailed schedule yet."

Sunday morning? Rick frowned at the vice president, who held up a hand asking him to be patient.

"Yes, I know," Charlie continued. "And we appreciate it. As far as I'm aware, Evelyn and her people are taking care of everything. But I'll tell her." Charlie listened. And nodded. "Yes, sir. We will. See you in a few days." He looked at the phone thoughtfully and clicked off. "He's worried about us, Rick."

"So am I. What's this about getting in Sunday morning?"

"They're sending four planes to evacuate us. Two will leave Friday and two on Saturday. The last flight will get away just an hour or so before impact."

"You *lied* to the president. You said they hadn't worked out a schedule yet."

"The schedule's tentative. My question to you, Rick: Which of the planes should the vice president be on?"

Rick sensed doors closing. "You *can* be a son of a bitch, Charlie."

Charlie held out his hands. "What choice do I have?"

Rick shook his head. "None that I can see."

The president wasn't in a very good situation either. Overnight, Moonbase had turned into a monumental political liability. And it would get worse in direct proportion to the size of the disaster. They would hope no one got killed, although it occurred to Rick, as it must have to the president, that a heroic VP going down would have a distinct upside. Or even, he thought with a chill, his media advisor. Valiant bureaucrat lost on Moon. But God forbid any innocents get hurt.

Charlie pursed his lips thoughtfully. "How about you?" he asked. "Do you want an early flight?"

Yes, Rick thought. *By all means.* "I'll stay until Saturday," he said. "But I don't think I want to go out on the late flight."

"Nor do I. But I'm not sure I'm going to be able to avoid it."

"Charlie, the campaign's not worth your life." Rick was angry, but not sure at whom.

"In the meantime, Rick, I'd like you to keep close. I'm going to be dealing with the press constantly over the next three days and I'll need some ideas. You know, comments on the courage and coolness of the lunies under extreme stress. Of, uh, the American personnel, especially. Can we find a way to say that without offending anybody?"

"Sure."

"Okay. And make sure we mention Evelyn Hampton. Get the names of some of the other women here, too. Brave women. Credit to their sex. Their ability to meet even this kind of emergency shows us, and so on."

"Charlie, that's a trifle sexist."

The vice president laughed. "That's why I need *you*, Rick. We're going to salvage what we can. So we'll want to point out that we still have the means to go on. Mustn't quit. The Dream. Invoke the *Challenger* accident. And Rick—"

"Yes, sir?"

"For God's sake, give me some poetry."

Georgetown, Washington, D.C. 12:03 P.M.

George Culver wasn't particularly unhappy that the flight had been canceled. He took advantage of the unexpected day off to have lunch with friends at Hurst's Turn of the Century on Wisconsin Avenue. Hurst's had opened just after Christmas, 2000, and its murals incorporated scenes from those closing years of the Clinton era. Here was a gaudily outfitted band and there an antique Toyota Corolla. A bearded father and his son sat in a crowd, waving pennants for the old Washington Redskins. The grand opening itself had been captured in oil, with people dressed in the quaint fashions of the time, standing in line for the first day's fare.

Culver's friends were also pilots. Mel Bancroft flew for Continental; Rich Albert was an air force colonel. Usually they talked about their profession, or about women, but tonight the topic was the incoming comet, and the heavy outbound traffic they'd seen on the highways around the capital. People were afraid that pieces of the moon might fall into the ocean and that Chesapeake Bay would spill over. Mel was not unsympathetic with those who'd chosen to head inland for the duration. He admitted he'd probably clear out too if he lived here. But he didn't, and he had a flight in the morning. Saturday night, he'd be in Indianapolis. "So if a piece of the Moon really does fall into the ocean," he said, "I plan to read about it in the paper."

Rich worked a desk job at the Pentagon. He didn't like the assignment or the bureaucracy, but he was getting his ticket punched for a star. He looked older than he was, and George thought part of that might have been the result of the peacekeeping operations he'd been involved in. A lot of people got killed during the African missions, and Rich had been captured and held for four months by Tibaki rebels. It was an event he would not talk about, but he walked more slowly than he used to, and sometimes winced when he got in and out of cars. He sipped his drink and admitted that he'd put his wife and kids on a plane as soon as he heard. "Nothing to lose by going to Vermont to stay with her folks for a few days."

"What about *you*, Rich?" George asked.

"I'm on duty over the weekend." He was thickset, short, with a sand-colored mustache. Rich was a poker player and a golfer, and he was quite capable of being the meanest son of a bitch in the world. He was designed by nature to fight wars. "But if anything happens," he grinned, "we'll call in the choppers and get the hell out."

The waiter took their orders, chicken fingers for Mel, a tuna sandwich for Rich, a Caesar salad for George.

"I saw a tidal wave once," said Mel. "We were flying medical and food supplies into Ahmadabad. There'd been some sort of outbreak, and I was in Saudi Arabia between flights. They were scrounging pilots who were certified for the 328s. So we took one on, and we were coming in out of the Arabian Sea just as a wave went ashore. Most terrifying goddam thing I've ever seen. Apparently, there'd been warnings, but nobody had gotten them to the general population. I read later that fifteen thousand people drowned or disappeared." Mel's eyes turned bleak. "They were just standing around when the wave hit."

George had been fortunate. "I've led a quiet life," he said. "Never seen anything like that. Never hope to."

The subject turned to the infant baseball season, and they were still arguing over predictions when lunch arrived. George took one bite of his salad and his cell phone beeped. He excused himself, slid the instrument out of his jacket pocket, and spoke into it. "Culver."

"George?"

"Yes, this is Culver."

"We need you, George. Right away."

He recognized the voice. "Pete, is that you?" He could hear control tower sounds in the background.

"It's me."

"I'm in the middle of lunch. I'm supposed to be off today."

"Life and death, buddy. For real. Get down here. Pack for a couple of days."

"*What?* What's going on?"

"Tell you when you get here."

"Pete, where am I going?"

Pause. Then: "The Moon."

•   •   •

NEWSNET. 12:30 P.M. UPDATE.
(Click for details.)

BRENKOV CHECKMATES WIDE-EYE
Russian Scores First Human Victory Ever Against MIT Program

Psychology:
INTELLIGENCE IS LEARNED BEHAVIOR
Graham: The Role Of Genetics Has Been Vastly Exaggerated

BRITAIN SENDS ASSISTANCE TO FLOOD-RAVAGED SUDAN

NEW BATTERY SYSTEM FOR CARS ON HORIZON
Thousand-Mile Charge To Be Available By '27
But New Units Are Expensive

JASON RILEY DEAD IN FALL FROM PENTHOUSE APARTMENT
Creator Of "Pat and Mary" May Have Been Pushed
Cartoonist Had Received Threats From Angry Readers
Accused Of Blasphemy, Racism, Anti-Elderly Attitudes

COMET TO HIT MOON
"It's Only A Reprieve," Says Michaelson
Collision With Earth Would Have "Killed Us All"
Moonbase To Be Evacuated

SEXCOMS AT TOP OF RATINGS AGAIN
Cop Shows Distant Second

FREE LUNCH GANG ROUNDED UP IN FLORIDA
Preyed On Handicapped

4.

Moonbase Spaceport. 12:33 P.M.

They were just beginning to admit passengers onto the boarding ramp when Tony Casaway arrived. He had originally been scheduled to carry the vice presidential party on the Micro to L1. But the schedules were in chaos today. He understood that management was trying to move as many people as possible to L1. The comet was coming, and people were excited, the way they got on roller coaster rides when they knew they were in for a deliciously scary time but one that ultimately would be safe.

Tony wasn't so sure. He'd caught a sense of worry when Bigfoot had brought him in to tell him about his shuffled assignments. Not desperation, by any means. But there had been a tightness in the air. He'd assigned it to the simple fact that Moonbase was going to get blitzed. But it might have been more than that.

Tony Casaway was an old test pilot, which is the best kind. He was different from the other pilots, who'd come to the Moon for reasons he could never understand. They talked a lot about frontiers and going to Mars. Tony came because Gina had gone shopping one day at a supermarket and walked into a hail of gunfire when a couple of goons tried to knock the place over. She was buried in a green hillside outside her native Kansas City, and Tony had gotten as far from that hillside as he could.

The Spaceport, like the rest of the facility, was submerged in the regolith. The hangers and pads were designed to accommodate a multitude of vehicles: the buses that connected Moonbase to L1, and a variety of space trucks and moon-hopping cargo carriers called lobbers that could haul equipment and products between the central complex and outlying factories and research posts.

A group of evacuees were milling about in the passenger lounge while technicians ran preflight checks on the two vehicles—a bus and the Micro—that were scheduled to depart within the half hour for L1. Most were middle-aged movers and shakers, VIPs who'd come to Moonbase for the ceremony. These included an eminent historian, a world-famous sculptor, and two Hollywood types. Wolfgang Weller, the German foreign minister, and his three-person entourage were also here.

Weller was tall and imposing, with cold gray eyes and an imperious manner. He looked annoyed, and Tony wondered whether the source of his irritation was the impending destruction of Moonbase or the fact that he was being herded about with the commoners. He looked like an easy man to dislike. Curious quality in a diplomat.

Or maybe the trouble was in Tony's mind. He didn't like high-powered types. They always seemed to need special attention, and to expect people to fawn over them. He made it a point therefore to seem unaware of the rank of any such passenger.

The passengers parted to let Tony through. He strode up the ramp and was greeted inside by Shen Ka-tai, the flight attendant. "Saber's on board," he told Tony.

Tony nodded and passed into the snug passenger compartment. There were four seats on either side of the aisle, set in pairs. The nature of traffic between L1 and Moonbase dictated the need for a compact, fuel-efficient vehicle to transport small groups and occasionally single persons. That vehicle was the Micro. Two more microbuses were currently under construction and were to join the fleet within the month.

His passengers were coming in behind him. Weller and three aides, and a family with two kids. Eight people in all. The manifest described the family as tourists and indicated their final destination as London. The two kids, a freckled girl about ten and her slightly younger brother, looked excited.

The parents, however, were brusque and nervous. They issued sharp commands to their progeny to sit down, buckle in, and please don't make so much noise. Tony reassured them, explaining that they'd be safely home when the comet arrived, a state of affairs that clearly disappointed the kids. The mother began a lecture about how this was not funny and they were lucky to be on their way.

Tony climbed the ladder and slipped through the overhead hatch onto the flight deck.

Saber was going through the preflight routine. "Hello, Tony," she said, smiling at him over one shoulder. She was tall and lean, almost six feet, with a boyish build. She had black hair and luminous blue eyes, and despite her lack of dimensions, never seemed to want for male escorts. Her name was Alisa Rolnikaya, and she'd been born in Florence into a Russian diplomat's family. She'd learned to fly when she was fifteen, returned to her family's home in St. Petersburg for her education, learned to fly jets, and spent several years with a NATO squadron whose pilots had been mostly Italian. There she'd acquired the code name "Saber," which had followed her to the Moon. The name fit, Tony thought. There was an edge to her personality, and to her sense of humor. She'd been with the Lunar Transport Authority three months, and her assignment to the Micro was her first. So far she seemed competent enough.

"Have you seen the comet pictures?" she asked.

He nodded. He was already making retirement plans. Below, Shen was getting the passengers seated.

"Switch to internal power," said Saber.

"Micro." Moonbase Control on the circuit.

"Go ahead, Control."

"You are unplugged and ready for departure in six minutes."

The Micro was a sphere set on top of a pair of landing

treads. The flight deck was located inside a blister at the top of the sphere. At that moment Tony was looking out across the bay, where he could see the power and fuel umbilicals dropping away. The indicator lamps on his status board blinked yellow. Depressurization in the bay had begun.

The pad clamps released.

Tony listened to the sounds in the cabin below: footsteps, voices, luggage being placed in the overhead bins. Then the closing of hatches, inner and outer. The air pumps picked up a notch.

Shen reported the passenger cabin ready for departure.

Control again: "Micro, your turnaround time at L1 is going to be as quick as they can make it. Sleep when you can. It doesn't look as if you're going to have any down time until Friday."

"That's what I hear. It's going to get rank in the old Micro."

Saber smiled and shook her head. They both knew there'd be a quick break while the vehicle was being serviced after each flight. Not a lot of time, but enough to get scrubbed off and change into a fresh uniform.

"It's *always* been rank in the old Micro," said a new voice, which Tony recognized as that of the operations supervisor, Bigfoot Caparatti.

"Hello, Bigfoot," he said.

"See you when you get back, Tony," said Caparatti. "Good flight."

The overhead doors began to open.

"Green board, Tony," said Saber.

"Countdown to ignition. On my mark. Ten . . ."

The Micro mounted a single General Electric 7RV engine, capable of providing a steady one-g acceleration. At zero, Tony started it. It roared into life. The flight deck trembled and the Micro began to rise. Then they were out of the illuminated bay, ascending into the night.

White House, Truman Room. 1:27 P.M.

"Al, is everyone here?"

The president had summoned his cabinet for a teleconference about the comet with two scientific experts.

Kerr had been talking with the secretary of defense when Henry entered. He glanced around the table, did a quick count, and nodded. "Yes, Mr. President. Only one missing is Hopkins."

Armand Hopkins, the secretary of the interior, was on the West Coast. Henry took his seat, trying not to show that he was in pain. He hurt all the time now, but only Emily knew. And probably Al.

Henry had been a vibrant, energetic head of state during the first two years. He still tried to maintain the pretense, but it was getting harder. The disease was sucking his life away. He'd have kept the story quiet if he could, but there'd been no way to do that. Still, as long as people didn't *see* it happening, he could continue to function. He'd become almost a tragic figure, perceived as a kind of saint, a man confronting eternity, with no motive to do anything other than what was right for the nation. Everyone treated him with deference, more or less as though the entire nation were attending a bedside vigil. It was a situation unique in American history. Other presidents had received the country's adulation in retrospect. Henry enjoyed it while in office. In the United States of 2024, it was not considered sporting or decent to attack the president. On the other hand, he was the ultimate lame duck.

"Mr. President," Kerr said, "unless you have a preliminary comment, we're ready to go remote."

"Do it."

Split-screen images, a man and a woman, flickered onto a wall display. Henry had seen the man's face before, but he couldn't put a name to it.

He had caught a second breath since his meeting with

Juarez, and his basic philosophy, that everything turns out okay if people just don't panic, had taken hold. One of the TV images, the man, wore a graveyard demeanor. *We don't want that dumb son of a bitch talking to the media,* Henry thought. *Who brought* him *in?* But Henry thought his cabinet members and advisors also looked gloomy.

"Before we go any farther," said Henry, "let me caution everyone that we need to be careful what we say outside this room. The Moon story's already out, but the public reaction is going to depend to a fair degree on what comes out of this meeting." That wasn't so, of course. Henry knew that the media would be the ultimate influence and *they* would decide how to play the story. But he needed his people to do their part. And he particularly wanted to impress the outsiders that they should be careful what they say. "When we get out of here and talk for the record, let's try to think about the impact our words will have. Things are going to be difficult enough over the next few days. We don't want panic on our hands if we can avoid it." He saw his secretary of state frame the word *panic* on his thin lips as if the thought had not occurred to him. Henry pushed back in his chair and removed a gold pen from an inside pocket. "Now, Al, why don't you introduce our guests."

Kerr nodded. "Professor Alice Finizio from the Jet Propulsion Lab." An African-American, she wore bifocals attached to her lapel by a silver chain. Her orange blazer seemed a bit loud to the president, who believed that the inner self, and not one's clothing, should be the source of attention. She was a slim woman, with silver hair, probably close to seventy. She reminded him quite forcibly of his late grandmother. Kerr described her as an astronomer.

"And Professor Wesley Feinberg of the AstroLab." That explained why the face had seemed familiar. Feinberg was a leading scientist, had won at least one Nobel prize, and had been on the cover of *Time* or *Newsweek* recently. He'd even been a guest at a White House dinner, although Henry couldn't recall speaking with him.

Feinberg was thin, short, bleary-eyed, with a crop of gray hair pushed back on a balding skull. His expression suggested he had more important things to do.

"I'd like to welcome you both," the president said, "and we thank you for taking time to be with us today. I'm sure you were introduced earlier to the people at the table." He knew that wasn't so, but it didn't matter. "Mercedes," he said, "where are we?"

"We are now projecting a ninety-seven percent probability that Tomiko will strike the Moon."

"Any conflicting views?" This was aimed at the faces on the wallscreen.

Finizio's eyes were slits. "I'd say it's more like ninety-nine six. There's no question about this that I can see."

"Okay." Henry took a deep breath. "It's going to hit. What does that mean?"

"If it comes in the way we expect it to," said Feinberg, "it'll splash the Moon."

Finizio confirmed the estimate by her silence.

"I'm sorry," said Jessica McDermott, his secretary of defense. "I didn't catch that. What do you mean *splash*?" McDermott had been CEO at Rockwell before moving over to the Pentagon. She was in her sixties.

"It means that after Saturday night there probably won't *be* a Moon."

The men and women around the table shifted uneasily. Chairs creaked, people cleared their throats. Harold Boatmann, secretary of transportation, glanced up at a portrait of a smiling Harry Truman. "I guess we can get by without a moon," he said. "Are there any other *consequences*?"

"The Moon," said Feinberg, "will probably become a mass

of loose rubble, plasma, dust, and gas. Some of that debris can be expected to come our way."

All eyes turned toward the president. Henry felt his mouth going dry. He'd spent the last couple of hours convincing himself that a collision occurring a quarter-million miles away could not present a serious threat to the well-being of the United States. He looked down the table at a line of worried faces. "What are we talking about, exactly?" he asked. "Are we in trouble?"

"Probably not a great deal," said Finizio. She even *sounded* like his grandmother. She looked directly at him. "I think the primary danger here is not from lunar debris, but from panic."

"That's nonsense," said Feinberg. "There's going to be a lot of rock flying around and we don't know where any of it will be going. Mr. President, *anything* can happen."

"Define *anything*."

"Earthquakes. Tidal waves. God knows what conditions will be like Sunday morning. But I'll give you an example of the possibilities: If a big enough chunk of rock were to fall into the Pacific, we'd all go for a swim. Damned near the whole planet."

Kolladner heard fingernails tapping. Someone coughed.

Finizio rolled her eyes. "That's a *remote* possibility, Wesley," she said, "and you know it."

"It's not at all remote."

"Of course it is. Listen, you've always had a tendency to exaggerate, but I think you need to curb yourself a little here."

Henry broke in before it could develop into a food fight. "Professor Finizio, tell us what *you* expect to happen."

"Very little, Mr. President. Understand, with an event like this, Wes is right. *Anything* is possible. But none of it is very likely. What I expect is that there'll be increased meteor activity. But I suspect we'll come through it quite nicely. You may have to deal with a few isolated incidents. But probably nothing worth getting alarmed over."

"There'll also be a problem about the axis," said Feinberg, as if Finizio hadn't spoken. "The obliquity of the ecliptic is, to a degree, sustained by the relationship between Moon and Earth. Take that away—"

"Oh, for heaven's sake," said Finizio.

"In English, please," said the president.

Feinberg nodded. "The seasons depend on the tilt of the Earth's axis. You know that, of course. We're farther from the Sun in July than in December. But that could all change now. Take away the Moon, and we're going to see a much more pronounced wobble."

"Do we care?" asked Patricia Russell, the press secretary.

"Summers will get hotter, winters colder. Higher latitudes will become unlivable. There'll be a problem with farming."

"Farming?" asked Henry. He looked back at Finizio for help.

"He means the wheat belt will move south," she said. "But that's something that won't happen for a very long time. Not anything we'll have to worry about."

"The next administration?" asked one of the political advisors.

Finizio laughed. "Maybe the next millennium," she said. "Certainly not earlier. Probably considerably later."

"That's true," admitted Feinberg, "but we need to think about the future."

"Let's *stick* with the present for now," said Henry. "Is there anything else?"

"Be assured," said Finizio, "that the Moon is not going to go flying off in all directions. Gravity will still be present, and whatever else happens, most of the rock that now composes the Moon will stay right where it is. Oh, it'll get moved around a little. Broken apart. But no worse. I think the government's wisest course is to simply keep everyone calm." She glanced off to her left, where she must have been looking at an image of Feinberg.

The president wanted to applaud.

"I think that's an extremely optimistic view," said Feinberg.

"What do you want me to do?" asked Henry quietly. "Evacuate both coasts?"

"I'll tell you what you *should* do," said Finizio. "For starters, evacuate L1. It's too close to the collision. And maybe Skyport, for good measure."

Evacuate the stations. Well, that at least was easily done. And best of all, it wasn't his responsibility. But he'd pass the advice along.

Seeing he could get no farther with the experts, Henry broke away from them at the earliest opportunity, thanked them for their advice, and turned to his aides. "We don't have much time," he said. "I propose to answer the critical questions first." He looked at Mercedes Juarez. "Can we stop this thing? What about nuking it?"

"It's too big," she said, "and it's coming too fast. Johnson Space Center says we might as well try to hit it with a stick."

"Should we issue a warning?"

"I don't see how we can," said Amos Pierson, his counsel. "Can you imagine trying to evacuate L.A. and New York by *Saturday*? Where would we put everybody? How would we *feed* them? We'd get giant traffic jams, people would die in accidents, and others would die because emergency vehicles wouldn't be able to get to them." He thumped two fingers on the table. "And there'd be a lot of looting unless we plan to leave the cops behind to take their chances. I guarantee you, Mr. President, call for an evacuation, and we'll see a disaster of monumental proportions."

Harold Boatmann had folded his arms in a defensive posture as Pierson came to his point. "I can't believe," he said angrily, "that we'd tell people everything's okay when we know damned well it might not be, and then sit back and hope nothing happens."

"It won't matter what we tell them," said Russell. "They're going to hear about it on TV anyway. Nobody's going to pay much attention to what *we* say. People will panic, and it'll be Katy bar the door."

"I keep thinking," said McDermott, "what'll happen if you try to evacuate and it all just blows over. *The sky is falling.* I can see the editorial cartoons now."

Afterward Henry returned with Kerr to his office and lowered himself into the leather chair that had been designed specifically to ease his chronically aching back. "You know, Al," he said, "it doesn't matter a damn what we do unless the media cooperate. If those sons of bitches decide to play everything up, we'll have the biggest panic on our hands this country's ever seen."

They stared at each other. "Have Grace get McConnell on the line for me."

5.

Ronald Reagan Washington National Airport, Washington, D.C. 1:33 P.M.

The space plane resembled a rocket ship out of a 1950s science fiction film. It was long, silver, bullet-shaped, with stubby retractable wings and tail fins. It was fueled by a mixture of hydrogen and oxygen. The Reagan flights were propelled by a rocket booster along a seventeen-mile-long tunnel, traveling northwest beneath the Potomac into Maryland, and launching near Glen Hills. A nuclear-powered version was on the drawing board, but until someone could figure out how to allay environmental concerns, it was going to stay there.

Alexander Drummond, the operations boss for LTA Reagan, was short, fat, and bald. He wore chain jewelry and his tie was pulled down and his shirt was open at the neck. He had bushy eyebrows and thick lips. His type had appeared in a thousand cop films as Mister Big. He was staring out his office window, from which he could see both the SSTO and the launch track. "George," he said without turning around, "your mission profile is on the desk."

George Culver glanced down at the folder but made no move toward it.

"It asks you to do double duty," Drummond said. He came back to his chair, waved George into the divan, and sat down. "*I'm* asking you to do double duty."

Drummond had hired George, had looked after him, and George understood it was now payback time. "I'm listening," he said.

"There'll be four planes on the mission. Two of them will leave Skyport today and arrive in lunar orbit tomorrow around noon. Both will start back Friday, bringing as many people with them as possible.

"A third plane will go into lunar orbit Friday evening and will leave late Saturday afternoon. By then, there shouldn't be too many people left.

"We want *you* to go to L1. You'll get there at about eleven A.M. tomorrow. Pick up your passengers. Expect a full load. Return to Skyport. Your TOA should be about seven A.M. Friday."

George shrugged. So far so good.

"Unload and refuel. As soon as you're able, you'll turn around and head for the Moon."

"You're not serious," said George.

"You'll be in lunar orbit by noon Saturday. Shortly after you get there, the third plane will leave. *You* pick up whoever's left."

"How many are going to be left?"

"Probably fewer than a hundred. But you won't have them all on board until roughly nine-thirty. I'm sorry; I know that's not much lead time."

"You mean before the comet comes in."

"Yeah. That's what I mean."

No wonder the son of a bitch was looking guilty. "Alex, what the hell are you setting me up for? You want me sitting out there when the place goes up?"

"You should be well on your way back before the event."

"*Well on my way back?* What are we talking here? Twenty minutes?"

"An hour, George. I think I can promise you an hour. Minimum. Listen, I know it's tight, but we don't have any choice."

"Sure you do. You've got a half-dozen or so other SSTOs sitting around. Use one of those and speed things up."

Drummond's chair squeaked. "Sending a fifth plane wouldn't speed *anything* up, George. The bottleneck's with the moonbuses. Getting people off the surface and up to the planes. It's a slow process. So it doesn't matter whether we use four planes or five. The last flight out is still going to be leaving at around nine-thirty P.M. Saturday.

"Now, we're doing it the way we are for two reasons. One, you're the best I have. You might need to do some jinking on the way back, and there's nobody I'd rather have in the left-hand seat. Two, sending you out to L1 will give you some experience in how the vehicle handles beyond earth-orbit."

"Great," said George. "I'm honored."

Outside, a fuel truck moved across the concrete apron. "You don't have to do it. I can't force you. But there'll be roughly a hundred people coming back with you. Their lives will depend on the pilot we send them. I want *you*. If you want to back off, I'll understand and I'll get one of the others."

"Son of a bitch," said George.

"Thanks." Drummond picked up the mission profile and held it out to him.

•   •   •

Moonbase, Grissom Country. 3:05 P.M.

Evelyn took the call in her private suite. She was not a physicist, but she suspected what was coming, and the suspicion was confirmed when she recognized Kermit Hancock's voice. Hancock was her second-in-command at corporate headquarters in Boston. "We got a call from the White House," he said without ceremony. "They're recommending we evacuate both space stations. Especially L1. They think it might get totaled."

Totaled. The term somehow trivialized the potential loss of so much. But at least they had the plane going out there. Just as well to get everybody off. "Do it," she said. "I'll make the calls."

There was a long pause. "Evelyn, I'm sorry."

"Me too, Kerm." She felt very tired. "Me too."

Microbus, approaching L1. 3:10 P.M.

The station floated against a background of stars. As Tony Casaway watched, it disgorged a ferry. The ferries were boxy vehicles, capable of carrying between twelve and forty passengers, depending on the model. Their sole mission was to move passengers and cargo between the space stations. This was the *Christopher Talley.* Tony was close enough to see people in the passenger cabin. They were probably dependents being sent to Skyport as a precaution against the comet.

Digital readings blurred on his screens as thrusters fired and the main engine, which had been braking the ship, went silent. They were rotating in sync with the satellite. The Moon, enormous at a range of only sixty thousand kilometers, and Earth drifted slowly across the windows in apparent pursuit of each other as the microbus turned on its axis.

Like Skyport, L1 used counter-rotating wheels to enhance stability and simulate a sizable fraction of lunar gravity. L1 was smaller than the Earth orbiter by almost a third, and because it had no tourist pretensions, it was a far more spartan facility. Several thruster clusters helped maintain its position at the unstable Lagrangian point.

"Seven minutes to dock," said Saber.

"Roger." He locked onto the short-range beacons and manuevered into the designated guide path while Saber talked to the flight controllers and started providing minute-by-minute course adjustments.

Then a new voice came on the circuit. "Tony."

"Go ahead, L1."

"Update. FYI, Tony, we just got word we're evacuating the station."

Tony thought he meant Moonbase. "Say again, please."

"They're looking for major trouble when the comet hits. We're clearing out L1."

Evacuating *L1? "By Saturday?"*

"Roger. You're instructed to unload your passengers and start back posthaste."

The terminator arced across the lunar surface, dividing it sharply between dark and light. Tony glanced over at Saber.

"We're a long way from the Moon," she said. "How much damage can Tomiko do?"

6.

Skyport. 4:04 P.M.

The two planes making the early flight were from Berlin and Copenhagen. The pilots had left their flight attendants home. George had allowed his to come on the *Arlington*, with the understanding that they would make the first flight, to L1, but not the lunar mission.

The fourth spacecraft, they were informed, would be coming from Rome.

The three flight crews spent an hour with operational personnel in a ready room talking over details, setting up emergency communication protocols, trying to foresee what might go wrong, discussing the handling problems they could expect. The SSTOs weren't designed to fly to the Moon, and if anyone had foreseen the eventuality, there was no evidence of it in operational contingency plans. They would drag a lot of mass in the form of airframe, atmospheric engines, and landing gear, making them sluggish. If they really were going to have to dodge flying rock, they would have their hands full.

They would go into their assigned orbits, and moonbuses would come to them. The lunies also had two trucks available. The trucks had no in-flight docking capabilities, but would have to employ extravehicular activity (EVA) to transfer passengers. These would, of course, be operational personnel. And there'd only be one or two at a time. Carrying capacity for passengers was small.

"Nonexistent is more like it," said Nora Ehrlich, the British-born pilot of *Copenhagen*. "How tight is this operation?"

"You got it," said the briefer. "We have no room for screwups."

Shortly after he'd arrived, George had learned that other planes had been brought in to evacuate Skyport. Only operations people would remain to service the planes and take care of their passengers, and a few others deemed necessary to keep the station running. This was purely a precaution, management was saying.

After the conference, George and his crew went to Mo's Restaurant for dinner. At six he called Operations. They were still taking care of the details, they told him. But he should be ready to leave by eight P.M.

One of the details consisted of writing the navigational programming. The assignment was given to an overworked and underpaid technician whose job was to communicate with one of the astronavigators, and translate his instructions into code for the onboard computers on the three spacecraft. This technician was Kay Wilmont, who was in her second tour on board Skyport, and who had just put in for a supervisor's job.

The original plan had been to refuel the tanks to about half capacity, the level necessary to make the round-trip to either lunar orbit or L1. (There was no real difference.) But late planners had informed Operations that the SSTOs might have to do some maneuvering on the way home. Better be safe than sorry.

This was another breakdown. The only planes that might be forced to do violent maneuvering would be the two that would return Saturday. But no matter: The decision was taken to fill all tanks to capacity.

However, no one told Kay, or the people on her watch, of the change in plans. Consequently, the programs assumed a fuel weight that was fifty percent less than the amount actually carried. This was an error that, once caught, would require a series of midcourse corrections. In and of itself, it would involve no danger to the mission.

Transglobal Executive Suite, Manhattan. 4:47 P.M.

Twenty-seven years ago Bruce Kendrick had been the weatherman on the Channel 11 news out of Topeka. He'd been noticed by Captain Raymond L. McConnell when a Kansas City blizzard forced McConnell's plane to divert and he'd had to spend the night at the local Sheraton. McConnell had liked the way the kid handled low-pressure fronts, had offered him a job with the network, and the rest, as they say, was history.

Transglobal was filled with stories like that. Most of the top brass, and virtually all of the top performers (which was what TV journalists had evolved into), had been handpicked by the Captain. He owned the network, he had an unerring talent for turning huge profits out of news and features, and he was arguably the most powerful person in the United States. Quite possibly in the world.

The Captain did not owe his title to a naval heritage. According to Transglobal lore, it had begun as a joke, a designation suggested by his autocratic manner. McConnell nevertheless liked the title. He encouraged its use, and it consequently became the accepted form of address by all. He was fond of telling public gatherings that it had derived from subordinates who wished to impress him. And he always got a laugh by adding that he would have preferred "Judge," or better yet, "Excellency," but that his staff had drawn the line.

Everyone who knew the Captain was aware there was no line.

Bruce Kendrick was no stranger to the eleventh floor of the Transglobal Building. McConnell customarily had him in on Thursday afternoons, along with his immediate boss, news director Chuck Parmentier. The purpose of the meetings was to allow the Captain to keep involved with the news operation. *Let's take a look at where we've been this week, what we're emphasizing, what the slant has looked like, what's coming up. And perhaps most important, what we want to achieve and how best to go about it.*

If McConnell was a dictator, he nevertheless knew enough to ask questions and listen to the answers. He withheld his own views until the very last, and as far as Kendrick could judge, kept an open mind until the time for decision arrived. He was even willing to entertain objections after a decision had been made, and had been known to reverse himself in the face of a compelling argument. It was a quality, Parmentier maintained, utterly unique in the executive suites of the giant newsgathering corporations.

But this was Wednesday, a day early. Kendrick went first to the news chief's office. "It has to be the comet," Parmentier said.

The Captain was not a physically imposing man. He was

an inch or two under average height, his hair still black despite his seventy years. He was a lawyer by training, although he'd never practiced. He was standing by a window as they were shown into his suite, looking down at Central Park. The office was immense, decorated with original artwork, including a Remington and a Jardin. "Gentlemen," he said unceremoniously, "we have work to do." A steward wheeled in a tray of donuts and danish, and poured coffee all around.

The Captain circled his desk and sat down. His brows were heavy, his eyes scarcely visible. "Take a look at this," he said. He punched a button and the four o'clock news roundup began to roll.

The daytime anchor's girl-next-door features smiled out from the screen. *"This is Janet Martin at the news desk,"* she said. *"There's more fallout from the Comet Tomiko story this afternoon. People along both coasts and near large bodies of water around the world have begun to flee their homes. As Tomiko zeroes in on the Moon, scientists are warning of the possibility that debris might fall into the oceans, generating enormous waves."* (Cut to pictures of jammed highways, traffic moving at a crawl.) *"How serious is it? Dan Molinari is at the Beaver Meadow Observatory in New York with one of the people who are trying to find out. Dan, how's it look?"*

Molinari was standing with a bespectacled little gray-haired man wrapped in a frumpy blue sweater. *"Janet, this is Wesley Feinberg of Harvard's AstroLab. He came up here for the total eclipse and hasn't gone home yet. Professor Feinberg, I wonder if you can tell us what's going to happen this weekend."*

Parmentier was watching the Captain to try to guess what was wrong.

". . . really hard to say, Dan. Anything could happen. There's just no way to predict accurately the aftermath of an event this explosive."

"Professor, we've seen that a lot of people are worried about the oceans. How do you feel about that? Is there a real danger for those who live in coastal areas?"

"Certainly. If I lived on a beachfront, I'd want to be away from it for the next few days. Wouldn't you? Denver's nice this time of year."

McConnell muted the sound, leaving the two images to continue their conversation silently. He looked across the vast expanse of his cherrywood desk, directly at Parmentier. "Well, Chuck," he said, "what do you think?"

"It's a damned good story," said Parmentier. "I don't think I understand what you're driving at, Captain."

Kendrick looked from his boss to the Captain. Parmentier was usually pretty quick on his feet, but when he thought he had a story he could run with he sometimes became obtuse. Kendrick knew right away where this was going, but he was far too shrewd to embarrass the man who signed his paycheck.

McConnell's eyebrows drew together. "Have you considered," he asked, "what will happen if we succeed in panicking two hundred fifty million people? Not to mention our overseas audience?"

Parmentier's face reddened. "Captain, this is a very big story. What do you want us to do? Sit on it?"

"I don't like the way we're playing it, Chuck. We could instigate a major disaster. There've already been deaths out there."

"Accidents."

"They happen when people go around the bend. We are in the process of driving a lot of people around the bend." He spared a glance for Kendrick, who tried to look as if he'd thought all along they should be going easy on this.

"We have a responsibility to the public," Parmentier said.

"Goddammit, Chuck, save that kind of talk for the politicians. This is *me*. I will not be responsible for creating several nights of mayhem. For killing God knows how many people before this is over. And maybe inviting a few lawsuits."

Parmentier was not a man to be threatened lightly, even by the Captain. "We have no choice, *sir*," he said, pronouncing each word deliberately and with a touch of outrage, "but to present the truth to our viewers. The truth is that there may be major disruptions over the next few days. Places like New York are vulnerable. It's our *job* to tell them what we know."

McConnell's eyes grew hard and he looked at Kendrick. "Bruce, I wanted you in here because I thought this was something we all need to agree on. What's your opinion?"

Kendrick cleared his throat and started to talk in circles. "Never mind," said the Captain. "I can see you'll try to protect your boss. And that's good, Bruce. Up to a point. But this—" He got up and studied a Remington on his desk. "The truth is, Bruce, that we really don't *know* what's going to happen. Everything is speculation, and speculation should not be passed off as hard news. Do I make myself clear?"

"I suppose," said Parmentier, "we could shift the emphasis."

"Yes," said the Captain. "That's exactly what we *will* do. We will shift the emphasis."

His tone suggested that, unless anyone wanted to debate the issue, the interview was over. Parmentier and Kendrick rose. Kendrick said he'd get right on it. And both men started for the door.

"One more thing," said McConnell. "Over the weekend—"

"Yes, sir?"

"We'll do the network broadcasts from field stations. See Jim. He's already setting it up. I don't want any of our people in the building, or anywhere near the city, after tomorrow."

White House, Oval Office. 4:48 P.M.

Feinberg smiled innocuously out of the screen. "*Certainly. If I lived near an ocean, I'd want to be away from it for the next few days. Wouldn't you? Denver's nice this time of year.*"

Henry killed the picture. "Sometimes I wish for the old days," he said.

"How do you mean, Henry?" asked Kerr.

"When national leaders could have nitwits shot. There's a lot to be said for that." He'd just finished a conference call with his counterparts in Japan, Britain, Germany, Russia, and China. Everyone was adrift. Germany and Russia were acting, moving people inland. They could do that. They didn't have thousands of miles of coastline to concern themselves with. Others were taking moderate measures, stockpiling supplies, planning for disaster relief, and putting the military on standby. Britain and Japan, without any interior to speak of, were at the mercy of events.

Henry didn't like his own policy, which consisted of watching, waiting, and trying to reassure everyone. Of hoping he could ride it out. *We'll deal with the consequences as they arise*, he told himself. *Maybe we'll get lucky.* Some religious leaders were urging him to declare a national day of prayer. That was all the nation would need during a crisis, to see its president on his knees.

Nobody makes it to the Oval Office without taking a lot of heat. By the time he arrives, he's scarred, cynical, tough, single-minded. And he doesn't believe anybody or anything can't be handled. (Or *she* doesn't. The United States had had its first woman president. She'd served one term, 2017–2021, and refused the nomination for a second with the comment, *Not worth it.*)

She was wrong, of course. It *was* worth it. Henry knew that. And every other politician in the country worthy of the name knew it. Even in times like this, when so much depended on his decisions, and the way was so murky, it was worth it. Especially in times like this. There was no chance at greatness without a decent challenge. He'd been concerned that he would disappear into the history books with people like Polk and Cleveland, effective presidents who might have ranked high had a sufficient misfortune risen to confront them. You can't be a Lincoln without a civil war. It now appeared he had his civil war.

Despite the overwhelming nature of the problem, he'd thrown aside his dark mood of the morning. He needed to get everything right. And he needed to be lucky.

But there was no reason to believe that would not happen.

7.

TRANSGLOBAL WORLD REPORT. 6:45 P.M.

"An Indonesian plane crashed in the Bay of Bengal today with all aboard, two hundred seventy people, believed lost. Rescue operations are hampered by bad weather.

"Rebels in Patagonia admitted responsibility for the bombing of a government office building, where eleven people, including an American diplomat, were killed last week.

"Here at home, people continue to take to the roads in unprecedented numbers, frightened by reports that pieces of the Moon might fall into the oceans Saturday night. We should remind our viewers that many scientists have said that such an event is unlikely. This is Bruce Kendrick with the *World Report.*"

White House Rose Garden. 7:44 P.M.

In the evening, Henry could see the comet. It was a bright, blurry patch in the west, lingering for a short time after sunset. It would, astronomers noted, move rapidly up the sky over the next few nights.

STATEMENT BY THE PRESIDENT. 8:00 P.M.
Delivered over all networks.

"My fellow Americans,

"As you're aware, Comet Tomiko is approaching the Moon, and is expected to collide with it Saturday evening at approximately ten thirty-five P.M. eastern daylight time.

"I'm pleased to tell you that evacuation of Moonbase, and as a precaution, of the two space stations, is going ahead with all deliberate speed. We do not anticipate any difficulty getting everyone out of harm's way.

"There's been some concern about pieces of moonrock being jarred loose and coming our way. It appears that the force of the impact may be sufficient to severely disrupt the Moon. As a result there may be some debris. But there is no immediate cause for concern. Your government has been monitoring the situation, and the angle of the strike is such that scientists are confident we have nothing to fear.

"While I will not underestimate the gravity of the situation, the most serious danger we face right now is the possibility that some Americans will overreact. This is a time when we must remain calm and not allow ourselves to be stampeded by fear or rumor. We are in this together and we will come through it together. I have directed that federal agencies and military units be put on alert to render assistance, should that become necessary. Meantime, the safest place for you and your family this weekend is at home.

"Thank you very much. And good evening."

Moonbase Spaceport. 11:28 P.M.

Tony had ferried two loads of passengers to L1 in record time. During the second run, the Micro completed its six-thousandth hour in flight. That imposed a series of routine service requirements on the maintenance crew. When he arrived at Moonbase, they went after it with their checklists. They examined thrusters and docking assemblies, inspected life support, and set themselves to replacing those parts that were subject to a high degree of wear. Among these parts were the actuator valves for the attitude jets.

The evacuation planners intended to abandon the micro-bus, along with the other two moonbuses, after they'd completed their mission and everyone was aboard the space planes. Consequently, much of the six-thousand-hour maintenance routine should have been unnecessary. But in the communication between the command function and the operational crews, that detail was lost.

Tony's Micro was subjected to the full treatment. Workers knew only that they had ninety minutes to perform a maintenance that normally required five hours. The result was, as one might imagine, that thoroughness was sacrificed.

Like all pure space vehicles, the Micro was equipped with a single engine and a group of attitude jets. It was fueled by a mixture of powdered aluminum and liquid oxygen. After a cumulative burn time, the jets were inclined to slag, and therefore required periodic replacement.

The jets were mounted on a bracket between ring-shaped fuel intake manifolds circling the ship. One ring carried fuel; the other, oxidizer. The pitch/yaw assembly consisted of four jets facing out, equally spaced around the ship. The roll assembly was the same except that the jets were locked in the bracket so they faced tangentially, two clockwise, two counter. The Micro had four assemblies total, pitch/yaw in front and back, roll around the center, and a fourth set mounted along the thrust axis, two forward and two back, used for fine position maneuvering.

Wherever possible, parts converged. All pipes, fittings, and manifold outlets were identical for all ferries, buses, and cargo haulers, even though the haulers used larger engines. Consequently, the piping was oversized for the smaller engines, and could deliver more fuel or oxidizer than necessary. Flow was controlled by an actuator valve. Moonbase manufactured two types of engines: large for the cargo carriers, and small for the buses. In the big engines, volumetric flow was doubled.

Because of convergence, both units looked identical. Those designed for oxidizer were rounded; those for fuel had flat surfaces. But the only way to distinguish between valves for large and small engines was to look at the part designator. There was no throttle in the vehicle; current opened the valve, lack of current closed it.

The technician charged with installing the units was a thirty-year-old engineer from the University of Texas. His name was Elias Tobin, and up until that time he had a perfect work record in a job that required absolute attention to detail. But Elias was under pressure to finish, because lubricants needed to be replaced, engine lines inspected, and the engine recalibrated. Later, an investigation team would determine that under the circumstances, the only essential task among those assigned to Elias was the replacement of the actuator valves.

He got it wrong.

Fortunately, it was not in itself a serious error.

LUFTHANSA ADVISORY TO U.S. TERMINALS. 11:47 P.M.

Lufthansa Airlines announces that, as a precaution against expected celestial events this weekend, all flights will be grounded after 8:30 P.M. EDT, Saturday, April 13. Resumption of service is tentatively scheduled for 12:01 A.M. EDT, Wednesday, April 17, but will depend on existing conditions.

CHAPTER FOUR

FLIGHT
Thursday, April 11

1.

L1, Pilots' Quarters. 3:06 A.M.

The phone brought Rachel Quinn out of a deep sleep. She flicked on the table lamp and looked at her watch. "Quinn," she said into the speaker.

"Rachel." The voice was familiar, but she couldn't immediately place it. "I'm sorry to wake you at this ungodly hour."

The station director. "It's okay, John. What's wrong?"

"I wonder if you could come by my office."

"Now?"

"Please. It's urgent."

She slipped out of bed and fifteen minutes later emerged from an elevator in the executive suites of the administration section. Lights were on and people were working. The director's secretary looked up as she entered. "Please go in, Colonel."

John Barringer was arrogant, ruthless, and capable of throwing tantrums. When she walked in he was bent over printouts with an aide. He signed for her to take a seat, dismissed the aide, and came over to her. "Rachel," he said, "When were you planning on taking *Lowell* back to Skyport?"

"Tomorrow," she said.

"I wonder if I could have you move your schedule up a little bit?"

All she needed to do was get some supplies on board. Food and water. "I don't see why not," she said. "When did you want us to get under way?"

"ASAP. We've got our hands full with the evacuation, and you can help."

"Sure. What do you need?"

Barringer leaned back and crossed one leg over the other. "There's a crunch at Moonbase. They have a lot of people to get out. Right now they're shipping them over here. You could go home by way of Luna, pick some of them up, and get them clear. Help take a little of the pressure off."

"I didn't realize it was that close," she said. "I understood there was no problem."

"Let's say they've tried to keep the public statements optimistic. In any case, we'd appreciate the assistance."

"Sure," she said. "We'll do what we can. But keep in mind that *Lowell*'s only designed to carry six. Lee and I are two. That means we can only accommodate four more. That doesn't sound like much help."

Barringer leaned forward. "Why only four?"

"We'll be squeezing life support. But we can manage maybe a couple extra. Make it six."

"Good," he said. "That's a start. Suppose we put oxygen masks on board. *Then* how many can you take?"

"I don't think I want to risk carrying people all the way to Skyport using individual breathing gear."

Barringer nodded. "I don't think you quite understand what I'm trying to say, Rachel. People you don't take might get left."

"My God, is it that bad?"

"It's tight."

"How many do you want to put on board?"

"About twenty. Maybe a few more if you can manage."

"They're not going to be comfortable."

"We're not worried about *comfortable*."

"Okay," she said. "Give me twenty. No, make it twenty-five."

Barringer was a man easily lost in a crowd: round face, receding hairline, unremarkable features. She'd never thought much of him, truthfully. Rachel believed that a man was best judged by what he cared about, and Barringer, in her presence, talked only about accounting techniques and personnel procedures. He visibly toadied to visiting VIPs, and (if reports were accurate) rarely had a kind word for his employees. But this morning she felt sorry for him.

"I'll have the tanks and masks loaded within the hour," he said. He studied her briefly. "I know there are only two of you. Do you need a spare pilot?"

"No," she said. "Thanks."

"Thank *you*, Rachel."

She nodded, got up, and started for the door.

"One more thing." He hesitated. "Have they officially canceled the flight yet?"

He was talking about Mars. The mission. "No," she said. "Not yet. I guess they have other things to think about."

"I'm sorry," he said.

She understood: Barringer had been around long enough to know that if the mission went kaput, there'd be another crew on board when NASA finally sent it out. And the mission was certainly kaput.

"Yeah," she said. "Thanks."

Micro. 3:52 A.M.

Tony deposited his third load of passengers at L1 and started back. He was getting bored. He had now spent almost fifteen consecutive hours on the flight deck of the Micro. With two and a half days to go.

As he accelerated away from the station, he passed Hal Jenkins's bus, inbound with another sixteen refugees, which was how he'd begun to think of the people fleeing back toward the home world. The bus blinked its lights. Tony returned the greeting, but his attention was captured by Tomiko, which hovered just above the other ship's cabin lights. It had moved out of the Sun's glare and become a fuzzy star.

Coming fast and coming faster.

It looked harmless enough. "Where's its tail?" asked Saber.

"I heard somebody on TV saying you can't see a tail because it's pretty much pointed in our direction. They also think it's moving too quickly and the Sun isn't getting time to heat it up."

He put the scopes on it and went to full mag. The comet seemed to have a pulse, a rhythm that brightened and dimmed with his heartbeat.

There won't be much use for moon pilots after this weekend.

She must have read his mind. "Will you retire, Tony?"

"Yeah," he said. "I might. I don't think I could go back to flying groundside. Not after this."

Her lashes looked damp.

"You okay, Saber?"

"You're lucky," she said.

Saber aroused Tony's paternal instincts. It was a bitch to get this far and have somebody just yank it away. He'd heard a story about one of the medieval popes getting angry at a comet and excommunicating it. He didn't know whether the story was true or not, but he could understand the gestures of humans whose lives were upset by a visitor they couldn't touch, couldn't ward off. He stared at the image on the overhead display, glowing and peaceful and even *beautiful*, and he wished he could reach out, cast a spell, *crush it*.

"I wonder if they've been able to track it back," Saber said.

"To where?"

"To where it started."

"I doubt it's possible. The thing's probably a billion years old."

"It's strange," said Saber. "A billion years, and all this time it's been running hot and true for the Moon." She stared at the image, and Tony could see emotions rippling through her eyes.

He released his restraints and got up. "How about something to eat?"

"Sure," she said.

He opened the hatch to the passenger cabin and dropped down. The galley was located aft in a separate compartment. He walked back on grip shoes, opened the refrigerator, took out a couple of cheese sandwiches, and put them in the microwave. He sliced some tomatoes and onions, made up a salad, picked up the ranch dressing, filled the thermos with coffee, and carried everything back up to the flight deck.

"Thanks," she said, digging in. "I didn't realize I was hungry."

"I miss Shen," grinned Tony. "Not used to getting our own stuff." They'd left the flight attendant at L1. One less to carry.

Saber took a second helping of the salad. "I wonder if it's alone," she said.

"How do you mean?"

"Sometimes these things travel in clusters. There could be more of them out there, coming this way."

"That's a cheerful thought."

"Isn't it?"

When they'd finished, Saber offered to clean up. But Tony wanted an excuse to move around. He took the remnants of the meal back down to the galley, put the salad into a plastic bag, and stacked the dishes.

L1, *Percival Lowell* Flight Deck. 4:18 A.M.

"What frustrates me," said Lee Cochran, "is that we could still run the mission."

"Isn't that a little selfish?" asked Rachel.

"No, I don't mean that," said the geologist. "We could

make the Moonbase pickup, deliver them, collect the crew at Skyport, and be on our way. There's really no reason we couldn't do that." His eyes, which were usually pretty sexy, just looked empty now. "We haven't received any direction yet, I guess?"

"No," she said. "Nothing yet. But we're certainly going to get scrubbed."

"Why? The launch window's open. Why not salvage the mission? There's no reason to scrub."

He was right. The brute work was done, the ship ready to go. There was no *operational* reason they couldn't leave from earth-orbit. Still, she understood the political realities: the *Lowell* couldn't go sailing off to Mars while people at home were scrambling to avoid a disaster.

Her cell phone bleeped. "Colonel?"

"Go ahead, Jim." James Hoffer was the rescue coordinator.

"The cushions are here."

"Okay. Put them on board. I'll be back to show you where."

"Cushions?" asked Cochran.

"For our passengers."

Cochran sat down beside her. "After we drop these people off at Skyport, why don't we keep going?"

She grinned. "Steal the *Lowell*? We'd better plan to stay on Mars."

But it wasn't really funny, and Cochran looked genuinely in pain. This was the professional culmination for all of them. For Lee and herself, for their four crewmates who'd just arrived at Skyport prior to shipping over to L1.

"Look," she said, hoping to end the discussion, "Moonbase is going down and the gloss will be off the program. The politics won't be right for a launch."

"Goddam politics. If they scrub, it'll be *years* before we go. Or before *somebody* goes."

"Lee," she said, "let's concentrate on the immediate problem: Where do we put our passengers?"

"Damned if I know."

"I think it's time we figured it out. Let's go take a look."

She wanted the passageways clear. They could put six people in the tiny cubicles that would have served as crew's quarters. Two more could be seated at unused duty stations. There was room for another six in the rec/community space, and the rest would be safest in the equipment locker. There they could sit in the Mars rover and the mobile laser drill, where they could belt down.

The drill looked like a tractor with a praying mantis astride the hood. Lee paused before it, and Rachel could read his thoughts. It was designed to reach a hundred meters beneath the Martian surface and bring back samples. He would have been in the saddle, wielding the ruby beam, sending the collector deep, and retrieving Martian history.

Now they both knew it was never going to happen. When the *Lowell* went, in two or three years, if it happened at all, there would be a whole new crew.

"Look at it this way," she said. "We have a chance to demonstrate the usefulness of a nuclear-powered vessel. Maybe when this is over, somebody'll realize the advantage of having a *Percival Lowell*. I mean, we've built the first one. *This* is the one that cost all the money. Now it's just nickels and dimes."

Micro Flight Deck. 6:51 A.M.

The Micro was approaching the Spaceport. They were on auto, following the beacon down, when the radio came alive. "Tony? This is Moonbase." Bigfoot's voice.

"Go ahead, Moonbase. We copy."

"Change in plans. They're sending the *Percival Lowell* over this morning. You and another of the buses are going to rendezvous with it. You'll have about forty-five minutes' turnaround time. You'll take nine people up." That was the usual eight, plus one for the vacancy they'd created by losing Shen.

"Roger that, Bigfoot. We get to see the nuke in action, huh?"

"Nothing but the best for the jocks."

"I wonder how many people they have to move off," Saber asked.

Tony didn't respond, and she switched her attention to the comet, which was showing a second tail in the scopes.

"Maybe it's breaking up," he said. "Maybe we'll get lucky."

"That would be nice." Saber looked at her screen. "But don't count on it. It says here that two tails are common."

"Oh." The comet had begun to take on a personal aspect, as if it were a living thing. It would have given Tony a great deal of visceral pleasure to watch it come apart.

The green lamps, the GO indicators, were blinking on Saber's board. Lights were coming on in the center of Alphonsus as the Spaceport opened its doors to receive them. The attitude jets fired, fired again, and the Micro rotated, aligning itself to the approach corridor. Had either Tony or Saber been watching closely, they might have seen traces of gray haze outside the bus. Whether the haze would have been recognized as unburnt fuel, as powdered aluminum being forced into an engine at twice the rate it could be used, is doubtful. But it would have given someone pause.

Alphonsus was pocked with numerous rills and secondary craters. The central uplift, which was characteristic of large craters, threw a harsh shadow across the terrain. Moonbase itself was safely tucked beneath the regolith, its location marked only by its lights.

"Micro," said Moonbase, "you are looking good."

The jets fired again. Tony felt the bus turning on its axis. And again.

"Hot and normal," said Saber.

"Micro, you are cleared to land."

Forty-five minutes. Just enough time to eat. "Want to try for breakfast?" he asked.

"Yeah." She nodded. "Good idea—"

An orange warning lamp blinked on. Saber looked at the overhead display. "Fuel consumption's up. Attitude jets."

Tony followed her eyes. They'd lost a few pounds.

"Something loose maybe," he suggested.

"Don't know. It was all right before the six-thousand maintenance."

Tony grumbled about Moonbase techs. "We'd be better off if they'd just leave it alone." He flipped the comm switch. "Moonbase, this is the Micro. Attitude jets are using excess fuel."

"Roger."

"Check it out for me during the turnaround, okay? It's probably just a leak."

2.

BBC WORLDNET. 7:07 A.M.
Interview with Dr. Alice Finizio of the Jet Propulsion Lab by Connie Hasting.

Hasting: _Dr. Finizio, you've seen the pictures of people fleeing from coastal areas across the country and around the world. What would you say to those who have a beachfront home?_

Finizio: _I'd tell them to stay in their living rooms, and watch pictures on television of all the foolish persons stuck in traffic jams._

Hasting: _Then you don't think there's any danger?_

Finizio: _There's always danger, Connie. I can't promise that a piece of rock isn't going to come through somebody's window. Or land in the_ ocean. But I'd be willing to bet that the odds of getting killed are higher on the roads right now than they are along any shorefront.

Hasting: Is there anything you are worried about?

Finizio: Oh, yes. I think we're about to lose our tides.

Hasting: That doesn't seem like a major problem.

Finizio: It could be serious. This isn't my field, but we can be sure there'll be an impact on the ecosystems. Quite a few species won't survive when there are no more tides. Egrets, for example, will almost certainly become extinct.

Hasting: I don't want to seem insensitive here, but I'm sure you'll agree, Doctor Finizio, that the loss of the egret will not be a serious problem for most of us.

Finizio: Probably not. But everything is interrelated. There'll be a ripple effect. Remember, this won't be a gradual die-off, but an excision. On the order of introducing rabbits into Australia. Or shooting birds in the Dakotas until mosquitoes all but took over the area. We just don't know what'll happen long range. Or at least, I don't.

Hasting: Is there anything else we need to worry about?

Finizio: A substantial amount of particulate material will probably settle in the atmosphere. We could get an ice age.

Hasting: Would that happen right away?

Finizio: (Hesitates.) If it were to happen, I'd think the effects would be felt pretty quickly, yes.

Hasting: I guess we wouldn't have to worry about greenhouse gases anymore.

Finizio: Well, actually, there's a scenario that could lead into that area as well.

Hasting: It doesn't sound like good news, Dr. Finizio.

Finizio: (Cheerfully.) Well, there are always dangers. Which is why I advise your listeners not to worry. If the worst happens, we won't be able to do much anyway. But I think, in the short term, we'll be fine. The long term is what'll probably not be so good. But the long term is very long.

•   •   •

Moonbase Spaceport. 7:10 A.M.

Moonbus AVR/2665, designated *Wobble* by its crew, lifted off with twenty-six passengers, whom it would deliver to the Copenhagen-based space plane when it arrived. A couple of scales had been brought in and station personnel were weighing everybody and calculating totals. The flight had come up with a tolerance for another three hundred pounds terrestrial, so two passengers, one adult and one child, had been added.

When they made their rendezvous, two flight attendants would debark along with the passengers, thereby increasing the number of people the bus could carry on subsequent liftoffs.

A half hour after *Wobble*'s departure, Tony and Saber were back in the passenger lounge at the Spaceport. They too had to submit to getting weighed, one-ninety-eight for Tony, one-thirty for Saber. *So we can tabulate accurately*, they were told.

Following Tony's suggestion, the maintenance people had checked the fuel lines for a leak. "Nothing," Bigfoot told him. "We probably pulled the hose too soon last time. Left you a little short of fuel. It happens." He shrugged. "Our fault."

"I don't like not knowing what the problem is," said Tony.

"Not like it's critical," said Bigfoot. He was the most muscular man Tony had ever seen up close. His name was Elrond Caparatti. The nickname dated from football days. He'd been a defensive lineman, briefly, with the Packers. The story, according to Bigfoot, was that someone had come down hard on his knee on his very first play. Tony suspected the story was embellished, but it was a fact that his career had ended early. He still limped.

"It's only a few pounds light," Bigfoot shrugged. "Look, if I thought it was serious, Tony, we'd give it a complete rundown. But it's not, and we're already behind. It won't matter anyway. We're just going to abandon the damned thing Saturday."

Tony nodded. He trusted Bigfoot. "Okay," he said. "Thanks."

Bigfoot gave him a thumbs-up. In the waiting area, they opened the doors and the passengers started up the boarding ramp.

On board, they ran quickly through their preliminary checkoff. Tony reported he was ready to go, and Bigfoot showed up on the circuit again.

"Don't you ever sleep?" asked Tony.

"Not lately. And neither will you. When you download your schedule you'll notice that you're going to be flying continuously between now and impact. Try to divvy up duties where you can. Sleep when the opportunity offers. Tony, I have to tell you, we'll get everybody out, but it'll be close, and it'll only happen if everything goes like clockwork." He paused. "You're cleared to depart."

Saber had gone below to make sure the passengers were ready. They were still hauling families and visiting VIPs. She reported everything secure in the cabin and hurried back up the ladder while Tony got his final countdown. Overhead, the roof divided and rolled back.

"They're really excited," said Saber. "Especially the kids."

"About getting away?"

"About riding on the *Percival Lowell*."

He lifted away from Moonbase. It was a near-perfect launch, requiring only a few brief bursts from the attitude jets, not enough to reveal that one was firing rich, using twice the amount of fuel as the other eleven. He felt relieved when the main engine shut down with no telltales or warnings on his board, and no suggestion that fuel usage had risen. Maybe they *had* failed to fill his tanks; or maybe it had been a computer glitch.

Once they were in orbit, Tony went down to say hello to his passengers. He always made it a point to visit the cabin.

Usually, during the five-plus hours between L1 and the Moon, he did it at his leisure, welcoming people aboard, lending his calm demeanor to the inevitable one or two who were making their first flight. He wore grip shoes even though he'd long since learned to move with ease through zero-g. Those who might already be a little skittish reacted more positively to a captain who seemed to have his feet planted firmly on the deck.

The VIPs were seventy-year-old Kwae Li Pak, listed as a world-renowned expert in long-term low-gravity effects on musculature; a United States senator; a nineteen-year-old student from the Polytechnical University of Catalunya, whose trip to the Moon had been first prize for a science project; and a Russian industrialist.

All were excited, even Pak. The senator, who was from South Carolina, wished aloud that the hand of God would reach out and strike the comet down. He seemed to be in much of Tony's state of mind. The Russian made it a point to thank Tony and to inquire when the pilot himself would get clear.

"I'm not sure," he answered. And after a moment's thought: "As soon as I can."

Lowell showed up on the scopes right on schedule. Tony put a visual on the overhead and Saber gazed at it admiringly. "It's the only way to travel," she said.

Tony shrugged.

The first time Tony had seen the *Lowell*, docked at L1, he'd felt mixed emotions. Great-looking ship, all dressed up with nowhere to go. Mars was just a desert with a big volcano and some very old riverbeds. Hardly worth two years on plastic rations.

The Micro closed gradually with the interplanetary vessel. Tony exchanged operational data with a female voice.

"That'll be Rachel Quinn," smiled Saber. There was something forlorn in her tone.

"You wouldn't really want to make that trip, would you?" he asked.

Saber smiled. "I'd kill," she said.

Lowell's docking port was located on its underside in the after section. Tony swung the Micro into position, setting it almost crosswise with the larger ship, and handed control over to the autopilot, which took it across the last fifty meters. He switched on the intercom and warned the passengers not to remove their harnesses until they were advised to do so. A light jarring underscored the admonition.

But the magnetics had taken hold and amber lights were coming on, signifying that the connecting chamber between the docking grips was sealed and beginning to pressurize. Minutes later the lights went green, and Saber went below to stand by the airlock.

Tony heard the hatches open, heard Saber talking with another woman, who must have been Rachel Quinn. Then he slipped out of his own seat and went below to say good-bye to his passengers.

They filed out happily, and he heard cries of delight as they arrived on board *Lowell*. Then he caught a glimpse of Quinn.

"See you at Skyport," she said. And the hatch at the other end closed.

Tony was mildly irritated. It was true the Micro didn't have much glamor, but it was a tough little workhorse, and these people weren't treating it with proper respect.

"Damn," said Saber.

"I know what you mean," said Tony.

"I wanted to climb through and get a look."

"Oh. Well, you saw it at L1. Hell, you've been inside it a half-dozen times."

"It's different out here," she said. "It's *alive* now."

"I don't think we have time to spare," he said.

"I know." She keyed the disconnect and watched their own hatch close.

He used the thrusters only twice during the withdrawal.

SSTO *Berlin* Flight Deck. 7:12 A.M.

The faulty navigational programming created a problem for all three space planes. *Berlin*'s pilot, Willem Stephan, was placidly watching Moon and comet growing larger when the alert came in from Moonbase: "We show *Berlin* and *Copenhagen* off course."

"Negative," his flight engineer told him. "Flight profile looks good."

"Moonbase," Stephan said, "we do not show variance." *Copenhagen*, eighty kilometers off to starboard, was a bright star.

"Wait one," said Moonbase.

Stephan switched over to Nora Ehrlich in *Copenhagen*. "How do *you* look?"

"Same as you, Willem. Right on target."

The voice came back: "Both birds, this is Moonbase. We want you to go to manual. Switch to Channel Eleven and pick up the beacon. Acknowledge when you've complied."

His flight engineer was Gruder Müller, a friend who went all the way back to his University of Hamburg days. Gruder brought the beacon trace up on the screen. "*Berlin* acknowledges," said Stephan.

"Roger. Stand by for course correction."

"Roger, Moonbase." He exchanged glances with Gruder. Maybe piloting between Earth and the Moon wasn't quite the exact science he'd thought.

"*Berlin*, this is Moonbase." A new voice. With authority. Probably the watch supervisor. "We are going to slot you into a different vector from the one planned. We think there's a glitch in the programming, so we'll do the rest of this hands-on. Do you read?"

Stephan acknowledged.

He entered the new data into the computer, and six minutes later executed his course change. *Copenhagen* followed suit.

Berlin's first scheduled pickup was to be from the microbus. He ran a simulation of the rendezvous. "We don't match up so well now," he said. "The Micro's going to have to finagle a bit."

Washington, D.C. 7:22 A.M.

Harold Boatmann hadn't slept all night. The gray dawn was seeping through the curtains of his Georgetown apartment. He gave up and got out of bed, scrambled some eggs, put a half-dozen strips of bacon into the microwave, made a pot of coffee, and checked with his duty officer. Things were calming down a bit. People had been soothed by White House assurances and by the tack adopted by the media, which were downplaying the comet and portraying those who took to the roads as cranks.

The transportation secretary should have been gratified. But the truth was that the administration's position was a gamble. Tens of thousands of lives might be lost if they guessed wrong. Boatmann wondered how he would live with that kind of burden.

He picked at his breakfast and finally gave up on it, taking his coffee into the living room, where he sank into an upholstered chair. He propped his feet on a hassock, set the cup down on a side table, and stared at the row of framed photos on the mantel. The room was still dark, the shades drawn against the morning light, the photos hidden in shadow. They were his son and daughter and a bevy of grandchildren, in-laws and cousins, friends from earlier days now scattered around the country. And a photograph of himself and Margaret and the president, taken on the White House lawn during a signing ceremony. His thoughts kept returning to yesterday's White House meeting.

We'll ride it out. We'll hope for the best, ride it out, and look to get lucky.

Boatmann couldn't get past the reality that if he were living in Miami, he'd want the truth. The notion that the president and his advisors were sitting on dangerous information, not sharing it with the people most at risk, had potentially appalling consequences. If things went the wrong way, that could be enough to bring the government down.

Boatmann's vision blurred. He divided the people in the mantel photographs into two groups: those who were safe, and those who were not. He had already warned some. Several, for one reason or another, he had not been able to find on short notice, and he was too discreet to leave messages on answering machines. But he'd try again today.

He stirred himself, got up, drew the curtain aside, and peered out into the morning. The sky was slate-colored and the air smelled of approaching rain. Wisconsin Avenue was unusually quiet.

His anguish was compounded by the knowledge that the president was right: A mass exodus from the coastal cities would cost lives. What were the odds that cometfall might indeed amount to nothing more than a few late-night meteor showers? There seemed to be no answer to that question. He had spent much of yesterday, after the cabinet meeting, on the Web and on the phone. Nobody knew.

But it seemed inherently dishonest to withhold what they really believed. No matter the motivation. The system only works when there is an honest compact between government and governed.

Easy to say. But how was he going to justify it to himself if he set off a panic?

His coffee had gotten cold. He poured another cup. After a while he reached for the phone.

3.

Moonbase, Grissom Country. 8:05 A.M.

The vice president's call had come late the previous night, with the suggestion that Rick prepare appropriate remarks for a televised news conference today. *A good opening statement. We want to be upbeat*, Charlie had said. *We should probably admit the uncertainties of the situation. But we're in the hands of good old American technology. We and our foreign friends are going to come through, blah, blah, blah. The president wants us to focus attention on Moonbase problems. He's hoping we can divert the public's attention and stop them from jamming up the highways at home.* His voice had taken a strange tone. Charlie rarely showed negative emotions about others, but he'd sounded irritated with Kolladner. *While you're at it, prepare a list of likely questions I'll be asked. And recommended responses.*

Not that you'll use any of them, Rick had thought.

Anyhow, Rick arrived at the vice president's door loaded with suggestions. Charlie's voice invited him in. He was sitting on the sofa, turning pages in a notebook. "Good morning, Rick," he said. "I have some ideas how this should sound."

"Are they that nervous at home?" Rick asked.

"I understand the situation's improving. But the Man is uncomfortable. And he has reason to be. You ever play poker with him?"

Rick hadn't. But he knew the president's reputation. Kolladner didn't play now, of course. There'd be no way to keep it from the media, and the public could be made to frown on a poker player in the White House. It would be the kind of thing the talk show hosts and the late-night comedians loved.

"He's always claimed," Charlie said, "that he never bluffs. It isn't true, of course. But it makes the bluff effective."

"He's bluffing now? About Saturday night?"

"Yeah, I think so. He's scared."

Rick nodded. "If the worst happens, he could lose both seaboards."

A muscle moved in Charlie's jaw, but he said nothing.

Rick, who had an elemental dislike for downbeat conversations, waved it away. "I made some notes on how I think we should handle the news conference."

"Good. It's scheduled for eight. Prime time, all networks and Weblinks. There'll be several guests, including some groundside scientists who think there's really nothing to worry about. They've even got one who swears the comet's going to miss. They're going to have Kendrick anchoring the thing. He'll ask a few questions. I'm sure you can imagine what they'll be. And we want soothing answers." He sat back and looked closely at Rick. "Henry wouldn't admit this, but if I'm reading correctly between the lines, I think the fix is in. I wonder if the president has heard more than he's admitting."

"It's the wrong move," said Rick.

"Why? What makes you say that?"

"It's just going to stir up the people who think there *is* a major problem. I guarantee you, within an hour after the telecast, every Ph.D. who disagrees will be holding a press conference of his own. Our best bet would be to say as little as possible, photograph the president going about routine business, and for God's sake make sure they get pictures of his wife and grandkids down on a Florida beach."

"It's too late for that now."

"I guess. You know, I hate to criticize a colleague, but the president needs a decent press secretary." Rick sighed. "I saw some reports from your home state. Everybody's clearing out. Headed west."

"I think I would, too," said Charlie.

"Yeah," said Rick. "Especially after we tell them tonight there's nothing to worry about."

•   •   •

Percival Lowell Utility Deck. 8:14 A.M.

Rachel received the mission postponement order while her second shipment of passengers were coming aboard.

MARS FLIGHT CANCELED. NEW DATE NOT ESTABLISHED.
REGRETS.

Lee Cochran was in back getting everyone settled. Rachel ran a copy, and when the bus had pulled away, she strolled back and showed it to him. He nodded, showing no emotion. "I wonder," he said, "if the mission will ever happen."

Lee's comment stuck in Rachel's mind while she stayed to help get everyone settled. *It won't be that way,* she thought. *We have the instrument to break out into the solar system; and whatever happens here, we'll go.*

We will *go.*

The passengers had been informed they'd be required to wear a breathing apparatus, but they looked askance at the devices anyhow. Several wanted assurances there were enough oxygen tanks to take care of everyone. Rachel thought how odd it was that people thought nothing of boarding a ferry or a moonbus without asking whether the life support system was adequate. But here, of course, they were holding the life support system in their hands and it worried them. There were other questions. How would they eat? In shifts. What if the mask came off while they slept? Don't worry, if we develop a problem you won't sleep through it. But in any case, we'll check on you regularly. When I have to change tanks, do I have to hold my breath until we get another one? It's a three-second changeover. You'll be fine. Why don't *I* get an oxygen mask? Everybody doesn't need one because there's enough air in the cabin to support eight people and then some. We'll take turns, Rachel explained, and everybody will get some time out of the mask.

They had a passenger list in advance and they assigned the older travelers to the astronaut quarters. Several families were with the group, four officials from various governments, one Russian industrialist, and two NASA heavyweights. Rachel knew both of course, and one, the comptroller, told her wryly that he was glad to see they'd found *some* use anyhow for *Lowell*.

Lee was acting as flight host. He'd collected a dozen viewers from L1 and had jacks installed throughout the ship so their riders could tap into the onboard library. He showed everyone where the galley and washrooms were located, and which buttons to punch if they needed help. He demonstrated the restraint systems in the various seats, and gave webbing to those who did not have seats. He stayed with them, helping them tie down, until he was satisfied they were safe.

Rachel put on her most reassuring manner. Flight time to Skyport would be about nineteen hours. They'd arrive around four o'clock Friday morning, have breakfast, and would then be able to board one of the space planes that would be waiting to take them home. Nothing to worry about, she said. Sorry about the inconvenience. Just remember to keep the mask on and breathe normally and we'll all do fine. If you need to take the mask off for any reason, go ahead, it's no problem. If you feel you have to *keep* it off, please be sure to let us know.

"You've got real talent for this," Lee told her.

She went back to the flight deck and looked out at the comet. It was east of the Moon, getting bigger. The tails were now easily visible to the naked eye.

She switched on the PA. "Ladies and gentlemen, we're about to get under way. We'll be taking it slow and easy, but you'll still feel some push. The ship will be accelerating for about ten minutes. Please don't try to move around until after we tell you it's okay to do so." She could still see the lights of the second bus, pale and lonely, drifting into the dark.

Lee came in and sat down beside her. "All set," he said.

She nodded and pushed the throttles forward.

The nuclear plant was quieter and smoother than a chemical rocket. NASA had done extensive testing of the nuke in the Mojave and at L1 and had run hundreds of simulations. The ship's crew had taken *Lowell* on a few local test flights. Around the Moon and back, that sort of thing. But this was the first time that a nuclear-powered spaceship could be said to be operational. "We live in historic times," Lee observed.

"Yeah." Her wrist was pale in the glow of the instrument panel. "That we do, lad."

Arlington, Virginia. 9:16 A.M.

Mary-Lynn Jamison of *Washington Online* was working on the Arnold Cloud story when her phone rang. Cloud was a Midwestern congressman who had apparently hired a hit man to murder his wife. In this case, it appeared that the motive had not been another woman, nor even insurance. Rather, Cloud was in trouble in his home district, and he planned to claim that organized crime had wanted to send him a message. The cops were suspicious, but the congressman had the goods on a lot of people around Washington, and those persons, in a minor panic, were calling in favors. The authorities were under pressure to look the other way, but Mary-Lynn had enough thread to begin unraveling the entire story.

"Jamison," she said into the phone.

"Mary-Lynn, how are you?"

She recognized the secretary of transportation's voice. "Hello, Harold," she said.

"No recordings, Mary-Lynn."

She shut the machine down.

"Can we meet somewhere?"

"For lunch?"

"One o'clock," he said. "Willoughby's."

•   •   •

Moonbase Spaceport. 10:03 A.M.

"Any problems, Tony?" Bigfoot was waiting for them as they debarked.

Tony shook his head. "Running like a good little puppy," he said. The program for landing at Moonbase was standardized, and the attitude jets were therefore not extensively used. They did generate enough vapor that Tony got more bogus readings on his way down. But it seemed trivial, and time was now of the essence.

"Okay. Glad to hear it. We've got enough to worry about." Bigfoot made a rumbling sound deep in his throat. "The space planes are here. And so are your passengers. Take ten minutes and be ready to go."

Saber smiled. "Plenty of time to relax, huh? Couldn't ask for more, Bigfoot."

"Sorry, babe," he said. "We're a little pressed."

SSTO *Berlin* Flight Deck. 10:17 A.M.

Willem Stephan arrived on station and reported in. *Copenhagen* had already rendezvoused with one of the buses, call sign *Wobble*, and was taking on its first passengers. The schedule called for the buses to load as the most efficient windows came open. *Copenhagen* would depart lunar orbit Friday afternoon, and *Berlin*, Friday night.

He looked down at the lunar terrain. "I never thought I'd get here," he told his copilot.

The copilot was Kathleen Steadmann, from Bremerhaven. Kathleen squinted at the comet. "Just in time, looks like," she said.

L1, SSTO *Arlington* Flight Deck. 10:23 A.M.

Arlington had also required a midcourse correction to compensate for the programming, but nevertheless she arrived at L1 almost exactly on time.

The station did not have standard docking facilities for the SSTO. Station personnel had converted a truck bay, and George guided the rounded prow of the big spacecraft into it. An airtight fit wasn't possible, so the area couldn't be pressurized. He still had red lights on his board when he'd gotten in as far as he could. He killed the engines on command and watched a group of technicians in p-suits swarm over the wings and hull, using cutaway cables to secure the spacecraft. The bay was located in the hub, which was stationary and therefore a zero-g area. The plane swayed and occasionally bumped against its mooring. Now a second team appeared, drawing a Fleming tube out from the boarding ramp. They connected it with the main airlock.

The Fleming tube was a pressurized, flexible, accordion-like walkway constructed of metal and plastic, designed to gain access to vehicles whose normal means of entry had been damaged. This one was about thirty meters long. George went back and stayed by the main door, which was somewhat forward of the center of the spacecraft. When the lights on the door went green, signifying pressure on the other side, he opened up.

A young woman in a dark blue uniform, similar to the one worn at Skyport but with an L1 patch, smiled out at him. "Welcome to LaGrange One, Captain," she said. "We're glad to see you."

An hour and a quarter later, George and his crew had cleaned up and returned to their plane. Two hundred twenty-four passengers were now on board. A few of the operational people remained at their posts until *Arlington* was clear.

"Do you have transportation?" George asked the radio voice with whom he'd been talking.

"Oh, yes. We've got the *Antonia Mabry* warmed up and ready to go. We'll be right behind you, *Arlington*."

"See you at Skyport, then," said George. He guided the

plane onto its return heading and began to accelerate. Behind him, the lights of the space station were going out.

4.

Manhattan. 10:36 A.M.

Marilyn Keep was a copy editor for GrantTempo Publications. She was attached to GrantQuasar, the historical novel division. Her husband was an account executive for Bradley & Boone, a rising securities firm. They had a comfortable, but not lush, two-bedroom apartment in Manhattan, just off Central Park West. Marilyn was twenty-nine years old, had been married four years, and wanted more than anything else to get pregnant. When we're in a little better shape financially, Larry had been saying.

She worked at home. Her assignments arrived every other Wednesday toward the end of the afternoon. Currently she was trying to get through *Shadow of the Betrayer*, a murder mystery set in the court of Charles XII of Sweden. Although she enjoyed her job, and liked reading historical novels, she could not appreciate the subtleties of GrantQuasar titles in the same way as those she might casually pick up in a bookstore. She was too caught up in detail for that, ensuring that eye colors and speech patterns stayed consistent, assembling time lines, running down anachronisms. What she did was more technical than literary. She knew that, of course. But she did her job well, and she'd saved more than one high-priced writer from a red face. Although nobody seemed to appreciate her efforts.

Ordinarily she worked against a background of nativist stereo music, the kind of stuff that sounded like mountain streams and windblown forests set to drums and chants. But that day the drums and chants had given way to CNN, which murmured contentedly in the background. While she imposed her magic, her subconscious listened for words like *comet* or *falling rock* or *possible tidal waves*.

There was almost nothing else on except reaction to the coming collision. Was New York safe? a host was asking a needle-nosed man. Was there a coverup?

The needle-nosed man thought there was.

A woman on one of the talk shows originating in Los Angeles, in a voice just this side of hysteria, proclaimed that everyone near the Pacific was going to *die*. She was not an expert, merely someone in a studio audience, but her fear so unnerved Marilyn that she called Bradley & Boone to ask Larry whether they shouldn't think about getting out for a few days.

"Everything seems normal," Larry said maddeningly.

She looked out the window. The streets were certainly normal, which is to say, jammed with commercial traffic. (Private vehicles had been prohibited from coming into the city in 2010.)

"I think we ought to get away until it's over," she said.

She could hear him breathing on the phone. In fact, she could *see* him staring at the instrument with that look he got when he concluded once again that he'd married an alarmist. "Why don't we talk about it tonight?"

"I'm not sure we should wait to talk about it tonight. If we're going to get out of town, maybe we should do it while there are still airline tickets available."

"Oh, come on, Marilyn." He sounded annoyed, as if this were somehow *her* fault. "We can't just take off in the middle of the week and go run into the woods. We don't have the money for something like that. And anyhow, I've got commitments here. I'm not able to just walk out the door because everybody's getting excited about a comet."

"It's *not* the middle of the week. It's *Thursday*."

"Shoot me. I missed by a day."

"They're saying New York might get hit by tidal waves."

"Marilyn, listen to yourself. The city's going to be here next week, just like it always is. But I tell you what: Get tickets for tomorrow night. Where do you want to go?"

She didn't care. As long as it was higher ground.

"Try Columbus," he said, his voice suggesting that she had panicked, but that it was all right, he'd go along with it. "We can stay with my folks."

She called TransWorld. They were booked through the weekend. So was every other airline at JFK, LaGuardia, and Newark.

So was Amtrak.

NEWSNET. 12:30 P.M. UPDATE.
   (Click for details.)

SSTOs, *LOWELL* JOIN RESCUE EFFORT
   Space Planes Make First Flight Beyond Earth-Orbit
   Lowell Enroute To Skyport With Evacuees
   Moonbase Not Expected To Survive Collision

PACRAIL TO SEEK NEW FARE INCREASE
   L.A. Monorail Still Losing Money In Third Year Of Operation

SIDNEY PAUL DIES IN COMMUTER PLANE CRASH
   47-Year-Old Actor Remembered As Octavius In *Battle Eagles*
   Wind Shear Blamed

CONGRESS APPROVES SOCIAL SECURITY FUNDING BILL
   $30 Billion Infusion To Keep System Afloat Until '28

PRICE OF GAS DROPS FOR NINTH STRAIGHT MONTH
Solarcars, Public Transport, Powersats Credited With Turnaround

COMPOSER RESCUES CHILD IN LONG ISLAND FIRE
Karen Baker Won Emmy For "I Left My Heart On The LTA"

WOLFZIGER INDICTED FOR GENETIC RESEARCH VIOLATIONS
Madison DA Will Ask Maximum 20-Year Sentence

FBI SURROUNDS ANTI-TAX GROUP'S ENCLAVE
Church Of The Universal God Does Not Recognize IRS
"Caesar Has Forfeited His Right To Tax"

CLINTON RETURNS TO WHITE HOUSE FOR EDUCATION BILL CEREMONY
78-Year-Old Former President Applauds Bipartisan Effort
"This Time We Must Make It Work"

San Francisco. 9:31 A.M. Pacific Daylight Time (12:31 P.M. EDT).

Jerry Kapchik was chief of the personal tax branch for Bennett & McGee accountants. He was young and energetic, and was on the inside track for the department manager's job when it would become vacant at the end of the summer. Jerry made friends easily, enjoyed Wednesday night bridge at the club, and was a rabid 49ers fan. Life was good. But the host on the radio in his office was talking about the comet, and his listeners were calling in and saying things were a lot worse than anybody knew. *Get away from the ocean*, they were saying.

Jerry wasn't much inclined to take his talk shows seriously. But one of the file clerks had gotten a call from home and asked for the rest of the day off. Before she left, she told Jerry that the situation wasn't good, and she didn't think she'd be back next day either. "Tell you the truth, I'm getting out of town until everything blows over."

Worst possible time, of course: Filing day was Monday.

"It won't help your career," he'd warned her, but she only shrugged.

He'd wondered if she understood how absurd she looked. And it *was* absurd, like one of those movies about the Middle Ages where there's a comet or an eclipse and everybody falls on the ground in a panic. Still, he'd heard the reports that they might lose the Moon. It was hard to believe that pieces from the Moon could fall all the way into San Francisco Bay. But what did he know?

For Jerry, the world was a happy place. He'd learned from his father to make sure he lived in the present and not exclusively in the future. So he took time to smell the roses. He had Marisa, two bright kids, a lovely Tudor home in Pacifica, a clutch of orange trees, a two-car garage, a perfect lawn, a playhouse for the kids, and a healthy bank account. The only thorn in his side was a series of allergies against which he was constantly taking medication.

He could see the Bay from his office window. It was a beautiful, sun-splashed day. A few sails were sprinkled across the calm blue sea, and a freighter moved against the horizon. It was impossible to believe anything was amiss. But he wondered whether it wouldn't be a good idea to put some things in the cars, to get ready to clear out. Just in case.

Micro Flight Deck. 12:36 P.M.

Tony needed two orbits instead of one to achieve rendezvous with *Berlin*. The Micro came up from behind and off the port quarter. The sight of the big SSTO ahead, its wings and tail fins gleaming in the sun, introduced a surreal quality to the moment. It was like the automobile commercials that show a small family van jouncing across a cratered moonscape.

He exchanged greetings with the pilot, and turned docking over to the onboard computer. Then he activated the PA. "Ladies and gentlemen," he said, "as you can see if you look out the right-hand windows, we've caught up with your ticket home. It's going to take a while, though, before we can hook up with her. As you're aware, the space plane has been running a little behind, and we've come in on a course that's going to require some maneuvering on our part. It'll probably be forty minutes or so before we dock. So just relax. If you need to go to the rest room or leave your seat for any reason, this is a good time. Once we begin to move, we'll want everyone buckled down. I'll be putting on the warning light shortly. Enjoy your flight home."

"You know," said Saber, "these people are going to be on that plane a long time. It'll be thirty-some hours before departure. Plus whatever the flight time is to Skyport."

"Yeah," said Tony. "I hope they brought a lot of sandwiches."

Saber made a face. "I hope they have good ventilation."

The computer announced a countdown to the maneuvering sequence. Tony went down into the passenger cabin and affected a studied casualness with the passengers. He had sensed during boarding that some of them were uneasy, and he wanted to reassure them that nothing unusual, and certainly nothing dangerous, was going on here.

The Micro would move into a position perpendicular to the space plane's long axis. That wasn't a problem for the computers, but it presented a point of view guaranteed to sicken the passengers. He explained that they might experience some queasiness if they watched the operation, and suggested they draw the blinds on their windows. When one of the fathers tried to do so, his son complained loudly. The father backed off, but picked up a magazine and buried his head in it.

Tony returned to the flight deck for the approach. The autopilot made a minor adjustment to the intercept course, using a series of short bursts from the main engine. Then it began firing the attitude jets in a long, complicated sequence.

This was the first time since the faulty valve had been installed that extensive maneuvering was required.

The Micro rotated and brought the docking port into line. Its sensors scanned the SSTO while the onboard computer communicated with its counterpart on the space plane and compared the Micro's actual and ideal approach attitudes. Meantime, unburnt fuel again leaked out of the twelfth jet.

It was in the form of a fine haze, which began to interfere with the sensors, introducing a degree of uncertainty, and occasionally of contradiction, into their readings. The onboard computer, trying to compensate for the contradictions, fired and then refired the jets, pumping still more powdered aluminum into the Micro's immediate environment.

Tony gradually noticed the unusual activity. He frowned, but assigned it to the fact that they'd changed the flight plan and had come at the plane at less than an ideal angle. He was puzzling over it when Saber called his attention to the radar returns.

The space plane's image on the display had lost its sharpness. The returns were still timed right, but they'd begun to fade in and out.

"What's going on?" he asked, running a quick instrument check. Everything seemed okay.

The jets fired again. Stars burned in wisps of fog. Saber shook her head. "Something's wrong," she said.

Tony finally saw the gray haze of powdered aluminum just as the fuel warning lamp lit up again. He checked his board. The radar returns were getting worse, spreading out all over the screen.

"We've got a burst line somewhere," said Saber.

The radar screen was becoming pure soup.

He switched to manual and looked out into a sheet of fog. "Where's the goddam plane?" They'd been within fifty meters, but now it was lost in the haze, invisible to both their eyes and their scanners. He opened a channel. *"Berlin,* this is the Micro. We have a problem."

Static. Then the pilot's voice. Tony could make out only a few words over the interference: ". . . read you, Micro . . . drifting . . . advise."

"Can't see a thing." Saber switched from screen to screen. Everything had clouded over. The viewports now looked like poorly silvered mirrors.

Tony went to manual and tried the radio again. The transmission broke up completely. He needed to get away from the cloud, but he was too close to the plane to try his main engine. If he guessed wrong . . .

"What do we do?" asked Saber.

"I hope they can see *us,*" he said. "We stay put, and let him pull away."

5.

Lunar Orbit. 2:51 P.M.

The cloud that had settled around the Micro did not dissipate. The SSTO pilot, unable to communicate with the blinded vehicle, accelerated away to a distance of six hundred kilometers. Bigfoot dispatched one of the moonbuses, after it had offloaded onto *Copenhagen,* to help. But chasing down, and then getting close to, a vehicle that couldn't see and couldn't communicate but might decide to move at any time, was a tricky, time-consuming business. It looked as if the situation would require sending someone across. The bus's copilot was in the process of getting dressed for the attempt when Tony roared out of the haze, still leaking fuel.

By then Bigfoot had located the problem.

There were only so many things it could have been. And Bigfoot nailed it on the first guess by the simple expedient of checking the inventory.

Fortunately, no one had been injured in the incident, and repairs would be simple enough. But they'd lost several hours. And he knew whose fault it was.

They made up part of the time by transferring the Micro's passengers to the moonbus, which, after another two-hour chase, delivered them to *Berlin.* "Not in a very good mood," Stephan reported from the plane.

Since the Micro had already docked successfully at both Moonbase and L1, Bigfoot knew there was no risk bringing it directly back.

No problem, he told Tony. *You're probably a little short of fuel, but not enough to matter.*

Well, there was *some* good news. The Micro would be operational again as soon as they installed the correct valve.

But it was scant consolation. The flight schedule, with its carefully arranged windows, had been trashed; and by six P.M., Bigfoot still had not been able to devise a new one that got everybody off.

Wrightstown, New Jersey. 2:58 P.M.

The Pine River Furniture Company occupied three and a quarter acres of prime land. It manufactured handcrafted leather chairs and sofas and teakwood desks and tables for the well-to-do. "Every Piece An Original," its flyers proclaimed. "No Finer Furniture At Any Price."

A small, family-run organization, it had resisted pressures to expand and diversify since its institution in 1961. The result was that while its competitors evolved away into other lines of business, or occasionally collapsed, Pine River chugged along, providing exquisite furnishings for the affluent, and consolidating its customer base. At last count it had logged forty-seven consecutive profitable years. At Pine River, conservatism was the faith.

Its chief operating officer was Walter Harrison, namesake

and great-grandnephew of the founder. Harrison was a family man, a member of the Rotary, a devout Presbyterian, a contributor to dozens of good causes, an officer of the Coalition Advocating Decency in Media, and a Little League coach. He'd served in the army, had been with the peacekeepers in Africa and in Central America, and had alarmed everyone in his family except his father by marrying a Jew.

He had a tendency to overreact. He knew that, and understood it did not fit well with his conservative soul. Consequently, when trouble seemed to threaten, he treated his own instincts with caution. Today his instincts were screaming.

"What I would like to know, Marshall," he asked the short, gray-haired man seated in the leather chair (Bulhauer model) in front of his desk, "what I am concerned with is, where will we be if any of this actually happens? Are we insured against flood?"

Marshall Waring had been the company's lawyer for thirty-five years. He was a solid man, both feet on the ground, well versed in corporate law and product liability, a competent if unimaginative bridge partner, and an occasional luncheon companion. "Walt," he said, "we are *twenty-five miles* from the ocean. What are you worried about?"

The afternoon stillness was giving way to the roar of helicopter rotors. From the direction of Fort Dix. "They've been going all day," said Harrison. He leaned back in his chair and gazed steadily at the smaller man. "Why do you think they're doing that?"

"They always do that. There are *always* helicopters flying back and forth here."

"Not like this," said Harrison. "I think they're getting out." He caught the lawyer rolling his eyes. "I *live* here. You think I don't know something's happening?"

Waring, unsure how to respond, just held out his hands, like a supplicant.

"Okay." Harrison waved it away. "I've been looking over the policies. Paragraph sixty-six of the property and equipment coverage specifically excludes acts of God. Paragraph seventeen of the product policy contains the same exclusion. *Now*, am I safe in assuming that, if the worst happened, if a tidal wave came this far inshore, that we would be left with *nothing*, no factory, no product, *nothing?*"

Waring nodded slowly. "That's essentially correct, Walt. Yes. We are not insured against tidal waves. Or flooding. This is not a flood area. We'd also be cleaned out by an earthquake. Or if a volcano erupted." He frowned and crossed one leg over the other. "Why don't we look at it this way: If things get so bad that the tide comes all the way in to Wrightstown, you won't have to worry about the company. The *country* won't survive."

"I'm not trying to be funny here, Marshall." Harrison glanced around the office walls. They were covered with photos of himself supervising soapbox derbies, receiving the Chamber of Commerce Man of the Year Award, sharing a microphone with the commanding general of Fort Dix, shaking hands with the governor. "I'm not responsible for the country. But I *am* responsible for Pine River and its employees and customers, and I am damned well going to see the company and its people through this."

"How?" Waring asked.

"By biting the bullet." He punched his intercom. "Louise, would you send Archie in, please?"

"Be careful," said Waring.

"That's exactly what I'm trying to do." More helicopters roared overhead as the door opened and Archie Pickman came in. Harrison looked out the window, trying to follow the choppers. Then he turned and looked pointedly at the man standing in the doorway. "Come in, Archie. Sit down." He drummed his fingertips on the desktop. "What do *you* think about the helicopters?"

"Hell," Archie said, "they're getting out."

Archie Pickman was the plant manager, and Harrison's most trusted subordinate. He'd come to Pine River thirty years before with no particular skills, newly married, and in need of a job. The company traditionally hired only experienced craftsmen, but Harrison's father had seen something in the boy.

The CEO's eyes found the lawyer. "My brother-in-law," he said, "works at the Franklin Institute. He called this morning. Says there's reason to worry."

"I suggest we not get excited," said Waring.

"No one's getting excited," said Harrison. "But we're going to close down the operation tomorrow. Archie, I want to get the merchandise, all of it, onto trucks and moved over to Reading or somewhere in that area. Onto high ground. If there aren't enough company trucks, rent some."

Pickman's eyes opened wide. "I don't think the problem's all that serious," he said.

Harrison pushed back in his chair. "By God, I hope not. But if it is, we're not going to get caught here with our tails in the fan. If it's a false alarm, all the better, and we'll haul everything back next week. Figure out how many people we'll need, and have somebody call around, make arrangements for food and lodging. Okay?"

"Yes, sir," said Archie.

"Walter," said Waring, "you are overreacting."

"It's a safety measure, Marshall."

"You'll be a laughingstock when it's over."

"Maybe. I hope so." He turned back to Archie. "One more thing: Advise our full-time employees that if anyone wants to take his family to high ground—draw a line somewhere and figure out where we're talking about—the company will split the motel bill fifty-fifty for Friday and Saturday night. Okay? After that, we should know where we stand, and they're on their own."

Moonbase, Press Briefing Room. 3:00 P.M.

Rick Hailey was satisfied they'd thought of everything.

Eight reporters had been chosen to ask questions. Two were at Moonbase. Others were on feeds from across the nation and around the globe: the BBC's Charles Young in London, and Erik Lachman in the Berlin office of *NEWSNET*. Chiang Tien was in Beijing for the New China News Service; Ali Haroud was in Egypt for the *Cairo Times*. Ellen Randall represented PBS; and Mark Able, CNN. Transglobal's Keith Morley and Pacific's Tashi Yomiuri were both at Moonbase, seated in the conference room with a small crowd, facing a lectern on which was suspended the vice presidential seal.

Hampton did the introduction, and she kept it simple: "Ladies and gentlemen, I have the honor of presenting Charles L. Haskell, the vice president of the United States."

Haskell entered the room, shook a few hands, took his place at the lectern, and smiled into the cameras. He looked good, far more presidential than Kolladner had ever managed, Rick thought. And self-possessed. He was obviously relaxed. He greeted his worldwide audience, announced that he wanted to make a statement before the questioning began, smiled that *aw shucks* smile, and said, "Well, I know you're all a little worried about us, but I think everybody should know, first off, that we're in good hands." He looked across at Evelyn, who did what she could to appear on top of things.

Charlie was good that day. In Rick's view, he'd never been better. He sounded calm and reflective, utterly confident that the situation was under control. He even managed a few bad jokes. ("I hate to leave Moonbase. After all these years struggling with my weight, I finally get it down to thirty-seven pounds and they show me the door.") The jokes were part of his public persona, not clever—people didn't like clever jokes from their political leaders—but self-effacing. The vice president had a gift for playing off his audiences. This one seemed especially responsive. They laughed at his one-liners and warmed to him quickly.

When he finished, the reporters tossed him softballs. How was the morale at Moonbase? And then got a little more serious: In light of this unfortunate occurrence, had the space program proved after all to be a mistake? The Mars mission had been postponed, possibly indefinitely. If elected, would he support a new attempt?

Haroud wanted to know whether they were going to get everyone off the Moon safely.

"Certainly," said Haskell.

"I mean safely *away*, Mr. Vice President. It looks as if one or two of the rescue vehicles will not get much of a running start before the impact."

"If you're asking whether we're concerned, Ali, then my answer is *yes*. Of course we're concerned. But everything that can be done is being done." He paused to think it over. "Look, let me put it this way. I expect to be home in a few days. And I intend to be the last person to leave Moonbase. I will personally lock the door and turn out the lights."

Rick knew he meant it, but he wished he hadn't made it a public commitment.

WASHINGTON ONLINE. 3:18 P.M.

by Mary-Lynn Jamison

Sources close to the White House said today that the president has been advised that the Saturday night comet impact on the Moon may eject debris that could land on Earth with deadly consequences. Large pieces of falling moonrock might devastate entire cities, the president has been told by high-ranking scientists. Another major concern: Fragments crashing into the oceans could generate giant waves. If that happens, population centers in coastal areas in the United States and around the globe are at risk. The sources indicate that a conspiracy of silence exists among world leaders, the scientific community, and the media regarding the probable consequences of the impact.

TRANSGLOBAL SPECIAL REPORT. 4:22 P.M.

"This is Shannon Gardner in downtown St. Louis with Tomiko Harrington, who discovered the comet that bears her name. Tomiko, how has life changed for you during the last few days?"

"Well, it's really been very exciting. I've lost count of the number of interviews I've done today. I'll be on the *Jack Kramer Show* tonight on CNN, and on *The Today Show* tomorrow morning. I've even been called by some people who want to work with me on a book."

"Any plans along those lines?"

"Oh, I don't think so. What's to tell? I . . . just happened to find a comet."

"You were going to say something else?"

"I almost said I was lucky enough to find a comet. But it really hasn't been very lucky, has it?"

6.

Moonbase, Director's Office. 6:27 P.M.

Jack Chandler hadn't slept since the emergency started. He was no longer young and just couldn't keep going indefinitely. But he wasn't aware there was anything left he needed to attend to, so he turned the operation over to his aides, announced he'd be at his desk if he was needed, turned down the lights, and lay down on the sofa in his office. Of all the people at Moonbase, of all the careers that would be lost, investments dissipated, dreams blown away, no one was going to take a harder hit from Tomiko than the director.

For the first time in almost ten years, there was no lead weight in his chest, no painful awareness of his bruised heart's constant struggle with gravity, no sense of his lungs struggling for air. Jack Chandler loved his life on the Moon. He'd come to stay.

Evelyn thought they were at the end of the human attempt to expand off-world. What was it she said she'd told the vice president? *You get a window when the technology, the money, and the will are all there. We had it. Briefly.* They were already scrambling at the LTA to salvage what they could from their fleet of space vehicles.

For Chandler, it meant a return to one g.

He closed his eyes and listened to the soft, steady rhythm of his heart. His body remembered what it had been to be twenty-five.

The distance between Earth and Moon was measured, not in kilometers, but in *heartbeats*.

Someone knocked. The door opened. "Mr. Chandler?" His secretary.

"What is it, Susan?"

"Phone, sir. It's Elrond Caparatti. Says he has to speak with you. Says it's urgent."

Moonbase, Grissom Country. 11:53 P.M.

Evelyn was wrapped in an oversized bathrobe. "You're sure," she demanded.

Chandler hesitated. If the average weight went miraculously down so they could squeeze an extra person on here, and another one there, they could still make it. But realistically speaking, that wasn't going to happen. "Yes," he said. "It looks like about six people."

Her eyes bored into him. "Overload the buses," she said.

"They *are* overloaded. One of them damned near crashed an hour ago. They aren't built to carry a lot of excess weight, Evelyn. I'm sorry: A few of us are not going home and I think we better start getting ready to face it."

"Show me," she said.

Chandler produced his numbers, the maximum weight allowances for the individual vehicles, departure and rendezvous times, the windows. He watched the muscles move in her throat as she studied them. "We can't do any better than this?"

"I've been over there, working with them all evening. We've tried everything we can think of. This is the best we can do."

Her eyes moved away from him. "You can get the Micro back here by about ten," she said.

"What good's that going to do? The last of the planes'll be out of here by nine-thirty. We couldn't even get back up to it before the comet hits. Couldn't even get out of the Spaceport, for that matter."

"Six people?" she said.

Chandler felt the weight in his chest. "Make it five," he said.

FRANK CRANDALL'S ALL-NIGHTER. 11:59 P.M.

Crandall:	Go ahead, Bill from Nashua. Welcome to the show.
First Caller:	Frank? Frank, am I on?
Crandall:	You're on, Bill. But you want to turn your radio down.
First Caller:	Oh. Okay. Listen, about this comet thing?
Crandall:	Yes.
First Caller:	It's another government coverup. You know what I mean?
Crandall:	Why do you say that, Bill?
First Caller:	They claim they put all that money into the Moon—
Crandall:	You mean Moonbase?
First Caller:	Yeah. And now this comet comes out of nowhere, and they're telling us it's gonna whack the place. Completely. Doesn't that sound a little strange to you?
Crandall:	Well, I think it's pretty unlucky.
First Caller:	Unlucky? Come on, Frank. They've given the money away. Handed it out to their friends. And all these welfare types. So now they have to come up with a way to hide what they did. Get rid of the body, you know?
Crandall:	Okay. Thanks, Bill. Appreciate your calling. Jeanie from Clarksdale, Alabama. Hi, Jeanie.

Second Caller:	Hi, Frank. Hey, you know, I can't believe I actually got through. I've been trying for two years.
Crandall:	Well, we're delighted that you were so patient. So, what are your thoughts on the comet?
Second Caller:	You know how people are saying it's weird that it comes the week we're opening the place? Well, I don't think it's a coincidence.
Crandall:	In what way, Jeanie?
Second Caller:	I think it's pretty clear. We open the moonbase, and God sends a comet. Same day, we see it. What does that mean to you?
Crandall:	Anything can happen?
Second Caller:	The Lord's trying to tell us something. You know what the Good Book says: "He that has eyes, let him see."
Crandall:	What's the Lord trying to tell us, Jeanie?
Second Caller:	We got no place on the Moon, Frank. It's too close to heaven. We got no place, and he's tellin' us so. I hope we're smart enough to listen.
Crandall:	Okay, folks, we'll be back after a break.

Chapter Five

EVACUATION
Friday, April 12

1.

Evelyn Hampton stood in Charlie's doorway. Her usually placid features were unsettled.

Under other circumstances, Charlie would have been grateful for the company. One of the disadvantages of his office was that, if he didn't travel with an entourage, he had no one to talk to. Except reporters. Reporters always wanted to talk, of course. And that was okay. But it was business. Politics. And despite his good relations with the press, Charlie understood the need for caution. There was no such thing as a casual conversation with the *Washington Post*.

"Hi," he said, wondering why she was there, knowing it was not good news.

She pushed the door shut behind her. "Problem, Charlie."

He made room for her to sit. "How did I guess?" he said.

Her eyes were dark pools. "We're running behind."

He nodded, feeling the world close in. "How far?"

"Looks like six people."

That wasn't possible, and Charlie wanted to believe he'd misunderstood. "Six who won't get off?"

"That's what it looks like."

"So few," he said. "Surely they can be squeezed in somewhere." Her features remained unyielding, and Charlie started thinking about political implications. But when he saw that her cheeks were damp, he felt a twinge of embarrassment. "What are you going to do?"

"Jack says he'll stay."

"Maybe it won't be as bad as we think." He didn't know what else to say.

"I doubt we can count on it. Anyway, you need to think about covering your own rear end."

I will personally lock the door and turn off the lights. Yeah, he was in an uncomfortable situation.

She turned back to the door. "I've got to go."

"What will you do about the others?"

"I haven't decided yet."

"Ask for volunteers," Charlie said. "You only need five. I know this sounds harsh, but you can always find people who're willing to be heroes if you phrase the request right." That was a corollary of Rick's primary principle that most people can be talked into damned near anything if you find the right emotional icon to appeal to. God, country, whatever.

Her eyes hardened. "You're a cynic, after all, aren't you?"

"No. I . . ." He squirmed under that dark gaze, saw contempt creep into it. "That's not what I meant . . ."

She started for the door. "Doesn't matter. Anyway, I only need *four*."

He stared at her. "You don't have to do that," he said. "You're not assigned here."

Evelyn looked suddenly vulnerable. "You can't do that speech, Charlie, unless you're willing to stay yourself. You know, captain of the ship and all that."

Something passed between them, a communication at a level so visceral that Charlie shuddered. He groped to recover the situation. "Is there anything I can do?"

"Get us another bus," she said. Her hand was on the doorknob. "The problem's the buses."

He felt *unclean*. "How many know?"

"Jack's over now telling his people. We'll deny everything until this evening. That should give you time—"

"—to get myself bailed out."

"Yes." The word was like a knife, although her tone was gentle. "I'm sorry. I gave you bad information before. I thought there'd be no trouble about the evacuation. Maybe it was wishful thinking."

Charlie was back to the problem he'd faced earlier: A man hoping to lead the United States could not afford to be perceived as hightailing it when danger threatened. But the game had changed. Somebody wasn't going to *get* out.

"I suggest you inform the president immediately. You have a private channel, of course?"

Sure. Let him know the situation and he'll order me back to D.C. But it has to be done before the bad news breaks.

"I suspect," she was saying, "he'll discover he needs you immediately, and we'll get a request to put you on the next bus." She looked up at him and her eyes were unreadable. "Nobody'll ever know."

"Thanks, Evelyn," he said. Relief mixed with guilt flooded through him.

She smiled. It was a bland, emotionless smile. "Good luck, Mr. Vice President." She opened the door and paused. "When you get the order, let me know. I'll see there are plenty of witnesses."

After she had left, Charlie sat a long time, staring at the door.

Moonbase, Main Plaza. 6:06 A.M.

Evelyn rode the elevator up to ground level and stepped out into Main Plaza, where the soft gray light reflected the early hour. (The illumination panels kept pace with the twenty-four-hour cycle.)

She felt empty. Drained. The end of her life had come upon her with desperately little warning, and she was wondering whether she'd ever really lived. What was missing?

She really didn't know. She'd accomplished all the goals she'd set for herself, had gotten one good husband out of two tries—not bad, on average. Her countrymen were better off because of her efforts. She'd wielded the kind of power most people only dream about. And she'd even contributed substantially to the effort to start the human race on the road to the stars.

What was missing?

Why had she felt a kind of cruel satisfaction in going before the vice president of the United States and demonstrating her superiority of character over him? In watching his discomfort? Was she so uncertain of her own virtue?

She had no quarrel with Charlie Haskell.

A group of technicians, wearing Moonbase jumpsuits, came up one of the ramps and strolled along a walkway, headed for the administration building. One of them recognized her and smiled.

Maybe, she thought, *when you get without warning to a point from which your life can be counted in hours, and you're not ready to go out of the daylight, it has to be like this. Maybe it doesn't matter who you are or what you've done.*

Evelyn, only in her late thirties, had already experienced more sheer joy and gained more of a sense of accomplishment than anyone has a right to expect. Maybe that was the reason that, when the tears came, she could not quell them.

Moonbase, Director's Conference Room. 6:55 A.M.

As director of Moonbase, Jack Chandler wore a second hat: He was also head of the Department of Management, which included administration, personnel, finance, security, matériel, education, and public relations. There were two other departments: Health and Safety, and Technical Services, each with its own group of divisions.

He hadn't slept since talking with Caparatti, and he was bleary-eyed, his senses dulled. But the adrenalin was still pumping and he could feel his heart pounding as he looked out over the nineteen faces that represented his co-department heads and their division directors. He'd put out coffee, rolls, and bagels; and he wandered through the group, warning key people by his demeanor that the news was bad. Finally, at seven, he walked to the lectern. The room quieted. His private secretary slipped in, carrying a handful of papers.

"Ladies and gentlemen," he said, "As you probably know, we had a problem last evening. One of the buses suffered a delay and threw us off schedule. It now appears that we will not be able to evacuate everyone prior to impact."

They'd known it was coming. There'd been no way to keep it quiet. Still, the official confirmation froze the moment. Chandler listened to the low hum of the ventilation system. There was the financial division director, her thin, worn cheeks suddenly bloodless; and the head of Technical Services, staring down at the table; and the public relations chief, nodding as if he'd just outlined an admirable strategy. Each in his or her own way tried to hold the reality at arm's length.

The expressions of shock metamorphosed into dismay. "We've adjusted the evacuation schedule somewhat," Jack continued, "and each of you will be given a copy as you leave this morning. Senior personnel will stay behind until everyone else has been gotten off. It now looks as if six people are going to have to ride out the impact at Moonbase. We're carrying maximum weight load on every bus, and we're making the best possible flight times. I'm sorry this is happening. I honestly do not know how we could reasonably have foreseen this kind of eventuality and provided for it.

"If your name is among the last six, please stay a few minutes. The rest of you please confirm your departure time with Transportation. Miss a flight, you get to stay." He felt close to tears. "Thank you." He wanted to say more but he didn't trust his voice.

His own name, and Evelyn's, were at the bottom of the list. The other four were Angela Hawkworth and Herman Eckerd, the two department heads; Jill Benning, the personnel director; and Chip Mansfield, director of the engineering support division. "I want you to be aware," he told them after the room had cleared, "that we'll do whatever we can. But I don't want to hold out any false hope."

Benning was a small woman, about forty, trim, dark-haired, intense. "By what right," she asked, "do you decide for us that we should be left behind?"

"What would you suggest?" asked Chandler evenly. "That you and I clear out and leave a few secretaries to deal with it?"

"This is not in my contract," she said. "I've a family at home. Others are dependent on me. I can't just let you throw my life away." She looked desperately around for support. The faces of her colleagues were masked. They would, he thought, be delighted to see her win her argument. But they weren't anxious to take her side openly.

"The corporation," said Chandler, "will see that your family is looked after. Scholarship funds will be established, and other matters will be taken care of, as appropriate. I'm sorry to be so cold-blooded about this, but we have neither options nor time."

"And what happens if I go down and get on one of the buses?" she demanded, glaring at him.

"They won't let you on, Jill. If your name isn't on the list, they won't let you on."

Eckerd cleared his throat. "I'm willing to stay," he said. "I can't say I like the idea very much, but I don't see that we have much choice."

Benning turned a furious stare in his direction. Then she swung back to Chandler. "You'll hear from my lawyer," she said.

He looked at her and couldn't be angry. "If we get home,

Jill," he said, "I'll be more than happy to debate this in court."

When they'd left, he sagged into a chair. He had thought, when he came here, that he would never return groundside. He didn't want to go back, not to the dead weight in his chest and his heart fluttering with every breath.

So maybe it was unfair. It was harder on them than it was on him, and he was playing a heroic role, volunteering himself, expecting them to follow his example. But he didn't dare tell them how he really felt, didn't dare do anything that would complicate his need to get them to stay voluntarily. Or as voluntarily as he could arrange.

Skyport. 8:17 A.M.

Tory Clark had heard that the *Percival Lowell* was approaching, bringing the first group of evacuees from Moonbase. She took a break and went up one deck to the Earthlight Grill, picked up some cinnamon buns, and looked out the window. It was there, skimming the planetary haze, long and gray and lovely. It was smaller than the SSTOs, and not as sleek, but somehow it encompassed a greater aura of *power* within its frame.

"Headed for the junk pile," said someone behind her.

THE TODAY SHOW. 8:30 A.M. SEGMENT.
Excerpt of an interview with Wesley Feinberg by Jay Christopher.

Christopher: *Why does it have two tails? Isn't that unusual?*

Feinberg: *Not at all, Jay. Comets often have two tails. One's composed of dust, which is more or less blown off the comet head. Unlike the ion tail, it's illuminated only by reflected light.*

Christopher: *An ion tail is not dust, obviously.*

Feinberg: *That's right. It consists of ionized molecules, so it glows on its own.*

Christopher: *Professor Feinberg, you spoke with the president about the comet?*

Feinberg: *That's correct, Jay.*

Christopher: *Can you tell us what you told him?*

Feinberg: *I don't think that would be appropriate. That's probably a question you should ask him.*

Christopher: *All right, then. What can you tell us about the collision? How much real danger is there?*

Feinberg: *Well, we'll undoubtedly see some meteors. If the Moon breaks up, as now appears quite possible, the situation could become serious. There are several scenarios that raise the question whether life on Earth could survive.*

Christopher: *(After a long pause.) Are there others who agree with this assessment, Professor? Other scientists, I mean?*

Feinberg: *Oh, yes. I'd think most would.*

Christopher: *Are we talking about tidal waves?*

Feinberg: *That's certainly a concern. But a major impact anywhere on the planet could cause immense damage, trigger an ice age, or a runaway greenhouse effect. This is really not a comfortable situation, but we'll just have to wait and see what happens. On the other hand, we're fortunate as regards the position of the Moon and the angle of the strike.*

Christopher: *Can you explain that?*

Feinberg: *Of course. (Graphic appears.) If the worst happens, and the Moon is destroyed, you can see that most of the material will be blown away from the Earth.*

Christopher: *What's going to happen to it?*

Feinberg: *Oh, the bulk of it will remain in orbit. You know, we talk exclusively about safety concerns. And that's certainly understandable. But we shouldn't overlook the fact that this is a priceless opportunity.*

Christopher: *You mean to watch the collision close up.*

Feinberg: *More than that. We tend to forget, because our lives are very short and nothing around us ever seems to change, that the universe is really a very violent place. It's not necessarily a bad thing that we be reminded of that periodically.*

Christopher: *Provided we survive it.*

Feinberg: *Of course.*

<u>*BBC WORLDNET.*</u> 9:05 A.M.
Report from Skyport:

" . . . evacuation was completed at the L1 space station this morning. In a daring rescue, the SSTO *Arlington* brought off two hundred and eleven persons and returned them safely to Skyport moments ago. The same spacecraft will leave shortly to join three other planes orbiting the Moon in the continuing effort to bring out Moonbase personnel."

Moonbase, Grissom Country. 10:05 A.M.

Charlie listened on his private channel to an enraged Henry Kolladner. It was bad enough that Feinberg was trying to panic the nation. But someone in the administration was telling the media that Henry knew how dangerous the situation was, that he was recklessly playing with the lives of Americans. He'd find the leaker, the president swore, he'd run the bastard out of the administration and see that he never worked in this town again (by which he presumably meant the United States government). Not ever. He would even consider criminal action. Furthermore, he thought he knew who was doing it.

He went on in that vein for a while, but didn't name anyone. Charlie had a couple of suspects in mind, but he understood the turmoil that must have been generated in a meeting in which they decided to stand aside and risk a general disaster without issuing a warning. He understood why the decision had been taken, and was not inclined to be judgmental because he wasn't sure what the correct action should have been. *We'll know Sunday morning, won't we?*

"Charlie, they won't just hold this against *me*. I'm sorry to say it, but they'll remember the *party* in the fall. *You'll* probably end up paying the bill."

Considering the president's unspoken opposition to his candidacy, the remark was disingenuous. But the thought had occurred to Charlie too, although he suspected charges of a coverup wouldn't matter much. His connection with Moonbase would probably be enough to sink him. Still, he knew he needed to put a cheerful face on the situation. "Maybe not, Henry. If the rocks don't land on New York, everybody will say you did exactly the right thing. If they *do*. . . ." He stared at the scrambler he'd plugged into the wall unit. "If they do, there probably won't *be* an election."

"We're doing what we can, Charlie. Moving supplies, equipment, getting troops in place. In case. . . ."

"What about the rest of the world?"

"Everybody's scrambling. There's even some cooperation out there, believe it or not. North Korea, for God's sake, has offered to pitch in. But the mechanisms aren't in place. The major alliances may be able to coordinate mutual assistance efforts; elsewhere it'll be hit or miss."

"Well," said Charlie, "if we get lucky, get a near miss, something that just scares the bejesus out of everybody, maybe some good will come of it."

"I hope so." The president was briefly silent. "How are you holding out?"

Charlie hesitated. "Not so well, actually."

Henry went cold on the other end. "Spell it out, Charlie."

The vice president told him everything he knew. "They haven't announced it yet."

"You've got yourself into a box."

"I know."

Charlie listened to static on the line. "Okay," said Henry. "We'll have an emergency in, uh, the Everglades. Needs the administration's point man for environment. You get the hell away from there. I'll send written confirmation and give the directive to the media so everybody knows you're being ordered out."

"Nobody'll believe the Everglades story."

"Then we'll think of something else. When you get the directive, you might protest publicly. Demand to stay on at Moonbase. That'd be a nice touch."

2.

Seattle. 7:27 A.M. Pacific Daylight Time (10:27 A.M. EDT).

Matt Randall had no intention of getting caught when the tidal waves roared ashore. He lived on Vachon Island in Puget Sound. He habitually got up at six and ran for an hour before catching the ferry over to the mainland for his job with the Coastal Marine Insurance Company, where he managed the general casualty division. This was the unit that insured the uninsurable: teen drivers with bad records who'd been assigned to CMI under the Special Risk Plan. He felt as if he'd acquired another special risk, a very bad one, after watching the early news reports. The gray-haired man from Harvard was calm and almost dispassionate, and consequently very believable.

Matt made up his mind, skipped the run, and hustled his wife out of bed. She watched the interviews for a few minutes and agreed. They collected the kids, twin girls three years old, loaded up the station wagon, and managed to squeeze onto the ferry. Despite the early hour, there was already a small horde of their neighbors packing and clearing out. Once on the mainland, he threaded his way through downtown Seattle onto I-90, and headed east. At eight-thirty he called the office and got a strange voice. His secretary had called in sick.

Traffic was uncharacteristically heavy. It crawled along, mostly eastbound like them. The day was overcast and gloomy, laced with occasional showers. The fifty-mile drive out to Lake Easton State Park took almost three hours. There, just after they'd passed a rest area, the twins announced they needed a bathroom. Matt pulled off at the next exit and swung into a McDonald's. He bought a round of burgers and fries. It was midmorning, but the place was filled anyhow.

Getting back onto the expressway required a difficult left-hand turn across two lanes of southbound traffic, followed by a quick swing into the right-hand lane. He sat several minutes, watching for a break in the flow, saw one, and cut across the highway. He tucked into the left-hand lane and never saw the Voyager van that simultaneously pulled out to pass, expecting to make a left turn just ahead into a charge station. It hit him in the right rear panel and nudged him into the oncoming traffic. The girls screamed and his wife threw her hands against the dashboard. There was only a flicker of stark terror, and then the sky crumpled into darkness.

Four vehicles, carrying eleven people, were involved in the pileup. Of these, only the driver of the van escaped injury. Matt lost his wife and one of the twins.

For the Washington State Police, it was the beginning of a day filled with carnage.

Skyport Flight Terminal. 11:03 A.M.

George's dozen flight attendants came by to wish him luck. They stood uncertainly in the passenger lounge, two or three in uniform, most not. Several offered to come if he wanted them along. He thanked them and said he'd see them Sunday when he got back.

Then he boarded the plane and ran through the preflights

with Mary. He and his copilot would be carrying only about a hundred passengers, the last group of evacuees, on the return flight. He was happy that the load would be relatively light, because the spacecraft would be easier to maneuver. If, in fact, the giant spacecraft would be able to maneuver at all.

"Green board," said Mary.

George nodded. He began to ease out of the bay.

He felt *good*. For years he'd done nothing but fly back and forth from New York to London, and Kansas City to Miami, and then he'd made the big jump from Washington to LEO. Yesterday he'd flown out to the Lagrange One point. Now he was going the rest of the way to the Moon, and he was on a rescue mission. "Okay, Mary," he said, "let's do it."

Moonbase, Grissom Country. 11:04 A.M.

"We need to think about what kind of spin we'll put on it."

Rick nodded. "This whole thing's a nightmare. Next time we'll know not to make pledges off the top of our head, won't we?"

Charlie squelched his irritation. The man, after all, was right.

Rick was sitting disconsolately, his hands thrust into his pockets, his jaw propped on one fist. "Who's getting left?" he asked abruptly.

"Evelyn. Jack Chandler. Other than that, I don't know. Some of their senior people, I think."

"*Hampton's* staying behind?"

"That's what she says."

"Gutsy woman. She's not in the chain of command out here. Doesn't have to do that." Rick looked as if he were about to say something more and thought better of it. Instead he took out a notebook and flipped it open. "We're scheduled out at one-twenty. Our plane leaves orbit around midnight tonight."

"Okay."

Rick shook his head. He'd tried to get them on the flight that was leaving orbit at one, but the White House orders hadn't come through yet and it was already too late to get to it. "We'll get through this, Charlie," he said.

The vice president stared at him a long time. "Some of us will," he said.

Moonbase, Chaplain's Office. 11:27 A.M.

Mark Pinnacle was the product of a well-to-do, old-line Northumberland family. His recent ancestors, most of whom he knew by name and likeness, had been scholars, soldiers, and statesmen for the British Empire. When things went downhill for the landed aristocracy, the Pinnacles moved into trade and eventually into software development. George Pinnacle, Mark's grandfather, had secured fame and fortune with a wide range of games and practical applications for the home.

Mark was only the second Pinnacle in modern times to don the cloth. That he did so was less a tribute to his faith than it was irritation with his father Avery, who attended church each Sunday and liberally supported it with donations, while explaining to his children that there wasn't a word of truth anywhere in Christian dogma. The sole value of the Church, he contended, was to entertain the rabble and make them keep their socks up.

When in a fit of exasperation Mark charged his father with hypocrisy, the old man had laughed. *Without Christianity, or some similar system*, he said, *civilization would be impossible. It teaches us, for example, to lie.*

To lie, Father?

Imagine, my boy, what life would be like if we all blurted out what we really thought on every occasion. And then he'd grown serious. *Think of the alternative: Suppose there were not a mechanism in place to scare the savages into behaving.*

Every child who's worth a damn eventually issues a statement of independence. Mark's consisted of applying for entry
to divinity school. He'd intended to limit himself to a year or
so while his father squirmed. But in the end, impressed by the
faith of his teachers, he'd stayed. And if the personified God
who walked through Galilee seemed always somewhat remote
to him, he never allowed any but his closest associates to
glimpse his doubts.

When an uncle asked whether he was interested in becoming the first chaplain at Moonbase, he accepted immediately.
He would be nondenominational, the uncle explained. No
proselytizing. All faiths to be considered equal. *We know better,
of course,* the uncle winked. *But we won't let on, shall we?*

It was a natural situation for Mark. He had taken to it with
enthusiasm, and had now been at Moonbase two years, minis-
tering to its collection of workers, technicians, and researchers.
There were few among the lunies who could be described as
devout, but they too needed someone to talk to on occasion,
someone to take care of the ceremonies that mark life's various
passages.

He performed the first lunar wedding, and poured water
for the first lunar baptism. He presided over the first formal
Hannukah celebration, and read the rites at the burial of the
Moslem Isbn ben Mihal, who died when a faulty p-suit burst.
No one seemed to mind that prayers were led by a man who
might not formally have subscribed to the doctrine from
which they sprang. It seemed to Mark that, on the Moon, the
sharp definitions between the various faiths tended to blur.

Fortunately, there weren't many funerals. In fact, one of
the joys of being Moonbase chaplain was that he blessed children and unions far more often than he had to console the
bereaved. He discovered something else as well. At home, the
majority of his parishioners went through the motions of their
faith, but seldom thought about it in any meaningful way. It

was merely something that was there, rather like the weather or the dial tone. But the people who came to Luna tended to have strong negative views about chapels and yet were inclined to gaze into the infinite and admit their doubts. These, Mark believed, were the ones especially worth saving.

Now that the comet had come, he wondered what purpose it was intended to serve. He shared the general dismay, the concern that went beyond whether this or that individual would get off in time. For the chaplain, as for many at Moonbase, something significant was drawing to a close. End of an era. And it was a painful time for him particularly, who subscribed to the notion that nothing happened by chance. How often had he listened to people argue that it is after all a Darwinian universe, cold and neutral? An *engine* that doesn't know we exist, cranking out stars, squirrels, and astronomers with equally insensate industry.

It was, they said, only our frustration at seeing this truth, at having it written large across our skies, that drove the invention of religion. Yet it seemed we had drawn *someone's* attention. The nucleus half-hidden in the ruddy glow of streamer and mist looked like nothing so much as a devil's eye.

Moonbase, Communications Center. 11:46 A.M.

The young woman who'd attracted Rick's attention on his first-day tour of the public relations suite was Andrea Bellwether, a communications technician. She was British, a native of Portsmouth, where she'd grown up in sight of Nelson's *Victory*. She was the daughter of Frank Bellwether, commander of the *Ranger* on its fateful first voyage. Andrea had been six when her father tried to bring down the crippled vessel and had skimmed off the atmosphere and ricocheted in the general direction of Canopus.

That had been the darkest time of her life. She remembered the phone conversations with her father, she remembered not understanding why he could not come home, she remembered most of all his telling her to be brave. *Your mother will need you.*

After a while the calls stopped. Years later Andrea learned that when the crew began to run out of air they opened the hatches.

When she'd arrived at Moonbase, her coworkers assumed the appointment had been political. Something for the hero's daughter. In truth, it had been, but that didn't mean the appointment was weak. After a year and a half, Andrea was as good as anyone they had.

The commcenter had never been busier. The usually steady flow of traffic had become a torrent.

They planned to stay functional until midday Saturday. It would mean some of the technicians would have to go home on the late flight Saturday, the one that would barely get out before the collision. Andrea felt she should offer to stay. But life was sweet, and she wasn't sure she was ready to put it on the line quite so cavalierly.

Under ordinary conditions, four people were sufficient to staff the operation. But there were already seven technicians working when Andrea arrived. The supervisor set her up at a temporary routing position. "Just do the best you can," he advised.

Usually the work involved a run of administrative traffic, personnel data sheets, financial updates, confirmations of supply orders, advertisements hawking equipment that would be of value to Moonbase. There were responses to queries by Moonbase research people for project information of one kind or another, studies of chemical components in Arizona soil, comparisons of apparent magnitude of various stars as seen from Australia and the Moon, new information on ocean currents. Much of it had nothing to do with the Moon per se, but researchers were curious people, and they tended to try to keep up with everything.

But today every news service in the world wanted to know how Moonbase was doing, whether morale was holding up, whom they could interview. There's a great human interest angle, they were saying, people in a remote place facing a danger unlike anything we've seen before. How did it feel? Was anyone breaking under the strain?

The personal mail alone exceeded their usual total traffic. The voice channels were overloaded, which meant that person-to-person conversations simply weren't happening, unless you happened to be Evelyn Hampton or the vice president of the United States. Consequently, alternate channels were piling up. Thousands of requests for information about relatives and friends had already overloaded the buffers. They were also getting advice, warnings, suggestions from everyone with access to a keyboard.

"YOUR BEST CHANCE IS TO PUT THE SPACE PLANES ON EXACTLY THE SAME COURSE AS THE COMET, BUT WITH THE MOON DIRECTLY BETWEEN."

"YOU'LL BE SAFE IF YOU STAY ON THE MOON. ITS SPIN WILL REDIRECT THE ENERGY FROM THE COLLISION HARMLESSLY INTO SPACE. BUT STAY OFF THE PLANES."

"YOU PEOPLE SHOULD BE ASHAMED OF YOURSELVES. THIS IS ANOTHER EXAMPLE OF GOVERNMENT WASTE."

The bulk of incoming traffic came with distribution codes. But the rest of it could be anything, so Andrea had to look at each message, determine a recipient, and send it on. The obviously crank transmissions normally went to the chief of the watch, who dumped them. But today Andrea had been told to use her judgment. Get rid of the crazy stuff.

A programmed response was put together for the news organizations:

MOONBASE APPRECIATES YOUR INTEREST, BUT REGRETS THAT IT IS UNABLE TO ANSWER INDI-

VIDUAL QUERIES AT THIS TIME. CORRESPON-
DENTS ARE ASSURED WE ARE MAKING
PROGRESS IN OUR EFFORT TO EVACUATE
EVERYONE SAFELY, AND ARE REFERRED TO OUR
HOURLY NEWS BULLETINS.

There was a message for *her*, from her mother, who lived in
Edinburgh: *"I KNOW HOW MUCH THE JOB UP THERE MEANS TO
YOU. BUT WE'LL BOUNCE BACK THE WAY WE ALWAYS DO."* And to
her surprise she found one from an old flame, from whom she
hadn't heard since college: *"ANDI, I STILL LOVE YOU. COME HOME
SAFE."*

That had been a long time ago.

A bell signaled the arrival of a priority message, to be
signed for by Vice President Haskell. That meant a hard copy.
She ran it off, looked at it, and saw that the VP was being
ordered out early. On the next flight. *To facilitate communications
and assist in organizing the emergency response effort.*

She had heard that not everyone was going to get out, so
she wondered whether the White House was trying to rescue a
heroic vice president who was determined to stay. Or get one
out who'd talked too much and walked into an embarrassing
situation.

She showed it to the chief of the watch.

"Okay." He took it from her. "I'll see that it gets delivered."

FINANCIAL TIMES, WORLDWIDE EDITION. UPDATED 11:53 A.M.

Major market indices dropped sharply again for the second day
in a row. Concern for the financial stability of Moonbase International
and the Lunar Transport Authority fueled steep declines across a broad
range of issues. . . .

3.

Charlie was alone when the message came. ". . . just received in the commcenter, Mr. Vice President. For you." The messenger was a boy, probably not eighteen. "I need you to sign for it, sir."

Charlie complied. "Why are you still here, son?" he asked. "When are you leaving?"

"I'm scheduled out tomorrow." The boy was an African-American, and he gazed at Charlie with the almost wistful respect that vice presidents automatically command from all except those who know them well. "The early flight."

"Good luck," said Charlie.

He smiled shyly. "You too, sir."

Then he was gone and Charlie was alone with his escape hatch. What a terrible break the Micro incident had been. They'd been close to turning all this around. *Haskell hangs on until the end.* It would have been dynamite, and might have carried him all the way to the nomination.

But now people were going to die. And he knew the other candidates would beat him into the ground with his early exit. In fact, he'd have little choice when he stepped off the plane except to withdraw from the race. Rick pretended not to think so, but Rick had a tougher skin than he did.

Charlie was tired.

Evelyn was going to stay.

Jack Chandler was also going to stay. Chandler was only a passing acquaintance, but Charlie had shaken hands with the man. Talked with him. Wished him luck.

Charlie had come face to face with himself and he didn't like what he was seeing.

He looked at his watch and thought about calling Evelyn. Wish her luck, ask if there were anything he could do. *Say good-bye.*

Son of a bitch.

However he tried to squirm out of it, he would remain forever the man who ran away.

Moonbase, Chaplain's Office. 12:09 P.M.

A substantial number of people came by the chapel on this last full day to say good-bye and to wish Mark Pinnacle well. They all knew that some of the senior staff were staying behind, and Mark noted a range of reactions. People were pleasantly surprised, some maintaining that they'd expected the heavyweights to be the first ones clear. Others were skeptical, and suggested it was a hoax and nobody was really in danger. Most, however, were saddened.

There were rumors that those staying hadn't all been volunteers, that they'd been strong-armed to a degree by Evelyn Hampton. If true, it wasn't a heroic picture. Wouldn't look good in the history books, having to hold a gun at people's heads to get them to do the right thing. But no one was stepping forward and saying *take me*.

And why would anybody do that? Why would, say, a young man with his future before him, offer to sacrifice himself so his boss could escape? It was asking too much of human nature. At least in its Western manifestation.

The chaplain was struck by what he'd heard of Hampton's behavior. She had a reputation for ruthlessness, and he assumed it was well earned, in the way he assumed no one could rise to the top of any organization without incorporating in his, or her, soul a little DNA from Tamerlane. Still, Mark had a gift for looking at situations through other people's eyes, and he felt sorry for her when he considered the choices she'd faced.

They'd put him on the Saturday afternoon flight, so he'd be well on his way before the comet hit. But he'd known as soon as he heard the rumors about people having to stay that it presented a special problem for him. Would Christ have climbed on board one of the buses while others waited to die? How could he possibly do that? What did he really believe, anyway?

He'd struggled with it throughout the morning. Once, he'd picked up the phone, intending to call Jack Chandler, make the offer. But he'd only stared at the instrument while his heart pounded.

Once done, it could not be recalled.

Mark Pinnacle was thirty-one. He loved life, enjoyed a good drink, and had a wide circle of friends. He spent invigorating evenings with them in lively debate about life, death, and politics. He probably had a stronger interest in women than was proper for a man of the cloth. He looked forward to finding someone with whom he could share his life. He understood what the grand passion could be, and he'd determined to settle for nothing less.

He was thinking about that when he almost casually concluded that, if he went home, left someone else to die in his place, he'd be denying everything he thought he stood for.

He sat down beside the phone and picked up the instrument. His hand trembled as he punched in the director's number, which he'd not forgotten from his earlier attempt. The secretary wished him good afternoon, informed him that Mr. Chandler was busy, but passed him along when Mark insisted the call was important.

"Yes, Chaplain," said Chandler's gruff voice. "What can I do for you?"

Mark's blood pounded through his arteries. "I'll stay," he said.

Chandler seemed baffled, not sure what Pinnacle was talking about.

"Put my name on the list. Give my flight to someone else."

"Oh," Chandler said. "You're sure?"

Afterward the chaplain hung up and sank exhausted onto his couch. But a strange thing happened: The fear drained away and a startling sense of inner peace filled his soul. He began to understand that his mission had ended, his earthly existence (he smiled at the phrase) was drawing to a close, and there remained now only to keep his courage and await the judgment of his Creator.

He poured a drink and toasted his own valiant act. The thought crossed his mind that he had fallen into excessive pride. But he felt entitled.

When the first rush of emotion had passed, the fear came back. What a weak thing, he thought, is the unfortified soul. Even when guaranteed salvation, he was frightened in the baleful light of the approaching comet. Yet he had Christ at his side. What must it be at a time like this for unbelievers?

The room had grown cool, as if the life support system had shut down. He put on a jacket and went out to Main Plaza, where there were still people gathered in the parks and outside the shops, almost all of which were closed. He greeted acquaintances, and those whom he did not know but whose eyes rose to meet his, wishing them a good flight, and saying, yes, he'd look forward to seeing them again when they all got home safely. He smiled at his little joke.

He sat down finally on a bench outside a dark cookware shop with a red banner stenciled OPEN fastened diagonally across the show window. A row of newly planted saplings lined the walkway. The people sprinkled throughout the mall area did not give the impression that anything was terribly wrong. There was occasional laughter and the talk seemed light-hearted enough. Yet they *did* cling together.

Herd instinct.

His decision had done something to him, cutting the chain that joined him with his fellow creatures. He felt quite alone.

NEWSNET. 12:30 P.M. UPDATE.
  (Click for details.)

MBI DENIES SOME WILL BE STRANDED
  "Everything's Under Control" — Hampton

BARBERSHOP QUARTETS TO SING IN TULSA
  Pageant Will Run All Week

Science:
  NINETIETH ANNIVERSARY OF "BIG WIND"
    Highest Velocity Natural Wind Ever Recorded April 12, 1934
    Gusts Reached 231 MPH

  HISTORY BUFFS GATHER AT FORT SUMTER
    Commemorate First Shots Of Civil War
    VR Simulation Planned

  MICHAEL HARMON WILL SPEAK AT FDR CEREMONY IN WARM SPRINGS
    Only Four-Term President Died April 12, 1945

  HASKELL VOWS TO BE LAST OUT
    "I'll Lock The Door And Turn Off The Lights"

  PLANES, TRAINS, CARS: TRANSPORTATION GRINDS TO HALT
    Airlines Cancel Flights; Highways Jammed
    Don't Plan To Visit Aunt Sue This Weekend
    (See Related Reports: 'Chaos on Roads' and 'Japanese Head for High Ground')

  LIBERATION DAY IN UGANDA
    Twentieth-Century Dictator Idi Amin Overthrown On This Date

SEASIDE RESORTS LOSING LUCRATIVE WEEKEND
Tourists Flee Southern Vacation Sites

Washington Online. 12:33 P.M.
by Mary-Lynn Jamison

The White House announced a few minutes ago that it has ordered Vice President Haskell off the lunar surface and into one of the space planes now orbiting the Moon. Press Secretary Pat Russell explained that the move was necessitated by the president's need to keep in close contact with Haskell while communications at Moonbase are being transferred to the SSTOs. Haskell, who had publicly pledged to be the last person to leave the lunar facility, has been reported as "unhappy with the directive," and has asked to stay on the ground, but permission has apparently been denied. Last night, in a nationally televised press conference, the vice president said . . .

4.

Moonbase, Main Plaza. 12:36 P.M.

Rick's unruffled inclination to calculate the political implications ahead of more humane considerations did not spring from callousness so much as a simple unwillingness to believe that anyone was actually going to die at Moonbase. Rick lived in a world of image and manipulation, a world that was essentially free of violence. Nobody ever really got hurt. Not physically. For him, the issue was how the vice president would look while the senior executives were trying to sort things out.

Maybe the experts were wrong and it would just be a matter of coming back later to pick up whoever got left. The comet, after all, was coming down on the back side of the Moon. *His* job was to see to Charlie Haskell's nomination, and therefore to avoid the potentially devastating political fallout from the event. He obviously couldn't stay, so the sooner

Charlie Haskell was on board the plane and headed home, the better.

There was a small crowd gathered at the tram station in Main Plaza, waiting to be taken over to the Spaceport. He stood off to one side, the few possessions he could salvage packed in a briefcase. People were talking about what they would do when they got home. Whether there would be an effort by Moonbase International to find jobs for them. About how sorry they felt for the six who were staying.

The tram arrived and everyone climbed aboard. A recorded voice warned them to be seated. When they had, the vehicle began to move.

Two professorial types took seats in front of Rick. One wore a black woolen sweater against the swirl of air in the open vehicle. He was speaking intently, but Rick caught one word: *chaplain*.

The tram moved into a thick patch of forest. Rick edged forward.

"You're sure?"

"Yes. I saw the list just before I came over. Did you know him?" Both speakers wore glasses, and both were neatly barbered.

"Just from the bridge club."

Rick recalled the nervous-looking man on the speaker's platform and wondered why they were talking about him in the past tense.

A fair approximation of sunlight filtered through the overhang. The air smelled of spring.

Rick leaned forward. "Pardon me," he said, "did something happen to him?"

Both men turned. "To whom?"

"To the chaplain."

"He's staying behind," said the man with the sweater.

Birds sang, and a chipmunk stood atop a log, watching

them pass. The two men returned to their conversation. And Rick found the news disquieting.

The tram entered a tunnel. Lights blinked on and shadows raced along the walls. After a few minutes they turned into a curve and began to slow. The recorded voice advised them that the vehicle would be stopping momentarily.

He leaned back.

"None of this is your responsibility, Monica." Female voice behind him, husky, angry. "You're just like me. We're low-graded employees. We take our paychecks and we do our jobs. We never got paid for anything like this. It's not our responsibility."

"Whose responsibility is it?"

"People like Hampton. Look, the executives of the world take the money, give all the orders, get all the perks, and when the load of shit comes in, they're supposed to deal with it. *They* are. Not you. Not me."

The tram began to slow. It glided to a halt, rocked gently from side to side, settled onto a platform, and stopped. The gates whispered open.

"You want to go down there and sign on? I'm sure they'd be glad to have you," the husky voice said.

Rick watched the two women get off. They were both in their twenties. Both attractive. One black, one white.

"Just don't forget," said the black woman, "dead's forever."

The passengers filed out and rode an escalator up to a higher level, where they followed a passageway and divided into waiting areas marked YELLOW and GREEN. Rick's boarding document indicated GREEN.

The launchpads were visible through wall-length Plexiglas. The Micro crouched in its network of umbilicals and screening. Jets of steam escaped from its underbelly. Technicians were going over her, checking off items on notepads. He heard static on the public address system, and then a voice: "Passengers on the yellow flight are boarding now. Green flight is running about ten minutes behind."

A few people got up, said their good-byes, and wandered out through a doorway.

The vice president of the United States was standing off to one side of the service desk. He looked lost. Rick glanced at Sam Anderson, who made a sour face and shrugged. Rick felt as if he were living in one of those alternate realities so popular in the cinema.

"You okay, Charlie?" he asked.

Charlie shook himself. "Yeah," he said. "I'm fine."

Rick produced a sheet of paper. "I've put together a statement for you. I think we should release it as soon as we're on the plane."

He glanced over it but did not appear to read it.

"It just says you're leaving under protest, that you want to stay on here but the president insists you return immediately, and that you see no recourse, and so on."

"Good." Haskell looked as if he'd aged overnight. A couple of people came over and asked to shake his hand. *Pleasure to meet you, Mr. Vice President*, they said. And, *Good luck in the primaries.* No assumption here he'd get the nomination. When they left, Charlie shook his head but said nothing.

Rick was silent for a time. "I heard," he said, "that the chaplain's staying, too."

"The chaplain?" Charlie's eyes narrowed.

"Yeah," said Rick. "I thought the same thing."

More hand-shakers appeared. The vice president was his usual cordial self. He had the gift of making the person to whom he was speaking feel as if his entire day had been directed toward that meeting. He was happy to make their acquaintance, he said. And he was proud of what they'd accomplished.

"What *same thing*?" he asked Rick when they were alone again.

"Well, you know. The chaplain doesn't look like the kind of guy who'd *do* that."

Haskell closed his eyes momentarily. The public address system announced that GREEN flight was ready to board.

"Time to go," said Rick.

The vice president didn't move for a long time. Finally he shook his head. "No," he said. "I can't do this." He turned to Sam, who was developing a horror-struck expression. "You and your people get on the flight," he said. "See that someone gets my ticket."

"I can't do that," protested Sam.

"Do it. I'll see that your protests go on record." He shook hands with Rick and thanked him.

"What are you doing?" asked Rick.

"I'm not sure," said Charlie. "But I know what I *can't* do."

Copenhagen Flight Deck. 12:51 P.M.

Nora Ehrlich ignited her engines, and let them idle while she glided along her orbital path. Then, at precisely at 1:02 P.M., she applied thrust, and the space plane, carrying 136 passengers, lifted out of orbit and started for home.

Moonbase, Grissom Country. 1:47 P.M.

Evelyn Hampton had left Moonbase evacuation to Jack Chandler, and had devoted her time to preparing Moonbase International to deal with the situation. She'd nominated the person whom she wished to succeed her, had developed a strategy that might allow the corporation, after going Chapter Eleven, to revive itself in a new form. "We can't just give up," she'd told the board of directors. "The technologies now exist to expand beyond Earth. The experience with Tomiko should not deter us; rather, it should serve as a warning." For a start, she thought, there was Project Skybolt, an orbiting laser system that would have been capable of slicing incoming asteroids into rubble. But the program had inevitably been perceived as pork. It was an easy target for budget cutters, and after fifteen years and several abortive starts, it had still not gotten off the drawing boards. Even Culpepper had opposed it. *We don't need it at this time.* It would not, of course, have been much use against Tomiko, but it might have been nice to have in the aftermath of the collision if pieces of the moon began drifting earthward. *If we learn nothing else from this, we now know that the hazards are very real and there's a legitimate need for planetary defenses. But there's more to it. A lot more.*

Expansion seemed to be built into the genes of the species. Expand or stagnate. But the Western governments were heavily in debt. If there was going to be a drive off-planet, private interests would have to show the way, would have to demonstrate a payoff. It would have to become a moneymaker.

That hadn't happened yet. Wouldn't have happened for years to come. But there were still off-world industries to be developed. *And if the Moon has been here just long enough to allow us to use it as a springboard, then we should be grateful for that.*

The important thing now, she told MBI, *is that we do not go back into the shell. The current generation has the equipment and the knowledge to begin the process. If these people are forced into other lines of work, if the buses and ferries and SSTOs are mothballed, then it'll be over. Certainly for our lifetimes. Maybe forever.*

She prepared a few farewells that she'd send out tomorrow, if necessary. She was spending much of her time now in Jack Chandler's company. Unspoken communications passed between them, a glance, a smile, a shrug. They'd always been close, but now she felt a connection that went beyond anything she had ever felt with another human being. It was as if a psychic link now existed, enabling her to read his thoughts and share his emotions.

And the chaplain. Mark Pinnacle. Mousy little man who'd looked so frightened on the speaker's platform. Who would have thought? She'd been delighted to hear of his offer. It had allowed her to call in Chip Mansfield and tell him he was off the hook. And if somebody else would agree to stay, she could get rid of Benning, who was next in line. She hated the notion of spending the last hours of her life with people who'd stayed only because someone had forced them into it. Better to die with the valiant.

She climbed out of her jumpsuit. It'd been a long day and she ached for a shower. She could justify it now: There was no further need to conserve water.

The telephone rang as she stepped into the stall, but she didn't bother with it. Get it when she came out. The ultimate emergency had broken over her head and nothing was going to rush her again. Not in this life.

Evelyn had been born in Dakar. Her father had been a British missionary, her mother a teacher of French literature at Senegal University. Evelyn had announced early that she wanted to become a physician. She'd seen firsthand the living conditions of the tribes, and she was going to do what she could. It was an admirable ambition, but one that faded in high school when she discovered a distaste for chemistry and physics.

She went to the University of Versailles, where she concluded that a great deal more money was to be made by bringing fantasy to the middle class rather than medical repairs to the poor. Virtual reality was about to arrive on African shores in all its manifestations, diagnostic, cinematic, therapeutic, analytic. Evelyn did not yet have her bachelor's degree when she founded MicroTech, Ltd., hired a secretary, and secured licenses from poorly informed bureaucrats.

From that moment she controlled the growth of the industry in and around Senegal. She profited handsomely from her monopoly, expanded into Mauritania, Ghana, Sierra Leone, and the Ivory Coast. Organized crime tried to move in on her, but she hired her own elite security force, and in the end she was tougher than they were. All of this took place just before the African boom. When it came, Evelyn parlayed it into a seat on the board of Global Communications, Ltd.

She was in the right spot when the nations decided they wanted to establish a permanent presence on the Moon and they needed a corporation to help them do it.

For a while it was MicroTech all over again, except on a global level. She was *Time*'s Woman of the Year in 2022, she employed a half-dozen Nobel prize winners, and she was on first-name terms with prime ministers and presidents. Her ghostwritten book, *Moon Over Wall Street*, was enjoying its fifty-seventh week on the *New York Times* best-seller list.

She'd married twice. Marcus Hampton had been gunned down during the war with the east African thugs. William had gotten the wrong idea about her, thinking she'd consent to be part of a harem. She didn't know where he was now.

She had one son by Marcus, who lived with her in Roxbury. He was at MIT, working on a doctorate. Old enough to deal with the loss of his mother. Should it come to that.

The phone was ringing again when she shut the water off. She strode out of the bathroom, toweling herself as she went. "Hampton," she said. Her name, spoken by her voice, activated the instrument.

"Evelyn." It was Chandler. "I just got a message from Ops."

"What's wrong, Jack?"

"The flight left without Haskell."

She needed a moment to digest that. "How'd it happen?"

"He and his party apparently *walked*. One of them delivered the tickets and told our people to give the seats to somebody else. He was up here several minutes ago."

"Did he explain why? Why he didn't go?"

"No. But he's on his way over to see you."

"Okay," she said. "Thanks, Jack. I assume we filled the seats."

"Yes."

"Okay. Put them on the morning flight tomorrow."

"Yes, ma'm."

She heard raised voices in the corridor. "I think he's here, Jack. I'll talk to you later."

She grabbed a robe, drew it around her shoulders, and turned to face the door.

Moonbase, Grissom Country. 2:06 P.M.

Charlie Haskell was no hero. He admired heroes, was always ready to quote TR or Churchill, and had twice presided over the Veterans Day ceremonies. But he'd never in his life been called on to perform an act that could be described as heroic. He'd confronted a bully or two, and once stood up to a tyrannical geometry teacher. The memory of that long-ago day had flashed briefly, absurdly, through his memory as he sat on the tram, surrounded by Rick and his frustrated agents, riding back to Main Plaza.

Frustration had been the order of the afternoon. He'd insisted his agents board their scheduled flight. They'd refused. And Rick, who usually looked after himself first, had picked this moment to step out of character. He'd argued that Charlie couldn't possibly stay, couldn't consider it, owed it to the American people to get home, was too valuable to lose. Which is to say, even Rick couldn't come up with a compelling reason for him to save his skin.

Charlie had no family that was dependent on him, no one who would be terribly hurt if something happened to him. And no real reason for existing, other than his job, which someone had once described as consisting of three duties: to go fishing, to preside over the Senate, and to wait for the president to die.

Rick had argued all the way down to Evelyn's apartment.

But it seemed to Charlie as if his whole life had been a preparation for this terrible moment. He thought of himself as a national leader. He enjoyed the trappings of his position, luxuriated in the celebrity, rubbed shoulders with the powerful, toured the country clubs. Now had come the moment to lead.

He'd sat on the tram, listening to Rick. He pictured himself in the White House next year, if he got lucky, trying to drive from his mind the knowledge that someone braver than he had died in his place. He couldn't even remember the chaplain's name. His heart had been pounding. Later he would come to believe that the decision had been taken hours earlier, that it had been a left-brain thing, that it was just a matter of waiting for his conscious mind to catch up. And maybe there was some truth to that.

Charlie had tried to call the president from the tram. He had a code that got him through the Moonbase commcenter without a hitch, but Henry had been in a meeting. *He'll call you back, sir.* So he left a message explaining what he had done. *That*, of course, had put him across the Rubicon.

Then he'd gone looking for Evelyn. If he was going to take this kind of step, he wanted at least to relish the pleasure of telling her personally. He wondered why it was so important to him to gain her respect. But now he stood outside her door, telling Rick and his embattled agents to go away, waiting for her to answer, feeling elated and terrified and very pleased with himself.

He was surprised when the door opened. He'd detected no movement on the other side, but feet padding across a floor were harder to hear in lunar gravity. Evelyn was wrapped in a yellow terry-cloth robe, standing in a puddle, and looking curiously at him. "What's going on, Mr. Vice President?"

"I'm not sure," Charlie said. "May I come in?"

She stood aside. "They tell me you missed your flight."

He glanced back at Rick and Sam, and walked across the threshold. She closed the door behind him.

"I'm staying," he said.

"*Staying?*"

They looked at each other across a gulf.

"Got any coffee?"

"You and the chaplain," she said almost dreamily. "Why?"

"I kept thinking about MacArthur," he said.

"MacArthur?"

"Twentieth-century American general."

"I know who he was." She frowned. "What's Douglas MacArthur got to do with anything?"

"Are you angry with me?"

"Why would I be angry?" Her voice was icy.

"I really don't know. You sound hostile."

"Tell me about MacArthur."

"In 1942, when the Philippines were about to be overrun by the Japanese, Franklin Roosevelt ordered MacArthur, the commanding general, to slip out. It was the right thing to do because the Allies would need MacArthur. He was worth a couple of divisions. They sneaked him past the enemy fleet, and afterward he became a major force in the war. He was directed to abandon his troops. To save himself. He did, and nothing he did after allowed him to live it down. They called him 'Duck-out Doug.'"

Although Charlie was almost a foot taller than Evelyn, she seemed to be looking down at him. "Forget politics," she said. "You don't have any troops here." She picked up the phone and punched in a number. "Are they confirmed?" she asked.

"Don't," said Charlie.

"Good," she said into the phone. "He'll be on the flight." And she turned to him: "Twelve-fifteen liftoff from the Spaceport tomorrow morning. I've got six seats for you."

Charlie felt a rush of anger. "I'll only need five."

She looked at him for a long moment, glanced at the phone, and sank into a chair. "You're sure?" she asked.

"Yeah. I'm sure. It's harder to cut and run than it is to stay." It occurred to him that history would remember the six who stayed. Probably more clearly than it remembers most vice presidents.

5.

Moonbase, Administrative Offices. 2:08 P.M.

Andrea Bellwether had never before seen her boss in so grim a mood.

Her boss was Teresa Perella, who was usually congenial and animated, and who'd never seen a problem that couldn't be solved or got around. Today she looked beaten. She stared out over the heads of her communications specialists, as if her mind had drifted far beyond the confines of the meeting room.

"We're ready to begin moving out," she said. Teresa was a tiny woman, with dark eyes and a persona that radiated presence. She'd buried two husbands. Exhausted them, the joke was. "We're going to keep the commcenter running until midafternoon tomorrow. I'll need three people to help. Those who stay will be on the late flight out. They're saying it's safe, but who knows?" She gazed at them, lips parted as though she had more to say but was hesitating. *Those with no families.*

Tommy Chan signaled he would wait.

Those with no future.

Eleanor Kile. Eleanor was a spectacularly beautiful woman, the loveliest at Moonbase, Andrea thought, but one of those who seemed to frighten males off. All but the wrong types.

Anybody else? Teresa drew herself up a little straighter. "We need one more."

Andrea Bellwether was riffling mental files, studying the texture of the wall, thinking of all the people she'd like to see again. Parents, uncles, a niece.

What would Teresa do if no one came forward?

She looked at Chan, and at Kile. Well, hell, they'd have an hour start. Andrea caught Teresa's eye and nodded. She was rewarded with a glimmer of respect.

Wrightsville, New Jersey. 2:11 P.M.

The Pine River Furniture Company convoy was finally under way. Archie would have preferred an earlier start, because he wanted to get around Philadelphia before the rush-hour traffic began. But they'd underestimated the complexity of loading the stock safely, and overestimated the ability of the temporary help to follow simple instructions. There were eighteen trucks, filled with executive desks and leather divans and carved swivel chairs. The company had assigned its entire fleet, fourteen dark blue vehicles with white piping, carrying the logo designed by the original Walter Harrison, depicting a debutante curled into an overstuffed armchair on a riverbank. Four other vehicles had been rented from Wrightstown U-Haul.

Archie rode in the lead truck. Claire Hasson, a company driver, was behind the wheel. In the side mirror, Archie could see the convoy stretching back around a curve. They were on Route 68, which would connect via I295 with the Pennsylvania Turnpike. They were headed for Carlisle and the Blue Mountains. Ridiculous, in Archie's mind. But, by God, it would take one very large tidal wave to sink them up there.

Carlisle hadn't been the first choice. But they'd been unable to find commercial accommodations anywhere in Pennsylvania's mountain country. After hours of fruitless calls, Walter had pulled strings with lodge brothers who'd agreed to take the drivers into their homes. Archie wondered what the boss had promised in return.

The lack of motel vacancies had served as a warning. Archie dispatched his family that morning in the Buick station wagon to stay with his wife's sister in Troy, New York. Susan didn't like being separated from him, although she too maintained that nothing was going to happen. But she became visibly worried when Archie reported that Harrison took it all very seriously. We'll be back here next week joking about it, they'd agreed. Then she'd gotten into the Buick with their teenage son and daughter, both of whom had objected loudly to the forced removal, and driven off.

The convoy was moving at a brisk pace along the four-lane road. Now and then, Archie saw other caravans. Macro Electronics. Sonya Precision Timepieces. SolarWorks Complete Auto Power Systems. Occasionally clusters of new cars with dealer plates sped past.

Being out on the highway, watching people heading west, undercut Archie's self-assurance even more. "What do you think?" asked Claire.

"It's crazy," he said. But he knew he was saying it because he was a boss and skepticism was expected from him. "This is just the chief playing it very safe."

"I'm glad to hear you say it."

"I don't think there's anything to worry about." And a minute later: "Where's your family?"

"Home. We thought about going to my sister's for a few days, but it means pulling the kids out of school, and Ed couldn't get the day off."

"Yeah. I know how it is."

And after another long silence: "But I'll be glad when we're through it, Archie. The stuff on the TV scares me."

His cell phone beeped. "Pickman," he said.

"Archie, this is Brad." Brad Cabry was a staff assistant, riding at the rear of the convoy. "I don't know whether you've been listening to the radio, but they're saying traffic's already heavy on the Pennsylvania Turnpike. More than rush hour. They're cautioning people to stay off."

Archie looked out at the long line of cars and trucks ahead. "Too late for us," he said. "We'll stick with Plan A. If it takes all night, it takes all night."

Claire nodded. "Absolutely," she said. "I can use the overtime."

Archie shifted his weight and tried to get comfortable. The truck felt as if it had a broken spring. "Has this damned thing been serviced?"

She reached into the glove box, pulled out the maintenance record, and handed it to him. He looked down at the numbers, but he had trouble focusing on them.

Manhattan. 3:36 P.M.

Marilyn Keep had looked at the pictures of jammed expressways, had watched news commentators smile condescendingly at the people who were on the run, had seen Chicken Little cartoons on *New York Online*. Anybody who was trying to head upstate was being portrayed as an idiot. Well, to those who were stuck in the city, it was comforting.

She was back working on *Shadow of the Betrayer* when the phone rang. It was Larry: "What are we doing tomorrow, love?"

She looked away from her chart, which recorded every physical and psychological detail of each character from the novel, and frowned at the phone. "Watching the Moon get plunked, I guess," she said. "What did you have in mind?"

"Louise is throwing a comet party tomorrow night. She'd like us to come."

"It's kind of last-minute, isn't it?"

"Well, it's kind of a last-minute comet. I think it'll be a kick."

Louise was one of Larry's colleagues, an economist at Kraus

& Cole. Marilyn had socialized with her on a few occasions. She was twice divorced, a woman who claimed to have thrown out both husbands, although Larry said it had been the other way around. She was the unofficial office social director, putting together pot luck lunches, bowling teams, and mass trips to dinner theaters. "Sure," she said. "Let's do it."

The world seemed to have returned almost to normal. Late-night comics were doing comet jokes, and a TV preacher had announced that Tomiko had been headed originally for Alabama until he'd prayed it away. Political pundits were analyzing its effect on the fall campaign. (Most thought it would hurt Haskell's chances, despite what they perceived as his adroit grandstanding, because of the national investment in Moonbase, which was now irrevocably lost.) The Yankees, who were at home this weekend against the Tigers, announced that if the Saturday night game had not yet been completed by ten thirty-five, the time of impact, they would call a delay to proceedings and put the celestial show on the replay screens. The Moon would be in the west, not visible to the fans other than those in the right-field seats. Some fans objected, and suggested that management could put the show on the screen, but that was no reason to hold up the game.

Marilyn's third-floor apartment looked out across Central Park. Everything seemed as it always did: A couple of kids were trying to fly a kite while their mothers looked on, joggers moved along the pathways, and the usual number of people occupied benches. Panhandlers were working pedestrians, and the streets were filled with taxis, buses, and delivery trucks. The schools were open, and Wal-Mart had announced a big comet sale. ("Get your tail down here while the savings last.")

Shadow of the Betrayer struck her as one of the less imaginative murder mysteries to arrive on her desk. The killer was transparently visible from about Chapter Three, and only marginally motivated. The red herrings were all quite plainly red herrings. The pacing was off, the characters were dull. The narrative had a breakneck quality out of keeping with what should have been an atmospheric mystery. The reader never had time to stop and think about implications. And the novelist himself seemed to have missed several opportunities to create real drama. It was as though he'd been double-parked.

Unable to concentrate, she opened the balcony door and stepped outside. It wasn't much of a balcony, just big enough to accommodate two chairs and a small table. She stood for a while, leaning against the concrete rail, watching three men move furniture from a rented truck into the apartment building next door.

San Francisco. 1:20 P.M. Pacific Daylight Time (4:20 EDT).

Everybody in the third-floor office of Bennett & McGee was staring at the TV. It was a split screen. A map of the Bay Area filled one side, from Richmond in the north to Santa Clara and the Los Altos Hills in the south, from the Pacific over to I680, encompassing more than eleven hundred square kilometers. An image of the comet's head, somewhat longish and irregular, cratered and torn, occupied the other. One huge crater took up about a fifth of the comet's visible surface. While Jerry watched, the outline of the Bay Area was superimposed over the comet nucleus. Then it was reduced until San Francisco and environs fit neatly into the big crater. A legend blinked on at the bottom of the screen: ACTUAL SIZE.

In a voice-over, Senator Mark Caswell was speaking with PugetWeb anchor Jane McMurtrie.

". . . impeachment," he was saying. "It's absolutely unthinkable that a president of the United States would downplay this kind of threat. I think you'll see an appropriate congressional response in the near future."

"But Senator," said McMurtrie, "isn't that really an idle threat? I mean, if there's substance to the charge that the information is vital to the nation's survival, the damage is pretty much done. The rocks will fall and there won't be a Congress Monday. If, on the other hand, he's simply trying to control the alarmists, which is to say, if nothing happens, what will the charge be? I mean, he'll have been right, won't he?"

"Not at all, Jane. We don't intend to let Mr. Kolladner play fast and loose with the safety of the people of this nation. And I can assure you that when this is over, there will be a Congress, and there will be a United States. And there'll be a reckoning."

Half the staff had called in sick. They'd had to man the trouble desk with people from the equity branch. Manny's Coffeehouse across the street, where Jerry usually stopped to have toast and read the *Chronicle*, had been closed this morning. A sign on the window read: BACK MONDAY.

Jerry and Marisa had spent the previous evening with friends, exchanging quips about people they knew who were leaving town. They'd laughed a lot, but the general uneasiness had been noticable.

His division head was Leo Gold, who'd been with the firm when the wagon trains came west. Leo's hair was snow white, and he had a voice like an electric saw. He was a model-train enthusiast. He called Jerry into his office. "Can you work tomorrow?" he asked without preamble.

Tomorrow was Saturday. It was the Saturday before April 15, which was a busy time for accounting firms. But Bennett & McGee had always prided itself on its ability to get the job done without having to go into crash mode during the tax season. No one below the level of general manager had *ever* worked the Saturday before the tax deadline. It was a matter of pride.

"But not this year," explained Leo. "All these people taking off the last couple of days, Jerry. It's put us in a bind."

Ordinarily, Jerry wouldn't have thought twice. But he

knew Marisa was nervous about the comet. There was a possibility she'd want to leave, get out of its way, and they wouldn't be able to do that if he were committed to coming into work. "I was planning on a weekend out of town," he said.

Leo pressed his lips together. "Jerry." He canted his head. "Jerry, you're not serious."

How can you be so naïve, Jerry? "It's not the comet, Leo," Jerry hastened to explain. "This trip's been planned for several weeks. We're going to see my wife's sister Helen."

"Jerry, we're all going to be here Monday. San Francisco will be here. Bennett & McGee will be here. And I need not tell you what date Monday is."

April fifteenth. It occurred to Jerry that if the worst predictions played out, the last official act of the United States government might be its annual mugging of its citizens. "You have a bright future with the firm," Leo went on. "Don't jeopardize it over . . ." He seemed at a loss for words, and settled for drawing a circle in the air with his right index finger.

In the end Jerry agreed, not because he feared for his career. Rather, Leo's demeanor made him feel he had to prove he wasn't afraid of the comet.

6.

Point Judith, Rhode Island. 7:21 P.M.

Luke Peterson was a retired printer. His wife was twenty years dead, and his kids were scattered around the country. He owned a spacious brick home in Point Judith, with a lovely view of the sea. He had wide lawns and a paved driveway and plenty of room for his grandchildren, who loved the place and arrived in flocks every summer. He'd come to the ocean when he lost his wife, bought the property for $110,000. Now it was worth three-quarters of a million, and he wouldn't have been able to afford to keep it except that he was over seventy and there was a special provision in the tax law to protect home-owners against runaway real estate values. He'd run the print shop out of it for ten years, had published commercial and tourist flyers, and done various custom jobs, business cards, stationery, whatever. It'd been a nice living, but he'd gotten bored with it. Life was too short to spend in a print shop, and when he was able to close it, he did.

Luke had invested well, so money wasn't a problem. He played pinochle Wednesdays, and attended a great books club on the second Monday of the month. (They were reading Marcus Aurelius for the May meeting.) He played golf two or three days a week, as the mood hit him; and he usually ate lunch with a few guys from the Rotary. The Lunch Bunch, they called themselves.

He still got lonely. He missed Ann, and most days the house was quieter than he liked. But he'd adjusted reasonably well. She wouldn't have stood for his moping around and feeling sorry for himself, and he did what he could to follow the advice she'd written on the last birthday card she'd sent him, to treat life like an overripe grapefruit, and get all the juice out of it he could.

So he watched the TV reports with interest and a little trepidation. (Fear was part of the grapefruit, too.) But the ocean looked reassuringly calm and flat.

Pennsylvania Turnpike, northwest of Philadelphia. 7:33 P.M.

The traffic, which had moved sporadically for three hours, had now stopped altogether. State police channels reported that the turnpike was a parking lot all the way out to Valley Forge.

The convoy had long since dissolved. Archie could see four company trucks strung out behind him. The rest were gone, swallowed somewhere in the crush.

"Claire," he asked, "do you know what the justification

was for building the interstate highway system?"

She had no idea.

"Eisenhower said he wanted to be able to move troops quickly from one place to another. In case of invasion."

She looked around at the gridlock and smiled. "There were fewer cars then."

Pickups, station wagons, vans, all were loaded with cartons and blankets and kids. Furniture was piled on top. Lamps stuck out windows, and trunk lids were tied down atop chairs. Archie had been in the Caucasus during peacekeeping operations, when local strongmen had tried to eliminate minority ethnic groups and the Turks hadn't cooperated in the rescue. He remembered people on the roads, headed south and east, away from the killing zones. There had been a lot of cars, and the roads were decent. Not the Pennsylvania Turnpike, certainly. But there was something in this automotive crush that reminded him of those frightened multitudes.

Something.

Maybe the kids huddled in the back seats; and scared drivers getting out to push stalled cars off the road; and even occasional gunfire. In the Caucasus it had been snipers posted along the highways. Here he didn't know what it was.

Ahead, a blinker rotated slowly on a cruiser, but the cops were as helpless as everybody else.

Old cars were overheating or running out of gas. Electrics were exhausting their batteries. The Pine River trucks had been charged before leaving the plant. But even they would not get through the night.

"How you doing, Claire?"

She shrugged. They were inching past an off-ramp. It was loaded with vehicles trying to exit. There was an extra lane of traffic along the shoulder, but it wasn't moving either.

He'd tried several times to reach Susan on his cell phone. But the circuits must have been jammed and he couldn't get through. The roads were probably bad everywhere. He thought about her trying to navigate I-287 around New York, and regretted having encouraged her to go. "These people are crazy," he said finally.

She grinned. "We're out here with them."

"Yeah. But we're being paid."

THE MOLLY SINGER SHOW. 8:00 P.M.

Excerpt from an interview at the WXPI-TV studios in Richmond, Virginia, with "Colonel" Steve Gallagher, Commander, Thomas Jefferson Legion.

Singer:	*Colonel, why does Virginia need a militia?*
Gallagher:	*We all know the answer to that question, Molly. Some of us don't want to face up to the truth, and some of us are in bed with the traitors at the top. But we all know.*
Singer:	*Why don't you tell us?*
Gallagher:	*The Legion is all that stands between oppressive government and the people. If the federals are ever successful in putting us down, you and the other people out there might just as well put on your leg irons.*
Singer:	*So you really think there's a wide-ranging plot to enslave the American people?*
Gallagher:	*You can joke about it all you want, you and the rest of the liberal media, you've always been up front, egging these traitors on and hiding the truth. But when you turn the country over to them, they'll swallow you whole too. Just like the rest of us.*
Singer:	*Who precisely are we talking about?*
Gallagher:	*Start with Kolladner.*
Singer:	*What's he done?*
Gallagher:	*Government without representation, Molly. Open your eyes. It's the same reason we fought the first revolution. Look, it's not really about individuals. It's about*

the machinery of government. It's about a system that allows people like Kolladner to get their hands on the levers, that tries to hold down the rest of us.

Singer: *We have the vote.*

Gallagher: *Who do you get to vote for? Usually you can choose between two puppets. Molly, Molly, most men and women are born to be slaves. We both know that. At any given time on the planet, there are only a few who can truly be said to be free. The others, the great mass of your audience for example, are enslaved because they believe what they're told by their schools and their churches. By society, and particularly by shows like this. These are all corrupt institutions with a stake in ensuring correct behavior. Maintain order, that's what you want, isn't it? So you can keep your two-hundred-thousand-dollar-a-year job. You were born to be a slave, Molly. You've got some ability and you've sold out. Your job is to see that anyone who thinks for himself gets isolated, banished to the fringes, and rendered impotent.*

Richmond, WXPI Studios. 8:36 P.M.

Tad Wickett and the colonel's younger brother Jack were waiting for him in the lobby. "How'd it look?" Steve asked.

"You were damned good, Steve," said Jack. "Maybe we can wake some of these people up."

Tad nodded. "You put the bitch down real good, Colonel."

Steve stood for a moment, not moving, looking back the way he'd come as if they might call him for an encore. "She deserves to be put down a lot harder," he said. "It's people like that who are the problem. They cover for the sons of bitches who are draining this country dry. I can't believe she doesn't know she's being used."

"Whether she does or not," said Tad, "she's in the way.

Why don't we just put her out of business? Teach the rest of them a lesson."

Jack felt a chill. He didn't like Wickett. Twice in Jack's experience he'd almost gone off the road trying to run down dogs. He was an ex-Marine who talked a lot about eliminating people. You couldn't tell whether he meant it or not. The colonel laughed whenever Jack voiced his fears. *Don't worry about Tad. He only does what I tell him to. And we need people like him. Day's going to come. . . .*

"What did you have in mind?" asked Steve, who was far too smart to use violence except as a last resort. Still, he knew that dismissing suggestions peremptorily was poor leadership technique.

"Take out the station," said Tad. Jack could see he relished the prospect. "You know how at the end of the show she always says, 'This is Molly saying goodnight and good fortune'? Let her get the line in and then blow her and the station to hell. Right on cue."

The colonel grinned. Tad claimed to have killed several people in military service, and everybody knew he'd finished Scratchy Ellsworth in a fight last year. Police screwed up the investigation or Tad would be in jail now.

"I don't think we need to do that yet," Steve said. "But in time, Tad, we'll get around to Molly Singer."

7.

PENNSYLVANIA STATEWIDE RADIO/TV/NET HOOKUP. 9:00 P.M.
"This is Governor Adcock, speaking to you from the state capital at Harrisburg. I want to urge you to stay in your homes. I understand your concern about the Tomiko Comet, but I remind you that the Moon is a quarter-million miles away, and everything else is speculation.

"Traffic on the streets and highways of eastern Pennsylvania has all but ground to a halt, despite the best efforts of state and local police.

The safest place for you is at home. We have fully mobilized the resources of the Commonwealth to deal with any problem that might arise. I will add that I do not expect any, other than the ones caused by frightened citizens. Bear in mind that emergency vehicles cannot get through if private vehicles crowd the streets and roads. I would also ask that you refrain from tying up telephone lines unless absolutely necessary.

"I'll be leaving here within the hour to join Mayor Hanson in Philadelphia. I plan to stay at City Hall there tomorrow and through the weekend, to be with you until we can put this behind us.

"Please do not misunderstand me. I recognize the uncertainty of the situation. But be aware that this is a problem for all of us. The best thing we can do right now to help one another is to keep calm. I will continue to inform you of developments. Thank you and good evening."

Micro Flight Deck. 10:18 P.M.

They were chasing *Berlin*. It was a long run this time, almost an hour and a half, and Tony took advantage of it to try to sleep. But the incident with the leaky valve haunted him.

Unlike Bigfoot Caparatti, he wasn't given to guilt, and he in no way blamed himself that they were now perhaps fatally behind schedule. He knew what he might have done differently, knew he could have blown out of the cloud, or climbed outside and shut down the leaky valve, and finished the mission. But he couldn't have been expected to make those guesses. It would have been reckless, for example, to risk colliding with the plane. A small voice somewhere told him he should have realized the other pilot would draw away. But he couldn't be certain the other pilot wouldn't have thought he was in deep trouble, and would have expected the Micro to keep still while the plane approached.

Anyway, that was all past now. A waste of time to think about it. The question was, how to repair the damage?

There *was* a way.

"You okay, Tony?" Saber was looking at him, worried. *Berlin* was around the curve of the Moon. They were running over Farside, beneath the baleful glow of the comet, which now looked like a second sun. Not a real sun, but a cool, wispy apparition. Something seen at night in a forest.

"Yeah. I'm fine."

"What are you thinking?"

"You know," he said, "we can deliver our last pickup tomorrow night and still get back down before the comet hits."

Their last launch from the Spaceport would take place at about seven-thirty P.M., Saturday. They'd rendezvous with *Arlington*, which by then would be the only remaining plane in Luna's skies, at about ten after nine.

"We could get back down to the Spaceport by a quarter after."

"Ten?"

"Yeah."

"Tony, that's only twenty minutes before the comet hits. Not even time to get off the pad. Anyhow, *Arlington* would be long gone."

"So we'd have to stay with the Micro, wouldn't we?"

She stared at him. "We couldn't get out of there in under a half hour. We could skip the maintenance, but we'd still have to refuel."

"I know. Saber, I don't want to leave anyone on the ground."

"Hell. Nobody does. But all that would happen if we went back is that *we'd* get caught down there with them."

"Not necessarily." He picked up their passenger manifest, and looked over the names. There were three private vendors on board and three dependents. He also had two geologists, a hydroponics expert, and an astrophysicist. Total of ten. (The hydroponics expert was heavy, the kids were light. They'd been able to put an extra child on board.)

The astrophysicist should be just what he needed. He asked Saber to go below and invite her onto the flight deck.

Janet Koestler was middle-aged, slightly overweight, with a plump, apple-pie expression. It was easier to imagine her surrounded by grandkids than working with telescopes. "How can I help you, Captain?" she asked after he'd seated her in Saber's chair.

"Professional question?"

"Sure."

"I wonder if you could describe for us precisely what'll happen when Tomiko gets here? When it hits the Moon?"

Ahead, the Earth was rising.

"In what way?" she asked.

"Is the Moon going to explode?"

Her brow furrowed. "No," she said. "The Moon *can't* explode. It's really a fairly cohesive body."

"Then what's going to happen?"

"I haven't seen the calculations, but this comet is very big. It's an anomaly. And it's coming at a velocity I'd have thought impossible.

"A comet this size, if it were hitting Earth, would carve out a crater roughly thirty-six hundred kilometers in diameter. That's more than the diameter of the Moon." She paused for effect. "That tells me the Moon will be broken apart." She looked down at the lunar surface. "Everything in the immediate neighborhood of the impact will be vaporized, probably well toward the core.

"The comet's going to melt a lot of rock. *A lot.* Some of it will be blasted clear of the surface. Or maybe a more correct way to put it is, ejected from the gravitational center. Some will even be blown clear of the Earth-Moon system and go into solar orbit."

"But the Moon, or most of it, will still be here? Is that what you're saying? Because that's not what we've been hearing."

She frowned. "It's just very hard to predict this event. Look, the comet will fracture the Moon. There's no question about that. It'll convert it into a cluster of loose rock. Everything that *can* be broken *will* be broken. The shock will cause the rock to drift apart. It'll spread out around the Moon's orbit, and some of it will probably form a kind of shell around the Earth, at about the lunar radius. I'd want to do some work on this, but I imagine, given enough time, the particles will reform. And there'll be another Moon. Smaller, I would think." She took a deep breath. "There's another interesting possibility."

"Which is?"

"The Earth will acquire a set of rings. Over the long term."

Saber asked how long was the long term.

"Several million years. Certainly nothing we need concern ourselves with."

Tony leaned toward her, attentive. "Doc," he said, "I'd like to ask a hypothetical question. You've had a chance to look at the Micro?"

"I beg your pardon?"

"*This* vehicle. The one we're in."

"Well, yes. I've seen it, more or less. I'm *in* it."

"If it were a few thousand feet over Moonbase at the time of collision, what would you think about its chances of survival?"

"Not good."

"Can you be more specific?"

She shrugged. "Well, if the bus were directly over Moonbase, it would have one thing going for it. Impact will take place on the far side. But there's going to be a very large fireball. My guess is that the fireball will come right over the pole and engulf the entire northern hemisphere."

"Moonbase is at Alphonsus," Tony reminded her. "Thirteen degrees south."

"Maybe I should have said it will engulf the entire Moon."

"How high would I have to be to be safe?"

"Preferably halfway to Earth. At least. Captain, none of this is my field of expertise. I really don't know." She looked at him, and the smile, which had seemed a permanent part of her features, faded. "You're not planning on doing anything like this, are you?"

Moonbase, Director's Office. 11:03 P.M.

Chaplain Pinnacle hadn't been the first volunteer. A mechanic named Tamayaka had offered to stay in exchange for payment of future college expenses for his three kids; and a young optics expert, distraught over the philandering of her new husband, had asked to remain. Chandler had accepted neither. He was disappointed at the reaction of his senior people. Only Jill Benning had openly opposed him. But the others had stood by and left him to defend the only reasonable position as best he could. Eckerd was behaving as if he was doing Chandler a favor. Hawkworth walked around looking like a martyr.

Eckerd, who headed Health and Safety, knew about the director's heart problems. Chandler wondered whether he had pursued his knowledge to its logical conclusion: that it was far less difficult for Chandler to play the hero than it was for the others. And that hard reality chilled him. Still, it did not ease his smoldering anger. With or without the heart problem, he would have done the right thing. He knew that.

After the chaplain called, Chandler simply put out an amended list, inserting the chaplain's name directly above his own. That bumped everybody else, except Evelyn, up one slot. Then had come the shocker: The vice president was staying!

Chandler had his doubts that Haskell wouldn't change his mind. But he'd duly inserted the name, scheduled Benning for a flight, and moved the others up another notch. Benning had told him that he shouldn't think for a minute that this would get him and Hampton and the corporation off the hook. She was going to sue everyone in sight.

He wondered what they'd do if Haskell *did* change his mind. Call her back and tell her she was going to get to stay after all?

<u>*BBC WORLDNET.*</u> 11:07 P.M.
Excerpt from an interview with Dr. Olive Ellsworth of the Anglo-Australian-Observatory in New South Wales, conducted by Connie Hasting.

Ellsworth:	*The section we've highlighted is the impact area. It's on the far side, about a hundred miles west of Mare Muscoviense. It'll be coming in at roughly four hundred fifty-five kilometers per second, which is a slight decrease in velocity since we first saw it. That's due to the gravitational influence of the Sun, of course.*
Hasting:	*And it's the center of the comet that we have to worry about. Right?*
Ellsworth:	*Yes, Connie. It's the center, the nucleus, that will do the damage.*
Hasting:	*And the coma is the part that glows?*
Ellsworth:	*The coma's a cloud of gas and dust. When a comet gets near the Sun, it begins to heat up, and we get a coma. And a tail. Or, as in this case, sometimes two tails.*
Hasting:	*How big is the coma?*
Ellsworth:	*This one's about three hundred thousand miles across.*
Hasting:	*Three hundred thousand miles? That's pretty big.*
Ellsworth:	*Actually, it's smaller than you might expect from an object this large. That might be because of the composi-*

tion of the comet: There simply may not be that much material to burn off. Or it may be that its passage through the solar system has been so quick, the Sun hasn't had time to work its way. Probably a combination of the two.

Hasting: In these pictures it has a pair of tails.

Ellsworth: Yes. The ion tail, this one, is about six million miles long.

Hasting: But when I look at it in the sky, all I see is a large fuzzy patch.

Ellsworth: The tails are running in front of it, so they're not easy to see for an earthbound observer.

Hasting: The tails are in front?

Ellsworth: Oh, yes. Comets' tails always point away from the Sun. The solar wind causes that. (Displays images.) These were taken from the Venusian probe.

Hasting: It is lovely. . . . I wonder if you can tell us what's going to happen tomorrow night?

Ellsworth: Let's look at the graphic. You understand, this comet would be less destructive if it were moving at the velocity comets usually move in the solar system, at thirty or forty kilometers per second. But this is going much faster, and consequently it will hit the Moon very hard. You'll observe, it's approaching the Moon now.

Hasting: (Nods.)

Ellsworth: Here, it breaks through the outer lunar mantle. What's actually happening is that the area where the comet impacts is being vaporized to a depth of several hundred miles.

Hasting: It almost looks as if it's splashing in.

Ellsworth: Oh, yes. Splash is the right word. That's how craters form, you know. The material melts under the impact. This comet is unlike anything we've seen before.

•   •   •

SSTO *Rome* Flight Deck. 11:10 P.M.

At Skyport they'd corrected the programming glitch. John Verrano rode his spacecraft into lunar orbit on a dime. He opened a channel. "Moonbase, this is *Rome*."

"Go ahead, *Rome*."

"*Rome* is on station and ready for business."

Moonbase, Director's Office. 11:11 P.M.

It was, of course, the story of the age. Keith Morley of Transglobal was outraged when his link with the news desk was severed by the Moonbase commcenter. Jack Chandler had said yes, yes, he understood how Morley felt, but they couldn't give Morley an open channel because there just weren't enough circuits available.

"Circuits, hell!" Morley compained. "You're going to lose some people and you don't want me blowing the coverup."

"We're not certain yet we'll lose anybody."

Morley didn't care much for Chandler. He was the perfect bureaucrat, evasive, deskbound, a man who thought in terms of constraints and methodologies. From whom it was next to impossible to get a direct answer.

"What does that mean, Jack? Do you *expect* to lose some of your people?"

Chandler ran his hands through his thinning hair. "Yes," he said. "We do."

"Why are you sitting on it? Do you think it's going to change anything tomorrow night because you don't tell anybody?"

Chandler leaned forward, braced his elbows on his desk, and set his chin on his hands. "We're not sitting on anything, Keith." He glanced at his phone. "I'll call the commcenter and see that you get a link, if that's what you want."

"Of course it's what I want." He took a deep breath. "How many people are going to be killed?"

"Possibly none."

"Right. We've been through that. If you lose some, how many is it likely to be?"

"Six," he said.

Six. Well, it wasn't as bad as he'd thought. Assuming the old bastard was telling the truth. "Names?" he asked. "Who's getting left?" He did not take out his notebook, of course. He'd been in the business too long and knew that you never, ever conducted an interview with a notebook or recorder.

Chandler rattled them off. Himself and Hampton. Hawkworth, Eckerd. Pinnacle."

"The chaplain?"

"He offered to stay."

Morley called up his image of Mark Pinnacle. "Did he say why?"

Chandler shook his head. "No. I didn't think to ask."

"Okay. That's *five*. Who else?"

"Charlie Haskell."

Morley did a double take. "You're not serious. He left this afternoon, didn't he?"

"No. He stayed off the flight."

"But he was directed out."

"He's still here."

Morley started for the door. "Can you arrange for me to talk to him?"

Chandler shook his head again. He was very good at saying no. "I've no control over his appointments, Keith."

Damn. Either this was legitimate and Haskell was really going to try to ride out the comet, or something was going on. Either way, it was a *huge* story. But Morley's throat caught when he thought about his options. Nevertheless, he needed only a moment to make up his mind. "Jack, I'd like to stay, too, if you don't object."

Chandler's eyes widened. "You don't mean that," he said.

All of Morley's instincts told him there was no way the vice president would hang in if there weren't a way out. Politicians don't do things like that.

And it was a hell of a story. *Pulitzer*, Morley was thinking. *Maybe posthumous. But a Pulitzer.*

FRANK CRANDALL'S ALL-NIGHTER. 11:53 P.M.

Crandall:	*Hi, Jason from Coos Bay.*
First Caller:	*Hey, Frank. Cheers from the white beach capital.*
Crandall:	*Thanks, Jason. What's on your mind?*
First Caller:	*What's the straight stuff about the comet, Frank? The media always lie, and I keep hearing conflicting stories. I'm looking out my window now at the ocean. What's going to happen tomorrow night?*
Crandall:	*Don't know, my man. I don't think anybody knows for sure.*
First Caller:	*Should I get out?*
Crandall:	*That's your call, Jason.*
First Caller:	*What would you do?*
Crandall:	*Ol' Frank'll be on top of a mountain tomorrow."* (Laughs) *"Seriously, Jason, I'll be right here in Miami, doing my routine, and hoping for the best. I think the media have a tendency to be very careful what they report. Everybody has to look out these days, and I'll tell you why: There're lawsuits everywhere. So we're all supercautious. . . . We have time for one more call before we go to commercial. . . . Harry in St. Louis, hello.*
Second Caller:	*Hi, Frank. Say, I'd like to change the subject.*
Crandall:	*Go ahead. Talk about anything you want.*
Second Caller:	*I was wondering if you've noticed the Cardinals have started the season with six straight wins.*

Crandall: *Yeah, they're loaded with pitching, and it looks like they've got a serious team out there this year. . . .*

SSTO *Berlin* Flight Deck. 11:59 P.M.

Willem Stephan moved the throttle forward, and the spacecraft began to pick up velocity. He informed Moonbase that he was leaving orbit, and was relieved to watch the lunar surface begin to drop away. He'd been in orbit thirty-eight hours, and was starting back with 162 passengers. Not quite as many as he'd expected, but the incident with the *Micro* had slowed the operation down.

But *Rome* was in orbit now, and she would collect passengers during the night, until she was joined by the American plane early tomorrow morning.

Gruder looked at him. "I'm glad to be away," he said.

"Yes, old friend. As am I."

IMPACT

Saturday, April 13

1.

White House. 1:15 A.M.

The president had been at a party at the Polish embassy when Haskell's message reached him: UNABLE COMPLY YOUR LAST. HAVE TO LOCK UP.

Henry read it several times. *Damned fool.*

The Iraqi ambassador, standing beside him, asked what was wrong.

"Nothing of significance, Oman," he said, sliding the paper into a pocket.

People had talked about Senator Butler's latest gaffe (calling the voters "morons" without realizing the mike was hot), the ongoing food fight between two of Washington's top journalists which had nothing to do with politics and everything to do with a fashion model, and the discovery that a respected late-night political commentator had been buying child pornography. But Henry could not stop thinking about his beleaguered vice president.

At around three, back at the White House, he called Kerr aside and showed him the news. "This is Hailey's idea," said Kerr. "They want more drama. They want you to go on TV and tell him to quit monkeying around and get on the plane."

"That's what *I* thought at first, Al. But he knows I can't do that. They've admitted they can't get everybody out and they're starting to release names of people who're staying behind. How will it look if I demand they send him back, and then we find out that a father with three kids had to stay instead? No. The damned fool had to get out before all this became public information. It's too late now." He shook his head. "You've got to admire him. I guess it's that goddam Teddy Roosevelt schtick."

Ephrata, Pennsylvania. 1:50 A.M.

Claire was asleep in the cab of the Pine River Furniture truck. They'd stopped in the parking lot of the Old Rock Bank on Route 322. The rest of the convoy was God knew where because the phone system was overwhelmed and Archie couldn't patch through to anybody. Moreover, the truck's power cells had begun to weaken. Lines at the charge stations were a mile long, so they'd given up and pulled over to wait for morning. Weather permitting, the sun would recharge their cells.

The sky was lost in the glare of security lights. The rain had finally stopped, but the night was still damp.

The parking lot was small, with a chain drawn around its perimeter. A sign proclaimed: PARKING FOR BANK PATRONS ONLY. VIOLATORS WILL BE TOWED. They were sharing space with a half-dozen other vehicles. There was still occasional traffic, but the general crush had dissipated.

Archie admired Claire's ability to sleep in the truck cab. He'd tried every position he could, but he was still uncomfortable, dead tired, and wide awake. At no time during the entire exercise had the threat from tidal waves seemed more unreal.

The cell phone chimed.

Archie fumbled for it, trying to remember which pocket he'd put it in. "Hello?"

"Archie?" Susan's voice, obviously relieved.

"Hello, love. Are you okay?"

"I'm fine. I'm at Helen's. But it's been a nightmare. I've never seen anything like this. I've been trying to call all night. Couldn't get through."

"I know. I'm glad you're off the road."

"Archie, the expressway was terrible. It was bumper-to-bumper all the way from South Jersey. Where are you? Are you in Carlisle?"

"No. Traffic's been bad here too. But we're okay. We're parked for the night. The road looks pretty clear now. If it stays that way we'll be in Carlisle by noon."

"All right, champ. Be careful."

SSTO *Arlington* Flight Deck. 5:50 A.M.

George brought the big spacecraft into lunar orbit precisely on schedule. He was three thousand kilometers above the surface, and it was a good feeling, watching the moonscape turn beneath him, watching Earth disappear beneath the horizon. For the first time in his life, he was out of sight of the home world.

And the comet looked very close.

Twenty minutes later, a moonbus arrived alongside, and his first passengers began to file aboard.

TRANSGLOBAL NEWS REPORT. 6:14 A.M.

Police have reported isolated incidents of overnight looting in the Baltimore suburbs of Catonsville and Edgemere. At least eleven people have been jailed, and another dozen, including three police officers, hospitalized in related incidents. Baltimore mayor Patricia Godwin, in an effort to head off the kind of disruptions that accompanied the breakdown of public order after the Gandar execution two years ago, has put on extra police and announced that violators will be dealt with severely. She added that she could not guarantee that citizens wouldn't take matters into their own hands and shoot would-be thieves. This has been widely interpreted as a suggestion that homeowners who contemplate using deadly force to defend their property need not fear vigorous prosecution, as happened after the Gandar riots.

•   •   •

SSTO *Copenhagen.* **6:17 A.M.**

After a nineteen-hour run, *Copenhagen* established visual contact with Skyport. When the space station appeared in the windows, people in the passenger cabin began to applaud.

TRANSGLOBAL COMMENTARY. 9:03 A.M.

"Actually, the end of the Moon, if that's what we're really about to see, would be a very good thing. People need to be reminded periodically that a living world is a changing one. And we resist change with all the ferocity we can muster.

"This instinct, this love for the status quo, this conviction that the world is a stable and reliable place to live, is an idea left over from an era when people lived exactly as their grandparents had. When change was always bad news: that the Nile had overflowed its banks again, that the barbarians had arrived, that the plague was in town. We are wired to maintain the status quo.

"This need to conserve the present is a survival instinct that now works to our detriment. We see it in our failure to pursue nanotech research, in our fear of biotechnological enhancement techniques, in the resistance to the Mars mission. We see it in our daily lives in our inability to use the technologies that lie at our fingertips. Do you know how to program your VR player? A recent *USA Today* poll showed that sixty-five percent of those surveyed did not believe that life had improved since the end of the twentieth century.

"If the Moon truly disappears from our skies tonight, it will serve to remind us that nothing is forever, that the world keeps changing, and that we'd better learn to change with it. This is Judy Gunworthy with the Transglobal News Service, at the Johnson Space Center."

Moonbase, Grissom Country. 10:47 A.M.

Charlie shook hands with each of his agents, thanked them for efforts in his behalf, and tried to reassure them he would be all right. He explained that he'd notified their superiors that they'd left under protest, that he'd ordered them out, and that under the circumstances they had no choice but to obey. "I've recommended in-grade increases for all of you."

They smiled. Isabel momentarily lost her professional demeanor and embraced him. "I wish you'd change your mind," she said.

After they left, Rick came by and tried so hard to talk him out of staying that he lost track of time and had to dash out to catch his own flight.

Then Charlie was alone.

Pacifica, California. 8:35 A.M. Pacific Daylight Time (11:35 A.M. EDT).

Jerry Kapchik watched the images of crowded express-ways on his TV. Fortunately, the scenes were all east of San Francisco. Route 1, which he could see from his front porch, was quiet. After the first wave of nervous reaction, few of his neighbors had left town. It might have been they were more worried about looters than moonrock. There'd already been reports of break-ins in San Mateo and Palo Alto.

He could see Marisa setting up the water sprinkler out back. She'd be leaving in about forty-five minutes, taking the kids to the park. She was not happy that Jerry had volunteered to go into work, but she understood that such things were not entirely within his control.

The big news this morning was that the vice president was staying behind at Moonbase. Jerry had watched a brief inter-view in which Haskell said he hadn't given up hope that they'd all get out. *Hadn't given up hope.* How could we allow a vice president to get put in that kind of position? It didn't make sense, and Jerry wondered if the government was even more incompetent than it looked.

There were other stories. Terrorists had seized an embassy in Djakarta and were demanding the release of several hundred criminals from Indian prisons. Red Cross workers had been murdered in the Transvaal. There'd been a shoot-out in the

Japanese Diet. In a group action, several thousand families were suing the Los Angeles school system for failing to educate their kids. Everything seemed normal enough.

Jimmy came down the stairs. Seven years old, bright-eyed, big smile. He had his mother's blond hair. "Dad? Are we going to watch the comet tonight?"

The kids had stayed up late last evening, and they'd stood out near the garage with neighbors. The comet was out over the ocean. It was *big*, several times bigger than the Moon, and misty, like a big blob of fog caught in moonlight. It looked out of place, and Jerry'd had a sense that it belonged in another sky.

"Sure," he said. "If you want."

"Dad, I was wondering if we could do something."

"Like what?"

He hesitated. "Could we get a telescope? Like the Ryan's have?"

Actually, Jerry had been thinking about investing in one. He saw a chance to interest his kids in astronomy, and he'd been looking at an inexpensive telescope in the downtown Wal-Mart yesterday. "Sure," he said. "I think we can manage that."

Then there was Marisa. She'd been in a strange mood, saying she felt fine but refusing to meet his eyes.

Jerry, fortunately, was hard-headed, down-to-earth, eminently practical. Whatever might be happening a quarter-million miles away, the real world would continue to be caught up in tax law and mortgage payments and Little League games.

NEWSNET. 12:30 P.M. UPDATE.
   (Click for details.)

NATION BRACES FOR MOONWRECK
   Tens Of Thousands Flee Coastal Areas
   Carnage On Highways

PALADINI, CORMAN, ALMYER ATTEND PRAYER VIGIL FOR LUNIES
Almyer:"A Time To Put Politics Aside"

BUSES EVACUATE INNER-CITY SAN FRANCISCO
Poor People's Crusade Mobilizes Volunteers

TELESCOPES TO SEARCH FOR FALLING MOONROCK
NASA Coordinates Early Warning System

SPACE PLANE BACK FROM MOON
Evacuees Celebrate Arrival At Skyport

AID WORKERS MASSACRED IN PUNJAB
Two Chicago Nuns Among Victims

BOBBY RAY HUTTON MAY FACE TAX, FRAUD CHARGES
Televangelist's "Flights For Faith" Sold Bibles, Medical Supplies

HOCKLEBY, BRAXTON CHARGED IN GENETIC SOFTWARE CASE
Does First True Artificial Intelligence Live In Minneapolis?

WHITE FEMALES IN U.S. CONTINUE TO LEAD LONGEVITY CHARTS

Hockey:
RANGERS MOVE TO ALBANY FOR PLAYOFFS
Start McCormack Against Flyers
Wife-Beating Defenseman Has "Learned Lesson"

MANUSCRIPT MAY BE NEW LAMB ESSAY
Found In Desk Once Owned by _The Quarterly Review_

Moonbase Spaceport. 1:02 P.M.

Bigfoot's new crew had just come on. There were five of them, two short of a full complement. They'd stay through the rest of the day, and ride up to orbit on the last flight. He made it a point to thank everyone on the outgoing watch and wish them well.

He was out on the bay floor helping set up for the next refueling operation when the radio operator reached him. "Tony wants to talk to you, Bigfoot."

The *Micro* was on its way down, having completed a rendezvous with *Rome*. It was noisy in the bay so he walked into one of the offices to take the call.

"Yes, Tony, what can we do for you?"

"Bigfoot, I think we can get everybody off."

Bigfoot was tired of thinking about it. If they could make up a few hours somewhere it could be done. But they'd run every conceivable launch pattern in simulation, and they had the best they could get. The only other way was to try packing extra people on board the buses, which were staggering under their current loads. Chandler had ruled out going over the limits they'd set. He had no intention, he told Operations, of allowing a minor disaster to turn into a major one.

"How you going to do that, Tony?" he asked.

"My last flight lifts off tonight at seven thirty-fve. I take my passengers up to the plane and deliver them. Then I'm supposed to get on the plane myself and ditch the Micro."

"Go ahead. So far, you're doing fine."

"You've got two more busloads leaving shortly after I do. And that's it. But I can get back to Moonbase by ten-ten. Give or take. That's twenty-five minutes before impact. If we cut the usual routine to bare bones, we can get the vice president and the rest of them on board and skedaddle. We bypass all the usual procedures. Don't close the roof to refuel. Instead, put somebody in a p-suit to handle it. Have the passengers ready to go. We can be out in twenty minutes."

"Five minutes ahead of the event. *That's* good. And where would you take them? The plane will be gone."

"Anyplace is better than here."

"Whom do you suggest I ask to hang around to fill your tanks?"

There was a long, uncomfortable silence at the other end. Then Bigfoot sighed. "I'll see what I can do," he said.

Moonbase Commcenter. 1:21 P.M.

Andrea was the last of the nonsupervisory personnel to be relieved. She hurried back to her quarters, where her bags waited beside the bunk. They weren't going anywhere. No luggage other than light carry-ons was allowed on the flight. But she'd packed anyway. Just in case.

She opened one and took a zero-gravity coffee mug out of it. It carried the *Ranger* logo: a full Moon resplendent on a windblown U.S. flag. She pushed it into her pocket.

The apartment was cramped and not much to look at, but she felt as if she'd lived here a long time. It housed a lot of good memories. And a few not so good: a failed romance and some lonely evenings. Nothing earth-shattering. It had been home for much of her adult life, and she was going to miss it.

She stood on the threshold making one last survey. A peculiar feeling came over her that she'd been through this before and that she'd be back to do it again. In this life or in another.

An hour later she boarded a crowded moonbus. Her fellow passengers were subdued. They were all MBI employees, like herself. The dependents, visitors, consultants, and assorted VIPs were long gone. She settled into her seat and drew the harness around her. She realized she was glad to be leaving, not only for the obvious reason that the comet was coming, but because Moonbase suddenly seemed *alien*, unquiet.

It was an impression that had been growing, fostered probably by the increasingly empty malls and walkways and the closed shops and whispered conversations. During the few days since the crisis had begun, she'd been constantly in other people's company. But almost all her friends were gone now, either already in orbit, or well on their way to Skyport. She looked around the bus and saw Eleanor Kile, who'd stayed with her to work the last shift. Eleanor smiled. She looked scared.

"Ladies and gentlemen." The pilot's voice crackled over the intercom. "We'll be departing within five minutes. The ride up to the plane will be brief, not quite two hours. Once there, we'll transfer through the same door by which you entered the spacecraft. The plane will leave orbit at nine-thirty this evening. My copilot and I will be with you on that flight, and we're looking forward to a spectacular show.

"We know the ambiance on the bus isn't what any of us are accustomed to, or what we would like to make available, and I regret to announce there are no flight attendants. One of us will be along after we've gotten under way to see if we can do anything to make your trip more comfortable. I'll let you know when we're ready to leave."

Andrea closed her eyes and tried to sleep.

TRANSGLOBAL SPECIAL REPORT. 1:31 P.M.

"This is Frances Picarno in Rome, reporting from outside the Vatican. It's early evening here, Bruce, and a huge crowd has gathered at St. Peter's to pray. The pope is expected to appear momentarily at his third-floor balcony."

"Frances, what's the mood there?"

"Somber. They're very quiet. I could almost say frightened. But these are believers, and they feel very much in the hands of their Creator tonight.

"Vatican officials have told us that Innocent will do what he can to reassure everyone. This couldn't have come at a worse time for the pontiff, as we all know. He has been in failing health for the past year, and his doctors have apparently advised against his appearance here

this evening. But this pope, the *People's Pope*, is said to be quite concerned, and — wait a minute, Bruce. There he is now. . . . "

2.

Moonbase, Grissom Country. 1:32 P.M.

Haskell was just returning to his quarters when his cell
phone jingled.

"Charlie?" Evelyn's voice. "I'm glad you're there. I
thought I was going to get the recorder again."

"I was out touring the facility, Evelyn. Seemed like the
right time. What's going on?"

"Some good news. We might have a chance to get out of
here."

"*Wonderful.* I knew somebody'd come up with *something.*"

"The chances probably aren't very good."

"What's the plan?"

"One of the buses is going to come back for us tonight.
Take us off. But it's strictly last-minute stuff."

"Anything's better than just sitting here. Tell the pilot I
said thanks." He felt weak with relief.

Moonbase Spaceport. 1:35 P.M.

Bigfoot had struggled with his conscience since the incident with the valves. It was he, after all, who had checked the
fuel lines when Tony first reported a suspected leak. He'd
found nothing, because he'd taken Tony at his word and looked
for a leak and nothing else. In his own defense, he thought,
finding the improper valve would not have been simply a matter of opening the manifold and looking. Both sizes of valves
were identical in external appearance. He would have had to
remove each unit and inspect it. And, of course, they'd been
under extreme time pressure.

But now, despite the fact that he'd put himself at risk (or

maybe because of it), he was feeling good again. Maybe they could pull it off.

It didn't occur to him that he wasn't the only person carrying a burden of guilt. Elias Tobin, the engineer who'd installed the wrong valve, left a note saying he was sorry, and took an overdose of tranquilizers. He survived because a worried friend came by to check on him. Later Elias asked to stay with the Chandler group, but Jack refused the offer when a therapist gave his opinion that Tobin was incapable of making a rational decision.

They'd put him on a moonbus at about the time Evelyn was talking to the vice president.

Moonbase, Director's Office. 1:57 P.M.

Chandler looked across the desk at Angela Hawkworth. "We've got another volunteer," he said. "So you're off the hook. You'll be on a flight later this afternoon. See Susan about the details."

She avoided his gaze. "Jack," she said, "I'm sorry—"

"It's okay." She was the last of the people Evelyn had dragooned.

"I was willing to stay. You know that."

"I know."

She rose, anxious to be away before something changed. "Who is it?"

"Caparatti. We're going to put everybody in a bus and make a run for it. They need Caparatti to take care of the details, so he's staying on."

She nodded and started to back away. "I'd have stayed."

"It's okay, Angela. Everyone knows that."

Carlisle, Pennsylvania. 2:15 P.M.

Claire eased the truck under a line of elms and parked outside a restored turn-of-the-century country home. It had broad lawns and a driveway that curved around the house. The air was colder here than it had been in South Jersey, and smoke was coming out of the chimney. There was a backboard mounted over the garage door and a swing set was just visible in back.

Archie climbed down, feeling stiff and unclean and not really presentable. But the occupants were already at the front door: a middle-aged woman and someone else, an older man, behind her. Walter's lodge buddies, who were opening their home to two of Walter's employees.

The woman came out, studied them for a few moments, and started in their direction. Archie raised his hand in greeting. "Hello," he said.

She didn't look particularly well. There was a fragility of both mind and body about her, an impression of a woman made of broken glass. "Archie?" She held out her hand. "My name's Mariel Esterhazy. I'm glad you were able to get here all right."

Archie had left a message on their answering machine to explain the delay. "Nice to meet you, Mariel," he said. He introduced Claire.

"My husband's at work," Mariel said. "But if you bring your luggage up to the house, we'll try to get you settled."

The man who'd stood with her in the doorway came out onto the deck. He was short, with an expression and posture that would have looked good on a Rottweiler. He wore thick glasses, a blue blazer, and loafers.

"We've been watching the reports all morning," Mariel said. "This Moon thing certainly has people stirred up. Isn't that right, Scott?" She waved impatiently at the man to help Claire with her bag.

Scott, it turned out, was her father-in-law. He allowed Claire to come to him before taking the bag from her. Archie saw that he did not entirely approve of his guests. "Several of your trucks have arrived in town," he said, making only minimal effort to hide his distaste. "How many are there altogether?"

"Eighteen."

"I think we can account for about half of them." He managed to look inconvenienced, hefted Claire's bag, and hauled it inside the door.

Mariel showed them to their rooms and invited them to come back downstairs when they were ready. Archie's room was far nicer than anything that had ever been put at his disposal before. It contained an ornately carved queen-size bed, a thick blue carpet, antique furniture, lush drapes the color of lemons, and a spacious walk-in closet. An original landscape dominated one of the walls. Photos of laughing children were displayed atop the bureau and on a side table, and several leather-bound books were stacked on a shelf at the head of the bed.

He washed, changed, and went back down to the living room, where Mariel and Scott were conversing in low tones. Mariel balanced a cup of coffee on her knee. Scott had a mixed drink.

"This whole comet situation has gotten completely out of hand," Mariel said. "People have no sense of perspective anymore." She shook her head, mourning the loss. "Can I get you something to drink, Archie?"

Scott agreed. "But it's got nothing to do with the comet," he added.

Archie asked for chablis. He wondered about Scott's comment. "In what way, sir?" he asked.

"The comet's going to hit the *Moon*, for God's sake, Archie. I don't care how you cut it, that just isn't a big deal. Listen, the truth is that the country's taking another step toward a collective nervous breakdown. In my profession, we've seen it coming for years."

"And what *is* your profession, Scott?"

"Same as my son's. I'm a securities dealer. Retired." He made it sound like fleet admiral, retired. "Everybody knows these are scary times. Terrorists with nuclear weapons, rebels everywhere, international corporations with no loyalty to any flag so you never know where they stand. Everybody's scared to death of technology. The country has no faith in God anymore. The government's just a pack of bureaucrats and politicians getting theirs while they can, the churches are dying, and the crazies don't know what to get into. Anything at all happens, it's a conspiracy. This's an age when you need a good account executive."

"I beg your pardon?" This was from Claire, who had just entered the room.

"What I'm trying to say," said Scott, "is that the old days were different. Whatever you bought, it went up. People said they didn't need the advice of the pros. Because they always made money. But that's not true anymore. You need an expert now—"

"I'm sure," said Mariel, "everybody knows that, Dad." She turned to her guests. "Are you two hungry? Can I get you something to eat?"

"Thank you," said Archie, "we ate lunch on the road." He was admiring the furnishings. The room was done in oak and leather. One wingback chair had come from Pine River. Another original oil painting, people on a hillside beneath threatening skies, hung over the mantel.

"It's by Tollinger," Mariel said, apparently expecting him to recognize the name.

Archie nodded as if he wondered how he could have missed the fact.

Claire had been circling the piece, and now she closed in on it. "It's the *Coeur deVivre*," she said, startled.

"Yes," said Mariel.

Archie understood from Claire's sudden breathlessness that the painting was worth quite a lot. "Scott," he said, "what do you like on the market right now?"

Moonbase, Chaplain's Quarters. 2:26 P.M.

"Chaplain? This is Jack Chandler. I wanted you to know that we've got a bus coming back for us. We're going to make a run for it."

"Thank God."

"To be honest, I'm not all that optimistic. But it's a chance."

"Yes. Anything's better than sitting here."

"But Evelyn thought it would be a good idea if we tackled the evening with a full stomach. We're planning a dinner. Will you come?"

"Certainly."

"Good. Excellent. We'll eat, have a few drinks, if that's agreeable. And then we'll go over to the Spaceport."

"Okay."

"Six-thirty."

Right. Very British, that. Tea and lamb chops on the eve of disaster. "I'll be there," he said.

TRANSGLOBAL SPECIAL REPORT. 2:31 P.M.
Distributed to participating networks via Pool Agreement.

"This is Keith Morley reporting live from Moonbase, where Comet Tomiko is now very large in the eastern sky, and where the vice president of the United States has announced that he is holding fast to his intention to "lock the door and turn out the lights." Drama is building as the comet approaches. It's due here in a few hours. According to Jack Chandler, the director of Moonbase, the last scheduled flight will depart at six-thirty P.M., leaving behind the vice president and several others, who will try to return to Skyport by microbus.

"But the bus that will carry Haskell and six other people will barely be off the surface before the comet hits. Operations people here are not confident the vehicle can survive the blast that is expected at impact. Bruce, I'll be staying with this story, and we'll just have to see how it plays out.

"This is Keith Morley at Moonbase."

SSTO *Rome* Passenger Cabin. 2:33 P.M.

They were about an hour and a half from departure out of lunar orbit. Rick Hailey had been watching Earth set while a moonbus approached. He bit into a tuna sandwich and turned his attention to the bus as it drew alongside. It cruised in tandem for a few minutes, a large black sphere with the pilot's blister at the top. The buses looked clumsy on the ground, but in flight they had their own special grace.

Light spilled out of the windows and he could see people moving inside. It drifted gradually closer, passing beyond his window's angle of view. Then the pilot announced that docking was imminent. "Please remain in your seat," he asked, "until we get the incoming passengers settled."

Rick felt the shudder that marked the moment of contact, heard hatches open, heard voices, and watched the new arrivals begin to file into the cabin, coming through the main airlock.

There were no flight attendants to help. Instead, at the captain's request, a dozen or so passengers had volunteered to act in that capacity and had been issued white armbands and given a crash course by the flight engineer in kitchen capabilities and whatnot. Now this group squired the newcomers to the bloc of seats reserved for them.

They were quiet, subdued, obviously happy to be at last on the plane. Slade Elliott was among them. Elliott, whose career, like Charlie's, depended on image, also knew enough not to take the first stage out of town. He'd hung on until near the end. But you didn't see *him* getting caught up in the general crash. He was Rick's kind of guy. And with the action hero on board, the man who'd escaped a thousand dangers, Rick felt safer.

Outside, the comet was rising, a great orange spume against the black sky. He looked at it and thought about the vice president. Charlie Haskell was going to die out there, and Rick wished he could prevent it. He knew there was a lesson to be learned here, but he hadn't quite sorted out in his own mind precisely what it was.

Charlie was genuinely likable. But the poor son of a bitch had been booby-trapped by events. Rick knew that when the time came to publish his memoirs, the loss of Charlie Haskell would be one of the more compelling chapters.

His own political career was now in dire jeopardy as well. None of the other candidates was likely to take him on. He'd had to burn a few bridges and he was now Haskell's guy. Some would even be inclined to believe Charlie's "turn out the lights" remark had been Rick's idea.

Rick wouldn't object to going to work for the other party if someone were to make the right offer. It was a pity really. You don't get many shots at the White House. And it was all gone. Blown out of the water just like that.

And Haskell's sacrifice was probably unnecessary. The voters have a short memory, *Charlie*. He wondered whether the vice president had even stopped to consider how much damage he was doing to his friends. Still, the road to the presidency seemed to run right through Moonbase. Right through the heart of that goddam comet.

More hatches closed somewhere in the bowels of the plane. Rick pulled down the shade.

PACIFIC NEWS NETWORK BULLETIN. 3:56 P.M.
Distributed to participating networks via Pool Agreement.
    "This is Tashi Yomiuri coming to you live from lunar orbit. I'm in

one of the space planes, the SSTO *Rome*, and we're taking our last passengers on board now before we start back for Earth. The comet is about eight million miles away, coming toward us at almost a million miles an hour.

"We've been orbiting the Moon three times a day at a height of about three thousand kilometers. Which means we see the comet rise and set every eight hours. We've been able to watch it grow.

"The mood on the spacecraft is somber. People are frightened, and they'll be very glad to be on their way."

WALL STREET JOURNAL, ELECTRONIC EDITION
Excerpt of Commentary by Melinda Bright.

"People speculate about how far the comet has come, how old it is, why it's traveling so fast. We've heard astronomers suggest that it might have been blown out of a supernova, and that if it was, the supernova must have happened millions, or perhaps billions, of years ago.

"If that's true, this thing has had the Moon's number for a long time. I remember as a little girl sitting in our backyard in Kentucky, watching the Moon from my swing, and thinking how long it had been in the sky, and how it would be there forever. Now we know that's not so. The comet's been on its way possibly since the first humans climbed down out of the trees, and this day was marked on some cosmic calendar with all the inevitability of a quadratic equation. We've been congratulating ourselves that the comet's going to hit the Moon and not the Earth. And I agree that's reason to feel fortunate.

"But it isn't reason to feel glad. The Moon is an old friend, far older than the species. It's an integral part of who we are, and the way we live. It softens us. We associate it with our most tender feelings. We have made it a goddess, and we have written songs and poems about it. We have pledged our love to each other in its silver light. Maybe only when we see it no more, when this visiting monstrosity has put out its light for all generations to come, will we understand what we have lost."

• • •

SSTO *Rome* Flight Deck. 4:04 P.M.

John Verrano eased onto his new heading, watched the clock run down to zero, and felt the engines kick in. The force they generated pressed him back into his seat as the spacecraft rose out of orbit.

3.

Moonbase, Main Plaza. 6:01 P.M.

The news that an effort would be made to get the last group out had fired Chaplain Pinnacle's soul. He'd tried to maintain a stoic attitude throughout his ordeal. *Into Thy hands, O Lord. . . .* But life was priceless, and God knew that Mark did not want to part with it.

He sat at a table beside a cluster of palms outside the Victor Hugo sidewalk café. No one walked now among the trees, the lights were out in the offices, and the artificially generated breeze, sharp with mint, blew through the parks. In all the vast wooded expanse of Main Plaza, he saw only a young couple, strolling quietly, making their way gradually toward the tram station.

A handful of people came off one of the up-ramps, hurried across the center of the mall, and joined them. The chaplain glanced at his watch. There would only be four more flights out, three to the single plane that remained orbiting. And finally *his* flight, whose destination was in God's hands.

He was nervous about the dinner, afraid his fear would show. He'd tried prayer, had begged for courage, but still his hand shook and his voice played tricks on him.

One of his parishioners, a young woman, had come to the chapel when she'd heard he was staying and offered him a narcotic. Something to quiet his nerves. Get him through the ordeal. The stuff they called "silver." It was illegal, and he'd been startled when she'd produced the packet. He'd said no, he wouldn't need it, thank you very much, but she'd held it out and in the end he concluded it was his duty to take it from her. Remove the temptation. She'd kissed his cheek, wished him luck, and hurried away. He'd actually considered using it. But he did not know whether he had a tolerance for such things, and in the end he'd dropped it into a trash receptacle.

His cell phone beeped.

"Chaplain Pinnacle," he said.

"Chaplain, this is Evelyn."

"Yes." He was thrown off a bit by her familiarity. "What is it, Dr. Hampton?"

"I just wanted to remind you that we'll be serving dinner in a few minutes."

"No, I hadn't forgotten."

"Good." She paused. "You *are* okay?"

"Oh, yes," he said. "I'm fine."

"The vice president will be there." As if he needed enticement.

"Yes, I—I was just on my way."

The tram glided into the station. Its doors opened and everybody got on. Then the doors closed with an audible click and the vehicle slid out into the trees. He watched until it disappeared into heavy woodland on the far side of Main Plaza.

San Francisco. 3:17 P.M. Pacific Daylight Time (6:17 P.M. EDT).

Jerry Kapchik left work as soon as he decently could and went looking for a telescope. Wal-Mart had sold out. So had Sears. There was a specialty shop on Ocean Avenue, Galileo's. They'd been cleaned out, too, except for a 90mm Grazier reflector. The Grazier cost five thousand dollars. "Worth every penny," the salesman urged. It came complete with an optical shield that permitted the viewer to look directly at the Sun; and it had a programmable system with over seventeen thousand celestial objects in storage. "Just look up the code in the

Grazier manual for whatever you want to see," said the sales-man, "lock onto the North Star, and punch the code into the keyboard. The telescope will automatically find the object, focus, and track until you tell it to do something else. Or, of course, until the object sets."

"Of course."

"With this," he added, "you'll want your own observa-tory."

Jerry tried to talk him down, but the salesman explained he wasn't sure he even wanted to sell it to Jerry because he'd had a call ten minutes before. Somebody was on his way, hop-ing to buy one. "You're lucky," he said. "Day like this, I had to tell him we can't hold anything." He looked at his watch, as if the prospective buyer was even now rushing up the street.

It was more than Jerry had intended to spend, and he wasn't sure how he was going to explain it to Marisa. But something had come over him. Maybe it had to do with taking advantage of his son's sudden interest in astronomy. Maybe years from now Jimmy would remember the Grazier as the turning point in his life. Anyway, this was going to be a special evening and they should have the right kind of equipment to follow the event.

It was packed in two cases, but the clerk assured him that assembly was really very easy. Jerry picked up a spare battery, hauled the cases outside, and loaded them into a taxi. The taxi carried him to the parking lot just off Skyline Boulevard, where Jerry left his car every day to catch the monorail into center city.

He stopped en route to call Marisa and get it over with. She was initially unhappy and urged him to return it, but by the time he got home she'd decided the investment *might* be worthwhile. "As long as it gets used," she told him. "But if it just sits in the attic, *you* are a dead man."

Marisa had been an emergency medical technician with

the Pacifica rescue unit for several years. Now she taught emergency techniques at the San Francisco campus of the University of California. "The rescue unit has been put on alert," she told him.

"The comet?" he asked.

She shrugged. "People are nervous. I'd call an alert, too, if I were running things."

After dinner they took out the telescope. The clerk had been right: It *was* easy to assemble. They snapped the tube assembly into the cradle and locked the cradle onto the tripod. They tightened a couple of clamps, attached the computer, inserted the battery, punched a button to initiate a series of self-tests, and they were ready to go.

Jimmy and Erin delivered a gratifying display of enthusiasm. The only problem was that the telescope was clearly designed to be put in one place and left there. Jerry recalled the salesman's remark that he'd want his own observatory.

Nevertheless, they dragged it out onto the side deck and pointed it toward the comet, which now overwhelmed the eastern sky. The Moon was just visible, a child's ball floating beyond a red-lit thundercloud. It was early evening, the Sun still a couple of hours from setting. The wind was cool and crisp off the sea.

Jerry set the scope to manual operation. "Keep it simple," he told Marisa. He used the viewfinder to sight the instrument while Erin placed a stool on the ground. Then he looked into the lens. He saw only a dark circle, and touched one of the knobs. The Moon jumped into the image, slipped out to the left, and finally settled in place. He turned it over to the kids.

While her brother fidgeted, Erin climbed onto her stool, looked, and aaaahed. "I can see craters," she said.

Jerry stood back and studied the sky. The comet was very large, and streamers reached out and caught the Moon in a gauzy embrace. It chilled him.

While the kids looked and made noises about how wonderful it was, he caught Marisa's eye. "I was wrong," he said.

"About what?"

"Let's pack up and get out of here. Just for the night."

Her eyes went wide. "Jerry, the TV says there aren't any motels left out there. And we can't just drop in on Helen without warning."

"We'll get our camping gear," he said. "But let's do it."

They owned two vehicles, a Mazda Superhawk and a Chrysler wagon. Marisa, despite her protests, had foreseen the event and prepared for a quick getaway. Both cars were already half-loaded. They added food, water, and clothes. Marisa found her emergency aid kit and put it in the Mazda. They also packed the computer and some rare books that Jerry had been collecting, and Marisa's jewelry and the silverware. And their bank books and passports and U.S. bonds. And the kids' favorite toys. And the Grazier telescope.

TRANSGLOBAL NEWS REPORT. 6:18 P.M.

"This is Keith Morley reporting live with the vice presidential party at Moonbase. It is now just over four hours until the Tomiko Comet arrives. As you're probably aware, there'll be a spacecraft racing it to try to get us out. The vehicle's a moonbus, but it's smaller than the regular moonbuses, so it's known locally as the Micro. Its pilot is Tony Casaway, who's from San Francisco; and the copilot is Alisa Rolnikaya. Alisa is a Russian, although she was born in Florence, Italy. They call her 'Saber.' I expect to be talking to them a little later on in the evening, live and by remote, from the cockpit of the Micro.

"With me now is Chaplain Mark Pinnacle, who's one of the six who've agreed to stay behind when everyone else was evacuated. At the time you volunteered, Chaplain, did you know that a last-minute rescue would be attempted?"

"No, Keith. We had no idea anyone was actually going to try to get us out. I must say I was delighted to hear the news. I hope we can do it."

"Are you confident?"

"I'd like to think God isn't finished with me yet."

"Chaplain, I wonder if you'd tell us why you elected to stay behind?"

"I suppose I could turn that around, Keith. Why are you still here?"

(Hesitates.) "I suppose because it's my job."

"Me too."

"Chaplain, I wonder if you'd tell us which faith you represent?"

"Well, I'm Church of England, of course. But on the Moon I represent all faiths. And not only Christian, I might add."

"I'm sure our viewers wonder how that can be, Chaplain."

"I'm not sure I understand it, Keith. People just seem to accept it. Accept me. If you know what I mean."

Moonbase, Main Plaza. 6:28 P.M.

Chaplain Pinnacle was drenched with sweat. He was glad the interview was over, but he wasn't pleased with his performance. He'd had a heaven-sent opportunity to explain to the world how it really was out here, how the great faiths came together and the theological disagreements tended to fade away. There were no heretics on the Moon.

Out here, the universe looks pretty big.

Theologians had been describing the creator as infinite right from the beginning. And for the first time, people were beginning to understand what that might mean. Maybe there's room for all faiths. They seem to coexist quite nicely once they get off-world.

Mark had never felt closer to his God than he did at that moment. Yet this giant comet was coming to destroy the entire place. Why was that?

●　　　●　　　●

Moonbase, Director's Private Dining Room. 6:30 P.M.

It might have been the most memorable dinner Charlie had attended during his entire political career. He'd gone in reluctantly, expecting a funereal atmosphere, with the participants exchanging doomed glances and peeking surreptitiously every few minutes at their watches. But it wasn't like that at all.

Jack Chandler and Evelyn seemed to be in high spirits. Keith Morley had been to the abandoned commcenter, where he'd opened a permanent channel to his producer. Then he'd sat down with the chaplain, set up his microcam, and done a program. "You were absolutely great," he was telling a pleased Pinnacle when Charlie walked in the door. "Faith, courage, and humility. They were all there."

The chaplain thanked him. "A worldwide congregation," he said. "I would never have believed it."

Only Bigfoot was missing. He'd promised to come if he could, but they had a message from him: *Thanks for the invitation. Hate to miss the sausage. But if I eat now, we'll sit later.*

Evelyn and Jack had cooked the meal. There was no sausage. But they did deliver Caesar salad, chicken fingers (real chicken), fried potatoes, mustard sauce, white wine, coffee, and, for dessert, the *piéce de résistance*, fudge nut brownie with ice cream. Not much maybe in Georgetown, but by Moonbase standards, it was a feast of major proportions.

The chaplain bowed his head. Under other circumstances, his companions might have done little more than pause awkwardly. But this time they all joined him.

Charlie had been reared as a Methodist by a skeptical father whose primary purpose in belonging to the Church seemed to be political. It was the power center for the movers and shakers, for those who wielded influence in his hometown. The vice president himself attended church on a fairly regular basis, Methodist or whatever else happened to be handy. Like his father, he did it out of political expediency. Voters expected pious presidents.

Also like his father, he believed the universe a clockwork mechanism; and if there was a clockmaker, he'd hidden himself too well and had therefore no justifiable complaint with unbelievers. Charlie cringed at the long sermons, when he'd have preferred to play golf. Or sleep late. Churches had another downside: The preacher who found out he had a vice president in the pews often used his opportunity to attack the administration on behalf of his favorite moral issue. Charlie had been pelted from the pulpit over fetal tissue, Social Security cutbacks, voluntary life-termination, biosynthetic research, and the failure of the public schools to include God in the curriculum.

"I've always envied people with faith," Charlie told Mark Pinnacle. "It helps at a time like this."

The chaplain looked amused. "I wish I could tell you it makes me less nervous."

The table was set with gleaming silver, cloth napkins, fine china, and exquisite long-stemmed glasses. It was a startling change of pace to the spartan lifestyle at Luna. Evelyn poured the wine and they lifted their glasses. "To Moonbase," she said.

The laughter and good spirits defied all logic. There was a fair amount of graveyard humor, none of it funny in retrospect ("Here I am with the story of the century and somebody else is going to get to do the wrap-up"), but hilarious at the time.

Charlie discovered how much he liked these people: Evelyn, black, beautiful, whiplash bright, wanting to look fearless, but concealing a trembling hand when she raised her wine glass.

Jack Chandler, the perfect bureaucrat. Reserved tonight, conservative, a man who measured life by precedent and regulation. An hour ago, Charlie would have guessed that Chandler had never learned to enjoy himself. Now the director roared with laughter at every opportunity. And at one point he exchanged glances with Evelyn, and silently formed the words *I love you*.

Keith Morley, TV journalist, professional cynic. Self-appointed defender of the public weal. A man who enjoyed sacrificing the reputations of political figures. But Morley offered a series of going-away wishes for the others: that Evelyn would avoid the bankruptcy that loomed over Moonbase International; that Chandler would land an even bigger bureaucracy to direct: the cleanup effort after Tomiko; that the chaplain would be transferred to a quiet parish on the banks of the Thames; and that Charlie would get the White House, but only if he still wanted it when he got home.

And the chaplain. This man who had seemed so fearful a few days ago, who'd admitted earlier to being nervous, appeared utterly at home. He thanked Morley, implying that he and the journalist had already discussed his future hopes. He confessed to enjoying himself thoroughly, and wondered whether such an extraordinary evening wasn't almost worth the risk.

For Charlie, a bachelor vice president, almost all meals not taken alone were, to a degree, working meals, or formal engagements. Tonight, for a few hours, he became just one of the crowd. And he understood Morley's comment: *only if he still wanted it.*

Chandler covered his french fries liberally with catsup, another product Charlie had not seen at Moonbase. Jack finished one of the morsels off with obvious pleasure and looked around the table. "Anybody ever been in a life-and-death situation before?" he asked.

Evelyn nodded. "When I was five, I was pulled out of a burning building."

"You remember it?" asked Chandler.

"Oh, yes. Clear as day. In fact, it's the earliest thing in my life I *can* remember. It's sort of the day I became conscious."

"Were you scared?"

She smiled. "Yes. But of the firemen rather than the fire. They were big and they wore those odd coats and hats and masks."

"Anybody else?"

Morley said, "I got assaulted and left for dead by a gang once. In New York. They broke me up pretty good. Told me they were going to cut my throat."

"But they didn't?" asked the chaplain.

Morley opened his collar and showed them a scar. "They just didn't do a good job of it."

Charlie was horrified. For all the political rough and tumble, he'd lived a sheltered life. "Why'd they do it?" he asked.

"Who knows? I took the wrong picture, maybe. Or maybe I just got out of my car in the wrong part of town. I can tell you, it was the worst moment of my life."

"Worse than this?" asked Evelyn.

"Oh, yeah. Much worse than this. It was personal. Those kids wanted me dead. That's a terrible feeling, to find out that someone wants to kill you for no very good reason. But the comet. Hell, the comet doesn't give a damn. It doesn't know we're here. It's just a big dumb pile of ice blown out of somewhere." He shrugged. "Yeah, this is a lot easier. There's no hate mixed up in it anywhere."

There was a pause in the conversation, as if a significant moment had arrived. Charlie refilled everyone's glass. The wine poured slowly in the light gravity. "Here's to us," he said. They joined in the toast, and Charlie studied their eyes over the rims.

Jack Chandler offered another: "To both Tomikos," he said. "The woman and the comet. The woman because she gave us a warning, and the comet because it's brought us together tonight."

4.

The microbus lifted off for its last scheduled flight precisely on time. Saber watched the moonscape fall away. Bigfoot's voice sounded in her earphones. "Saber, the director wants to talk to Tony."

"Wait one." Tony was on the circuit with the pilot of the SSTO. She got his attention. "Mr. Chandler," she said.

"For *me*?"

"Put him through," Saber told the microphone.

Tony signed off with the SSTO.

"Stand by," said Bigfoot.

A new voice, precise, measured, weary: "Tony Casaway?"

"This is Casaway."

"Tony, this is Jack Chandler. I wanted to thank you for what you're doing. We're grateful."

"We want to get everybody out, sir."

"Don't we all? But we appreciate it. And I have a request. There's a TV reporter here with us. Keith Morley. You'll be taking him off, too. He'll want you to patch him through to his groundside relay."

"You want me to comply?"

"Yes. Please. Give him what he wants."

"Yes, sir. Will do."

"Good. It's a pleasure to have talked with you, Tony. Good luck."

Saber noticed no one had thanked *her*.

She looked down at the lunar surface.

"Looks as if we're moving up in the world," said Tony.

"Yeah. Well, you pull the right people out of the fire, it can do wonders for a career."

He looked at her as if she'd gone over a line.

"Hard to believe," she said.

"What's that?"

She pointed down. The entire bulk of the Moon lay between the comet impact site at Mare Muscoviense, in the northern hemisphere of Farside, and Moonbase. "With all that rock shielding it, you'd think Moonbase would be safe."

There were nine people in the passenger cabin, operational types and technicians, the people who maintained the power systems, the commcenter, and life support. And a couple of Bigfoot's technicians. They were the last group the Micro would deliver to the orbiting SSTO. Two more moonbuses would follow, and it would be over.

Except for the Micro's last run.

Saber was charged with monitoring inputs from ship's systems during launch, but she always made time to watch the moonscape. She loved these altitudes and this place, remote and stark, illuminated by the blue-white Earth. A casual visitor, gazing down into the 117-kilometer-wide crater, would not have noticed that women and men had walked there, had *built* there. For a range of practical reasons, Moonbase was buried. It would have taken a sharp eye from an altitude as close as a thousand meters to observe the antennas and the solar cells and the monorail. She preferred to believe, however, that it was not practicality that concealed Moonbase, but a sense of the fragile beauty of this world and a reluctance to repeat the old errors.

Not that it mattered now. The comet's glow pushed up past the horizon in three directions, signaling the approach of the monster. It was as if a gigantic sun was rising everywhere. The definition of distant peaks and crater walls had been sharpened. Beyond the western ringwall of Alphonsus, the black regolith of Mare Nubium, the Sea of Clouds, curved into the glare.

"Look at this," said Tony, switching on a computer simulation. A dime-sized disk and a tiny crescent, representing

Earth and Moon, floated inside a white cone. The comet's tail.

"You'd think we'd be able to see it out here," said Saber. But the sky was black as ever. Only Earth seemed different. She wasn't sure, but it looked dimmer than usual, as if the sunlight were being turned aside.

"They're estimating the length of the tail," said Tony, "at seventy million kilometers. It goes all the way out to the orbit of Mars."

And it's the next thing to a vacuum, she thought.

As the Micro continued to rise into the lunar night, the summer-colored comet rose with them, and its light enfolded the Moon. Saber listened to the passengers react as they watched from their viewports.

She sensed that Tony's adrenalin was pumping constantly now. He actually seemed to be enjoying himself.

"Tony," she said, "do you think we can actually pull this off?"

He gave her a thumbs-up. "Sure," he said. "It'll be close, but we'll do it." He switched the comet display off the main screen. "Chandler says Keith Morley'll be with them. Broadcasting live from the Micro." He laughed. "We're going to be famous, Saber."

"As long as we're not dead."

He caught the tone in her voice. "Hey," he said, "Alisa. We'll be fine." Tony rarely used her given name. Only when he was striving for intimacy. In this case, to allow him to reassure her. "Bigfoot thinks we can do it."

"Bigfoot thinks he's throwing his life away."

Tony's expression darkened. He was usually amiable, but this was serious stuff. "That's not true."

"Of course it's true."

"He agreed to stay. Nobody held a gun to his head."

"Look, Tony. He was responsible for the screwup that put us in this position. What did you expect him to say when you told him you needed a volunteer?"

She knew that hurt him, but it was true. He denied it, of course. "Bigfoot wouldn't stay if he didn't think we could do it." He glared at her. "Goddammit, Saber, don't come if you don't think we can make this work. I can manage alone if I have to."

She looked at him a long time. "Tony, do you know you never asked me whether I wanted to do this?"

He paled, and she could see him thinking back, replaying the conversations. "Sure I did," he said. And then: "I'm sorry. I just assumed. . . ."

In fact, left to her own devices, she did not believe she would have been willing to make the attempt. She liked living, and she didn't think much of the odds on this one. It wasn't as if a rescue effort was mandatory. You did what was possible. But nobody should be asked to throw her life away for no good reason.

So she was tempted to take him up on his offer. Let him try it alone. "You assume a lot, Tony. It would have been nice to ask."

He went into a brief pout. "I'm sorry. I thought you'd *want* to do it."

"Look, don't try to pile a lot of guilt on me. I'll go." *And that quickly, with almost no thought, the decision was made.* "But next time, I want to be asked. Up front."

"Okay," he said. "I apologize. But I wasn't trying to make you feel guilty."

"Forget it." Dammit. Never take an assignment with a hero.

Moonbase Spaceport. 8:21 P.M.

The last three flights had gone out within fifty minutes of one another. Bigfoot stayed on the radio, talking to the pilots until they'd ridden their beacons into orbit. Then he handed them to *Arlington*, pushed back in his chair, and looked around the operations center. In all that vast complex of work-stations, boarding areas, launchpads, supply rooms, and communications gear, he was alone. Most of the lights were already off. The overhead doors to Bay Four were still open. Somewhere a steam fitting hissed.

Bigfoot had grown up in a blue collar family that had never been able to get into the black until he'd signed with the Packers. He understood what it meant to live from payday to payday, and he'd consequently learned not to waste things. *Put as much on your plate as you want, but don't take anything you're not going to eat.* When his injury in that first game had ended his career, he'd gone to work for the FAA, done a stint as an airline safety inspector, another as a controller, and demonstrated a capability to lead. People instinctively trusted him.

He felt he'd always deserved their trust. Until the incident with the microbus.

Considering the design of the valves, it had been an accident waiting to happen. It was just terrible luck that it occurred when it did. But it had been *his* responsibility.

The dinner would be over by now, but he supposed they were still up there, commiserating with each other on their mutual misfortune, trying not to think too much about what was coming. The fact that the vice president was supposed to attend, and that ordinarily Bigfoot would kill to eat with the number-two guy in the country, didn't change the fact that all these people expected to die. That was a social event he just didn't want to attend. Still, they'd invited him.

He closed the overhead doors to Bay Four and repressurized. That was where he'd receive the Micro when it came. But that was more than an hour and a half away, and the pumps would freeze if he didn't seal up. He tried to think what else needed to be done. But there wasn't much to do in advance that he hadn't already taken care of. There'd be no checkoff procedure this time. It'd be just refuel, board the passengers, and get the hell out.

Several of the monitors carried a computer simulation of the comet. He walked through the center, shutting them down, or if they were units he'd need later, switching to a different display. He decided the Spaceport was too quiet.

He tied in his phone to the radio so the pilots could reach him if necessary. Then he summoned the tram and rode it over to the Main Plaza, and took the elevator up to the administrative offices.

Skyport Orbital Lab. 8:44 P.M.

"I'm *not* going," said Tory. "And that's all there is to it."

Windy pressed his fingers against his forehead and made noises like a man with a migraine. "You are directed to leave," he said. "It's not my call, so it's not debatable. Your flight goes out at—" he glanced down at the piece of paper on his desk. "At nine-twelve. Be on it."

Tory folded her arms. "Windy, the biggest astronomical event in human history, by a wide margin, is about to occur and you are ordering me away from my post."

"Let me try again, Tory. It is *not* my order."

"*Whoever's.* But I'm not going to be sitting in a cloud bank at ten thirty-five wondering what's happening. You understand? I'm *not* going to do it."

"You don't have a choice."

"When did that happen?"

"Look, Tory, why do you think they're evacuating this place? It's not going to be safe here for the next few days. For God's sake, catch your plane and watch everything on the in-flight. What's the big deal?"

"Windy, please. I want to be here tonight. You owe me that."

"I don't owe you anything, Tory."

"Yeah you do. I've worked hard up here for two years and never asked for anything. Tonight I'm asking—"

"You're not listening to me. If the decision were mine to make, there'd be no problem. But it isn't."

They'd been evacuating Skyport all day. But it wasn't going to be a complete stand-down like L1. So-called essential operating personnel were remaining on board to keep the station running and to service the remaining SSTOs that would be coming in from Moonbase.

"How about telling them you need help?"

"Tory, the discussion's over."

"You *do*, you know. This place is going to be the center of the action for the next couple of days. Can't anyone *see* that?" The Orbital Lab controlled six satellite telescopes, as well as the automated observatory on Farside. The observatory was going to get bombed. But the others would become the early warning system for large pieces of debris headed, say, for Atlanta. "Things could get sticky here if the rocks come this way. And you'll be sitting here alone."

Winfield Cross was career Smithsonian, nominally a superstring specialist, but really more bureaucrat than astronomer. He'd stuck by the right boss at the right time and he'd been rewarded with a top job. He was okay, inclined to stay out of the way and give the technicians their head. All he really asked was that they keep him out of trouble. But he wasn't the man to butt heads for you. "I agree with everything you're saying, Tory. But it doesn't really matter. They want you out." He turned away from her.

"Off the record—" she said.

"There's no '*off the record*.'"

"Off the record, what would happen if I didn't show up at flight time?"

"It'd serve you right to get your silly ass hung out to dry. But I'll tell you this: I'm responsible for the safety of my people. You *will* be at the gate at departure time, or you'll face disciplinary action."

"Windy, aren't you overreacting a little?"

"I don't think so. You're not the first person in here today talking like this. I'm logging the incident, and I'm warning you: Don't give me trouble."

Tory loved her job and had no wish to put a dagger into her career. Furthermore, she was by nature compliant. All her life she'd respected authority (within reason, of course), tried to stay out of trouble, and been a good soldier. So she considered her response very carefully. "No," she said.

"I beg your pardon."

"I'm not going home. At least not tonight."

Windy removed his glasses and laid them on his desk. "I can have you *put* on board."

"Why don't you leave it alone? If you want my job afterward, you can have it. I'll tell anyone who asks that this conversation never happened, that you had no way of knowing I'd stay behind. Windy, there's never been anything like this in the whole history of the species. I am *not* going to sit in the forward compartment of an SSTO tonight watching in-flight telecasts."

FRANK CRANDALL'S ALL-NIGHTER. 8:49 P.M.

Crandall:	Linda from Anchorage, you're on.
Caller:	Hello, Frank. I wanted to tell you how much I admire you. Thank God there's somebody to get the truth out.
Crandall:	Thank you, Linda. What did you want to talk about?
Caller:	The comet?
Crandall:	Okay. What about the comet?
Caller:	Frank, doesn't it seem to you that the whole thing's a hoax?
Crandall:	In what way, Linda? Are you saying there is no comet?
Caller:	Oh, no. There's a comet, all right. You can see it. But I think

Kolladner and Haskell saw a way to turn it to political advantage.

Crandall: Tell me how.

Caller: Oh, come on, Frank. You don't really think they're going to leave a vice president on the Moon if it's going to be destroyed, do you?

Crandall: What do you think is going to happen?

Caller: Well, damn, the story's already beginning to come unraveled. First they said he was going to sacrifice himself, and now they're saying, well, maybe they can get him off, that they've got some hero space pilot who's going to make the effort, but how it's a thousand-to-one shot. You want to bet he makes it?

Crandall: You sound a trifle cynical, Linda.

Caller: Realistic, Frank. I'm just realistic.

5.

Moonbase, Director's Private Dining Room. 8:53 P.M.

At first Bigfoot thought they'd all been drinking a little too much. He could hear them from the elevator, singing and laughing. The song was "Stout-Hearted Men," and somebody was playing a guitar. He walked in and they cheered his arrival. The musician was Jack Chandler. He was wearing a party hat.

They were *all* wearing party hats. Charlie Haskell waved him in and pointed him to a chair. A couple of empty wine bottles stood on the table, and one had missed a trash can, but there was no sign of anything stronger. "How are things at the ol' launchpad?" asked Hampton. And they all laughed like banshees.

"It's okay, Bigfoot," said the chaplain, apparently noting his worried expression. "We can make it over there okay."

More laughs. Then, as if a switch had been thrown,

Chandler acquired a serious expression and put the guitar aside. "How are we doing?" he asked.

"Everything's as ready as I can make it. Tony's running on schedule."

The only one of the group Bigfoot knew personally was Chandler. The others introduced themselves, and Bigfoot got to shake the vice president's hand. Evelyn thanked him for staying behind to help.

Morley invited him to do an interview and they all laughed again. This time Bigfoot joined them.

SSTO *Arlington* Flight Deck. 9:05 P.M.

George Culver watched the microbus come in along his port side. The pilot laid it smoothly in position and began sending over his passengers. Two other buses were following close behind, and he had both in his instruments. He would load the passengers from all three as quickly as he could, make his window, and get out of the neighborhood.

That was the vehicle that was going to turn around, go back, and try to rescue the vice president. George admired the pilot. He looked out at the comet and tried to cover it with his hand at arm's length, but could not. He was happy *he* wasn't going to be here.

The Micro informed him that transfer had been completed. He watched the lamps signaling that the passenger cabin airlock was closing down. When it was sealed, Mary came forward. The Micro's thrusters lit and it arced away into the night.

"Heads up," he said. "Next one's coming in."

One of the passengers who'd volunteered to help now appeared at the door behind him. "Problem, Captain," she said.

"What's wrong?"

"I think they're getting a little nervous in back. Could you come back and talk to them?"

George couldn't leave the flight deck with a bus approaching. "Mary?" he said.

She nodded. But another voice broke in, deep and angry. Its owner appeared immediately behind the volunteer: "I don't think we need any talk. What we need is to get this goddam plane on the road." The speaker was a beefy man, thin hair, angry eyes. Lot of loose flesh. *Enough mass for two people*, George thought. He was barely thirty.

The flight engineer jumped to his feet. "Sir," said Curt, "you're not permitted in here."

"You people are going to get us all killed. You see how close that son of a bitch is?" He looked at the comet.

George got up. "We'll be out of here in plenty of time—"

"We damned well need to get out of here *now*. Everything's taking too long."

"I assure you, Mr.—?"

"Donnelly," the man foamed. "I was only here doing survey work. Nobody said anything about something like this."

"It's a surprise to us all, Mr. Donnelly."

"Why wasn't I put on one of the other planes?"

"We're already on course for home," said George. "Our window's up ahead. We'll be picking up more passengers on our way out. But we need everyone to sit down and stay out of the way." Curt took Donnelly's arm and tried to lead him back to the passenger cabin. But he shook free and began a string of invective.

George turned the controls over to Mary and got up. "Go back to your seat," he said calmly. "You're interfering with flight operations and endangering everybody."

"Screw you," said Donnelly.

It was enough for George, who delivered a short hard right to Donnelly's stomach. The man folded up and went backward. "Get him out of here," he told the volunteer flight attendant.

"Captain," she said, "he isn't the only one who feels that way."

Donnelly tried to get up and hit back, but he measured George's size—and maybe his anger—and thought better of it. He grumbled about bringing legal action and limped out.

George followed him back to the passenger cabin.

The SSTO had a capacity for two hundred and thirty-five passengers. They had seventy-four on board now, with thirty-seven to come. They were well distributed, and George picked a spot from which most of them could see him. He picked up a mike. "Ladies and gentlemen," he said. "I know this is unnerving for some of you. But we're on our way back home now. One bus is pulling alongside us as we speak; another's running right behind it. We'll pick up those people and that'll be the end of it. Meantime, I repeat, we're headed home at this very minute, and we can't do any better than this even if there were no more buses, because we have a window to hit. Please stay calm.

"This is a very tough and very reliable spacecraft. It's extremely fast, and we'll be gone more than an hour before impact.

"That'll be plenty of time. Now. . . ." He paused. "We can't afford distractions, because they endanger all of us. I'm going to be busy, and my crew will be busy. So we won't tolerate any nonsense." He looked across the rows of seats and found Donnelly, who was glaring at him. Most of the passengers wore Moonbase uniforms. Donnelly and four others, in civilian clothes, were clustered together. Non-Moonbase personnel, he decided, who'd been out on the surface and gotten back late.

"Don't worry about it, Captain," said one of the uniforms, looking meaningfully in Donnelly's direction. "Nobody'll get out of line."

"Thank you," said George. "I know we'll all cooperate."

•   •   •

Point Judith, Rhode Island. 9:11 P.M.

Luke Peterson cut a slice of cherry pie, poured a glass of cold milk, and listened to the soft rumble of the incoming tide. A couple of trawlers moved listlessly through the dark, and he could hear kids laughing on the beach. Otherwise, Point Judith seemed deserted. Its streets were quiet. The shops down at the mall had mostly shut down early. Even Kroger had closed.

The Hendersons next door had told him they'd been planning all along to go see their cousins in Woonsocket, and no, it didn't have anything to do with the comet. Pete Albuchek across the street had discovered that *he* had to go visit an old friend in Worcester.

Luke wondered whether there'd be anyone down at the lodge, which was where he usually spent his Saturday evenings.

He tasted the cherry pie. In the old days, he and Ann had made a ritual out of the late-night snack, often carrying it out onto the porch and munching away while the tide rolled in. Now, instead of Ann, he had a computer display.

It was set on a shelf overlooking the kitchen table. He aimed the remote and clicked it and the *Time* logo filled the screen, then faded to an image of the comet. The comet was overlaid by the vice president's picture. It carried the legend: WILL WE LOSE HIM?

Luke liked Charlie Haskell. Like most Americans, he instinctively distrusted politicians, but he thought Haskell might be an exception. Luke's friends laughed when he said that. No such thing as an honest politician, they maintained.

But he'd decided that, if Haskell got the nomination, he'd vote for him. Luke didn't have the energy to try to sort out the issues. Both sides seemed reasonable when they presented their arguments for reducing the debt or handling the influx of immigrants or dealing with nanotech. Hell,

Luke didn't really understand what nanotech was. So his philosophy was to do the next best thing: find a candidate who seemed honest and put him in charge and hope for the best. His son Christopher liked to say that the country wasn't governable anyhow. Problems were too big, too intractable. The nation was too deep in debt. The borders were a joke. Every now and then some terrorist group took out a thousand people with nerve gas. Meantime, everybody who was out of power leveled all kinds of personal attacks against the people who were *in* power. Maybe Chris was right. Maybe even Andy Culpepper couldn't have dealt with things anymore.

Maybe the comet *was* a sign.

Skyport Terminal. 9:12 P.M.

Tory Clark's flight left without her. It carried two hundred twenty-two passengers and a crew of fifteen. Prior to departure her phone bleeped for several minutes. She ignored it.

SSTO *Arlington* Flight Deck. 9:25 P.M.

Their window was coming up. George watched anxiously while the last of the moonbuses arced in to dock.

They were down to four minutes before he had to lift out of orbit. Or forget about getting clear.

He listened to the rattle of conversation between Mary and the bus pilot, which seemed to go on interminably. Finally he broke in with a sharp warning and she acknowledged. He debated whether the clamps would hold if he tried to accelerate out while the bus was still attached. It wasn't something he wanted to try.

Listening over Mary's cell phone, he heard the inner hatch open, heard voices, *gotta move, hurry up now, let's go let's go.*

The comet was as big as the Earth, visibly inching forward. "Let me know as soon as they're aboard, Mary."

There were nineteen people on this one, including the two bus pilots. Full load.

He could hear Mary's voice counting heads as they came through. Fourteen, fifteen. . . .

"We're down to two minutes, babe. Hurry it along." He switched to the public address system and warned the passengers to buckle in. "Departure is imminent," he said.

"*Arlington.*" One of the moonbus pilots this time.

"Go ahead."

"Not set up yet for auto."

The plan was to let the autopilot ease the moonbus clear of the SSTO, which didn't have much flexibility for maneuver. "Forget it and get over here," said George. "Or we're leaving without you." He leaned back and looked at Curt. The port wing might clip the bus on the way out.

"I'll have a solution in a minute," Curt said. He worked over his console.

The comet was sinking. Not good.

"Nineteen," said Mary. "All accounted for."

"Get everybody buckled in. And stand by to jettison the bus."

She repeated the order and waited.

Curt's numbers flowed across George's display. "Ready to go," the flight engineer said.

"Cut it loose," said George. His control board winked.

"Bus away."

George applied Curt's solution and the SSTO wheeled to starboard and began to climb.

"Bus clear," said Curt. "Return to base course. Go for the window."

George went to full thrust and the space plane rose swiftly out of orbit.

•   •   •

Micro. 9:26 P.M.

Tony and Saber, descending toward Alphonsus, over-heard most of the conversation between *Arlington* and the bus. Saber thought she saw a brief flicker of light against the velvet sky, a flicker that might have been *Arlington* starting for home.

They were now alone with the monster.

6.

Moonbase, Director's Dining Room. 9:27 P.M.

It was winding down. Jack Chandler felt a wave of regret when Bigfoot, after glancing several times at his watch, excused himself, explaining that he really shouldn't be here, that he should be at his station in case something went wrong.

What could go wrong? Chandler asked, but did not listen to the answer.

"We should probably *all* go," said Evelyn a moment later. "This isn't a good time to be late."

The others nodded, glanced at their watches, drained their glasses.

"Good luck," said Haskell, so low that the words were barely discernible.

Morley looked at the vice president and pointed to his throat mike. Haskell glanced at Evelyn, who shrugged. The vice president nodded and Morley withdrew to the far end of the room, took his microcam from his pocket and set it on the table. He aimed it at himself and began to speak into the mike. Chandler couldn't make out what he was saying.

The chaplain looked over at him and smiled encourage-ment. *We're going to be okay, Jack.*

"I know," said Chandler aloud.

He hadn't yet made up his mind what he was going to do. Or maybe he had, in some inner recess where no light lived.

And maybe that was why his heart pounded so fiercely, he thought the others must hear it.

"You okay, Jack?" asked Haskell. He was frowning.

"I'm fine. It's an emotional moment," he admitted.

They filed from the dining room into the adjoining passage, took the elevator, descended to ground level, and emerged through the front doors. It was, of course, night in Main Plaza. Post lamps provided pools of light, illuminating benches and shop fronts and walkways. It was a scene of almost painful tranquillity.

Chandler paused near an azalea bush. "Something I forgot," he told Evelyn. "Family pictures. I'll meet you at the Spaceport."

"Okay," she said. "But hurry it along, Jack."

He nodded.

"Want company?"

"No, no. You go with the others. I'll be right over." He felt his face growing warm.

She looked at him for a long moment. The others were walking toward the tram station. Their leisurely demeanor had been replaced by something more precipitate. "Make it quick, Jack. Okay?"

He nodded, turned away, and descended the ramp to level three, where he walked back to his quarters in McNair Country, an area reserved for Moonbase managers.

His footsteps echoed through the empty corridors. He seemed preternaturally aware of the texture of the walls and the geometry of the passageways. There was a sense the place was *alive*, as if everything that had ever happened here had somehow been captured and stored.

He found his room, inserted his keycard, and opened up. When he'd left it to go to the dinner, he hadn't known whether he would return or not. Even now he wasn't sure about his intentions. But he *was* sure he did not want to go back groundside, back to the crushing weight in his chest, back to the constant fear he took to bed every night that he would not wake up in the morning.

He could probably arrange to live at Skyport, but there was no job for him there. He'd be a hanger-on, a pathetic former paper shuffler, sucking up space and resources. And zero gravity would only mean further decay anyway. No. What he needed was a clean end. Cut it off and be done with it.

Moonbase Tram Station. 9:32 P.M.

The tram was waiting.

They climbed on board, Evelyn and Charlie, the chaplain and Morley. Morley asked if he could interview the vice president when they arrived at the Spaceport. Just get his reactions, very casual, very quick. Charlie knew that Rick would never agree to such an arrangement without preparation, fearing Charlie would say the wrong thing, admit to fear, express indecision, say *something* that would be used against him later. So he readily acceded. Then he sat back to take his last look at the interior of Moonbase. Beside him, Pinnacle looked distracted.

"You okay, Chaplain?" Charlie asked.

"Yes." His eyes seemed far away. "You're very fortunate, Mr. Vice President. However things go, you've accomplished a lot with your life."

Charlie thought about that as the vehicle drew away from the station. It navigated Main Plaza, penetrated copses and gardens, passed along rows of darkened shops that looked as if they'd been empty a long time. The smell of freshly cut green grass was in the air.

"I'm not so sure," Charlie said. "I'll admit I've done better than I would have ever thought possible. But it's all *position*. I don't know that I've ever actually *accomplished* anything." There were probably a lot of people out there who remembered the chaplain fondly for one reason or another. But whose life was better because Charlie Haskell had lived? "What would you change about your life?" he asked suddenly. "What would you do differently?"

The chaplain thought about it. "Veronica," he said.

"Veronica?" Charlie had expected an answer couched in piety, a failure perhaps to be sufficiently charitable. Not something as mundane as a woman's name. "An old girlfriend?"

"No. To my everlasting shame." Pinnacle smiled shyly. "I conceived something of a passion for Veronica years ago. When I was nineteen. I seem to harbor it still."

"What happened?"

"Not much. We dated a few times. Over a period of three months. She lost interest."

"Oh." Charlie looked past the chaplain's shoulder at a cluster of elms. "It must have been a pretty strong passion to survive for so many years. What happened to her?"

He shrugged. "I took her at her word and never went back."

"Not ever?"

Pinnacle chuckled and shook his head. "Pride's a deadly thing, isn't it? The most destructive of the vices, I think."

They rolled through manicured parks and clicked into stations where no one waited. Eventually the greenery dropped away. They passed out of Main Plaza, crossed a bridge over an excavation that would have become the operating area for the Mining and Industrial Department. Then they slipped into a tunnel. The tram grew dark and lights came on. They were climbing now.

"What about *you?*" the chaplain asked. "What would you change?"

Charlie considered the question. "I'd like to have had a couple of kids."

"Are you married?"

"No," said Charlie. "I never got around to it."

"Things undone," said the chaplain.

"I'm sorry?"

"Regrets always involve things undone. Never stuff we did that we shouldn't have. Always opportunities missed."

"Yeah," said Charlie. "I think that's probably true."

"Mr. Vice President, if we get clear of this, I think I'll be a different man."

"We better hide the women," smiled Charlie.

But the chaplain said nothing more.

The mood had grown sober. After a while the tram began to slow down. Its automated voice warned them to exercise caution, that a curve was coming. Minutes later they emerged into the terminal. Before the vehicle stopped, Morley got up and twisted round to face everyone. "What I'd like to do when we arrive," he said, "is to get off and set up. And I'd like to send you guys and the tram back into the tunnel. Just for a minute. Then I'll bring you out again so I can get pictures of the arrival."

Charlie started to protest but Evelyn squeezed his arm. "Go along with it," she said. "He deserves some pictures."

"If we get caught," said Charlie, "people will accuse me of staging shots."

"Nobody'll ever know," said Morley as they arrived in the station.

"Do we know how to back up the tram?" asked the chaplain.

Morley had done his homework. He went to a control box, opened it, and smiled at them.

TRANSGLOBAL SPECIAL REPORT. 9:51 P.M.

"This is Keith Morley at the Moonbase Spaceport. About three-quarters of an hour remains before Comet Tomiko arrives. We've received word that the vice president and his party are headed over here to board the microbus that will try to carry them to safety.

"They left Main Plaza just a few minutes ago and should be here any—wait, I think I hear them coming now. . . . "

Moonbase, McNair Country. 9:53 P.M.

Jack closed the door behind him and sank onto his sofa. It was getting late, and if he didn't leave soon the decision would become moot. He looked up and saw the photo of Jeanie and the three kids taken years ago on Cape Cod. They'd all been young then, Jeanie apparently in the bloom of health. But even then the disease had sunk its roots into her. She'd fought it until the last of the kids were gone, and then she'd collapsed. Six weeks later he'd lost her.

There were other photos: here, he was accepting a Special Performance Award from Evelyn; there, his features were superimposed over a graphic of the Moon. Over the desk was a citation from the Boston Chamber of Commerce; and by the door, a scroll from the U.S. Contract Bridge League:

OPEN CHAMPIONSHIP, PAIRS
WILMINGTON, DELAWARE, JUNE 2–4, 2017
FRED HAWLEY, JACK CHANDLER

He'd been reared a strict Baptist. It was a way of life he'd been happy to escape, but he envied now the quiet faith of his boyhood, the conviction that he would see again everyone he cared about.

Jeanie. Luminous eyes. Mischievous smile. He missed that most of all.

It occurred to him that he *had* known all along what his decision would be. He had, after all, left the photo on the shelf.

He went into the bathroom, opened the cabinet, and took down a container of tranquilizers. He shook a half dozen out into a trembling palm and looked at them a long time before he filled a glass and drank them down.

He'd sent messages of farewell to his children. They'd been phrased against the backdrop of events, couched in ambiguous terms suggesting he might be unable to escape.

Evelyn would, he knew, conceal the truth.

He laid his head back against the cushions, closed his eyes, and waited for the tranquilizers to take hold.

Moonbase Spaceport. 9:57 P.M.

Morley was talking into a microcam when they reentered the station. ". . . here they are now," he was saying. Following his directions, Evelyn climbed first out of the tram. And then Charlie. "Mr. Vice President," he said, maneuvering Charlie into the eye of the microcam, which he'd attached to a wall, "I wonder if I can get you to say a few words. What's your feeling at this moment?"

Dumb. But Charlie gave it his best: "They tell me that Tony Casaway and Alisa Rolnikaya"—he pronounced her name deliberately, taking great care to get it right—"are two of the best pilots we have. I'm confident this'll have a happy ending."

Bigfoot appeared. "The Micro's running on time," he said in the overdramatic, wooden manner of a poor amateur actor. Charlie decided he'd been cued. "We'll be leaving from Bay Four."

He waited a minute or so for a brief exchange between Morley and the vice president. Yes, admitted Charlie, this was an unnerving situation and he'd feel better when he was on his way. Then he turned the interview around, asking Morley for *his* thoughts. The reporter was amenable and laughed, and they recorded a conversation that Charlie knew was going well.

"This won't be the end of manned space flight," Charlie told the television audience, by way of rounding off the interview. "One way or another, we'll be back."

He didn't really think so, though it seemed like the right thing to say. But if "back" meant out in space again, it wasn't going to happen. The economics wouldn't support it. Maybe manned space flight would happen again one day, but it would be far down the line somewhere, so far down that he suspected the human race might have time to forget it had ever traveled to its Moon. He'd always been a supporter of Moonbase International and the Lunar Transport Authority and NASA, but he knew which way the wind would blow after this. The next campaign would be about fiscal sanity. Next time, they'd let another generation impoverish itself.

Briefly, they'd touched the sky. And it had been to no purpose.

A vast emptiness opened inside him. The White House seemed far away, as remote and unattainable as Mars. Tears welled up in his eyes, and he was not sure for whom they came—himself, or something far greater.

Bigfoot was gritting his teeth and looking at his watch. Charlie signaled that was enough. Morley thanked him on camera, signed off, shut down, and thanked him again.

Bigfoot led them into the passenger waiting area. "I'll be talking to you over the PA," Bigfoot said. "When I ask you to, go down that tunnel over there." He pointed. "The door'll be closed at the far end. It'll open when the Micro's down. There'll be a tube. Go through the tube and into the passenger cabin. As quick as you can. Okay? I don't need to emphasize that there'll be no time to waste."

"What about you?" asked Evelyn.

"Don't worry about me. I'll be going in through a different door." He started out of the room, but turned back. "Good luck," he said.

He left them and Evelyn looked at her watch. "Getting late. What do you think's keeping Jack?"

Moonbase, McNair Country. 10:01 P.M.

The medication obviously wasn't working. He opened the bottom drawer in a side table and extracted a bottle of Scotch. He filled a tumbler, straight, and drank it down. Its warmth spread through him and the tension began to dissipate.

His cell phone chimed. "Jack?" Evelyn's voice. "For God's sake, where are you? It's late."

"I've decided not to go, Evelyn."

"Jack, you can't do this."

"I don't want to go back."

"I think we should talk about this *later*. Where are you now?"

"My apartment."

"My God, Jack—"

"That's right. I couldn't get over there in time if I wanted to."

"Jack—" He heard her struggle to control her voice. It felt good to know she really cared about him. Other than professionally.

"Good luck, Evelyn. You'll make it. And thanks for everything."

He disconnected. When the cell phone chimed again he took out the batteries and laid it on a table. Then he pulled the jack on the table phone.

He walked over and looked at his certificate from the Wilmington bridge tournament. That had been a good weekend. One of his best.

He poured a second glass of Scotch.

Moonbase Spaceport. 10:02 P.M.

"I'm going after him."

Charlie had overheard Evelyn's side of the conversation. "There isn't time," he said. "You don't even know where he is."

"He's in his quarters. Where else would he be?"

"He's in his quarters *now*. It doesn't matter. He's made his choice, Evelyn. You have to respect it." He drew her to him and held her. Her cheeks were wet and she was trembling.

"I should have known," she said.

"How could you have possibly known?"

She started to answer, but broke it off and simply held him. And Charlie remembered the silent message he'd seen passed to her from Chandler.

"I love you."

"Damn him," she said quietly.

7.

Louise Singfield lived in a rooftop apartment in a four-story brownstone on 77th Street just off Central Park. It was perfect for a moonwatch party.

Marilyn and Larry arrived by taxi, identified themselves through the intercom, and were admitted. They rode a creaky elevator to the fourth floor and climbed a staircase the rest of the way. Louise's door opened off a narrow landing.

There was laughter inside and familiar voices. Marilyn immediately recognized Doug Cabel, Larry's boss. She didn't like Cabel, not because of anything he'd ever done, or even *was*, but because of the way her husband turned into a toady in his presence. Larry was a good man: He treated her well, made a decent living, didn't cheat, didn't demonstrate any major vices. Yet he seemed to be admirable for what he didn't do rather than for what he *did*. She'd been married three years and had come to realize that she was making do. The great romance she'd dreamed of in college, like the ones she read about every day in her job, had not happened. And now, she knew, *would* not happen.

Well, it could have been worse.

Louise's door opened and there stood the hostess herself. She wore a white blouse with navy collar and sleeves and navy slacks. The blouse was cut to reveal some breast. A bit much, Marilyn thought, for a casual office BYOB affair.

"Good to see you, Marilyn," Louise said, delivering a peck on the cheek. She accepted a kiss from Larry and introduced her boyfriend *du jour*. Mike Somebody-or-other.

Marilyn knew most of the people there. Larry's department did a lot of socializing. Doug believed it was good for morale and he encouraged it.

They contributed their bottle of Jamaica rum to the cache, made a couple of daiquiris, and went out onto the terrace. Larry paid his customary obeisance to Doug. Doug commented on this being quite a night, and then asked how the *Kiplinger's* report on BRK Merchandising should be handled. Or something of that nature.

The comet had grown appreciably from night to night. Now it commanded the sky east of the Moon. Nearby stars had faded, and when Marilyn walked to the far edge of the terrace, near the roof and away from the lights, she thought the illumination from the comet strong enough that she could have read by it.

Marv Taylor joined her. "Spooky, isn't it?" he said.

Marv, like Larry, was an account executive. He was quiet, introspective, gentle. His eyes were light blue, like the sky during late morning, and they seemed always amused and sad at the same time, as if he knew the truth about her. (What *was* the truth about her?) He was not married. There'd been a fiancée when she'd first met him. But the woman was gone and Marilyn, for reasons she did not entirely understand, had been relieved at her departure.

"Yes," she admitted. "I've never seen a sky like that."

He was not drinking. "This'll be a night to tell your grandkids about."

Marilyn tasted her daiquiri. It was strawberry. "Larry thinks it'll fizzle. He says astronomical stuff, comets specifically, *always* fizzle."

He smiled. "He's probably right," he said.

She looked into his eyes. *Marv Taylor, I'd like very much to bed you.* But she wouldn't. If she were sure she could get away with it, she'd think seriously about giving it a try. She felt entitled to one real passion during her life. But she'd get caught. Larry would know.

On the other hand, if this really turned out to be the end of the world, as some people were saying, what difference would it make?

White House, Oval Office. 10:04 P.M.

The Moon wasn't visible from his windows. Henry had set up a hot line for the state governors, had resisted nationalizing the Guard (which would only serve to encourage those elements in the nation that were given to panic), had talked with the heads of state of two dozen nations, had authorized full U.S. commitment to a UN Response Team, and had gone on national television with a fireside chat, FDR-style.

He was especially good in that format. Al Kerr had told him once that he oozed sincerity. He understood that people were upset, he'd explained. They were experiencing something quite disturbing. But Americans were not among those who would give way to hand-wringing and fear-mongering. (In fact, the media, he thought, had done quite a good job at keeping a lid on things.)

Should any effects of the distant collision (he emphasized *distant*) be felt in the U.S.A., he assured the nation that the government was ready to act with all the power at its disposal. The military had been deployed to lend assistance in the unlikely event it might be needed. Federal agencies were standing by. And he himself would spend the evening in the White House. He was planning to watch a good movie, and expected not to be disturbed.

He added, almost as an afterthought, that Vice President Haskell was still at Moonbase. He was proud of the vice president, and the five brave Americans who had remained with him. (He'd gotten carried away here. Morley was a New Zealander; Hampton was from Senegal; the chaplain was British; and, of course, one of the two pilots of the Micro, had they been mentioned, was Russian. But let it go. The nation needed pumping up.) A rescue effort was under way even as he spoke, and he was optimistic that everyone would be brought away safely.

Al shook his hand when he was done. It had been a masterful performance. The president had spoken from his living quarters on the second floor of the West Wing. The book-lined walls, the sputtering fire (a virtual effect, actually, because the evening was unseasonably warm), the family portraits, had all lent a sense of security and tranquillity to the proceedings.

There was, of course, no movie planned for the evening.

After the broadcast, Henry had returned to the Oval Office, taken a call from UN Secretary General Elie Kopacca on an unrelated matter, and then headed down to the situation room. In the holotank, a virtual comet closed in on Mare Muscoviense. Displays portrayed the comet from a dozen different points of view. On the far side of a glass partition, a dozen operators manned computers and phones. There were uniforms everywhere. He saw Mercedes Juarez deep in conversation with the liaison from the Federal Emergency Management Agency.

The situation room was essentially a military operation, usually a relatively blasé place run for the convenience of the commander-in-chief. When a crisis was in full swing, however, it could become the nation's nerve center. The officer responsible for it was Rear Admiral Jay Graboski.

Graboski was something of a crank. He didn't much like civilians, junior officers, reporters, or White House employees. He was convinced the nation was in a steep moral decline and that only military discipline, practiced across the land by all citizens and enforced by a tough national police force, would be sufficient to turn things around. He tolerated Henry Kolladner because he had to, but he was not reluctant to offer advice, usually in the guise of "cracking down" on some practice or other. For all that, Graboski was useful. He knew the equipment, its capabilities and its limitations. He never lost his head. He was brutally honest. And he had no private agenda that transcended his loyalty to the United States.

When Henry entered the area, Graboski was clustered with a couple of his lieutenants. He saw the president and came over. "Nothing's changed, sir," he said.

The clocks were counting down the last hour.

"Is the rescue effort on schedule?"

"Yes, Mr. President. The microbus made its SSTO rendezvous on the dime. They're in the descent stage now, approaching Moonbase." He went on to describe efforts on the West Coast to stock food and equipment in elevated areas.

Henry didn't care much about details. He was thinking instead about the last nine months of his term, what he hoped to accomplish, a few old scores he wanted to settle, the kind of mark he hoped to leave on history. And he was trying to calculate how tonight's events would influence all that. Whether, for example, the death of a heroic vice president would reflect well on him. Or put him into sharp contrast. After all, it might be said, the opening of Moonbase was a monumental event. The president should have been there. And how would *he* have behaved?

How indeed?

TRANSGLOBAL NEWS REPORT. 10:05 P.M.

"This is Keith Morley reporting live from Moonbase. I'm talking by remote with Tony Casaway, the pilot of the microbus that will make an attempt to pull us out of here in, uh, about twenty minutes. And with him is his copilot, Alisa Rolnikaya. Tony, where are you now?"

"Hello, Keith. We're close enough to see the lights. We'll be there in a few minutes."

"Good. I don't need to tell you that we're waiting anxiously. I wonder if you'd care to give us your assessment of the situation? How do things look from your perspective?"

"You want the truth?"

"Sure."

"I don't want to upset you, Keith, but they look scary. The comet is virtually on top of us. I'm showing you now the view from the cockpit."

"I see it. It looks lower in the sky than it did earlier."

"Just before it comes down, it'll drop behind the horizon. Or at least it would if you were sitting on top of the ringwall mountains. I don't mind telling you, I'll be happy to pick you folks up and be gone."

"I don't mind telling you, we share your feeling, Tony." *(Chuckles.)* "How about you, Saber? I should mention that Alisa is Russian, and she goes by her old NATO code name, Saber. You both volunteered to do this. Having any second thoughts?"

"I probably shouldn't admit this in front of the whole world, Keith, but I'm scared to death."

"Well, Saber, I want you to know we appreciate your coming after us."

"Keith?"

"Yes, Tony."

"How do you feel?"

"Same as Saber. We'll be standing by the launchpad with our lunches packed."

On board *Diligent*, USCGC 344, in the East River. 10:06 P.M.

Commander Peter Bolling listened to the rumble of his twin V16 diesel engines and watched the piers and wharves slip by. They were uniformly empty.

"It's eerie," said Dan Packard, his XO. The waterfront was lit up, like always. Here and there a solitary figure patrolled the docks, flashlight and clipboard in hand. Beyond, the towers of Manhattan rose under clear skies, unchanged and unchangable, mocking *Diligent* and her orders. It *was* eerie. Even Bolling, who'd been working the harbor for twelve years, had never seen it so completely deserted.

The *Diligent* was an ancient 210-foot cutter, known affectionately to her crew as *Dilly*. She was based at Governor's Island, had spent the earlier part of the evening directing outbound traffic into Long Island Sound. Now, in company with her sister vessel *Reliant*, she was moving south on the East River, one final patrol before clearing out through the Narrows into the Atlantic, where they would wait until higher authority was sure events in the sky would not create hazardous conditions in the cramped New York and New Jersey waterways.

Ships had been putting out to sea now for three days, taking no chances on getting caught near shore if high water developed.

Bolling was a graduate of Stanford, where he'd majored in history. He'd grown up around boats and joined the Coast Guard more or less as a lark, expecting to enjoy himself for a few years before settling down with a *real* job. He'd earned a commission at the academy and married a marine pilot. He'd liked the life, enjoyed the freedom, and now wondered that he could ever have thought seriously of working in an office.

His marriage hadn't lasted: too many irregular hours on both sides, no kids to bind the partners, and maybe too much money. They'd stayed in touch and managed to remain friends. Tonight, he knew she'd squired an automobile carrier out past the eastern markers and elected to stay with the ship. It was running coastwise, with stops in Philadelphia, Charleston, and Brunswick. But it would lie well offshore with the rest of the merchant fleet until the situation sorted itself out.

"I sent my family out of town," said Packard. "Soon as I heard."

Bolling knew several people who'd tried to do that but had

been unable to book transport. And more than a few who'd started out by car, given up, and come home. "I don't think there's anything to it, Dan," he said. "But it never hurts to be safe."

He was glad his ex was out, too.

Funny how night skies give credence to fear. When he'd reported for duty this afternoon and they'd begun to lay out the operational plan, it had all seemed ridiculous. The sun had been bright, the weather warm, and everyone was laughing over a long jaunt out into the Atlantic. But it felt deadly serious now as *Dilly* and *Reliant* moved past empty piers.

One vessel, the *Kira Maru*, was inbound. *Diligent* overtook her as she approached Throgs Neck Bridge. The Merchant Marine Academy was off to port, just beyond Kings Point Road. Automobile traffic seemed normal. Maybe even a little heavy for a Saturday night.

Dilly was loaded with medical supplies just in case. And it carried a couple of tanks of fresh water. Someone in the chain of command was taking the comet seriously.

The skies were about as clear as they get over New York. Comet and Moon had risen almost simultaneously during the late afternoon. They were overhead now, entwined in the bridge, almost visibly drawing together while he watched. He drew his jacket around his shoulders. On the river at this time of year, nights were always cold.

His orders were crumpled in his jacket pocket.

PRESERVE THE BOAT IN THE EVENT OF HEAVY WEATHER.

That was strange phrasing, he thought, considering what they feared.

RENDER ASSISTANCE AS NECESSARY.
MAINTAIN RADIO CONTACT AT ALL TIMES
AFTER 2200 HOURS.

REPORT PROMPTLY ANY UNUSUAL
HYDROLOGIC PHENOMENA.

Now the dark sky gave way to the Whitestone Bridge.

"Look," said Packard, pointing ahead toward a small flotilla of yachts, a few points to starboard. There were maybe twenty boats in all. Bolling could hear music drifting across the water. And laughter. But they were keeping together, and they waved as the cutter passed. Some of the coasties waved back.

The lead boat was a twin-engine white and maroon Mainship motor yacht with *Yankee Liz* painted on her bow. "Ramsey," said Bolling to his radio operator, "Bring *Liz* up."

Ramsey was not much more than a kid, just out of school. He spoke into his microphone, listened, nodded, looked at his skipper. Bolling gestured for the mike.

"*Yankee Liz,*" he said, "this is the Coast Guard. Where are you bound?"

He could see the boat's captain on its bridge, hunched over the radio. He was a short, dumpy man, but it was too dark to make out other details. "Getting clear of the Sound tonight," he said.

"Where are you headed?" asked Bolling again.

"Peekskill."

"All of you? Are you traveling together?"

"Some are going to Croton-on-Hudson."

"Nobody going to sea?"

"No, sir."

"Very good, Captain. Thank you."

Off to port, LaGuardia Airport was quiet. Bolling had seen it like that before, idled by a heavy storm or by a strike. The tower looked active, and he could see vehicles moving on the approach roads. But there were no lights in the sky.

They passed Rikers Island and Hell Gate.

Reliant was out of sight now.

The city crouched on the river, insensate, timeless, invulnerable. Headlights moved along both banks, climbed the approaches, and crossed on the Triborough.

They continued down to the foot of Manhattan, making perhaps better time than Bolling would ordinarily have allowed, but he felt crowded by the narrow channels of the East River. Governors Island and the Statue of Liberty came into view. The harbor looked serene, traffic flowing in an endless stream around its perimeter. A ferry nosed past them.

He checked his schedule. The ferries were going to discontinue service at 2230 hours. "I'm surprised they didn't decide to close the bridges until it's over," he said.

"I think that'd be a nightmare, Captain," said Packard. "I don't think you do that unless you really believe something's coming."

They'd been talking about it all day. Neither would admit to anything except skepticism. Another typical government hassle. But Bolling was nevertheless happy to get through the Narrows and out into the Atlantic.

8.

Micro. 10:07 P.M.

The landing lights at Alphonsus were bright and crisp, cheerful against the bleak landscape as Tony and Saber rode the beacon down. The Sun was below the eastern highlands, probably just a few hours from dawn. The crater looked different, unfamiliar, in the strange light.

As soon as the interview with Keith Morley had ended, Saber had gone down to the cargo deck to get into her p-suit. Tony was glad it was over. The prospect of speaking to millions of people had scared him more than the comet. Below, lights switched on and the roof doors began to roll back.

"Micro." Bigfoot's voice on the radio. "Tony, how are we doing?"

"On target."

"Okay. Everybody here's packed and ready to go."

"Roger that."

"But we've lost one."

"Say again, Moonbase."

"We lost one. Chandler's not coming."

"Roger." Pause. "Why not?"

"Bad heart." Bigfoot changed his tone. "As soon as you're on the pad, we'll proceed as planned. Is Saber in her gear?"

"She will be in a couple of minutes."

"Okay. I'm going to have to close down now. I need time to get through the airlock."

"Roger."

"When I get into the bay, I'll still be able to talk to you, but I won't be able to see any of the instruments. So you'll be on your own."

"I know." Manual descent into the terminal wasn't routine, but Tony didn't anticipate any problems.

"We'll have a beacon to ride out."

"Good. See you in a few minutes, Bigfoot." He broke the connection and buzzed Saber. "On final approach."

"Okay," she said. "I'm ready."

Moonbase Spaceport. 10:08 P.M.

The Spaceport accommodated nine service bays. Two of these were designed for cargo carriers; four housed the lobbers and hoppers that were used for short- or long-range lunar transportation. The remaining three served the buses that connected Moonbase with L1. Each, of course, could be depressurized individually and opened to the void through a set of overhead doors.

While he talked to the Micro, Bigfoot had been sitting in

a p-suit. Now he pulled on his helmet, checked his systems, picked up a remote and shoved it into a pocket, and entered the Bay Four airlock. He'd already depressurized the bay, opened its overhead doors, and turned on its touchdown lights.

When the board went green he opened the hatch and stepped into the work area. He'd laid out the umbilicals earlier, lox and powdered aluminum for fuel, others carrying an electrical recharge, water, and air. He'd also put out several transparent plastic bags filled with sealant, patches, wrenches, peanut butter (who knew how long this trip might take?), and spare parts other than those the bus normally carried. He studied them briefly, trying to think if he'd forgotten anything. Nothing came to mind.

He activated his radio. "Tony, I'm in the bay."

"Roger that. We're at twelve hundred meters."

He looked up. The tongue of flame from the main engine was moving against the stars. "I see you."

"How's the comet doing?"

"It's doing fine. It's inside a million kilometers," said Bigfoot.

Right on time.

Routine procedure called for Moonbase personnel to track incoming vehicles and maintain a constant flow of data exchange until they were safely down. But had Bigfoot stayed inside to do that, it would have taken too long to get through the airlock. Still, there was no real risk here. The bay was built to accommodate the much larger 2665 bus, so there was plenty of room, probably an average of ten meters' clearance on a side. Bigfoot wouldn't have worried at all except that he had a pilot in a hurry.

He released the stops on the umbilicals and laid them out close to the pad, setting each so he could activate the flow at the nozzle. When he was satisfied he could do no more, he recalled that Keith Morley had given him the microcam to set up inside the bay. He looked around, found a table, extended the instrument's legs as he'd been shown, and pointed it toward the pad. (He'd warned Morley that he might not have time to recover it, but Morley said that he didn't want it recovered, that he wanted shots of the Micro pulling in and leaving.) Then he climbed behind a heat shield and tapped into the public address system.

"This is Caparatti," he said. "Are you folks at the door?"

Evelyn responded. "We're ready to go, Bigfoot." She still didn't sound so good, he thought.

"Okay. We'll be opening up in about five minutes. Keith, you're all set and ready to go."

"Thanks, Bigfoot," said the newsman. "My director's asked if you can move it a little bit left. Just a few degrees."

Bigfoot complied, changing the angle until Morley said it was okay.

The rim of Earth was visible through the overhead doors.

Tony's voice on the radio: "How do I look, Bigfoot?"

Dammit, he didn't like trying to eyeball the Micro in from here. "Drifting east a couple of points," he said. "As best I can tell."

"Roger."

Bigfoot watched him compensate. "That's good. Keep coming." Safety regulations prohibited personnel from entering this area during landing or launch operations. The chance of getting caught in the backwash was high. The heat shield behind which he hid was designed to protect equipment.

One hundred meters.

A clock on the control room wall showed ten thirteen.

The bay brightened in the glow of the rocket engines. He heard the two pilots talking to each other, switched to another channel, and listened to Keith Morley reporting to his global audience. Damned if he didn't sound as if he were enjoying every minute.

Bigfoot had known people like that during his brief tenure with the Packers, guys who seemed absolutely fearless, who thrived on risk.

Forty meters.

"A little tight at the rear, Tony. Take it forward a touch. That's it. Not too much." Even through the suit he felt the heat from the motors.

Thruster clusters adjusted their angle and fired. The Micro centered itself. "That's good. Bring it in."

A gout of flame arrowed through the overhead doors.

"Passengers, ready up," he said. "The bird is almost down."

Treads and main engine nozzle cleared the roof and the fire licked the launchpad. Now the undercarriage, and finally the sphere itself bellied in. Its weight settled onto the treads, compressing them.

Clouds of steam formed and began to dissipate.

Through the lighted windows he could see movement on the flight deck. The Micro cut power and Bigfoot came out from behind the shield. He pointed the remote at a sensor on the far wall and squeezed. The pad rotated the vehicle until its main airlock lined up with a marker on the deck. Then he pushed a different button. A Fleming tube, considerably shorter than the ones used at L1, unfolded from the Bay Four gate, and like a caterpillar trundled across the bay and connected with the airlock.

Meantime, the ship's cargo hatch opened and Saber, in a p-suit, popped out. Bigfoot laid the remote on the deck. "Refuel first," he said.

"Okay." Saber moved quickly out to help with the umbilicals, while he got the latches up for the fuel receivers. With no wasted motions, they connected both lines and hit the switches.

Now, while Bigfoot went after the other umbilicals, Saber

retrieved the remote and checked the readings. She had a green light, which meant a good connection. She aimed the instrument again at the sensor and opened the door that would permit the passengers to enter the Fleming tube. On his radio, Bigfoot heard Morley's broadcast as they scrambled into the passageway: *"Bruce, as you can see, the door's open at last and we're moving down the ramp."*

Saber connected the electrical line while Bigfoot got the others. They hit the switches, and electricity, oxygen, and water began to flow. Next they threw the plastic bags into the airlock. When that was done, Bigfoot returned to the umbilicals. Flow was steady and normal. His gaze drifted to the clock—twenty after—and back to the gauges, where numbers flicked past.

At ten twenty-three, oxygen and water topped off and Saber disconnected the lines and threw them clear. They couldn't do much about recharging, of course, in the short time they had. Usually the operation needed close to an hour and a quarter. But they'd take what they could get.

The critical area was fuel. Tanks were now about forty percent full.

Tony reported the passengers were through the ship's airlock and filing into the cabin.

Saber spoke to Caparatti on the radio: "Bigfoot, when we're done, we'll go in through the cargo hatch. I want to try to get to the flight deck if I can. You seal the hatch behind us."

"Okay," he said.

Morley was still doing his broadcast, using the low-key voice that was supposed to suggest great drama: *"You're watching Bigfoot Caparatti on your screen now. And yes, if you're a football fan, that's the same Bigfoot who once played for the Green Bay Packers."*

Once is exactly correct, you dumb son of a bitch. Did you really have to bring that up?

Saber was watching the recharge. "How we doing?" Bigfoot asked.

"Okay. We'll have enough to power the systems. How's the fuel?"

"About halfway."

Tony came back on: "Everybody's in and the hatch is secure. You can disconnect the tube."

Saber aimed the remote. The walkway came loose and began to retract.

Bigfoot's entire world narrowed down to the two fuel counters and the clock. He let the numbers slip out of focus. Saber's eyes were dark pinpoints behind her visor.

The narrow patch of black sky visible through the entry doors had acquired a haze. He found himself torn between terror and an inclination to dismiss the entire affair as hysteria. Earlier, when he'd made the decision to stay, he'd gotten patched through to his mother, who'd cried and prayed on the phone; and an old friend with whom he'd played college football, who'd told him he was a damned fool but that he was proud to have known Bigfoot. It was said in the past tense.

"Can we get moving?" asked Tony.

"Almost done," said Bigfoot.

At ten twenty-six, the liquid oxygen tank reached full and the pump shut off. Bigfoot disconnected, and threw the umbilical aside. Saber decided she had enough power, and broke her line loose and dropped it.

"Get inside," Bigfoot said. "I'll be with you in a minute."

"Why don't we call it a tankful and clear out?"

Yeah. What the hell.

She started for the cargo hatch while Bigfoot shut down, jerked the umbilical out of the fuel receptacle, capped it, and closed and secured the latch. He lobbed the line as far as he could, which in lunar gravity was a substantial distance. Then he was right behind Saber, dashing for the open hatch while she told Tony that refueling was complete. They'd cut it a lit-tle short in the interests of time, she said, but he shouldn't start the engine yet. She was scrambling into the cargo deck airlock and simultaneously extending a hand to Bigfoot. "We're inside," she told Tony. "Go!" Bigfoot stabbed at the control panel and the outer hatch swung shut. Oxygen poured into the chamber. The engine lit and the bus trembled.

The inner hatch opened. Saber popped through and dashed across the hold, removing her helmet as she went. She was quite agile in low-g footwork and she left Bigfoot far behind.

She swung up the ladder and erupted into the passenger cabin, still carrying her helmet. The Micro began to rise.

Bigfoot meantime had closed and sealed the airlock. Then he tried to follow Saber into the passenger cabin, but the bus was moving quickly now and his weight was increas-ing. He struggled halfway up the ladder, realized he couldn't make it, and concluded his sole mission was to close the hatch between decks. He caught a last glimpse of Saber moving monkey-style up toward the cockpit as he pulled the hatch shut and secured it. Then he retreated back down the ladder.

They were on their way.

Moonbase Spaceport. 10:24 P.M.

Viewers around the world watched the scene in Bay Four through Keith Morley's camera as Saber flung her umbilical away and dashed for the open hatch. Then Bigfoot appeared in the picture, moving with deliberation through the light grav-ity, throwing himself up and into the airlock. Saber helped drag him inside. And the hatch closed.

Morley was still speaking in a voice-over, describing the passengers' coolness, admitting his own tensions. Later, many viewers would wonder how he'd managed not to get on the nerves of the others, especially during that final countdown, whispering in his coolly dramatic tone, *"six minutes to impact, five* minutes," and so on.

Occasionally the image switched to the comet, captured by a range of instruments on the ground and in space. Several had been placed at ground zero at Mare Muscoviense, where they looked directly up at the oncoming monster. In the lower right corner, a clock ticked off the remaining time.

News media estimates indicated that 3.6 billion people saw the first wisp of smoke from the main engine just before it roared into life. That number made it the third most watched telecast ever, behind Super Bowls LXX and LXXII.

The blast from the main engine blanked the screens. But Morley plowed smoothly ahead: *"I see we've lost our picture. Bruce, from this point on we're going to have to rely on audio. . . ."*

Transglobal went to a split screen, matching a live image of the comet with a photo of Keith Morley in a tropical shirt and a Panama hat, taken during the Rio conference in January.

"We're clear of the terminal, picking up speed. You can hear the roar of the engine." (Pause.) *"I should tell you, by the way, that we've switched over to internal relay so we won't lose the audio signal no matter what happens at Moonbase.*

"It's becoming a little hard to talk. I'm getting pushed into my seat. My weight's come back, but I feel as if I weigh an extra hundred pounds or so. The sky's different from the way it looked when I came last week. It's lit up.

"I can't see the pilot. The door to the flight deck is closed. Saber Rolnikaya came through here from the cargo deck minutes ago and went up to the cockpit. She was wearing a p-suit and carrying her helmet, which she handed to me. I'm going to hang on to it as a souvenir of the occasion.

"However this turns out, everyone should be aware, Bruce, that this is a group of very special people. You can't see any of them anymore, but they're hanging on pretty well. I don't know what's running

*through their minds right now, but I can tell you what's running
through mine. I'm scared."*

AstroLab. 10:33 P.M.

Feinberg had gone to the AstroLab, where he watched the
approach from the operations room. A dozen monitors displayed magnetic fluctuations, relative velocity, comet bright-
ness, spectrum analysis. The Farside observatory had used its
chemical oxygen iodine laser to vaporize a small section of
Tomiko. The analysis showed slight but significant amounts of
titanium and aluminum. What kind of comet carried pro-
cessed metals?

"I really wonder about it," Feinberg told an assistant
whom he trusted not to quote him. "We might be suffering a
loss of monumental proportions."

The assistant understood he was not talking about the
Moon. Or the hazards from falling rock. She nodded.

I wish we could have got a closer look," Feinberg continued. "Landed on it. Dug it up."

"It's moving too fast," she said. "Even if it were just passing through, we could never have caught up with it."

Feinberg stared at Tomiko's image in the displays. *What
are you?*

Tomiko had lost a substantial fraction of its initially
observed velocity. But it was still running with the solar wind
at almost twenty-four thousand kilometers per minute.
Halfway around Earth in thirty seconds.

Astronomers were still trying to account for the velocity.
A mathematician at the University of Hamburg, noted for
metaphysical ramblings, suggested that the comet had in fact
been *aimed*, that its velocity was intended to demonstrate that
it was not part of a natural event, and that the pinpoint strike
on the Moon was a warning. He did not elaborate.

The networks and the Web, during the final hours before

impact, had been filled with admonitions to get right with God.

The Moon was in its first quarter. Seen from New York, it was in the western sky. The comet was a magnificent sight, spread across the heavens, its tail leading the way, overwhelming the Moon, reaching across the Atlantic and diving beneath the horizon. The corona, on the other hand, was bright and solid, a sheath of golden light.

Marilyn Keep watched Tomiko closing in from Louise's terrace. Larry seemed content to talk finances with the boys, to leave her in Marv's company, to behave as if he were the only male in the world. By ten-thirty she'd had too much to drink. Marv was taking advantage of whatever occasional solitude they could find, a brief interlude on the terrace, a moment passing each other in a corridor, to brush lightly against buttock or breast. She didn't mind it at all, as long as they did not get caught. She liked the brief suggestion of possession, enjoyed the sudden fluttering excitement. It was the first time during her marriage she'd allowed anything like this. When she looked reprovingly at Marv, his eyes glowed with mischief. And his fingertips casually touched her hip, as if it were something they did all the time, as if they shared some mutual secret. So it happened that, as the comet touched the Moon, while all eyes turned skyward, Marilyn was really quite busy with something else.

At Point Judith, Luke Peterson watched from his backyard through a pair of field glasses. He'd read enough, and seen enough, to know there *was* more danger near the water. But the night was peaceful, and the sky was full of stars, except where the comet wiped them out. This was where he lived. If God had set the machinery in motion to take him tonight, well then, God would find him at home.

And no complaints.

It was raining in Carlisle, Pennsylvania, and no one was

going to see the Moon at all. Claire Hasson and Archie Pickman sat with the three Esterhazys, watching Keith Morley's report from the launchpad. It was all very exciting for Archie, despite the skepticism of his hosts. "See," said the elder Esterhazy to no one in particular, as the Micro fled the lunar surface, "what did I tell you? They're free and clear." His son Jeff was very much like him, except for a condescending smile that seemed to have become a permanent part of his features. Other than that, he had the same pinched face, the same bullet head, the same irritatingly self-confident expression. The male Esterhazys were not persons with whom one spoke; they were persons to whom one paid attention.

Archie was worried that the vice president was going to get killed.

"Ridiculous," said Jeff. "You don't really believe this, do you?" He looked sympathetically at Archie.

"What part of it don't you believe?"

"Archie," said Scott, speaking with the dry voice of experience, "this whole thing's an election stunt."

"You think the White House controls comets?"

"Don't get upset," said Jeff. "But these people saw their opportunity and took advantage of it. They've choreographed everything so Haskell comes out of it looking like a hero. There's no danger, never has been. It's going to look close, it *has* to look close, but they'll get clear okay."

Archie saw Mariel Esterhazy frowning and shaking her head at her husband. *Please shut up*, the gesture said. "I don't think so," said Archie.

"That's the payoff for them," glowed Scott. "You're an intelligent man, Arch, and they've even got you fooled."

The Kapchiks had gotten out of Pacifica and well out into the Diablos. They were on a two-lane mountain road, well above the floor of a valley filled mostly with scrub. The Sun was just dropping into the peaks behind them. The same

Moon and comet that lit the night sky over Rhode Island floated in daylight directly overhead. They'd been driving in heavy traffic since leaving San Francisco, carefully keeping both vehicles together. But they were high up now, certainly safe from any deluge, and they were looking for a place to turn off when they came across a cluster of tourist shops. A rusting sign proclaimed the area to be the Jenkins Point Shopping Center. There was a charge station, a Mexican restaurant, and a souvenir store. Although they'd been traveling several hours, Jerry's solar units had replenished the power and he was still carrying almost a full charge.

The electric cars of the Twenties were far more economical than their gas-fueled alternatives. They didn't have the acceleration most drivers would have preferred, and they needed to be plugged periodically into rechargers when operated at night or in gray weather. Recharging was the major drawback of the system because it took a half hour, and might be required every five hours or so when conditions weren't right. But in sunlight they could run almost indefinitely.

The Jenkins Point Shopping Center was located on an overlook on the western rim of the San Joaquin Valley. "Why don't we stay here tonight, hon?" Jerry suggested.

It was as good a spot as they were likely to find, snuggled against the face of the mountain. Other people had apparently had the same idea. Roughly forty cars were parked in a secondary lot on the south side of the road, across from the shops. Where there was still plenty of room.

Jerry turned off the highway. He found a space where they could put both vehicles side-by-side against an ancient plank fence. Beyond the fence, the mountainside rose almost sheer for two hundred feet. The kids asked if they could go to the top, but lost interest when Marisa pointed out there was no way to get there. They agreed to substitute the restaurant, called Pablo's.

Jerry had parked at the extreme eastern end of the lot. This got them to one side of the crowd and also looked like a good spot to set up the telescope. To Jerry's left, the land ran abruptly downhill into a gully.

The Moon looked soft and fog-ridden.

Tomiko was a bright nebulous blur, following the track of its tail, cruising down the sky. People were bunched together in the lot, looking up, no one talking. Traffic on the two-lane road stopped and the cars emptied.

Erin asked where Moonbase was. She wanted Jerry to set up the telescope so she could see the microbus. But there wasn't time, even if the telescope had the capability, which he doubted.

The only person at that moment who might have been able to see the Micro as it lifted away from the lunar surface was Tory Clark, who had redirected L1's ADCOM telescope array and instructed it to lock onto any moving object in the Alphonsus area. But the light wasn't favorable for high magnification at that range, so she too was unsuccessful.

Passengers on board the *Merrivale* would have had to look east to see the collision. But the sky was overcast and a light drizzle had slicked down the decks. Horace had not recovered from his disappointment over the loss of Amy, and on this night he was not at all aware of any unusual events in the sky.

Arecibo, which tracked the comet throughout its six-day run, estimated its impact velocity would be 417.6 kilometers per second.

At the AstroLab, Wesley Feinberg watched it move toward the Moon with both fascination and sadness. The collision would be intoxicating, an astronomical joy unique to this generation. But they were losing this most fascinating of comets.

Comet cores are often more solid than their "dirty snowball" appearance had led twentieth-century astronomers to believe. Whether this was the case with Tomiko, or whether Tomiko was an asteroid with a massive accumulation of ice and dust, or whether it was something else altogether, no one was ever going to know.

9.

Micro Passenger Cabin. 10:34 P.M.

They were also watching the comet on board the Micro, where the images from the Farside observatory had expanded into pure light. Even in the cargo hold, where Bigfoot had spread out some cushions left there for him by Tony, a wallscreen was picking up the Transglobal feed. Keith Morley's picture was on-screen, with a voice-over running conversation between the journalist in space and Bruce Kendrick on the ground.

"Here in the Micro, Bruce, everyone's quiet. We're just waiting now to see what's going to happen."

"Can you see anything yet, Keith?"

"No. The horizon's bathed in light. In all directions. I wish I had a camera to show you. But nothing's changed out there as far as I can tell."

"How high are you?"

"I don't know. High. Maybe six thousand meters."

They were closer to five thousand meters a moment later, when the light exploded.

Impact came at 10:35:17 EDT.

The world watched through its array of orbiting telescopes. What they saw resembled not a large meteor crash, but a lightning strike. Tomiko had filled the sky, filled the lenses, floating in the optical field until there was nothing but *comet*. And then it came silently down, not a giant piece of rock and ice, nor a falling star of immense proportions. Rather, it was a lightning bolt blasting the moonscape, melting the regolith and its underlying rock, crushing the mantle, vaporizing everything within hundreds of kilometers of ground zero.

The Moon spasmed.

The comet nucleus ripped deep into the ground before exploding in an enormous fireball that melted the mantle to a depth of more than six hundred kilometers, exposing the outer core. Shock waves rolled through the lunar interior at thousands of kilometers per hour. The fireball expanded over the fracturing surface, moving seemingly in slow motion, spreading around the Moon, cradling it, engulfing it.

Tony watched it come. From his perspective, it was a wall of fire racing in from the north. He sensed the sudden stillness in the passenger compartment, saw the moonscape break up beneath him, saw Alphonsus disappear into the ground. A curtain of dust rolled over the churning scene, and the darkened flight deck glowed red.

The Micro fled before the fire, crawling away at a constant one g.

The sensors exploded in a tornado of pings and bleeps. Debris rattled against the hull. The Micro rocked and dipped and swerved, a leaf caught in a vast wind. A tread came off and a warning lamp blinked on.

Fire filled the sky.

It seared his eyes and licked at the blister housing the flight deck.

Saber switched off the warning. "Rising external temperatures," she said.

Tony nodded and refrained from sarcasm.

Something hit from below, hurled them higher, snapped his neck back. Bulkheads and decks creaked.

"Water line," said Saber. "Cargo."

That meant Bigfoot was getting wet. "Shut her down," said Tony.

"Done."

The attitude jets were firing in frantic sequences, trying to maintain stability.

Tony was hurled against his harness and thrown back into his seat. The Micro rolled and fell and soared. The storm swept it along, a steel bubble in a sea of fire.

Morley's running account was broadcast from the Micro to a Comsat, relayed to his New York studio, where it was combined with the network signal and returned to Tony's console. But the signal, not surprisingly, had died. The monitor carrying the Transglobal telecast was a blizzard of interference. Tony thought about informing the journalist he was no longer getting through, that he might as well give it up, but decided to say nothing. It kept Morley occupied, and maybe served as a link to safety for the others.

"Engine overheating," said Saber.

"Roger." Let it overheat. They'd be lucky if that was the worst that happened.

Something inside let go with a bang.

"Passenger cabin," Saber told him. "CDS." That was the Coolant Delivery System. Nothing to worry about.

A tentacle of melted rock splashed across the blister. The glass began to bubble. Tony opened his channel to cargo. "Bigfoot, you okay?"

"Great ride, Tony."

"Doing what I can. We're almost out of it."

Saber glanced at him. The world outside was full of fire. "What makes you say that?"

"One way or another. We can't take much more of this."

"Engine's in the red," she said.

He couldn't shut down. The Micro needed two-point-four kps to avoid falling back to the surface. Acceleration was passing two-point-zero. He watched it climb, not knowing whether there was a surface to fall back *to*, suspecting he'd be carried along with the blast whatever he did.

Two-point-two.

The storm clattered and banged and raged against the hull.

He'd have to cut power once he reached escape velocity. Or risk losing the engine and possibly the ship.

"Tony, we're pushing it."

"Don't worry," he said. "There's always a certain amount of leeway built into these things."

Two-point-three.

Red lamps were blinking all across the status board.

Two-point-four. Tony gave it another minute and killed the engine.

Riding now in relative quiet, they listened to the storm beating against the hull, the squeals of the status board, and the electronic burble of the instruments.

Saber picked up the mike. "Everybody okay down there?"

Evelyn's voice responded: "Alive and well."

"Good. Stay with it. We know it's loud but we're doing okay." She explained why they'd shut the engine down. "But we're still moving. We'll relight in a few minutes and begin to accelerate again."

At that moment the flames fell away, and the Micro rose above great, dark, boiling clouds. A river of light exploded from one and arced gracefully across Tony's field of vision.

Then he was out among the stars. Earth, blue and serene, floated almost directly ahead.

Saber sighed happily.

"Too soon," he said.

To underscore the point, a slab of rock the size of a pickup spun out of a dark cloud and took off an auxiliary antenna. It would have done much worse, but Tony reacted quickly and rolled away.

•   •   •

SSTO *Arlington* Flight Deck, 20,000 kilometers from Luna.
10:36 P.M.

The leading edge of the blast was expanding at almost three hundred kilometers per second. Two other spacecraft were in its path, *Arlington*, a little over an hour away; and *Rome*, which had gotten about a six-hour start.

There hadn't been much George Culver could do to protect his plane other than put as much distance as he could between himself and the Moon. The short, stubby wings that supported the SSTO in atmospheric flight had retracted, antennas were down, passengers had been warned of approaching turbulence.

In this case, the term was a mild understatement. Behind them, the entire universe seemed to have lit up.

Mary wiped her lips with the back of her hand. "I don't know," she said, watching it roll toward them.

They'd stayed too long. There hadn't been enough time to get everybody off, but no one had wanted to admit it. They should have left with Rome, *just cut their losses and gone. But who was going to make that kind of decision?*

"Hang on." It was all George could think of to say in the instant before the wave washed over them.

AstroLab. 10:37 P.M.

The AstroLab was located in central Massacusetts, not far from the Quabbin Reservoir. It was housed in one of those garish ultramodern steel and glass abstract buildings, designed to demonstrate a kind of mathematical flow but which really only succeeded in marring the landscape. It would have looked good on Boston's Commercial Street. But among lakes and forest it was an abomination. It reminded Wes Feinberg of a swirl of lime Jell-O.

At the critical moment in the event, Feinberg did something that those who knew him well might have predicted: He left the turmoil of the Astrolab, where his colleagues were crowded breathlessly around the main display, watching raw data flow in through radio, infrared, and X-ray telescopes, from ACCD's CMM photon counting systems, and UV detectors. And he wandered out to the north walkway.

It was a cool night, and he was glad he'd worn his woolen sweater. He pushed his hands into his pockets and looked out over the trees. Where the Moon had been, there was now a blood-red cloud, lit by inner fires. It was expanding and it cast a ruddy glow across the forest.

The facility had filled up and overflowed with people from coastal areas and with some locals who sensed it was the right place to be on this night. Feinberg had talked with several. None admitted to believing there was serious danger to the world; yet here they were, well inland. *Better safe than sorry*, they told him. The American motto: *Safety first.*

He could see flashlights in the parking lot. People were herding together, watching the event, ooohing and aaahing. Cries of "Look at that," and "It's beautiful" filled the night air. Campfires burned in the surrounding hills and back on the picnic grounds. There were occasional flashes as people tried to take pictures of the event.

SSTO *Rome* Passenger Cabin, 143,000 kilometers from Luna. 10:38 P.M.

Tashi Yomiuri had thought about trying the stunt that Keith Morley had pulled, but in the end, prudence had held sway. Now, watching the eruption on her monitor, she knew she'd made the right choice to put a decent amount of distance between herself and that inferno. Morley's broadcast had just been cut off at the source, and while Bruce Kendrick talked as if contact would be restored momentarily, Tashi believed that her colleague was gone. Posthumous Nobel? Maybe. Probably. But it wasn't the price *she* was prepared to pay.

There'd been a Pool arrangement, and all networks had

been carrying the Morley report. But her producer back in New York had alerted her to be ready to go, now that Morley would no longer be a factor. "We'll want a blow-by-blow of what's happening," he'd said. "You're as close as anybody." He sounded exhilarated. "What can you see? What are the reactions of the passengers? Anybody breaking down?"

She didn't really know what was happening. The only view she had of events was what the networks were providing. A few minutes earlier she'd seen a flash outside her window, like summer lightning, but now there was nothing except a glow on her raised tray. Earlier, she'd interviewed Rick Hailey, the vice president's press advisor, who was up in the front of the plane. But it had been relatively tame. Hailey was too old a hand to say anything out of the way. The government would respond appropriately, he assured her, the nation was fortunate to have strong leadership at this critical juncture. That sort of thing.

She'd gotten a far better interview from Slade Elliott. He'd surprised her by admitting that, sure, he was scared, wasn't everybody, but he'd talked to the pilot, John Verrano, and Verrano seemed both competent and confident.

Would he like to have *Shadow* along this time? *Shadow* was the self-aware TV starship in which Captain Pierce and his oddball crew roamed the galaxy. "Sure," he grinned. "This kind of flight would be small potatoes for *Shadow*."

Tashi also recognized two of Charlie Haskell's Secret Service detail, the big one they called Sam, and an attractive young woman who looked like innocence personified.

There'd been some empty seats on the plane, so Yomiuri had been able to keep access to the aisle. She had a camera, and if the spacecraft started to rock, she'd get some good coverage and maybe come out of this pretty well after all.

Within minutes after Morley's signal had been lost, they

brought her up live on the Pacific News Network. She described the mood in the plane, making much of it up because there was no unified mood. Some people were merrily oblivious to the danger, others were terrified. But Tashi painted a picture of passengers hanging tough because it made good press, and because it wasn't that far from the truth anyhow, if you could draw a line more or less down the middle.

She was interrupted by the PA: "This is the captain. Ladies and gentlemen, we'll probably be doing some maneuvering during the next few minutes. It might get a little rough; we expect it'll be something like running through a storm. I want to assure you, however, that you're in a very well built plane, and we'll come out of this in good shape. Meanwhile, I'd like you to secure any loose articles so they don't injure you or anyone else. Please be sure your tray is up, and everything not fastened down is in an overhead bin. We'll let you know when we've gotten through this."

Yomiuri took a deep breath and went back to her play-by-play. Her earphones pinged and her producer spoke to her: "Tashi, we're going to switch over to the Pool."

She would be going global. "Okay," she said.

"In one minute. Clyde Sommer's your anchor. FYI, as far as we can determine, nobody's reestablished contact with the Micro or with the other plane."

That produced a chill. "I'm sorry to hear it."

"It's likely just the general turbulence. Maybe they're okay, maybe not. We expect to lose you in a couple of minutes, too. Your signal, that is."

Her heart skipped an extra beat. "Right," she said.

"Twenty seconds."

"Okay. I'm ready to go."

She listened to the countdown in her earphones, imagined Clyde Sommer, the network anchor, seated at the prime desk in New York. Just before she went on, she removed the right earphone and slid it up on her head so she could hear what was going on around her. "This is Tashi Yomiuri, on board a space plane approximately ninety thousand miles from what used to be the Moon. We are currently running at about fifteen thousand miles an hour before a hurricane of fire. . . ."

CHAPTER SEVEN

TRIGGER

1.

Micro Flight Deck. 10:40 P.M.

They'd survived the initial blast. Tony had run with the storm with consummate skill, reigniting the engine at the first opportunity and jinking the bus in ways that its designers would not have thought possible. Watching him, Saber had been grateful that she was riding that night with Tony Casaway.

The initial fury had subsided. They were still taking a lot of hits, but most were glancing shots that banged and clanged and did no serious damage. One tore into a storage compartment belowdecks, but the hatches held; another took out a power conduit and left the passenger cabin in darkness. Fortunately, the occasional boulders that leaped at them out of the dark, and the cascades of melted rock that slashed across the sky, did not have their exact coordinates, and so they lived.

It was as if a wave had passed. The void now was still filled with charging debris. But it was in quantities and at velocities that allowed the sensors to track major threats.

Morley asked whether the Micro had reestablished outside communications yet. The answer was no. "Damn," he said, "this is great stuff." But he added that he wouldn't mind if the excitement died off a little.

Evelyn wondered whether the captain knew the passenger cabin had no lights.

"We know," said Saber. "We'll fix it later. But we're a little preoccupied right now." She was pointing out an incoming fragment while she talked. Tony nodded and moved the Micro out of the way. The fragment was a long, thin sliver, maybe half the length of a football field, tumbling end over end. She heard the reaction in the cabin as it sliced past.

The short- and long-range sensors filled the screens with returns. Sometimes they were rock shards and storms of pebbles and dust; more often they were amoeba-forms that might have been belches of gas or plasma. The viewports revealed mountainous shadows and liquid fire. Occasionally the stars disappeared altogether, as if the Micro were passing down a red tunnel.

They continued to move steadily through the crowded sky at one g.

"Micro, this is Skyport." The voice crackled in his earphones. "Do you read?"

"We copy, Skyport. We are still here."

"What is your status?"

Tony relayed what he knew, fuel usage, damage report, passenger list. "No casualties."

"Micro, we're missing one name."

"Jack Chandler. He didn't make it."

"What happened?"

"Heart attack, we think. Died just before they were scheduled to come on board. His body was left at Moonbase."

The response broke up.

"Say again, Skyport. Do you read?" There was only interference.

Something hit the blister again and was gone too quickly to be seen. It left a crooked star, not unlike the type that a flying rock might put in a windshield.

"We okay?" asked Tony.

The danger was that the blister had to withstand 14.7 pounds per square inch of air pressure. The three decks, cargo, passenger, and flight, were sealed off from each other. So if the worst happened, and the canopy blew out, at least the Micro would only lose its pilots.

Only the pilots.

Saber touched the star with her index finger. She pushed gently at it and traced the individual lines. "I think it's okay," she said.

Micro Cargo Deck. 10:41 P.M.

Like Saber, Bigfoot was still inside his pressure suit. As a precaution, he'd put his helmet back on, but he was having problems with vertigo and got it off again just before throwing up. He'd secured himself to the ladder with his belt; and although the accelerated liftoff wasn't nearly as stressful as it would have been leaving Earth, it was nevertheless not comfortable, and left him with bruised ribs and an aching shoulder that he suspected had been dislocated.

C deck, the cargo deck, was a confined space: it possessed no viewports, and it rocked and fell and twisted until his head spun violently. He wished he'd moved more quickly and got to the passenger cabin.

But it could have been worse: since they were accelerating, the vomit had gone to the deck and wasn't floating around. He grinned and felt a little better.

SSTO *Rome* Passenger Cabin, 145,000 kilometers from Luna. 10:42 P.M.

Rick controlled fear by the simple act of cutting off the cause. His technique in this case consisted of lowering his blind and concentrating on other issues. Specifically, on how well things had gone so far. The vice president had behaved well, and if they all came through it, there would be an appropriate reward. For Rick, that reward would consist not simply in winning the White House in the fall, but in running a campaign for a genuine hero. Charlie Haskell, a long shot in his own party a week ago, was going to be unbeatable.

Haskell was off the Moon, riding a *bus*, for God's sake, and a little one at that. With any kind of luck, communications would be restored, Morley would continue to give Charlie a ton of play, and there'd be brass bands to greet the vice president when he got home.

Rick's juices flowed at the prospect of writing appropriately modest remarks to be delivered to the news services. The phrases were already running through his head: *We were fortunate to be flying with What's-his-name, who's one hell of a pilot or we'd all be dead.* And, *We've taken a heavy loss at Moonbase, there's no doubt of that. But no one's been killed, and that's what counts.* Or, *Yes, we've lost some people, and I'd like to ask you to join me in a moment of silence for these brave heroes who dared to reach for the future. . . .* Charlie was good at this kind of stuff, had a natural flair for it. Probably because he believed it. It was the secret to his success. He was naïve, everybody knew it, even *he* knew it, but it didn't matter. It was all part of his charm. It was what the voters *liked*.

For Rick, it was a clear demonstration of what the game was really about. The media often maintained that campaigns weren't substantive. But the media didn't understand about electioneering. When they complained that issues were seldom discussed, that the debate got too personal, that in the end a fog of obfuscation was thrown over everything, they were missing the point: An election is an art form. Its purpose is not to illuminate the issues of the day, but to box in an opponent. To watch him try to wriggle free of charges and innuendo. It was Charlie's special gift that he could perform the surgery in a friendly, inoffensive, down-home manner. People liked that. They *didn't* like vindictive politicians, or hard chargers.

Something smashed into the spacecraft, and the cabin tilted, first one way and then another. There were startled cries, and Rick white-knuckled the arms of his chair. But the plane straightened out and the pilot came on the speaker: "Nothing to worry about, folks. Just a piece of junk bouncing off the hull. There'll probably be more, but we're doing fine."

Rick forced himself to concentrate on the vice president's arrival at Reagan. He pictured the scene, Charlie coming out of the plane, waving to the crowd, moving to a platform for his remarks.

Politics was a struggle for power, in its purest and simplest terms. If the voters were lucky, the winner would go on to improve their lot, because he would need their votes next time. Or because he enjoyed being popular. But issues were irrelevant. Always had been, probably. Once the age of mass communications arrived, presidents became entertainers, celebrities, if they were smart. FDR used his fireside chats; Kennedy had allowed spontaneous questions at press conferences, relying on wit and charm. Reagan knew from the films exactly how a president should behave, and he had exactly enough acting talent to bring it off. In that sense, he was the first modern president.

It had taken a while for the country to get the point. But it had. Neither Lincoln nor Washington would have had a chance of election during the age of mass communications. And maybe that was just as well. Rick knew that neither would have taken his advice.

SSTO *Arlington* Flight Deck, 23,000 kilometers from Luna. 10:43 P.M.

George would have traded his soul for his old A-77 Blackjack. The space plane simply hauled too much mass, was too sluggish and too big a target.

He'd also discovered a disconcerting illusion. As an essentially earthbound pilot, he was accustomed to a sense of motion in flight: clouds whispering past, Skyport drawing near, Reagan falling away. Out here the environment, even the comet, had been frozen. Nothing ever moved.

Except for the explosive front that had ripped through and tried to tear the plane out of his hands. The tail assembly had been demolished and a rock had punched through one of the overhead compartments. He knew there was hull damage, but not how much. And there was still stuff coming at him. The pieces tended to be bigger than the dust storms and flying rocks in the first wave, but they weren't moving quite as fast now, so he had a better chance of getting out of their way.

He got on the circuit and told his passengers he knew the ride had been rough, but he assured them they would be all right.

Micro Passenger Cabin. 10:44 P.M.

The cabin was quiet. Morley's earlier monosyllabic burble had irritated Charlie, but now he missed it. It had been their last link with the mundane. With the lights gone and the surreal outside world trying to break through the windows, the mundane would have looked pretty good.

Fear was endemic. The vehicle continued to lurch wildly, and the sounds of stress in the bulkheads were all too threatening. Charlie sensed that no one expected to come out of this alive, and there was almost a wish that it should end. Get it over with.

But gradually the motions of the Micro became less severe, and there were extended stretches of relatively unagitated flight.

"Maybe we're through the worst of it," said Morley, seated behind him. They were separated, one in each pair of seats. *To gain maximum balance*, Tony had said. Charlie understood now why he'd wanted every advantage he could get.

"I hope so," Charlie said. Two emergency lamps were on, casting just enough of a pale glow to make out silhouettes. "You okay, Evelyn?"

"Fine." Her voice sounded odd.

He couldn't see her. She was behind him on the other side of the aisle.

The chaplain announced he was okay just as the Micro pitched forward and rolled. Charlie's harness grabbed at his shoulder. His stomach squeezed down into a dark wet place as the craft kept turning, and he gripped the sides of the chair. A shadow fell across his window and he looked out, saw only darkness crosshatched by fire. Morley yelped, the first indication of fear the journalist had shown. Charlie was pleased to see he was human. It was annoying to be caught in a desperate situation with someone who seemed unbothered by the hazards. *With the microphone,* Charlie thought, *Morley somehow transcended events, looked in on them from outside. Now it's gone, disconnected, and he's just like the rest of us.*

"Did you see *that*?" Morley was staring out the window and his voice was pitched an octave higher than the rich baritone with which Transglobal viewers were familiar.

"Yeah," said Charlie. He hadn't, not really. But they were cruising again and that was all he cared about.

SSTO *Rome* Flight Deck, 146,000 kilometers from Luna. 10:45 P.M.

Verrano never saw the rock. It glided out of the random clutter on his screens and nailed the number two engine. *Rome* shuddered, the fuel line sealed off, and the engine shut down. The spacecraft went into a slow spin. Before he could get it under control, his copilot whispered a warning: "Big one coming."

He went throttle up with everything he had.

The thing was behind them, barreling in, and he discovered that his rear opticals were gone, so he couldn't see it. But he *felt* its presence, estimated its size from the radar returns at several hundred meters. A mountain.

The changing radar image suggested it was spinning.

In the passenger cabin, Rick Hailey's heart was pounding furiously. He was pressed back hard in his seat, his eyes closed, listening to the crackle of debris raining off the hull, trying to think how he could put this experience into one of Haskell's speeches. But he knew this was a critical moment, had heard the change in tone in the engines, had felt the sudden jerky turns, and knew the pilot was trying to evade *something*.

Several seats behind him, the TV correspondent was still talking into her microphone. Behind and on his left sat Sam Anderson and Isabel. Slade Elliott was back toward the rear of the spacecraft. Captain Pierce, skipper of the *Shadow*, survivor of a hundred desperate encounters.

But not this one.

The world broke open and a terrible cold seized Rick's throat. He died wondering whether Charlie Haskell would be able to pay him an appropriate tribute.

Micro Flight Deck. 10:48 P.M.

"I think we're okay."

Saber cringed when he said it, knew instinctively that the remark would be unlucky. It sounded too much like an epitaph. And she was right.

The long-range scanners hadn't been worth a damn. There was simply too much free-floating junk in their rear, all of it coming too fast. The radar had settled down, was pinging more or less steadily, and then immediately after Tony's remark erupted into a cacophany of pings and bleeps.

"Son of a bitch," said Tony.

It looked like a solid wall coming up from behind. "Range two k," she said. "Closing at one-two-five." Kilometers per hour.

They had about a minute.

The wall shut off everything; it was a dark sandstorm. She could see no end to it in any direction.

Tony, knowing he couldn't outrun it, shut down the engine, rotated the clusters, and fired, changing the attitude of the bus. Then he relit, hoping to get above it, but Saber knew he wasn't going to make it. She picked up the mike: "Brace yourselves."

The SSTOs were more solidly built than the Micro, but their real advantage in this kind of situation was their capability to pile on the coal. The bus had only two speeds: one g and glide. It was the equivalent of trying to run from an avalanche in a potato sack.

Tony readjusted their angle at the last moment and cut power, turning the bus to face the storm. Keep the junk out of the engine.

It hit. Metal screeched, and a hurricane of rock and debris blasted the hull. An explosion rocked the Micro and sent it into a tumble. Klaxons sounded and red lamps blinked. Then as quickly as it had come, it was gone, leaving them spinning in its wake.

Saber needed a moment to clear her vision. When she did, Tony was trying to talk to Bigfoot over the intercom. And getting no answer.

She looked at the status board.

The cargo deck had been holed.

"My God," whispered Tony. "Was he in his suit?"

He'd still been wearing the helmet last time she'd seen him. "It might be the radio," she said.

Maybe.

A second warning blinker claimed her attention. "Losing air." Her voice tightened. "C deck again. Looks as if the line's blown." She closed it off, also effectively shutting down the oxygen supply for the rest of the vehicle.

Tony continued calling Bigfoot's name until Saber asked him to stop. "When we're reasonably clear," she said, "we'll have to go EVA." Can't wait too long. There'll be an air problem.

His gaze traveled down to her p-suit. "Where's your helmet?"

Where *was* it? She couldn't remember. She'd taken it off as soon as they were through the lock. Had carried it with her. She looked around the flight deck but didn't see it. They exchanged uncomfortable glances. If it was still in the cargo section, there'd be no way to make repairs.

She was out of her chair, searching furiously through cabinets and utility drawers. When she found nothing, she opened the hatch to the passenger cabin, saw the darkness below, snatched up a torch, and dropped down the ladder. "Everybody okay?" she asked, trying to mask her concern.

"Yeah," said the vice president. "We're fine. What's going on?"

She flashed the beam around the compartment. "Anybody see a helmet?"

"You mean this?" Keith Morley held it up so she could see it. "You gave it to me as you ran by."

Thank God. "Thanks, Keith." Dropping her professional demeanor, she hugged him.

"Saber." Charlie's voice had steel in it this time. "What's happening?"

She explained that the lower deck had been punctured. "We'll have to go outside to fix it."

"Outside?" said Morley. "In *this*?"

She nodded. "We've shut down life support temporarily. If it starts getting a little close in here, oxygen masks will drop from the ceiling. Use them."

"What about Bigfoot?" asked Evelyn.

She shook her head. "No way to know," she said, taking the helmet and starting back up the ladder. "We'll pass the word as soon as we do."

She closed the hatch behind her. "You think we can try this now?" she asked Tony.

The radar screen was quiet again.

The passenger compartment had a dozen masks, far more than enough to wait out a rescue coming from Moonbase or L1. Waiting would have been standard procedure last week. Keep the passengers safe, and sit tight till help gets there. That was the credo. But conditions had changed.

"We've got another problem," Tony said. He was digging into the equipment cabinet, from which he produced a wrench, a couple of screwdrivers, a bar, a torch, and two rolls of duct tape. "The airlock down there's got a trouble light. Outside hatch doesn't respond." He looked up to see Saber putting on her helmet.

"Not now," he said.

"You want to wait?"

"Yeah. We've got time. Let's wait till it gets a little less crowded out there."

"Okay. That makes sense."

"There's something else."

"What?"

"You're not going."

"Why not? I don't think we should chance losing the pilot."

"Hell, Saber, that's not the point. We might need some muscle to get the hatch open. You don't have a lot of heft."

Quebec. 10:56 P.M.

Twenty-one minutes into the event, streaks of light were seen over Saguenay Provincial Park in Quebec. It was the first recorded sighting of impact debris.

2.

SSTO *Arlington* Passenger Cabin. 10:57 P.M.

Andrea Bellwether had relaxed somewhat after those early terrifying minutes. She'd been literally paralyzed by fear, unable to stop imagining what it would be like if one of the rocks struck the plane, splitting it open and dumping her and her seat into the void. She'd never thought of herself as a coward. There'd been times during her life when she'd stood up to be counted, when she'd confronted bullies, and even once a mob when an IRA demonstration had turned ugly in London. But this was different, and she was left weak and shaken in the aftermath.

If the fire had not entirely drained from the sky, at least it seemed to have subsided, and the constant hammering and banging on the hull had stopped. Periodically the captain spoke to them, reassuring them. Just now she needed to be treated like a child. *Pat me on the head and tell me it's okay.*

Skyport Orbital Lab. 10:59 P.M.

Tory Clark was connected to a vast array of instruments in space and around the world, and data were pouring in. Windy Cross had gotten so excited, he'd forgotten his outrage at her. They were getting magnificent images, and the circuits were filled with excited voices. Infrared scans had penetrated the fireball. As predicted, the impact had shattered the Moon, had literally broken it apart. Pieces the size of Texas had torn loose and were adrift. It was too soon to ascertain where they were going, but theory suggested most of the debris would spread out at about the present lunar radius, with most of it remaining along the orbital line.

Some had argued that even if the comet did break up the Moon, gravity would soon draw the sphere back together. Looking at the images, Tory didn't think that was going to happen. Not now, and probably not in the foreseeable future.

At this point, one thing seemed certain: The world had received a scare, an object lesson far more impressive than the one Shoemaker-Levy 9 had delivered thirty years ago. Maybe Skybolt, which would be able to defend the planet with an array of chemical oxygen iodine lasers, would now become a popular cause. Moreover, Tomiko had demonstrated that we could not rely on having a year or two to get ready for an impact.

It struck her that losing the Moon might not be a bad trade-off if we got lucky and the Earth escaped without serious damage, provided we applied the lessons. Provided we made preparations for the next time.

Her displays carried images of the boiling cloud from several of the orbiters, from Mount Palomar, from Whipple and Kitt Peak.

One of her telltales began to blink furiously.

"POSIM-1," said Windy.

POSIM was *Possible Impactor*, the agreed term assigned to objects that might strike Earth. The determination that an object was potentially hazardous was made after evaluating approach angle, size, estimated mass, and velocity.

Tory tagged it for the Houston threat assessment unit. Houston might request more imaging, infrared, whatever; they might dismiss it as a nonthreat; or they might confirm and send out a warning to the good people of Tuscaloosa to clear out of town. It was going to be a nerve-wracking process because nobody knew in advance how fast the fragments would be coming, how many there might be, what would disintegrate and what wouldn't.

POSIM-1 was sixty meters in diameter, approaching at 180 kilometers per second. The front of the blast wave was just now approaching, and they were seeing mostly pebbles, gas, and dust. And a few rocks. POSIM-1 was the exception. Its trajectory would take it into the atmosphere at a wide angle, subjecting it to almost maximum friction before it hit ground. *If* it hit ground.

Tory watched a confusion of blips spreading across the displays. She wondered whether the instruments would be able to sort out the big rocks from the assorted rubble.

Houston responded to the hit: POSIM-1 would come to ground in the interior of South America, in the Gran Chaco Region. But not enough of it would remain to do serious damage, other than maybe scare a few cattle. Disregard.

POSIM-2 was slightly smaller, but on a tighter angle. Into the Pacific. Again, not big enough to do any damage.

At Zelenchukskaya, in the Caucasus, they were following the action. Someone, apparently annoyed that Skybolt had never been built, suggested sending the politicians up to beat the POSIMs off with sticks.

Radar put one fragment at a diameter of two hundred meters. But it did not get a POSIM listing because it was going to sail past the planet altogether and go into solar orbit.

The common wisdom was that the big stuff, if any was en route, would be moving more slowly and would therefore arrive later.

There had been speculation that nuclear missiles were being readied, but Tory knew there was no time for targeting. It was all happening too fast. They were just going to have to sit back and let events take their course.

The alarm sounded again.

"POSIM-3," said Windy.

Point Judith, Rhode Island. 11:26 P.M.

Luke Peterson had followed the reports coming in from the moon ships and around the globe. He'd felt a wave of regret when they lost contact with the vice president's party, and again later when the space plane had disappeared.

Transglobal's Bruce Kendrick had explained on both occasions that the LTA and NASA were still optimistic, and believed the problems resulted from the communications breakdowns one would expect under these conditions. Luke stayed with them for another half hour or so, but there was no more word on Haskell or the missing plane. When they started interviewing another astronomer about comets, he shut off the TV, made a rum and Coke, and walked out onto his front porch.

The Moon, or the object that had *been* the Moon, was visible up over the trees on the west side of the house. It looked like a bilious, red-flecked cloud, and it cast a sanguine light across his garage and driveway. His gray coupe, parked in front, had acquired a bloody hue that chilled him.

Beyond the dunes, the Atlantic lay quiet in a rising tide. Lights moved in the channel. A destroyer, possibly. Headquarters for the Atlantic Destroyer Fleet was located at Newport, as it had been as far back as Luke could remember, and the ships often made training runs out to Block Island.

A buoy clanged.

He and Ann had spent numberless evenings out here in the early years of their marriage. It was easy to imagine her spirit still hovering over the place, whispering to him in the running of the tide. She'd grown up in Woonsocket, an old mill town, and when he'd brought her to Point Judith, it was as if she'd arrived in India. *You're more interested in the ocean that you are in me*, he'd told her. And she'd laughed and thought about it. *It's all the same*, she'd said. *I can't imagine you anywhere else.*

Nor I, you.

The phone rang. But he wasn't in a mood to talk to anyone at the moment. He listened until it stopped, and then he listened to the voices, his on the recorder, and Del Clendennon's on the phone, asking him to call when he had a minute. That would be about the Wednesday night poker session. On or off? Probably on. They'd all be back in town by then.

The destroyer's lights were far out. If Luke had been watching closely, he might have noticed that they'd begun to rise, and kept rising. But he *was* looking at them a moment later when they abruptly went out, as if something had passed between them and the shore.

The telephone began to ring again.

Carlisle, Pennsylvania. 11:28 P.M.

Rain continued to fall, and the night remained overcast. Archie, who'd wanted to watch the show in the sky, was disappointed. He went out onto the deck and stared up at clouds and frequent lightning.

A stone mansion with turrets stood across the street wrapped in the dark. Lights blazed in the lower windows, and the turrets leaped into view with each lightning flash.

In the living room, the Esterhazys were watching a police show. He stayed outside and settled down to listen to the storm. After a while the front door opened and Claire joined him.

"Looks like the trip was pointless," she observed.

"Why do you say that?"

She shrugged. It seemed like such an ordinary night. "It's been an hour," she said. "Nothing's going to happen in Jersey."

"Yeah. Well, good." He did feel better, under the clouds.

She sat down in a rocker. "I can't imagine a piece of the Moon falling on anybody. Although I wouldn't mind if a chunk of it came through the ceiling in there and conked the Esterhazys."

Archie nodded. "I was thinking about trying to find a motel tomorrow. I can't stand another night with these people." Idly they watched a van drive down the street and pass in front of the house.

"If nothing's happened by tomorrow, we ought to be able to go back, shouldn't we?"

Before he could answer, her eyes widened and she looked up past his shoulder. He turned to see what had caught her attention. The dark skies were flickering, not in the rhythmic way that suggested more lightning, but in spasms. Abruptly a fireball streaked out of the overcast skies, came in over the trees, and plowed directly into the stone house. Archie was blown out of his chair. The world exploded around him, something knocked the wind out of him, and he went down in a fetal position listening to the roar go on and on. Small fires were burning everywhere, the deck had collapsed, and the van lay on its side in flames.

Slowly he got to his hands and knees. At that moment, he felt no pain, although his left shoulder had gone numb.

He didn't see Claire anywhere. The front door jerked open and Jeff Esterhazy's head popped out. He delivered a string of expletives, the only profanities Archie had heard from him. The mansion, its lawn, the iron fence that lined the front walk, and the street with its elms, had disappeared into a hole. A plume of black smoke rose over the scene. The van exploded, sending fire cartwheeling into the trees.

"What happened?" demanded Esterhazy in a tone that suggested Archie was responsible.

"Don't know," he said.

The front window was blown in. Inside, he heard Mariel: "Don't touch her," and "Are you okay, Claire?"

A second fireball floated down out of the clouds, lit up the entire landscape for miles, and landed out to the east somewhere with a distant *whump*. More flames leaped into the sky.

"My God." Esterhazy stepped through the door, let it close behind him, and walked to the edge of the porch. "Look what it's done to the property."

Archie never heard the third one come in.

•   •   •

Point Judith, Rhode Island. 11:30 P.M.

Luke could not account for the sudden uneasiness that settled over the house. It might have been the sense that he was alone, or virtually alone, in town. It might have been the accumulated drama of the evening's events, his concern for the people in the moon ships. It might have been an intensified perception of the sea that crouched only eighty yards from his front door.

The TV was muttering quietly in the living room. Luke had turned it back on and was looking for another snack, planning to stay up late and watch the news reports, knowing he wouldn't sleep no matter what. He'd just put on a fresh pot of coffee when he became aware of a new sound.

He listened, not able to place it, and went back out onto the front porch. The tide had gone out, and that was strange because it was supposed to be coming *in*. It was so far out that the water line was in darkness.

My God.

He hurried inside, grabbed his keys off the bookcase, thought about what else he should try to salvage, decided there was no time (although he sensed a degree of safety within the house), and sprinted for the car. The engine roared into life on the first try. He threw a U-turn and took off north on 108, past the beaches.

He floored the pedal, wondering how he could have been so complacent, so *dumb*. His rearview mirror showed neither stars nor sky. It was black back there, and the darkness *moved*.

He was past eighty-five, faster than he thought the car would go, when it caught him.

3.

Coast Guard Cutter *Diligent*. 11:32 P.M.

Dilly was in open water, about fourteen nautical miles southeast of Rockaway Inlet, outward bound with lookouts posted fore and aft and on both beams. Captain Bolling had been advised to put at least a hundred twenty feet of water under his keel. They were at ninety now.

His crewmen could not keep their eyes off the luminous cloud that had replaced the Moon. There was an unusual mood on the cutter. Bolling had seen his coasties in difficult situations, had seen them work to rescue the survivors of a yacht swamped by high seas, had seen them face down drug runners at night. This was different: They were quiet, thoughtful, intimidated. The usual banter that accompanied forays into risky situations was gone. Tonight they simply manned their stations and kept a weather eye on the sky.

Dilly's messenger appeared at his side, holding out a transmission. Bolling took it, glanced at it, and handed it without comment to Packard.

POSIM 06 APPROX 41°N LAT, 73°W LONG——ETA 140440Z.

"That's right down our stack," said the exec. He exchanged glances with Bolling. "Extra lookouts?" he suggested.

"I think it's time." The captain looked at his radar operator. "Keep on the scope, Ramsey. Anything unusual, anything at all, don't keep it to yourself."

Packard summoned the crew chief and passed the order. A minute later, more coasties with binoculars appeared on deck. "It shouldn't be hard to spot," observed the exec, scanning the skies.

The sea smelled clean and fresh. Bolling loved it out here, away from the greasy odors of the East River and Long Island Sound. If he'd been independently wealthy, he'd have bought a yacht and spent his life at sea. It had been a boyhood dream, and the Coast Guard was as close as he'd been able to come.

"There," said Packard. A long narrow light creased the

clouds dead ahead. Coming down. Pieces exploded away from it, and then it was gone, leaving only a few glimmers. "Didn't look like much, Skip." His voice reflected his conviction that he'd known all along they were on a fool's errand.

"If that was it, Dan," said Bolling, "it's running early." He scribbled the time and position of the sighting on a message sheet and sent it to the radio room for transmission.

The exec's face was blue in the subdued light of the bridge. A second streak trailed across the sky and winked out. The water was dead black. "They look like ordinary shooting stars to me," he said.

"I hope so." Bolling keyed the radio room. "What are you hearing?" he asked Herb Bitzberger, the operator.

"Nothing out of the way, Skipper," Bitzberger said. "The ships are talking to one another, but it's the usual kind of chatter."

"Anything from Breakwater?" Breakwater was Coast Guard Activities Command, New York.

"Negative, sir. They're quiet."

Bolling could see the lights of freighters strung out along the horizon.

"Coming up on a hundred feet, sir," said the helmsman.

"Very well," said Packard. "Steady on course. Reduce speed to one-quarter."

The boat settled into the water and the throb of the twin engines subsided. Bolling and Packard had agreed that the best course of action, once they were safely on station, was to assume there would be a major emergency, and to preserve fuel while simultaneously maintaining some headway. This was to prevent being capsized should a wave appear at short notice. Neither of the two had any experience with tsunamis. Nor did anyone else they knew. But Bolling had done some research. The books said there was nothing to fear in deep water. Tsunamis are barely noticable until they move into coastal areas or shallows, where the water tends to bunch up. Of course, *Diligent* wasn't exactly in *deep* water.

Another glowing track appeared in the sky. Coming their way. It got big, got *bigger*, and finally exploded and rained fire onto the sea. "Some of those hit the water," said the exec.

Bolling didn't think so. It was hard at night to know where anything was.

Fresh coffee came up from below. The crewman reported that contact had been reestablished with the moonbus carrying the vice president. "They aren't broadcasting from the bus itself," he explained. "But they say they're tracking them on radar."

Bolling was pleased to hear it. He liked Haskell. But more to the point, he thought that the nation would look bad if it couldn't rescue its number two executive from a disaster they'd seen coming for five days.

Another message came up from the commcenter:

TSUNAMI STRUCK COAST FROM NEW LONDON TO
MARTHA'S VINEYARD, NANTUCKET, AND THE CAPE.
140430Z. DETAILS TO FOLLOW.

How big? How much damage?

They picked up Transglobal coverage of the wave off the satellite. First reports were sporadic, but Bolling wondered whether the alarmists might not have been right after all. He snapped on the intercom and told his people what he knew. "We'll pass along whatever else we get as it comes in," he concluded.

They maintained a southeasterly course, beneath a now-quiet sky. Their depth reached one hundred twenty feet. The wind began to blow and the water started getting choppy.

At 1139 hours he was handed a general broadcast message from an oil tanker:

TEXACO QUEEN REPORTS SEA WAVE NORTHBOUND
40.7°N LAT, 71.8°W LONG—APPROACHING COAST.

He hardly needed to look at a chart; more trouble for
Rhode Island.

"Pass it to the station," he said.

"We've done that, Captain," said the messenger.

Bolling raked the horizon with his night glasses. It was
flat as a pancake.

Another fireball raced silently out of the clouds to starboard. The sea turned red in its glow. It passed overhead,
throwing off streamers, and plunged into the sea. A thunder-
clap broke over them. The sound had barely died to echoes
before the last of the fragments had fallen a few points to port
and the world was dark again.

"I've got the con, Dan," said Bolling. "Helmsman, come
to port fifteen degrees. All ahead standard."

"Aye aye, Captain."

He scribbled a quick description of what they'd seen and
handed it to the messenger. "Add our position and send it," he
said.

The cutter dipped into a deep trough.

"Captain?" Ramsey, on radar. "Look at this."

They were getting a solid reading almost dead ahead. It
looked as if a wall had been built across the ocean.

"It just *appeared*," he continued. "Range, six miles."

"Helmsman, make your course one-zero-zero. Right into it."

One of the forward lookouts shouted "Wave!" and pointed.

Bolling stared at it through his glasses. It looked *big*.

"Everybody tie down!" shouted the exec.

"Flank speed," said Bolling. "Let's put our lights on it."

Twin halogen lamps came on and their beams stabbed
through the night.

The cutter leaped forward.

"Three miles," said Willoughby.

It was visible now, a vast rolling surge without a crest.

"My God," said Packard, "I thought you said we didn't need to worry about anything like this in open water."

"Complain when we get home," he said. "Hang on." They tied the wheel down to ensure they stayed on course, and then he directed all crewmen to lash themselves to their positions. He followed his own instruction and watched Packard do the same.

Then it was on them, a dark roiling mountain. *Dilly* rode up its face. Bolling lost his balance and fell against the bulkhead. The prow bit into the ocean, and water thundered across the deck and crashed through the bridge. He was thrown down hard and lost track of direction, and for a terrible moment thought they were going to capsize, maybe *had* capsized. The ocean boiled around him. Then they hovered on the crest of the wave and the boat's lights looked down into a bottomless trough and lost themselves in mist.

Dilly slipped into the trough. It seemed to Bolling that they were free-falling, and the fall went on and on. Water roared over his head, and then it was gone and he was trying to wipe his eyes clear and get the sea out of his throat.

"You okay, Captain?" shouted Packard.

Their lights played across a churning sea.

"I'm fine. Radar?"

"It's out, Captain," said Ramsey. *"Blown."*

The helmsman was dazed. Packard took the wheel. Bolling could see nothing immediately threatening. He keyed the intercom. "Radio room."

"Aye, Captain."

"Get a message to Breakwater. That wave was forty feet. It's moving west northwest, approximately two-zero-zero knots."

"Aye, sir."

Bolling knelt beside the helmsman, but looked up at his exec. "We need a head count, Dan," he said. "Let's make sure we've still got everybody."

CNN NEWSBREAK SPECIAL REPORT. 11:33 P.M.

"This is Mark Able in the mobile unit above Groton, Connecticut. The lights are out down there and we can't see much yet, but here's what we know: A giant wave went through here a few minutes ago. There's heavy flooding on the ground. We can see overturned rail cars. There's debris everywhere, as if a big tornado had hit the area. Downtown is just flattened. John, I've never seen anything like this. It's just awful. There's nothing moving on the Connecticut Turnpike at all. And as far as I can see, there aren't any cars on it anywhere. There are some overturned vehicles north of the highway. And yes, John, I think that's what happened: The wave just swept the road clear.

"We have no estimates yet as to casualties, but I can't believe anyone down there could have lived through this. A couple of army helicopters have just arrived and are using spotlights to look for survivors. We're going to try to find a place to land, and we'll be staying on top of this developing story.

"Back to you, John."

Manhattan. 11:35 P.M.

The mood at Louise's rooftop party had been going severely downhill for about an hour. Party-goers gathered around the TV to watch pictures from the helicopter. As the images of ruined bridges and mud-covered streets and downed telephone poles continued, there was talk that maybe Manhattan itself wasn't safe.

Marilyn became uneasily aware of their proximity to the Atlantic.

"Maybe," somebody said, "we ought to head out."

"Head out *where?*" asked Marvin. "We're four stories *up*. Where could you go that would be safer than this?"

Where indeed? Marilyn looked down into the street, which was locked tight with trucks and taxis. They could hear the distant wail of a police cruiser. "Marvin's right," Louise said. "Anybody wants to stay the night is welcome."

Marilyn had spent much of the evening with Marv. It irritated her that her husband showed no sign of jealousy, nor even any indication that he noticed. It struck her as odd that the world seemed to come into clearer focus when she was moderately under the influence. She understood that night with cold clarity that she'd married the wrong person.

Maybe it didn't matter who she'd married. Her husband had been like Marv at one time. She could still remember the nights when they couldn't keep their hands off each other. The marriages of her friends, those that had survived, had all gone much the same way. Dull and listless seemed to be the best you could hope for.

Maybe she needed kids. Maybe this was how it was supposed to be until kids came along.

She was sure of one thing: The talk about tidal waves, and watching people try to get out of town, had all made her think about her own mortality. She wasn't really afraid of death itself. Death was too remote, something that happened to other people. But she knew that the clock was running, that none of the dreams that had brightened her teenage years had come true. Working on idiot manuscripts by other people was less than fulfilling. And she knew no one, not one person, who would be grief-stricken if she died. Her folks, maybe, but they didn't count. Larry would be sad, no doubt. He'd come to the funeral, sniffle at all the right moments, bounce back, and move on.

Marv.

If something were to happen to her, she wondered whether he wouldn't miss her more than her husband would.

There was a commotion inside, and the news was quickly

passed to the people on the terrace. *They were recommending evacuation of New York.*

She looked out at the Natural History Museum, its congeries of dull brick buildings spread across several blocks.

Below, along 77th, people were blowing their horns.

TRANSGLOBAL SPECIAL REPORT. 11:36 P.M.

"This is Bruce Kendrick in our Syracuse studios. We have more information now on the events at Carlisle, Pennsylvania, where Angela Shepard is standing by. Angela, what's the situation?"

"Bruce, early estimates are that hundreds died here when at least seven objects struck the ground in and around Carlisle at a little after eleven o'clock this evening. One demolished the center of town, which is now, as you can see, little more than a smoking crater. The town itself has been destroyed. An estimated three thousand victims are being evacuated to area hospitals.

"The Red Cross is setting up an emergency shelter, and the number that's running across the bottom of the screen can be used to get information about relatives. The military responded within minutes and is out in force.

"We're panning the area for you now, and you can see there are fires everywhere. The devastation is unlike anything you'd expect to see in peacetime. Everything's down, power's out, water's out. When we got here, people were wandering the streets, trying to help where they could. One man told us that the meteors just kept coming. Every couple of minutes, he said, another one would fall out of the sky.

"We have a video of one of them. Or we will have in just a moment. It was shot from a passing car in the northern part of town. Okay, there it is. You can see it coming in over the telephone lines. He loses it for a moment here. But there it is again. It looks as if it's approaching at about a forty-five-degree angle. This appears to be the one that hit the center of Carlisle, Bruce."

"Angela, let me break in for a moment. We've just been informed that the president will address the nation in twenty minutes, at eleven-forty-five. This has to be the shortest notice for a presidential address in U.S. history.

"We've also received reports that waves have struck Caracas and Trinidad. Everything so far has been in the Western Hemisphere. I assume that's because this is the part of the Earth that's turned toward the Moon tonight.

"We'll be staying at the Transglobal news desk throughout the night with this developing story. We hope you'll stay with us. Now, while we're waiting for the president's statement, we're going to switch to Charleston, South Carolina, where Peter Barton is standing by. . . ."

4.

Coast Guard Activities, Governors Island, New York.
11:44 P.M.

Captain Lionel Phillips looked up from his desk. The duty officer had burst into his office with a single sheet of paper. "Tidal wave, sir," she said. "Coming this way."

He snatched the paper.

YY 140442Z
FROM: USCGC *DILIGENT.*
TO: BREAKWATER.
SUBJECT: TIDAL WAVE ALERT.
WAVE ENCOUNTERED 41.3°N LAT. 72.8°W LONG. 140440Z X
APPROX FORTY FEET HIGH, SPEED 200 KNOTS RPT 200 X
COURSE TWO-NINE-ZERO.

He looked at it, felt his stomach go cold, and pushed the button. The klaxon began to wail. Everybody out. He'd not believed for a minute any of this sky-is-falling bullcrap, and consequently he'd encouraged his wife to ignore the threat. She was at this moment sitting with their five-year-old grandson in a pleasant Tudor home on Hylan Boulevard off Hugenot

Park on nearby Staten Island. Roughly ten feet above sea level.

The wave was four, maybe five, minutes away.

But thank God he'd been directed to assume the worst *here* and make preparations. "Janet," he said to the officer, "have we sent the general alert?"

"Yes, sir."

"Good. Let's go." He got out of his chair, headed for the door, and grabbed his jacket on the way past the clothes tree. "Everybody out," he said unnecessarily to the four others scrambling to shut down the center. "Go to mobile."

He fished his cell phone out of his pocket, punched his home key, and listened to it ring. His own voice clicked on: *"You've reached Captain Phillips's residence. Speak if you wish."* And the beep.

"Myra," he told it, "for God's sake get out. Wave coming."

Then he was half walking, half running, locking doors as regulations required, listening to the thwip-thwip-thwip of rotors. His people were all out now, scattering across the tarmac and climbing into the chopper. Except Janet, who was drifting behind, keeping pace with him. Damned women. "Go," he told her. She climbed aboard and he followed and the chopper lifted off.

Phillips looked east over the lights of Brooklyn toward the harbor entrance. Everything seemed normal. They activated *Bluebell*, the Coast Guard Command Center Aloft. One of the radio operators signaled for his attention. "Captain," he said, "we've got reports from a couple of merchantmen, too. They're saying more like *sixty* feet."

God help us. He directed the pilot to move south. At the same time, he tried to call home again. Still no luck.

It was on the radio now, all stations warning people to get to high ground.

Phillips was trying not to give in to panic. "Janet," he said, "get me Collins." The FEMA regional director.

Collins already knew, of course. "Doing everything we can," he said. The FEMA director had been another skeptic. "Maybe we'll get lucky," he added. That sounded ominous.

They talked for a minute, and then Phillips tried again to call Myra. This time she answered.

"Whoa, Phil," she said, "slow down."

He was gazing across the bay from about a thousand feet. Lights were moving down there. Two miles ahead, at the Narrows, he could see the Verrazano Bridge.

"Myra, there's a wave coming. Big one. Get out of there. Get on the interstate and head west."

"How big?"

"*Big.*"

"How much time do I have?"

"None—"

The phone went dead. He tried to call her back, but got a recorded message from the telephone company telling him the line was under repair.

Janet stared at him and said nothing.

He was trying to get the operator to check the line when the lights on the bridge blinked off.

SPECIAL BROADCAST FROM THE WHITE HOUSE. 11:45 P.M.

"My Fellow Americans,

"As you are aware, several tidal waves have struck the East Coast of the United States. The collision earlier this evening between the Moon and Comet Tomiko has filled the sky with debris. Pieces of the disintegrating Moon have been falling on land and into the ocean. Waves caused by these objects have struck several of our cities. New Haven, New Orleans, Charleston, have all been hit very hard. Even inland cities have been struck. So far most of the damage has been in the Western Hemisphere, because our side of the globe is presently turned toward the Moon.

"We have reason to believe the worst is over. And the news is not all bad. The West Coast, so far, has been spared. The nation's heartland is almost untouched.

"Tonight we will do what Americans have always done in times of crisis: We will draw together, and we will survive. We will work through this, we will maintain our faith in God, and we will still be here when the Sun comes up."

Later, Henry regretted that last line. Al had resisted it, but the president thought it had power and would become memorable. A line often quoted, and perhaps appealed to in future emergencies.

In fact, he realized too late it sounded unduly pessimistic.

Manhattan. 11:49 P.M.

The sea wave that hit the New York area wasn't at all the type that a lifetime of catastrophe films would have led the party-goers on Louise's rooftop to expect. There was no unfurling of the water, no crest, no foam. Every river and bay in the area simply rose and spilled into Manhattan, Queens, Brooklyn, Staten Island, and the Jersey shore. Standing toward the rear of the crowd gathered around the TV, which flashed pictures shot from helicopters, Marilyn watched the high seas surge forward over wharfs and ferries and riverside roads.

She was sipping her umpteenth daiquiri (a drink she favored because she could put them away all night without visible effect) when it occurred to her that maybe they *were* hitting her hard. The water was coming *here*. And 77th Street was still jammed.

She edged away from the crowd, went back out onto the terrace, and looked down at the traffic. They were bumper to bumper, not moving, a city electrical repair truck, a tanker, a beer truck, a city bus, a police car, a couple of taxis. The doors were popping open and the drivers were climbing out and people were pouring out of the bus and starting to run. But they really had no place to go.

Where was Larry?

Talking to one of the managers. She hurried past him, went out the door and took the elevator down to the ground floor.

She stepped out into a narrow lobby and hurried to the front of the building. Now she could hear screams and shouts outside. And the roar of a helicopter.

She reached the entryway. The inner and outer doors were about eight feet apart and designed for security. But the lock on the inner door would catch once she let it close. She'd be locked out. She looked around for a chair to brace it open, but didn't see one. Back near the elevator, a small table supported a lamp. She put the lamp on the floor, and used the table to guarantee her retreat. Then she opened the front door and looked out into the street.

People were running, walking, hobbling away from the river toward the park. A few sat in their vehicles looking bewildered. She stood on the top step, suddenly aware of a rumble. The ground shook and it felt like an approaching sub-way.

A middle-aged couple in evening clothes were hurrying past. The man looked up and saw her. "Run!" he cried.

The roar was coming from the west, over toward Broadway. And getting louder. People began to scramble out of the bus. Someone fell, but nobody stopped to help. A taxi, trying to get clear of the stopped vehicles, leaped the curb, ran down a young woman, and plowed into a hydrant. Water spouted into the air, gleaming beneath a streetlight.

At the same moment, a black flood turned the corner, roared over trucks and cars, swept away the Breyers Ice Cream signs on the third floor of the Carmody Building. The street-light went out. Air horns exploded.

"This way!" Marilyn called. "Up here!" But her voice was lost in the general chaos.

People streamed past, screaming. Someone was trying to climb atop a bread truck. Marilyn went halfway down the steps, tried to seize a woman's arm to catch her attention, but was pushed aside.

Now someone finally noticed the escape route she was offering: a boy, about ten, with his mother in tow. She thought they'd been on the bus, but she wasn't sure. They were threading their way through the stopped traffic and were still fifteen yards away when he looked up and saw Marilyn holding the door. The woman was terrified. They both called out to her and began to run.

Marilyn measured the distance and knew it would be very close. Their faces filled with fear. The woman tripped and went down, and to Marilyn's horror the boy stopped and ran back. He glanced over his shoulder at her, and she watched, knowing there was no chance. If she waited, the flood would take her, too. The moment congealed, froze before her eyes, the river rising and pouring over the trucks, swallowing everything, and the woman trying to push the boy in her direction. The child was sobbing, tugging at her, and Marilyn pulled the door shut as the water surged past.

The building trembled with the blow. Windows elsewhere in the house exploded and a torrent poured in. More gouted from an electrical fixture. She screamed her frustration and kicked the table away from the inner door, letting it close behind her, and splashed back down to the elevator lobby, the water already ankle deep. She pushed the button and sobbed and waited a long time for the elevator to come. When it did she lunged into it and the lights went out and she was plunged into absolute darkness. The doors started to close and her survival instincts took hold. She blocked the doors, held them open, and squeezed back out into the lobby. When she was clear, she let go, and they shut with a wet clack, but the elevator didn't move.

She stumbled through the dark, trying to remember where the stairs were. The building creaked and seemed to sink. The floor had gotten slippery and the torrent knocked her down.

She struggled to her feet, half swimming. The water swirled around her thighs. Something, a wooden lamp, floated past. She tried to feel her way along the wall. But the wall went on and on and did not open into the staircase. Had it been on the other side? Or was it at the other end of the corridor, near the front door? She couldn't remember, couldn't even be sure where the front of the building was anymore.

She cried out. The water roared. It was at her shoulders now and she was off her feet.

It stank of oil and dead fish and rotted wood. She kicked out of her shoes. Where was Larry? Didn't he even notice for God's sake she was missing?

The flood was coming in so fast now that she couldn't make any headway against it. She found the elevator doors again.

Something bumped her head.

The ceiling.

Somewhere above she heard shouts. Someone calling her name.

She opened her mouth to respond but it filled with water. Then, behind her, she saw light.

It was the stairway. Someone was in the stairway.

"Help!" she cried.

"Over here!" It was Larry!

The stairs had become a waterfall. She pushed toward it, fighting the current, fighting her own exhaustion.

He appeared, carrying a flashlight, hanging on to the handrail. He leaned out and reached for her, caught her.

"What are you doing down here?" he cried.

Under the circumstances it was an incredible question. "Drowning," she said, knowing he couldn't hear her. But he held tight.

Louise found a robe for her and offered her a bedroom. But she was hyper after the experience, despite being cold and bone-weary, and couldn't sleep.

They were alone in the bedroom. Louise had found some extra clothes for Larry too, a size too large, but that hardly mattered. He seemed as shaken by the experience as she, and that perception brought a glow she hadn't known for a long time.

"I thought I was going to lose you." He lay beside her, his features shrouded in shadow. An illuminated clock threw off the only light in the room.

She sank back into the pillows. "It all happened so quickly." She'd been crying and he kept trying to tell her everything was okay, that they were safe now. She hadn't been able to explain about the people on the sidewalk, about the boy and his mother, and every time she tried the tears came again.

"I love you," he said. "I didn't know I was married to a hero."

It wasn't as if he hadn't spoken the words in a long time. He told her religiously, faithfully, every day that he loved her. Much as he always commented that dinner was good. It was a courtesy, extended reflexively. But not this time. His voice sounded strange.

"I love you too, Larry," she said, feeling tides of emotion and remembering that less than an hour before she'd been contemplating the advantages of trading him for Marv.

His free hand insinuated itself into the robe. But she pushed it away and he looked hurt.

"Marilyn," he said again, bewildered, *"It's all right."*

But she was peering through the dark, looking again at the boy, into his accusing eyes. They'd been hazel, she thought. And she knew she'd be seeing them for the rest of her life.

5.

Micro Flight Deck. Sunday, April 14, 2:10 A.M.

"How about the g-suit?"

The *g* stood for gravity, and the suit was a kind of underwear worn inside the pressure suit. It was designed to keep blood from pooling in the extremities under high g-forces. They had only the one Saber had been wearing, now hung in a storage locker. Tony opened the locker and measured himself against the leggings. The suit was several inches too long. "I think I can manage without," he grinned. "Anyway, I'll be out and back in a few minutes."

The air in the cabin had become oppressive at about midnight, and Saber had distributed masks and air tanks. They switched to a second round of tanks just after two o'clock. By then the radar screen was quiet, and Tony decided it would be reasonably safe to venture outside.

He climbed into the p-suit (it too was a bit large), descended to the passenger cabin, and assured everyone there was nothing to worry about. Then he put on the helmet, did a radio check, stepped into the airlock, and closed the inner hatch behind him.

"Tony?"

"Go ahead, Saber."

"We've got a couple of pings on the screen."

"Anything to worry about?"

"Negative. But the neighborhood's not clear."

That was, of course, the danger: If something came at them she'd have to start the engine to evade. It wouldn't be a happy situation with him on the outside. "Okay. Let's get it over with, babe."

The outer hatch opened. He clipped a tether to his belt. The tether would unwind as Tony moved, and it was long enough to allow him to get inside the cargo deck. He snapped the torch onto his wrist, turned it on, reported himself ready to go, and stepped outside. The hatch closed behind him.

The hull was pocked, chipped, and scorched. He surveyed it and shook his head. "We're a little beat up out here," he told Saber.

The C deck airlock was out of sight below the curve of the hull. He pushed off, moved quickly down the face of the bus, aided by strategically placed handgrips. "Down" was the direction of the nozzle, and of the Moon-cloud, which came into view as he neared the cargo deck hatch. He could see the damaged tread floating off its mount like a broken leg. The entire lower section of the Micro had been battered, both by debris and apparently by the broken tread, which might easily strike the vehicle during sudden turns. He'd need to come back and get rid of it.

The hatch itself was bent; nearby, there was a baseball-sized eruption in the hull. A rock had gone in the other side and come out *here*. The metal was seared. Lights were still on inside. "I can see in," he told Saber.

"Do you see Bigfoot?"

"No. But there's something reflective."

"What?"

"It's a plastic bag."

"Oh," said Saber. "He brought a lot of stuff on board in plastic bags."

The bag drifted out of his line of sight, and then he could see only the far bulkhead. "Okay," he said, directing his torch toward the airlock, "time to get to work." He had just started for the hatch when something whispered against his faceplate. It might have been a handful of sand.

"Something just happen?" asked Saber.

"Negative," he said.

"Okay. Try to get inside as quickly as you can."

"Working on it." He reached the hatch control panel,

opened it, and twisted the key. A white lamp blinked on. Good. At least he had power.

He punched the ACTIVATE button and the status display lit up. DEPRESSURIZING, it said. The lamp went to red.

His suit registered a vibration. "More rocks?" he asked.

"Never saw it coming, Tony. Under the radar." The unit just didn't pick up pebbles. "Are you almost in?"

He was watching the display and the hatch. "I'll be inside in a minute."

"Roger."

He was thinking about Bigfoot. They'd never socialized, never spent time together, never even talked much, really. Just to say hello. There was a tendency among the operational types to spend time with their own kind. Tony fraternized with the pilots, and he assumed Bigfoot would have spent his time with flight operations personnel. Or with the managers. Probably the managers. He wondered what he'd been doing when the rock came through the bulkhead, what he'd been thinking. Tony hoped it had been a quick death. But there must have been a few moments. . . .

The status display was still red.

His suit display had no timekeeping mechanism, but the process seemed to be taking a long time.

"Tony?"

"Yo."

"Can you hurry it along?"

"Still recycling."

The red lamp finally went out, and the legend in the display changed: DEPRESSURIZATION COMPLETE.

He shifted his position, hanging on to the grip with his right hand, ready to slip into the airlock as soon as it opened.

But it stayed shut.

"Saber, I don't think this thing's going to work."

"It has to open."

"I'm glad to hear it." He switched to manual, took out the handle, turned it, and pulled.

Nothing.

He shifted his position and tried again. This time he felt something give. "Okay," he said. "Progress that time." He had a little space now between the edge of the hatch and its seating. He pulled the bar out of his belt and worked it into the space and began to lever it back and forth.

"Tony, you need to hurry. We've got stuff coming up on the screen."

"I hear you." He pulled hard.

"Maybe you should come back. Try again later."

He couldn't get good purchase, and when he pushed at the hatch it pushed back. The problem, he decided, was that he was trying to do the job while hanging on to the grip. So he let go, braced both feet on the hull, wrapped both hands around the bar, and pulled. It moved some more.

"It's coming now," he told her.

"Running out of time, Tony."

He set himself and tried again but the bar slipped and he floated away. "Uh-oh," he said.

"Uh-oh? What's uh-oh?"

"I'm adrift."

"Tony? I've got to move."

"Go ahead." He shoved the bar into his belt. "I'll be okay."

The engine lit and the bus leaped away. Tony plummeted backward until the tether caught and dragged him. It was short enough to prevent his getting fried by the main engine. But he crashed hard into the hull and jammed a wrist.

"You still there?" Her voice, worried, in his earphones.

"Yeah." He had to struggle to get the response out, and it occurred to him that he had the only suit. If he got in trouble out here, there was no way anyone could come after him.

"More coming in, Tony," Saber said. "We have to get clear."

"Okay. I'm fine."

Something splashed across his visor.

Liquid. He tried to wipe it away. But nothing happened, and in the strange light his arm didn't look right.

The liquid was coming out of his sleeve and he couldn't see his left hand.

Couldn't *feel* his left hand.

Darkness welled up around the edges of his vision. There was pressure in the sleeve. The suit was sealing.

But the light was slipping away.

Micro Passenger Cabin. 2:31 A.M.

Charlie was well along on his second oxygen tank. There were only a couple more available, which meant, unless they restored life support, they would begin to have problems around four o'clock.

It was impossible to see what was happening from the windows of the passenger cabin. Tony had gone down below the curve of the hull, and they'd heard the banging while he worked on the hatch. Charlie wanted to ask Saber how the operation was going, but he was reluctant to distract her. He'd learned the hard way that ordinary people can ask questions or make complaints and nobody thinks much of it. But a person with political standing becomes a jerk very quickly. So he waited, trading anxious glances with Evelyn, who was also trying to stay out of the way.

Morley sat gloomily, his hands pressed against his oxygen mask. He looked defeated, a sharp contrast to his positive and energetic on-air personality. The chaplain had been trying to adopt a fatalistic attitude to insulate himself against emotional rushes. "Not much we can do except ride it out," he'd say, or, "We're in the hands of the Lord."

They certainly were.

Charlie had been surprised when Saber warned them that

more turbulence was coming. *Turbulence* was a funny name for the rocks he watched whistle past his window. When she'd started the engine and rolled to one side, he'd concluded that Tony must have gotten inside.

But now the engine was quiet again. There was no sound belowdecks, and the Micro rode through an ominous silence.

Evelyn tried to radiate confidence. "It's okay," she said. "They know what they're doing."

Might not make any difference, Charlie thought.

The PA system clicked on, but no one spoke. Evelyn glanced at him again. The delay drew out until Charlie knew it could only be bad news.

The chaplain was peering through his window. "Houston, Houston," said Morley softly, "we have a problem."

The chaplain caught his breath. "Outside," he whispered.

They were dragging Tony at the end of his line. He looked deflated. Inanimate. He was spinning slowly, hands over feet.

As the angle changed, and the illumination from the ship's outboard lamps crept over him, Charlie saw that *Tony's left hand was missing.* At first he thought it was a trick of the light. But it wasn't.

Charlie Haskell wasn't yet old enough to have confronted, before this week, the imminent possibility of personal death. He assumed there'd always be a tomorrow. Now he looked out at Tony Casaway, he thought about Bigfoot in his airless compartment, and he shivered. Casaway had come back for them. Bigfoot had stayed behind to give them a chance.

Charlie was not a believer. He did not expect to be called to account and assigned a score for what he had done or left undone. His parents had believed in a mechanical world, a place of evolving hardware and software, no deities need apply. We just haven't figured it all out yet, his father was fond of saying. Things get more complex and we don't know why. But that doesn't mean we have to ascribe it to divine providence.

Charlie had endured a brief flirtation with Lutherans, as a result of joining a church basketball team. He'd been glad to escape. Later, when he entered politics, he'd been advised to pick a church. Any church. And just show up once in a while. He'd taken the advice and picked several. He could never take them seriously, but he discovered that they became more significant to his success as he moved higher in public office.

In Charlie's view, the bottom line was that if he died out here, it was all over. He envied Mark Pinnacle, who could face the worst dangers with relative equanimity because he believed that Paradise waited beyond the gate. He had only to explain to himself why Jesus had sent the comet. No big deal for a Christian.

For a realist like himself, life was a more complex game, in which one occasionally got run down by the software. Nothing personal.

"I have to tell you," Saber's voice said, breaking through his reverie, "that Captain Casaway is dead. I monitor no life signs from his suit." Her voice trembled.

The chaplain unbuckled and would have gone to her assistance, but Evelyn touched his arm and went up the ladder.

Nobody said much while she was gone. Charlie, Mark Pinnacle, and Morley ostentatiously avoided looking out the window. They heard low, intense conversation on the flight deck.

Morley's gaze touched Charlie's. "He never got to C deck," he said.

Charlie nodded. "I know."

"He didn't get to the air lines."

"I know."

"What are we going to do?"

It was a good question.

•   •   •

Skyport Orbital Lab. 2:33 A.M.

Windy, at the far end of the ops center, murmured an obscenity.

"What?" Tory asked.

"Big one." He pointed, enhanced the image, and brought up its numbers. It was sliced away on one side, as if someone had taken a hot knife to it, cut it the way you might cut a pineapple. It might have been a severed piece of fruit, flat along the bottom, somewhat longish, tumbling end over end and simultaneously rotating on its long axis, which measured—

—*One and a half kilometers.*

"My God," she said.

They relayed the data to their consumers.

It became POSIM-38. And quickly, *the* Possum.

6.

Cliff Beaumont reporting from Miami Beach:

"For God's sake, if you're within the sound of my voice, get under cover." *(Camera reveals a churning sea illuminated by lightning strikes. An enormous black funnel flickers in and out of the picture.)* "This thing will hit Miami Beach in a few minutes. If you have a storm cellar, get to it. If not, look for an interior room. We're several miles away, but we're getting some of the wash and we're going to have to set down. In any case, get out of the open."

AstroLab. 3:11 A.M.

As soon as the data from Skyport firmed up, Wes Feinberg was on the phone to the White House. They'd given him a code so he could talk directly with Mercedes Juarez. That wasn't his preference. Mercedes was too much a respecter of persons and authority. What Feinberg needed was someone who wasn't averse to crashing bureaucratic blockades and going right into the Oval Office. He'd wanted a line to the president (*"Impossible!"*) or at least to Al Kerr (*"Mr. Kerr is an extremely busy man."*). The world might come to an end, but Mr. Kerr would be too busy to notice.

"Can you put me through to the president?" he asked Juarez.

"I would if I could, Professor Feinberg. He's been in the situation room all night."

"Yes. Well, you might tell him he has a situation."

"What precisely is wrong?"

"This would work better if I could speak to him directly. He may have a worst-case scenario."

"You're probably talking about the report that NASA sent over a few minutes ago."

"I don't know. What did the report say?"

"It's classified."

"That makes it hard to talk about it, doesn't it?"

Juarez's tone stiffened. "Professor Feinberg, if you want to give me details, I'll see that they get to him." *Or don't waste my time.*

"All right. We have a big one coming in. Its catalog number is thirty-eight. It's going to pass through the upper atmosphere later this morning. The chances are good it'll slow down enough to go into orbit. If it does, tell him to expect the orbit to decay pretty quickly. What I'm trying to say is that I think the damned thing'll be coming down. You got that?"

For a long minute there was silence on the other end. Then: "How big? When's it coming? Where?"

He wondered what the NASA report had said. "It's one and a half kilometers across. You understand what that means?"

"Yes," she said. "I think so."

"Tell him. If he has any options, he may not have much time to use them."

"I'll get the word to him."

"He needs to talk to me."

Boston. 3:16 A.M.

The wave wasn't particularly big, in the context of the evening. It rolled across Logan Airport and Winthrop, which had been abandoned barely ten minutes earlier, after a warning had chased out the few diehards who remained. It was barely eight feet high when it swept through downtown Boston. Other waves went ashore at Plymouth on the south, and Gloucester on the north. The disaster was compounded at Marblehead when a major pileup blocked Route 114 and trapped thousands in the path of the sea.

At Plymouth, the Commonwealth Electric power station was destroyed. That caused an overload in Boston and Providence, and the system began shutting down. By four-fifteen the entire Northeast was without power.

Every major city on both coasts was now entangled in a desperate flight. Police forces disintegrated as officers scrambled to rescue their own families. Hospitals and other emergency services broke down for the same reason. Those who gave up trying to get out of town and sought refuge in local churches and community centers often found them locked. Military and National Guard units could move quickly only by air.

So far there had been no tsunamis on the West Coast. Experts were cautiously optimistic.

The media was perhaps enjoying its finest hour. Mobile news teams were everywhere, dropping out of the sky to record and interview the terror-stricken and the desperate.

"Where are you headed, Mrs. Martinik?"

"Anywhere. . . ."

People living in Denver, Kansas City, Indianapolis experienced a different kind of agony. There was hardly anyone who didn't have kids, friends, relatives in the path of the waves. But phone lines were down throughout the stricken areas.

Conditions elsewhere in the world were mixed. East Africa, the Middle East, and Asia had so far suffered less severely because they had not been directly exposed to the event. But debris was still falling, and the Earth's rotation was pushing them into the line of fire. Europe was being hit hard. Thousands were believed dead from Rome to the Gulf of Riga. Kiev in the Ukraine had, like Carlisle, been decimated by a meteor shower. Pôrto Alegre and Valparaíso had been inundated.

There was *some* good news: A tidal wave reported approaching Vancouver failed to arrive. At Pearl Harbor, the navy evacuated thousands of dependents onto warships in the face of approaching tsunamis. In Glasgow, city officials used trains, buses, and good planning to perform a similar feat.

Nations had already begun to assist one another with little regard to national borders. Russian military forces had arrived with food and medical aid at Kiev. While Poles rescued Latvians at Riga, Germans rescued Poles along the Pomeranian Coast. Italian relief agencies showed up in eastern France. Canadians were reported en route to New York.

There were some that night who were concluding, whatever else might happen, the human race would never be the same.

Skyport Orbital Lab. 3:18 A.M.

Skyport was a geostationary satellite, orbiting permanently above the Galapagos Islands. The sky over the eastern Pacific was alight with the fine webwork of meteor showers. Tory knew what was happening on the ground. Along the Gulf Coast and in Mexico, giant storms had been generated by abrupt changes in temperature and air pressure. Hurricane-velocity winds and driving rain struck Mobile, New Orleans, Tampico, and Veracruz. The TV carried images of crushed bodies and broken wheelchairs, of soggy teddies and over-turned buses. At Virginia Beach a desperate father tried unsuc-cessfully to save his kids from a wave by tying them to trees; at Wilmington a hospital attempted to ride out the rising sea, and lost its patients and virtually its entire professional staff. A Coast Guard helicopter off Atlantic City ran into wind shear at the wrong moment and went down in mountainous seas. Heroism and tragedy were everywhere.

Tory watched with eyes swollen from fighting back tears. Her own family lived in the area around St. Louis, so they at least were safe from the general devastation. But the POSIMs continued to go down, and she provided as much warning as she could. Usually it was thirty to forty minutes. It wasn't much, but it was a hell of a lot better than zero. And she was a big part of it, the woman they'd wanted to send home, at a time when they should have been beefing up.

She watched POSIM-27 sizzle into the atmosphere and disappear somewhere off Brazil. The cities of the Americas were usually ablaze with light, even at this hour. But tonight substantial sections of both continents had gone dark. Even the river of illumination that ran from Boston to Miami was at best patchy.

From here, from her perch thirty-six thousand kilome-ters over the Pacific, she sensed a rhythm to the strikes, a pat-tern of light and intensity and timing. Despite all that was happening below, this cosmic symphony was the most beau-tiful thing she'd ever seen.

White House, Oval Office. 3:20 A.M.

Henry was staring at the papers scattered across his teak-wood desk, and at the images coming in on his notebook screen from Miami. His eyes were blurred, his head was warm, his hands were trembling. Emily had pleaded with him to call his personal physician, to get something to calm him down. But the last thing he needed now was a tranquilizer.

How many had died tonight?

They'd never know; and if there'd been a revolver handy, Henry Kolladner would have done the right thing and put a bullet in his head.

The door opened and Kerr looked in. "Henry?" he said.

The only light in the room, aside from the notebook, came from his desk lamp. He looked at it, a memento from the president of France. "I made the wrong call, Al." He felt drained, empty. "We should've started evacuating the cities as soon as we knew." He'd learned his lesson. Minutes before the eleven forty-five address, he'd committed the resources of the government to a complete evacuation of coastal cities throughout the nation. Too late, of course. Far too late.

"Sir, we did what we thought was right."

He shrugged. "It doesn't matter, Al. We've got a lot of dead people out there. It didn't have to happen."

For a long time neither man spoke. Then Kerr said, "Feinberg's been on the line again."

The despair in his voice was evident. Henry swung the chair around slowly and looked at his chief of staff, transfixing him.

"What is it this time?"

"POSIM-38. The one we got the NASA report about."

The president took a long breath. POSIM-38 would pass through the skies over China later that morning. It was *big*, but it was going to miss. "It *is* still going to miss, right?"

"Yeah. I just got off the line with him. The problem is that he says it'll be back."

"What?"

"He says it'll slow down during its passage through the

atmosphere, and it'll start looping around the Earth. He can't say for sure, but he thinks it'll come down. Maybe pretty quick."

"My God. That son of a bitch is, *what*, ten blocks long?" Henry, for the first time, *felt* his disease. Like a living thing, it crept into his intestines and his lungs and curled around his spine. He found it hard to breathe.

"He says it's the trigger. If it lands, it's lights out everywhere. Ice age, famine, you name it."

"When?"

"He doesn't know. Depends on what happens to it as it passes through the atmosphere."

"Worst-case scenario?"

"Could be a couple of days."

Henry wiped perspiration from his brow and dug through the papers on his desk until he found the one he was looking for. "NASA says no immediate threat." His stomach felt as if it were wrapped in steel bands. "This *Feinberg*, is he—?"

"Our people think he's the best there is."

"Okay. Well, we're not going to sit here and take it. We'll nuke the son of a bitch." He tapped his finger on the NASA document. "It says here, closest approach at eight forty-seven. We'll take it out this morning and be done with it."

"I agree, Henry."

"Have NASA check Feinberg's numbers. See if they come up with the same results. Meantime, get Wilson on the line." Wilson was the air force chief of staff. "If NASA concurs with Feinberg, we'll do it."

Kerr violated his usual procedure by making a couple of quick calls while Henry waited, setting the process in motion. Then he turned again to the president. "There's something else we need to talk about, Henry. The District is vulnerable. I think we need to move inland ourselves. Just in case. I've taken the liberty of setting up an alternate command center at Peterson AFB."

Henry wanted to laugh, but his throat was dry. "Peterson? You want me to go to Colorado and sit on a mountain?"

"Peterson's not on a mountain, Henry."

"People hear Colorado, they think mountains. How's it going to look if the president, who told everybody to stay home, don't worry about the waves, everything's under control—if the goddam *president* clears out and heads for the mountains?"

"People are going to be too busy to think about how it looks, Henry. Afterward, they'll be glad the government still has a head."

"Like hell they will. Not *this* head."

"Henry, we've got aircraft out there, and satellites, more spotters than we know what to do with, but the waves are hard to see. Until they get close. They're coming, some of them, at three hundred miles an hour." His eyes got round and hard. "You've got a lot of people working with you, Henry. If you want to expose yourself, it's one thing, but you have your staff to think about."

And Emily. But Emily had recognized the dilemma, had refused to leave when he'd suggested it earlier that evening.

The president could hear voices outside. "Al," he said, "the country's hanging by a thread tonight. If we've got any nonessential people left here, get them out. That includes the agents. But I just don't have time to be running around the country. The operations team is mostly military. Their job's here. With me. We stay."

7.

BBC BULLETIN. 8:21 A.M. BRITISH SUMMER TIME (3:21 A.M. EDT).
"This is Sidney Cain reporting from London." *(His voice sounds unsteady.)* "You're looking at the old financial district from a point close to where Waterloo Bridge used to be. Eyewitnesses say the crest

of the wave was higher than Charing Cross Station. The downtown area is currently under about ten feet of water. Casualties are believed to number upward of a hundred thousand. And that may be a very conservative estimate. Emergency teams have begun to arrive, but they are going to have a very difficult time.

"Many—" *(Voice breaks momentarily.)* "Many of the landmarks have been destroyed. St. Paul's, as you can see, has collapsed. The roof is gone from the House of Parliament. The bridges are all down. Nelson seems to have survived. And Cleopatra's Needle. But not much else." (Another pause.) "Boats and supplies are already coming in from all over the British Isles. We've heard reports of a French flotilla en route across the Channel." *(Struggles to say more. Gives up.)* "Back to you, Clyde."

Micro Flight Deck. 3:22 A.M.

Evelyn had insisted on staying with her. Saber had been too numb to object. They'd sat silently for a time and then begun to talk. About how she felt, and later about Tony, and Saber's ambitions, and finally about life support.

There was still a lot of rock out there. Saber reacted automatically to the occasional warnings on the scopes, shutting down the engine when necessary, changing the angle of propulsion, doing a creditably good job of steering clear of hazards. Of course, it was getting easier. The outer edge of the blast had blown past them so quickly that it had been sheer luck they'd survived. Now the debris was moving far more slowly relative to the bus. The result was that a human pilot could hope to react in a timely fashion.

Whenever she had to accelerate, Tony's body fell aft, out of sight, but after they'd been running without thrust for a while he'd drift back, as if he were trying to stay close to the flight deck. To *her*.

It was eerie, and she was grateful for Evelyn's presence. Tony's death was hard to accept. He'd been endlessly com-

petent, the man who believed he could do anything. A waste-
land had opened inside her. She had not realized until she'd
seen him out there, trailing at the end of the tether, how much
she needed his support.

Now she was left in a bus with its life support shut off,
no hope of rescue, and no way to repair the damage. There
was one piece of good news: She had her communications
back with Skyport. She'd described her situation, described it
a second time for a supervisor.

They insisted she check the flight deck storage cabinets on
the possibility there'd be an extra suit. When there was none,
they told her they would stay with her and that their best people were working on a solution. She knew what that meant.

"No chance of a rescue mission?" asked Evelyn.

She shook her head. "No way anybody can reach us in time
to do any good. Fact is, they'd be hard-pressed to get to us
before we achieve Earth-orbit."

"When'll *that* be?"

"About twelve hours."

"We'll be breathing vacuum long before then," Evelyn
said. "We need an idea."

Saber had never stopped trying to devise one. And she
kept coming back to the moment when Tony had looked
through the puncture into C deck and seen one of Bigfoot's
plastic bags. "We might have a long shot," she said.

Micro Passenger Cabin. 3:29 A.M.

The mood in the passenger cabin had become bleak. There
had been talk of trying to go below without a p-suit, of using
one of the air tanks and just gutting it out, of ripping off the
hatch and recovering a suit from the lower deck and getting
back with it. How long would all that take?

Five minutes? Ten? Surely, one of them could stand *anything* for five minutes.

Depends how long it takes to get the hatch open.

And there was the roadblock: getting past the hatch. But they really didn't have much choice except to try it. Either try it, or just get ready to open the airlock in a little while and accept death gracefully.

Charlie was easily the most physically endowed of the persons on board, so he agreed to try, thinking that if no solution was possible he'd just as soon get it over. The happy camaraderie of the dinner party now seemed light-years away.

So it happened that when Evelyn and Saber climbed down the ladder from the flight deck, they found Charlie, with his oxygen tank shoved into his belt, standing at the airlock.

"You have the right idea," said Saber. She was carrying a rumpled gray jumpsuit. "But you'll freeze pretty quick."

"It's better than just sitting here."

"I think you'll also be holding your breath. I doubt you could breathe, even with the mask."

"Who's driving the bus?" asked Charlie.

"I guess we're taking our chances now," Evelyn said. "We have a more immediate problem." She looked at Charlie. "But we *do* need you to go. We talked about it, and Saber wanted to try it, but there's the problem of getting through the hatch."

Charlie surveyed the other males. They were both on the frail side. Two women, and good old Charlie Haskell at six-four. "So we need a little muscle." Ordinarily, Charlie would have made a joke of it, but neither the smile nor the tone would come.

"That's right," said Saber. "We just have to get you some better equipment. But first, let me show you where the spare suit is." She drew a map of C deck, and marked off the middle of three storage cabinets. "Just pull the latch and it'll open. It comes in two pieces: the suit and the helmet. Don't forget the helmet, right?"

Charlie frowned, feeling insulted.

"Charlie," said Evelyn, "Things are going to fog up on you out there. Both your vision and your brain. It's not going to be a milk run."

"Why don't I try getting into the p-suit down there instead of bringing it back?"

"Too complicated and too dangerous," said Evelyn. "Let's keep it simple. Just bring it back."

"Okay, now let's try to give ourselves a chance," said Saber. She reached up, punched the overhead, and shook out one of the two remaining oxygen tanks.

"I've already got one," said Charlie.

"You've got a *used* one. Everything we have is running on this, Mr. Vice President. Let's get you a fresh tank."

Charlie decided he liked her. She was under more pressure than anybody, she'd just lost her captain, but she was keeping her composure. Tough woman. "Okay," he said.

"The stored suit should be all right. But there's a chance that whatever tore up the compartment also got the suit. If it did, you'll have to try to strip the one Bigfoot's wearing."

"That doesn't sound easy."

"It won't be."

"Better idea," said Evelyn. "If the suit's damaged, forget it. It'll probably be easier just to repair the oxygen line than try to get the suit off Bigfoot."

"That makes sense," said Saber. She handed him a roll of duct tape. "Take it with you."

"Duct tape? I'm going to fix the leak with duct tape?"

"Best thing we've got. Anyway, Mr. Vice President, if it's more complicated than that, we're dead." She held out the gray suit, which wasn't exactly a jumpsuit but rather a top and a pair of leggings. Apparently made of Spandex. She measured them against him, adjusted them, and tried again. "This is going to be tight, but maybe that's just as well."

"What is it?" asked Charlie.

"It's a g-suit. It's mine, and it hasn't been washed and I apologize. It's underwear for a p-suit." She must have seen something in his face. "I'm serious," she said. "Look, air and temperature aren't the only problems. Your capillaries are going to burst. They'll go pretty quickly after you get outside. As that happens, you'll develop massive bruising. Enough of that and you're dead."

"How long's it take?"

"Don't know. I didn't pay enough attention because I never expected to go out without a suit. Or to send anyone else out. But not long, okay? The g-suit helps keep blood from pooling in the extremities under high g-forces. It also acts as a coolant. Which you're going to need."

Charlie looked at them doubtfully.

"Do it," said Evelyn.

"Not much respect here for the vice president," he told her. But he retreated to the washroom, climbed into the suit, and zippered up. It *was* tight. He pulled his clothes back on and returned to the cabin.

Evelyn inspected it. "Not much of a space suit," she said. There were no gloves, so the chaplain contributed a flannel shirt, which they tore up and taped to his hands. Saber produced a uniform jacket, cut it into strips, wrapped them around Charlie's feet, and secured them with tape.

She heard warning beeps from the flight deck and sent them all back to their seats while she hurried back up the ladder. Charlie sat down and buckled in. The engine roared to life and Saber moved them to a new course. Then she came back, carrying a wrench, a torch, and a pair of screwdrivers, which she set down beside the duct tape.

She looked at him and smiled. "Just the g-suit," she said. "You won't need your clothes."

"They'll help me keep warm," he protested.

"Keeping warm won't be a problem, Mr. Vice President.

Take my word." Charlie, embarrassed, stripped off his shirt and stepped out of his trousers. Neither he nor Saber wore their oxygen masks during the preparations for the EVA, and the deadness of the air in the cabin spurred him on.

Saber ran her hands over the Spandex and approved. "We need some more parts," she said. She went into the galley and rummaged around in the cabinets and refrigerator. She came back with a straw and a plastic storage bag.

Charlie watched curiously as she emptied the bag of several pounds of wrapped lunch meat, held it over his head, and pulled it down. "A little snug," she said, "but it should work."

Evelyn's eyes lit up. "Saber," she said, seizing the duct tape, "you're a genius."

"What?" asked Charlie.

They removed the bag and strapped the air tank to his back.

"Okay." Saber nodded at her handiwork. "Look out for the sunlight. You won't have adequate protection against it, and you'll get a bad burn real quick if you get exposed. I'll try to keep the bus turned away from it. But keep it in mind.

"You're going to be wrapped up with a bag over your head. That means you're going to feel constricted. Keep calm. Breathing will probably feel strange. Not inhaling. That'll be easy. But I think you'll have to work at it to *ex*hale.

"The g-suit won't cool you off because it's supposed to plug into the p-suit. So you'll get warm. That's another reason we want to keep you out of the sun. You're going to feel as if you're in a sauna."

"Go ahead," Charlie said. "I'm taking notes."

"I'm sorry. I wish it were easier. Somebody make a bandanna and wrap it around his head." She went on to explain, step by step, what he needed to do.

"One more thing," she said. "We don't have an extra tether. Before you do anything else, haul Tony in, disconnect his tether, and tie it to your belt. Tight. If we have to move the bus, I'll blink the outside lights twice, count to five, and go. *You* make sure you've got a good hold, okay? The tether won't save you from getting beaten up, or even popping the bag. And for God's sake, make sure you stay connected to the bus so we don't lose you."

They put the bag back on. Evelyn was about to tape it down when Saber held up a finger. "Not yet," she said.

"Why not?"

"He's got to exhale. There's no way for the air to escape. He'll fog up." She produced a straw.

"But," said Evelyn, "the air'll drain through that."

"Right. So we need a stopcock. Anybody got a paper clip?"

"Here," said the chaplain.

She took it, clipped it over one end of the straw, examined it, and then secured it with tape. Now she taped the straw, clipped side down, to Charlie's g-suit top so that the upper end would be inside the plastic bag. "If you have to, Charlie," she said, "open the clip when you exhale." She bit her lip. "It'll help to bleed a little of the air out through the straw, but do that very slowly. If the pressure drops too fast, you'll get a nosebleed."

Her eyes grew dark. "I think you're set now. And I'm sorry. I don't like doing this to you."

He nodded and smiled.

Evelyn wrapped a utility belt around his middle, handed him his tools, and strapped his lamp on his wrist.

They wished him luck.

And Charlie, his mouth dry and his stomach churning, went into the airlock and pulled the door shut. The activating presspad was white. He pushed it, saw the status displays change color, and simply sagged, already feeling clammy. His breathing was loud inside the bag and he checked the straw to be sure the clip was still in place.

The cycling procedure seemed slow. Charlie sat listening to his heartbeat. Saber had been right: Breathing quickly became a conscious effort.

A green light blinked on and the outer hatch swung open. He looked out into the void, expecting, despite what Saber had said, to be hit by a frigid wave. But he observed no immediate change in temperature. His nervousness ebbed and he looked out at the universe with a surprising degree of calm. No one gets to be vice president without developing a strong sense of self-confidence along the way, and a capability for responding under extreme pressure. These qualities, of which Charlie had not been particularly conscious, were nevertheless present, and they now came to his rescue.

He looked around and saw Tony's body, still quietly adrift.

Hauling him in would take time. And Charlie knew better than anyone, feeling the air in his lungs expand, that time was not on his side. Better to take his chances without the safety line and get on with it. Get Tony later. There was no safety to be had under present conditions, and it seemed the height of imprudence to risk himself pursuing it. He exhaled, heard the bag crackle, and leaned out of the airlock.

There was a handhold immediately to his left. He looked for more, and saw them spaced evenly at about two-foot intervals in both directions, up toward the blister and down toward the cargo deck.

It was an odd sensation, looking out and feeling no movement, knowing they were not anchored, seeing nothing below but void. He pushed the thought aside, seized the handgrip, and swung himself onto the face of the hull. He'd never liked heights, but this wasn't at all the same. The experience was easier than he'd anticipated, and he moved almost casually down the ladder. It occurred to him that he hadn't been very hopeful, walking into the airlock with his plastic bag, his straw, and his paper clip. But now his confidence soared.

Which reminded him: He'd stopped breathing. He exhaled, and his lungs refilled with no effort on his part.

Exhale.

He was warm. Getting warmer.

He kept moving. The broken tread came into view, and he could see the engine nozzle and the cargo deck hatch, which looked as if it had been jimmied partway open. He got to it quickly, tested the handle, pulled on it, and found no give.

But there was room for his fingers between the lip of the hatch and the seating. He shifted position, let go of the handgrip, got hold of the underside of the hatch with both hands, planted his feet against the hull, and pulled.

Nothing.

He tried again with the wrench and felt movement.

Okay. Progress.

He went after it, straining until sinews cracked. Sweat drenched the lining of the g-suit. A vapor formed across the inside of the bag and he had to stop. What had Evelyn said? Both vision and brain would fog? Maybe. But after this, *he'd* be the reigning authority on the subject.

He loosened the paper clip. Pressure forced air out through the straw.

The bag cleared.

He was about to begin again when a bank of lights, some spaced along the middle of the sphere, others near the treads, blinked on. They went off and came on again.

Count to five and start the engine.

Son of a bitch. He swung back to his handholds and grabbed for dear life.

He wasn't watching the nozzle, but he saw the glare from ignition on the metal in front of his face. In the same instant, the sudden acceleration threw him hard against the hull and tried to tear his arm out of his shoulder. Suddenly there was a *down*, very distinctly, and he dangled on the outside of the Micro, over an infinite precipice.

He clung to the handhold. Agony lanced through fingers and shoulders. He tried to cut a deal with whatever power governed the universe.

The grips had depressions, and he tried to find one with his foot so he could stand. Relieve some of the pressure. Don't forget to exhale. His wrench began to slide out of his belt.

He found a foothold, let go briefly with one hand, and repositioned the wrench.

Then the burn stopped and he was afloat again.

He didn't know whether it was over. They hadn't thought to make an all-clear signal, so he hung on, waiting. His legs drifted away from the hull.

He had to force himself to let go with one hand. He rubbed his shoulder and then, cautiously, let go with the other and repositioned himself over the hatch. He watched the lights the whole time.

They did not come on.

Exhale.

He waited for feeling to return to his arms, and then inserted the wrench under the hatch and pulled on it. If he'd worked feverishly before, he now applied himself with desperation. He felt springs pop and the wrench slipped and he banged his hand, but he ignored it and continued to work.

The hatch gave. And broke loose.

Micro Flight Deck. 3:41 A.M.

The voice snarled at her. "He's *where?*"

"Outside."

"Outside the *ship?*"

"That is affirmative."

"For God's sake—who am I talking to?"

"The pilot."

"What's your name, pilot?"

"Rolnikaya."

"Okay, Rolnikaya. I'll tell you what you're going to do. You get the vice president back inside. *Now.* Tell him Mr. Kerr wants to talk with him."

"At the moment he's busy, Mr. Kerr. I'll tell him when he comes in." She broke the connection.

8.

Micro, outside the Cargo Deck. 3:42 A.M.

Charlie pushed past the hatch, slipped into the airlock, and collapsed. He was breathing hard, literally panting, fogging the bag. He released the paper clip again, cautiously, remembering the warning about nosebleed. The bandanna was drenched.

Saber was right: It felt like a *sauna*. That was odd. He'd always assumed space was *cold*.

There was a status display on the bulkhead, and it had power. He found the white presspad, took a deep breath, and pushed. To his delight, the inner hatch opened.

Lights were still on inside.

Bigfoot's body, clothed in the p-suit, floated near the ladder, to which it was tethered. The suit looked broken and there were globules of blood drifting through the chamber. Charlie realized that every time Saber ran the engine, the body was slammed against the ladder.

He'd have liked to stop and secure it. But he felt extraordinarily weary. His bag wouldn't clear up, so he was having trouble making out details around him. And he suspected some of the blood was *inside* the bag.

It was hard to concentrate. Something touched his arm and his hair stood upright.

Bigfoot's helmet.

His hand closed on it and he had to think.

Hold on to it.

The locker. Where was the locker? He tried to remember. The part of his mind that remained clear seemed to be shrinking into a corner back in his head somewhere, somewhat like the effect that nitrous oxide produces in a dentist's office. He tried to fight it off. It occurred to him that he could no longer see the outside warning lights. But Saber could use the intercom to speak directly to C deck.

Right?

But there was no air. No medium to carry the sound.

There were three lockers, she'd said. It was in the middle one. He pushed past tanks, cables, shelving. Feeling his way.

He turned a corner. Drifted off the deck. Found a handhold, the side of a storage bin, something, and pulled himself back. And in this tortuous manner, half-blinded, operating out of a state that was neither rational nor deluded, he found the storage cabinets.

He opened the middle one and felt the suit. And another helmet. Take both. Bigfoot's might be damaged. Wouldn't want to have to do this again. No sir. This was too much even for the vice president of the United States. He wrapped the helmets in the suit.

He got back to the airlock, pushed the presspad, and watched the inner hatch close. He settled in to wait, and a minute went by before he realized he didn't need to bother because the outer hatch was already open, had *been* open.

Make sure you've still got the suit.

He did, and he felt for his ladder up the face of the moonbus. He didn't need it really. He could just lean out and *launch*. (He giggled at the thought.) Grab the hatch as he went by. Nothing to it.

In fact, he wasn't sure which way was *up*. The ladder went in both directions. Which way was the passenger cabin and which way the treads? He went back inside the airlock—*better safe than sorry*—found the control panel, wiped a smeary arm across his bag-helmet, and tried to read the markings. But he could see nothing.

Which way?

Then he remembered the airlock benches. They were for sitting, so they had to be near the floor. *Down*. He wanted to go the other way.

He found the benches, returned to the outer hatch, and checked the p-suit again. God help him if Saber had to start the engine. He seized a handhold and started up.

It had been a mistake not to count the handholds coming down. He thought there'd been eight or nine. Or maybe thirteen. (He chuckled again.) But he was counting now as he climbed, and at six he began feeling for the hatch to the passenger cabin airlock, although he knew it was too soon. At thirteen, he still hadn't found it. He considered tearing the bag off so he could see.

Exhale.

What would happen if he missed it? Did the handgrips go completely around the bus? He visualized himself climbing forever, going round and round.

Take off the bag. Roll the dice and settle it.

Could he get inside before the vacuum killed him? Who knew? Certainly not Vice President Charles L. Haskell. He wondered what Sam would think if he could see him now.

And his fingers closed around the hatch.

TRANSGLOBAL SPECIAL REPORT. 3:53 A.M.

"This is Keith Morley on board the vice president's moonbus. Just minutes ago, Vice President Haskell successfully concluded an incredible rescue effort outside the ship. . . ."

Micro Passenger Cabin, 4:07 A.M.

"Yes, Al, what is it?"

"Are you all right, Charlie?"

"I'm fine." That was hardly true, but considering the condition he *might* have been in, he was doing damned well. "I understand things are not so good at your end."

"Yes. Miami Beach, New Orleans, completely destroyed. Eastern seaboard hit from Maine to the Florida Keys. Not as hard. Not *total*. But it's—" His voice broke and he began to sob softly. *Al Kerr.*

Evelyn was climbing down from the flight deck, where she'd been in radio contact with Saber. She nodded and elaborately removed her oxygen mask.

"They're estimating tens of thousands of casualties," Kerr continued in a voice only slightly less shaky. "But God knows what the count really is."

Charlie's eyes squeezed shut. He thought of his own father and cousins, living at the Cape.

"It's a goddammed disaster, Charlie. I don't think any of us had any idea—"

"Okay." Charlie was trying to absorb what Kerr was telling him.

"Something else. I don't know whether you've heard or not, but the other plane is missing. Maybe it's just a radio failure. I know they lost contact with you for a couple of hours, too."

"The other plane? The one Rick's on?"

"That's what they're telling us. I don't think they're hopeful. I'm sorry." There was a long pause. "Charlie, right now it looks as if there'll be a million dead before this is over. The president would have talked to you himself, except that he's buried right now. You understand."

Buried.

"Charlie, you should be aware there's some doubt here whether the country can survive this."

"Yeah," he said. "I can see where there *might* be."

"Henry wants you to put the best possible face on things.

Stay upbeat. I mean, you're our point man on this. You've been there."

"Al, you sound like Rick."

"Yeah. I guess in the end we all end up sounding like Rick. Listen, what were you doing outside the ship? Isn't that dangerous?"

"It's a bus."

"Whatever."

"I was trying to get a hatch open."

"Okay. Don't do it any more, okay? Meantime, we'll get out a press release. *Haskell Takes Charge*, right?"

"Let it go," said Charlie.

"Charlie, I think the president will insist. Listen, we need all the PR we can get."

Charlie didn't particularly like the president. But he knew that Henry took the job seriously, and had to be suffering all the torments of hell now. He wasn't a man to write off losses, to recognize that there were some situations in which you simply acted the best you could and hoped for the best. Charlie knew that Henry would be blaming himself. He could almost hear the president's explanation: *Charlie, we should have started the evacuations right away. We were too worried about what we'd feed them away from their homes. We were worried about traffic jams, for God's sake.* So they'd guessed wrong and a lot of people had died.

But Charlie knew that if he'd been there, he'd have found no fault with the course of action. He'd have gone along, thinking they were doing the right thing.

For a few moments, the responsibility of the office touched him. He wondered now for the first time during his political career whether he really wanted to become president of the United States. Suddenly it was a dark and fearsome vision.

When he got home and things settled down, he'd rethink things. Maybe withdraw his candidacy. It wasn't really that he was frightened of the office, but he needed to recognize his own limitations. The next president was going to be facing a wrecked nation. The simple truth was that they'd need someone better than Charlie Haskell. Charlie might have been okay for good times; but the United States had been plunged into a monumental disaster. The nation needed a Lincoln. Or a Teddy Roosevelt.

Where in hell were they going to find one?

Immediately after Kerr got off the phone, Saber reappeared at the airlock. She looked pleased with herself, and Charlie was happy for her. "You can't beat duct tape," she announced. And then she looked at Charlie, strapped down, his seat lowered. "*You* don't look so good." She wanted to give him something to help him sleep, but Charlie refused. Not tonight, of all nights. As if he could do something to help.

"How bad *do* I look?" he asked Evelyn after Saber had gone back to the flight deck.

"As if you've been in a fight. And lost." She held up a mirror: His face was bruised and he had two black eyes.

"A lot of people dead tonight," he said.

She nodded. "We heard."

He hovered between exhaustion and horror.

And there was more bad news. Saber called Evelyn up to the flight deck. When she came back she said they'd received word that communication had never been restored with the early flight. It was presumed lost with a hundred and one passengers and three crew.

They were all thinking about it, running the names of friends and colleagues, trying to recall who had been scheduled on which flight.

One hundred four people. It was minuscule compared to the vast numbers who had died on the ground. But it personalized the losses. Rick and Sam and God knew who else and a million others.

It was the darkest night in human memory.

Manhattan. 4:01 A.M.

Larry stood by Marilyn's side, peering out over the rooftops and down at the new sea. Manhattan had become a cluster of concrete islands. The city was dark. The shattered Moon had long since set. "Goddam government," he said. "They told us there was nothing to worry about."

Someone pointed a flashlight over the side of the roof. Its beam bobbed up and down in the water. There were bodies.

Marilyn turned away. She'd been unable to sleep, and had eventually rejoined the quiet group gathered around a battery-powered radio.

The terrace doors were open and the curtains moved in a soft breeze. Approximately thirty people were still present. A few, who had drunk too much early in the evening, were asleep. The others looked listless and frightened.

Marilyn had relatives in Boston and friends on the Outer Banks. She'd tried to call them, but got only busy signals and recordings (*"The number you dialed is currently receiving maintenance. . . ."*) until about three. Now the phone was completely dead.

The rooms were lighted by candles. "I wonder what *our* place looks like," she asked Larry. Their apartment was on the third floor, a *high* third floor, and should have been above water. But it was an effort to care. "We should try to get home," she said.

"How do you suggest we do that, love?"

She was surprised at the sense of disconnectedness that had come over her. She almost didn't care about anything. But she knew there were things to be said, pretenses to be made.

Louise was in the kitchen. There was no running water, of course. Louise had broken open a bottle of spring water and was pouring out a small portion for one of accountants. "Make it last, Bill," she said.

"Is that the entire supply?" asked Marilyn.

Louise looked at the container. About a gallon remained. "This is *it*," she said. "We need to start thinking how we're going to manage if help doesn't come."

"Help'll come," said the accountant.

"I think," said Marilyn, "Louise is right."

Louise looked as if she hadn't slept all night. *She's been worrying about how she'll feed everybody*, Marilyn realized.

Larry came in behind her. "Maybe we should start by figuring out how we'll manage breakfast," he said. "Is there a grocery in the neighborhood?"

Louise nodded. Her customary energy had evaporated. "One block over toward Broadway. Across the street. It's called Barney's. But I'd think it's underwater at the moment."

"Listen," said the accountant, "the whole world knows we're caught here. Let's not go running off half-cocked. All we need to do is be patient."

"No." Marvin stepped into the candlelight. His voice sounded an octave deeper than usual. "I don't think we should just wait here to see what happens to us." He looked at Marilyn, and turned to Louise: "Is there anything in the building we can use for a raft?"

9.

White House, Oval Office. 4:07 A.M.

Nonessential personnel had been packed off and whisked away. Henry, who'd been on the phone with the Brazilian president, had watched them go with a sense of being on a sinking ship. The agents had refused to leave, and they now manned the front gate. All other entrances had been sealed. Save for the president, several of his top aides, the Secret Service, and the half-dozen officers staffing the situation room, the White House was empty. As a precaution, Kerr had brought in three Marine helicopters, which waited on the lawn, rotors slowly turning.

The president's phone rang. "General Wilson on the line, sir," said the army captain who'd replaced his secretary.

"Yes, Bob?" said the president.

"Mr. President, we're retargeting the birds, as you requested. We'll be ready to launch as soon as it passes."

"Good." Thank God. At least something was going right. "You have authorization to fire, Bob. But not until it's on the way out."

"Yes, sir. That's exactly how we'll handle it."

"Don't want any radioactive pieces falling on China."

"No, sir."

Others besides Feinberg had become aware of the threat offered by POSIM-38, and the story had seeped into the media. *The Rocky Mountain News*, in its electronic edition, noted that the object looked vaguely like a tombstone. Several editorial cartoons using the object had already turned up, including one that showed Henry contemplating his own gravesite, marked by a stone that resembled the Possum.

Well, they were right about that. Whatever happened now, Henry's obituary had been written and published.

Lightning crackled on the roof. It was as bad a storm as any Henry could remember in all his years in the District. The experts thought it was another storm spawned by moon-rock.

Kerr's familiar rap sounded at the door.

"Come," said the president.

The door opened cautiously and the chief of staff looked into the office. "Are you all right, Henry?" he asked.

"I'm fine." Kerr was standing awkwardly. The way he did when there was a problem. "What's wrong, Al?"

"More waves coming," he said. "Three to four hours. West Coast this time."

•   •   •

County Route 6, southwest of San Francisco. 1:19 A.M. Pacific Daylight Time (4:19 A.M. EDT).

The reports of the assorted disasters coming in from around the country, contrasted with the quiet wilderness in which the Kapchik family rested, lent the telecasts an air of unreality. It was as if they were watching an end-of-the-world television drama, running simultaneously on all channels. The glimmering mist that had replaced the Moon had itself gone behind a bank of clouds. A gentle wind blew out of the west, and the night was cool and pleasant. The mountainside on which they'd camped had filled up with people who traded food, coffee, and alcohol, and generally clustered together with the kind of community spirit that only shared risk could bring. They watched the images with dismay and pity, and they did not speak of the curious secret joy they felt for having escaped the disaster that had overtaken so many. After a while Marisa turned the set off.

She'd given up trying to sleep, and sat propped against a tree, wearing an extra woolen shirt. Her eyes drifted shut. She could smell campfires and coffee. A lot of people were still awake, talking to one another in subdued voices. Jerry had crawled into a sleeping bag with the kids, and now snored softly. Cars and trucks continued to roll east.

There'd been reports of waves approaching California, but they didn't specifically mention San Francisco. She thought of her home in Pacifica and prayed that it would still be there when they went back.

Abruptly the whispers turned to gasps. A fireball soared across the sky and exploded directly overhead. Fragments rained down. The hills brightened, and after a few moments she heard a crackle, like distant firecrackers. Then the world went dark again.

Jerry never stirred.

Somebody closed a car door.

Jerry wanted to go home tomorrow if nothing happened, but she thought caution was called for. In the morning, she would suggest they stay out one more night until they were sure.

The area in which the Kapchiks had parked was filled to capacity. Other vehicles lined the shoulder of the road. A police cruiser crouched in a patch of trees across the highway. It provided a sense of security, a kind of guarantee that the world would go on.

Marisa became aware of activity around her. The whispers turned to obscenities, and people leaned toward their TVs.

She pulled her earphones back over her head and switched on her own unit in time to hear an excited reporter describing an effort to evacuate Los Angeles. Hundreds of buses, organized by relief agencies and the military, were trying to get three million people to higher ground. Clouds of planes and helicopters were flying into private fields and small municipal airports to help. *Three million.*

A second report from a local news helicopter described conditions on the highways. Traffic was at a crawl.

God help them.

Then she realized they weren't talking only about Los Angeles. Emergency conditions prevailed the length of the West Coast, from Astoria on the north to Baja California on the south. Everywhere, panicked populations were trying to find higher ground, heading for mountaintops, breaking into skyscrapers, doing whatever they could.

It must be chaos.

In some areas, people were reported to be blowing up bridges and blocking highways to stop the flood of refugees. Lisa Monroe of CBS interviewed a man who claimed to speak for an entire municipality when he assumed the right to defend town land against the "hordes coming out of San Francisco."

"They'll overrun us," he said. "Look around you. They're

all going to want to sit on this mountain. Where are we supposed to put everybody? There's just not enough room. Not enough food. Not enough water." He spoke with an actor's precise articulation. A professional of one sort or another, she realized. "So, yes, we dropped a tractor-trailer on the road down there. And when they move that, we'll drop another one. I don't like it, but we've got our own to think about."

She looked at the relatively light traffic on the county route and wondered if it too had been blocked somewhere west. She shook Jerry.

"What's wrong?" he asked, looking dazed.

She told him. "They're saying everything's going to get hit."

"And we've got no flood insurance," he said. "Son of a bitch, Missy, we're going to lose everything."

They were nosed in against a hillside. Headlights moved rhythmically across the gravel every ten seconds or so. And lightning broke across the mountains.

But it wasn't lightning.

It was fire.

It came silently out of the sky and glided slowly across her field of vision. The highway and the mountain stood out white and stark. It seemed almost to float in, and then she could hear it, a succession of loud bangs and explosions. Pieces of it blasted away, and the thing itself passed out of sight behind the mountain. A roar shook the ground.

Lights came on across the highway above the souvenir shop. The shaking went on, stopped, and started again. More violently. The highway broke apart. Brakes screeched and cars piled into one another. There were screams and people running and flashlight beams lancing through the night. The lights in the shopping center, the security lights, the signs at the charge station all went out.

Engines were starting. A crevice opened near the foot of the cliff. A car slipped in and vanished.

"Quake," said Jerry.

Flashlight beams jerked up at the face of the mountain and faded into the dark.

The screams continued. Marisa heard a rumble. *Overhead.*

The cops were out of the cruiser, trying to wave people onto the road, away from the overhang.

Cars and trucks were trying to get clear, careening against one another, spilling into the highway. Air horns blasted. A Buick hit one of the cops and kept going. Another dropped its wheels into a hole and rolled over. The wheels spun and the occupants fought to get out.

"—out of here," Jerry was saying, scrambling for the front seat of the wagon.

Marisa was an EMT. Her first instinct was to reach for the first aid kit. She wanted to help the injured cop, but she was torn, knowing she should get her family to safety. And anyway, nobody was stopping and she couldn't reach him. While she tried to make up her mind, the face of the mountain exploded.

The kids had been sleeping in the back of the wagon. They woke now and screamed. The entire world was dissolving. Jerry rammed the tailgate shut while Marisa jumped in on the passenger side. Jerry dived in a moment later and climbed into the back to calm the kids. Rocks rattled off the hood and roof.

There was nowhere to go. The station wagon shook under an impact, and something shattered one of the windows. The landslide went on and on, and she couldn't see what was happening through the cloud of dust that had been kicked up. Then it was over.

"Everybody okay?" said Jerry.

They were fine. But the sound of moving earth had been replaced by screams and frantic cries for help and the sour blat of a jammed automobile horn.

"Take the kids," said Marisa. "Up that way, on the highway." She showed him where she wanted him to go. Away from overhangs.

Jerry looked helplessly at the half-buried line of cars blocking him in. "How'm I supposed to get out?"

"Walk," she said. "And make it quick. The rest of this thing might come down any time."

"Where are *you* going?"

She slid out the back, carrying a flashlight and the first aid kit. "To help," she said.

She picked her way through the carnage, punching numbers into her cell phone, and looking for the cop. He was unconscious, hemorrhaging, and had several broken ribs.

Nobody answered at 911.

Skyport Orbital Lab. 4:54 A.M.

POSIM-32 went down three hundred miles southeast of the Virginia coast. Tory relayed its coordinates to her waiting consumers, one of which was the U.S. Naval Satellite Tracking Service.

> <u>EMERGENCY *** EMERGENCY *** EMERGENCY</u>
> FROM: NAVSAT
> TO: ALLNAV
> DTG: 140956Z
> SUBJ: EARLY WARNING
> SEA WAVE INBOUND VIRGINIA-MARYLAND SHORE. RANGE SEVENTY-FIVE NAUTICAL MILES. SPEED TWO-NINE-ZERO KNOTS.

White House Briefing Room. 5:00 A.M.

The room was packed with reporters and cameras.

Henry looked grimly into the TV lights. "My fellow Americans," he said, "this has been a terrible night for the American people, and for people around the globe. As you know, despite our best hopes, giant waves have hit us very hard. More are coming. I wish I could tell you otherwise; I wish I could tell you that this national nightmare is over. But I cannot.

"In addition to the assorted calamities of the evening, we are also now threatened by a large object that we've come to call the *Possum*. Its real name is POSIM-38, and it's slightly over a mile long. POSIM-38 is a piece of moonrock that was blown clear during the collision, and it has the potential, should it fall to Earth, to do irreparable damage to the environment.

"This object will make a close approach to Earth at eight forty-seven this morning. It will pass through the atmosphere, and it is then likely to go into an orbit that will decay, that *will bring it back*.

"It will continue to present a major hazard unless we act. And the reality is that we'll never have a better opportunity to get rid of it than we have today. Therefore, I've ordered the air force to prepare a massive missile strike, which will be delivered *after it leaves the area of the Earth*.

"In this way—"

It was as far as he got.

A bolt of lightning exploded directly over the White House, the lights went out, flickered on and off a couple of times, and finally died altogether.

"We're off the air, Mr. President," said his producer.

"Can you get us back on, Herman?"

"In a few minutes. Maybe."

The emergency lights came on.

Henry glanced down at the crowd of reporters. "You can see how things have been." The remark drew a few tired smiles.

While he waited, he talked with them, explaining informally what the consequences might be if they failed to act against the Possum. Had he consulted with China? someone wanted to know. He hadn't; it wasn't a Chinese issue. CBS asked if the administration would now budget seriously for Skybolt.

He began to explain that the administration had always supported the concept, and was about to fudge history when a young navy lieutenant stepped into the room from a side door and handed a piece of paper to Al Kerr. Kerr glanced at it, came forward immediately and handed it to the president. It read: *TIDAL WAVE IMMINENT*.

"Ladies and gentlemen," Henry said, "we'd better continue the discussion elsewhere."

No one needed an explanation. The journalists scrambled for their cars. The president turned to an aide. "Get Emily," he said.

10.

AstroLab. 5:07 A.M.

Feinberg had been talking with Windy Cross about POSIM-38, requesting adjustments in the imaging process when *his* power failed. A minute later, the phone lines went out.

But Feinberg had become a very big player, bigger perhaps than he realized. Ten minutes after everything had gone down, an army helicopter descended onto the front lawn and a young captain introduced himself. His name was McMichael and he'd been assigned to provide whatever transportation or communication the professor might need. Then he asked confidentially whether the Possum was as dangerous as the president said.

Feinberg assured him that the danger couldn't be overstated.

Somehow, despite everything, Wes Feinberg had missed the human dimension of the catastrophe. He knew what was happening around the world, but his attention had been focused on orbital mechanics, and now, the dynamics of the Possum. He'd alerted the president as soon as he realized the danger. But he'd felt no real human involvement. Looking into McMichael's gray eyes, feeling the man's fear, he recognized his own detachment. He understood its derivation: his sense that there was nothing to be done about the rock, just as there had been nothing to do about the comet. His advice to the president that he act had been given despite the fact that Feinberg believed no action was feasible. That, lacking Skybolt, the world had no tool at hand with which to defend itself. The human race was caught in a game of cosmic billiards. It was probably going to lose, unless it got very lucky. And because he could only watch, he'd felt no emotional involvement other than his excitement at being here on this day.

The Possum would pass Earth by the barest of margins, literally roaring through the ionosphere, close enough to *see* with the naked eye. But it had enough momentum to avoid being dragged down. For him, the interest lay in the trajectory and velocity with which it would emerge.

"The president has made a public statement about the Possum?" he asked.

"Yes, sir. He was conducting a press conference, but it went off the air. Power failure in D.C."

"Join the rest of the country," said Feinberg. "What did he say about the Possum?"

"That he was going to nuke it, sir."

"*Nuke it?*"

"Yes, sir." He looked at his watch. "In a couple of hours, I guess. Right after it makes its pass over China."

Feinberg sighed. "Get me through to him, Captain."

"Sir, I'll do what I can."

Goddammed idiots. Don't politicians ever ask questions before they make decisions?

The White House. 5:09 A.M.

They hurried the president and first lady through torrential rain across the west lawn, where three choppers were waiting. One lifted away as they slogged through the drenched grass. Actually, Henry was in better shape, despite his illness, than most of the middle-aged officeholders with him, and he ended by helping some of them. Kerr in particular was gasping and heaving before he'd gone more than a few steps.

The military people stayed on the fringe of the group to assist where needed. As Henry arrived at the waiting helicopter, a bolt of lightning illuminated the Capitol and the southeastern sky for what seemed a full minute. And he saw the wave. It looked to be literally a mile high, its white crest breaking over the top, a mountain of water racing down on them. The people coming up from behind gasped and scrambled into the helicopter. The chopper crew helped, literally dragging some in by the scruff of the neck while a Marine officer redundantly shouted, *"Move move move."* Henry helped Emily up, and then he was unceremoniously hauled on board and passed none too gently from hand to hand. He heard Emily's choked voice crying out Al's name, saw Kerr stumble again, his legs twisted, falling forward while a young lieutenant tried to hold him up. Twenty yards beyond the chief of staff, a handful of reporters ran through the steaming rain. Now a voice behind Henry was saying, *"Go go,"* and the roar of the engines deepened and the chopper started to lift.

The president shouted for them to wait, *ordered* the pilot to set back down. Kerr was still on the ground, they didn't have everybody, there was room for more. But hands dragged him away from the open door and someone said it was all right, the other chopper would pick up the stragglers. But Henry knew there were too many for the remaining aircraft.

He was in one of the big cargo carriers. It rose so swiftly it threw him onto the deck. A crewman fell on him and held him. Someone else banged the door shut. "Hang on, sir," said the crewman.

Heavy winds beat on the aircraft. Henry couldn't see the wave anymore, couldn't see anything in the dark interior, couldn't get up to look because the deck swerved and rolled under him. Some of his aides had made it on board, some of the military people, a couple of the reporters, and one of the agents. But there'd been room for more. They'd left maybe twenty down on the lawn. Including Al.

The engines screamed. Henry found a handhold. There should have been a plan in place to get everybody out. Damn. His staff had screwed this up to a fare-thee-well. Or he had.

He felt especially responsible about the reporters. He'd called them to the White House, and had failed to make provision for them. As if he'd thought D.C. was a sacred place, somehow shielded from the catastrophe that was overwhelming the rest of the country.

The man who'd been on top of him, apparently satisfied that the president could no longer hurt himself, eased off. "Sorry, sir," he said. He wore single silver bars.

"It's okay, Lieutenant," said Henry. He looked around, found Emily, and was frightened by her empty eyes. He tried to talk to her but she could not speak.

Lightning flickered in the compartment. Sheets of rain hammered at the windows. The chopper lurched and dipped and rose again. The lieutenant leaned toward the cockpit, spoke briefly, and then nodded: "We're clear, Mr. President."

"Did the other helicopter get off?"

He spoke with one of the pilots again. "Yes, sir. They're in the air."

The roar of the engines eased and Henry got to his feet. The world below was full of liquid darkness and electricity. The lights were out, the ground was dark; he could see no streets, no homes, no monuments. He shivered.

Lightning glimmered against a black torrent pouring across the rotunda. The Lincoln Memorial, half-drowned, flickered in and out of existence.

He eased into the cockpit. "Pilot, can you contact the other aircraft? The one that took off behind us?"

The pilot nodded. "Welcome aboard, Mr. President," he said, and handed him a mike and a pair of earphones. "Bagel Three," he said, "the president would like to talk with you."

There was a long silence on the other end. Then: "This is Bagel Three. Glad you made it, Mr. President."

"Thank you. Were you able to get the people on the ground?"

Another long pause, long enough that Henry knew the answer. "No, sir. Not all of them. There wasn't time." The voice on the other end had become somewhat high-pitched. "There was nothing I could do, sir."

"I know, son. I was there."

"We just barely got off as it was, Mr. President. If I hadn't gone, everybody would have died."

"It's all right." He took a deep breath. "Is Al Kerr there?"

Emily squeezed his shoulder while they listened to people at the other end call Kerr's name. A jumble of voices, and then Henry heard him. "I'm here, Mr. President."

"Thank God, Al. Al, how bad was it? How many'd they have to leave?"

"Ten, fifteen. I'm not sure, sir." He didn't elaborate.

"Al, have you looked out the window?"

Another massive bolt of lightning hit. They were flying over a broad sea, with here and there a monument or a piece of the State Department projecting out of the water. "Yeah," said Kerr. "I saw it."

Henry wondered how many people had still been in the city. Taking his advice. "Al, where are we headed?"

"It's still dry at Camp David, sir."

They were turning to the northwest, running over the quiet waters, riding in relative silence now, save for the storm. "Mr. President." The pilot's voice again, breaking in, bringing him back from some other place.

"Yes. What is it?"

"You've got a call. Man named Feinberg."

"Patch him through, pilot."

Some clicks in his earphones. And then Feinberg's rasp: "Mr. President?"

"Hello, Wesley. You'll be interested in knowing we've just lost Washington."

"Mr. President, don't do it."

"Don't do *what?*"

"Don't nuke the Possum."

Henry looked down at the drowned city. "I think we've had enough, Wesley."

"*No!* If you persist, you'll only make things worse."

They were the last words Henry heard. He was about to reply, to ask how he could possibly make things worse, to observe that he was by God going to take the Possum out of the game, when someone screamed, the inside of the cockpit blurred, fire broke out, and the chopper's nightlights died. He was half-conscious, trying to find Emily in the dark, and he knew he was falling.

TRANSGLOBAL COMMENTARY. 5:10 A.M.

"The loss of power in the middle of the presidential press conference is the final straw in the assault against the public nerve. Probably never before in the history of the republic has the entire population stayed up all night. Millions have been driven from their homes, people have died in vast numbers, families are swept away in full view of TV cameras, and property damage mounts, God help us, into the trillions.

"The American people were surprised to see a presidential press conference only hours after two presidential addresses. If they were expecting Mr. Kolladner to announce Armageddon, they were carried along by his unexpected spirit of confidence and optimism. His clear goal of calming the nation might have been obtained had he not suddenly disappeared from the world's screens. In a hundred languages around the globe, voices explained that the transmission had been lost temporarily at its source, and that the telecast would continue momentarily.

"That news was followed, a few minutes later, by an announcement that a tsunami had struck Washington and continued all the way to Front Royal before exhausting itself against the Blue Ridge. The whereabouts of the president, as of this moment, are unknown. This is Judy Gunworthy with the Transglobal News Service, at the National Weather Service Office in El Paso."

Micro Passenger Cabin. 5:43 A.M.

"Charlie." It was Kerr again. But his voice sounded strange.

"Yes, Al. What's wrong?"

"Charlie, we've lost the president."

Charlie Haskell's heart began to speed up. What had Harry Truman said on hearing of FDR's death? *It was like a load of bullshit got dropped on me.*

Chapter Eight

BELL-RINGER
Sunday, April 14

1.

Manhattan. 5:45 A.M.

The effort to loot the local grocery store failed. Marvin and one of the accountants tore down a double-sized door to use as a raft, but their combined weight was too much and it capsized several times, dumping them into the flood. The accountant lost heart, and everybody else, including Larry, decided the smart thing would be to wait for the Guard. Finally Marvin set off alone. He came back an hour later, complaining that the store Louise had described was completely underwater. But he'd gotten off the raft, forced his way inside, and nearly drowned. He looked as if the story were true. He now joined those recommending they simply wait until help arrived. An unaccustomed whine had come into his voice, and Marilyn decided he didn't look as good this morning as he had last night. *Never start a romance with somebody,* she thought, *until you've seen him in a flood.*

Louise's refrigerator emptied out in a hurry, and the bottled water disappeared, despite all efforts at rationing. Her guests began to suggest that maybe they *should* make another effort to get canned goods out of the submerged store. "You can't tell how long we might be here," one of them said. Marv said he would not try it again under *any* circumstances.

A stock analyst who'd done a year at medical school pointed out that anybody going into the water, which was choked with corpses, risked typhus or some other ungodly disease. "Marv's right," she said. "We should wait."

They were cut off from the rest of the world. The batteries in the TV had died, and there was nothing to do now but gaze out over the city, gray and forlorn in the morning light. A stench had begun to creep into the air.

Larry tried to play the role of defender and provider that he must have felt was expected of him. He assured Marilyn everything would be okay, asked whether she was all right, and gathered her into his arms when she got teary. He didn't quite fit the part: Larry looked more at home in an office than in a crisis. But she felt it was nice of him to try.

She knew her husband would never have gone inside a submerged grocery store. But she also knew that, if he had, he wouldn't have come back and whined about it.

There was sudden commotion behind her: people pointing to the northwest. A helicopter, *several* helicopters, were coming in from over the Hudson, flying in formation, staying low. They penetrated the concrete valleys and divided into pairs as they approached the Central Park area.

There were other people atop other buildings, and everybody was waving. One of the choppers came in close and hovered directly overhead. It was olive-drab. Military. A voice spoke through a loudspeaker: "Folks, please clear the roof." Backwash from the rotors tore at her hair.

A soldier leaned out and gazed down at her. "How many of you are there?"

Quick estimate. "Thirty," Marilyn said, but the words were blown away. She spread both hands three times. Somebody behind her was saying, "Tell them fifty, get as much as you can."

The soldier signaled okay. The man who'd wanted to claim fifty muttered, "Dumb bitch." He was a little fat man with tufts of hair over his ears, framing a bald head. Larry heard the remark and went after him. The fat man started swinging wildly, and punched a woman who didn't get clear quickly enough. Then the circle of bystanders closed in to separate the two.

Marilyn felt proud of Larry at that moment. Not only because he'd defended her; but because the fat man was a department manager or some such thing at Bradley & Boone. Larry's job had just disappeared. For him, it had been a more courageous act than braving the flood to find his wife.

She hadn't felt this good about her marriage since the day she'd walked up the aisle.

The chopper came down until it was only a few feet overhead. Four cartons tumbled out. "Anybody need medical help?" asked the loudspeaker.

They glanced around at one another. "I've got a back problem," shouted a thin, weak-eyed man Marilyn didn't know. He didn't look like the type who would readily consent to ride in a helicopter.

"Can you walk, sir?"

"I think so."

"Good. Stay off your feet. The rest of you stay put. We'll be back."

The chopper lifted away. Larry made another lunge at the little fat man, and somebody told him to calm down. Marilyn could see that, under the indignant mask, her husband was quite pleased with himself.

TRANSGLOBAL SPECIAL REPORT. 5:47 A.M.

"This is Angela Shepard at Camp David, Maryland. An army helicopter carrying President Henry Kolladner was reported down minutes ago outside Washington. The president had been evacuated moments before a sea wave swept over the capital, and was en route here, where a command post had been set up to coordinate the government's response to the ongoing lunar crisis. The helicopter was apparently struck by lightning. Official sources are telling us that rescue units have been sent in, and that they still hold out hope.

"I talked to a member of the president's staff who was on board an accompanying aircraft, and who asked not to be named. She was in tears, Don. She said the president's helicopter caught fire and, in her words, 'fell like a rock.' She added that she doesn't believe anyone could have lived through it."

Micro Passenger Cabin. 5:48 A.M.

"Charlie, it's confirmed," said the voice on his cell phone. "They found the wreckage."

"He's dead?"

"Yes."

"Emily. What about Emily?"

"She was with him when it happened."

"My God. . . ."

Micro Flight Deck. 5:49 A.M.

"What is your status, Micro?"

"We are still here, Skyport. Life support looks good. The cargo deck has been penetrated again, but otherwise we're okay."

"We copy, Micro."

"Fuel is almost gone."

"Roger that. Continue to try to conserve. We'll get to you as quickly as we can."

They were currently moving at 8.1 kilometers per second, gaining speed as they fell toward Earth. Consequently, no rescue vehicle could be sent out to rendezvous until *after* they'd passed Skyport, which would happen around one-thirty P.M.

"Are you in any danger at the present moment?"

"Negative."

There was a hesitation at the other end. Then the bad news: "Micro, we project a solar orbit."

"Roger." Saber would have no fuel available for braking. So they would roar past the Earth satellite at present velocity plus whatever they picked up firing the engine and falling down the gravity well. "Skyport, I make it that we'll be moving too fast for a ferry to rendezvous."

"Keep the faith, Micro. You have a VIP on board. Two of them, in fact."

Saber ran the numbers through her computer. After they passed the planet, a ferry could chase them down, but the effort would require too much fuel. There wouldn't be enough left after the rescue, not nearly enough, to brake into earth-orbit. The ferry and the Micro would *both* sail out into deep space. To add to her worries, they would start running out of air again around six P.M. That was a long way off, but this time there'd be no onboard fix. Fortunately, however, there was an easy solution, and if Skyport didn't think of it, she'd suggest it herself.

She signed off, rubbed her eyes, and looked at the radar screen, which was mercifully quiet again. She'd recovered Tony's body and stored it below with Bigfoot. That had been a sad business. But at least his sacrifice hadn't been to no purpose. Unless something took a wicked turn on her, the Micro would bring in Charlie Haskell and the other volunteers.

She'd tried to get through to St. Petersburg, to see how her family was. The Russian city had been struck by a series of withering electrical storms and subsequent flooding. But telephone communications were impossible. So, since there was nothing else she could do, she put it out of her mind.

The Micro still had to burn fuel occasionally, to move out of harm's way. She wasn't seeing the storms of pebbles and sand anymore. The debris now tended to be limited to boulders and slabs. But they were relatively infrequent, and no longer racing past the Micro. The microbus was moving far more quickly than it had been during the early minutes of the event, and the rocks were traveling more slowly.

A few were enormous. One in particular measured out at

more than eighty kilometers across. A moonlet. She reported it to the Orbital Lab at Skyport, where it turned out they'd already tagged it. The woman she talked to told her it was going into orbit.

"Good," said Saber. "You wouldn't want *this* thing coming down."

The woman's name was Tory Clark. And Tory made herself memorable to Saber by passing on a news item: "By the way," she said, "they've confirmed the death of the president. Take care of Charlie Haskell."

It had been a long night and Saber needed about thirty seconds to realize she was now carrying the president of the United States.

She knew she should simply fly the bus, but she couldn't resist dropping down through the hatch to wish him well. To be the first to do so, because she was sure no one else in the passenger cabin had the information. Maybe even *he* didn't know, although the lamp over his telephone circuit had been burning continuously. Poor son of a bitch, he's half-dead up here and they still won't leave him alone.

She approached his chair. He had the phone to his ear, listening, taking notes. She stopped beside him and waited. He glanced up at her, held up his hand, signaling her to wait a moment, and then, when he could, asked the person on the other end to wait.

"Yes, Saber," he said, "what can I do for you?"

"Mr. President," she said, pronouncing the word with effect, and drawing the attention of everyone around her, "I wanted to wish you good luck."

That set off something of an explosion. Was it true? Had they found Henry Kolladner?

It had occurred to Charlie when he'd first gotten the news that Henry might have been fortunate. It was probably the only way he could have saved his reputation. Now he accepted their good wishes, embracing Evelyn and Saber and shaking hands with Keith and the chaplain. Then he went back to the telephone.

Saber tried to find him some privacy, but the only accessible sections on the microbus were the galley and the washroom. The galley wasn't very private and the washroom lacked ambiance. The new president would have to make do where he sat in the passenger cabin. He asked only that Keith Morley use nothing he overheard without getting specific approval.

Saber returned to the flight deck, and shortly afterward heard the hatch open. The chaplain's smiling face looked up. "I hope you don't mind," he said. "I was wondering if I could see how this thing operates."

She signaled for him to strap down in the copilot's seat.

He looked out at the luminous Earth. After a few inconsequential remarks he fell into a contemplative silence. "The universe seems very neutral," he said at last.

"How do you mean?"

"Not for publication."

"Of course not."

"Are you a believer?"

She thought about it. "I don't know, Chaplain. Probably not."

He nodded. "I cannot believe Jesus would permit what happened last night. Not the *Jesus* I know." Saber didn't know how to respond, understood that the comment needed no response. "Tell me, Saber," he said after a moment, "is there life on Mars?"

"Yes," she said, wondering what he was getting at. "But of a primitive order."

The chaplain nodded. "Doesn't matter how primitive. Conditions will allow what they will allow. Elsewhere conditions will be better. Right? Caribbean-style beaches. Cool, moist valleys. Rolling plains. Other Scotlands exist out there somewhere."

"Yes," she said. "I'd think that would have to be so. It's inconceivable that it isn't."

"Oh, it's conceivable that we're alone. *I* can conceive of it, and I wish it were so."

"Why?" she asked. Everyone she'd ever known had wanted the search for alien life-forms, alien civilizations, to succeed. The notion that anybody, *anybody*, would prefer an empty universe shocked her.

"Because then the story of Jesus would make sense. But in a universe like *this*, where we suspect there are perhaps *millions* of other races like our own, his sacrifice hardly seems applicable to the existing nature of things." The chaplain shook his head. "Either the crucifixion saves them all, or it does not. If it saves them all, we're asked to believe that out of this plenitude of worlds, He chose ours for His demonstration."

She could hear the chaplain's doubts, welling up from some long-blocked inner spring. She could hear the capitalized pronouns, could hear the plea for intervention. "If the crucifixion does *not* save everyone, then it must be carried out, in one form or another, countless times in countless places. What then becomes of His agonies, of the special sacrifice made for *us*?"

She thought about it for several minutes. "I never did understand the logic of the crucifixion," she said at last. "Maybe the point is supposed to be simply that he came."

2.

Skyport, Mo's Restaurant. 5:51 A.M.

Rachel Quinn hadn't slept. Like everyone else at the station, she'd been glued to the television. She recalled with mounting guilt her own anger that the Mars mission had been wiped out. But then, she'd had no idea the arrival of the comet would trigger anything like this.

Nevertheless, buried in the relentless accounts of waves, storms, and earthquakes, there were some encouraging stories; heroes were appearing everywhere. In Fort Lauderdale a man in a motor yacht picked up survivors and rode out several tsunamis. Doctors stayed at their posts in Baltimore, chopper-riding cops scooped people off rooftops in Houston, teenagers hurried toddlers to safety in Savannah. When a wave hit Vancouver Island, a man saved a group of his neighbors by piling them into a hydrogen balloon. He got clear with seconds to spare. In St. Augustine, a young woman helped several elderly couples climb an old stone tower to escape.

Even Skyport had been hit. Debris had blown out compartments on two decks, and three people were dead.

Rachel was in Mo's, having toast and coffee, watching CNN, when her cell phone trilled. The identifier indicated the call was from Operations. "Quinn," she said.

"Colonel, I'm Howard Chambers, special assistant to Belle Cassidy." Cassidy was the director of operations. "She'd like to see you if you could come by her office."

Ten minutes later Rachel was led through Cassidy's door. The director was standing in a corner of the room, bent over a console with two aides. She smiled at Rachel, dismissed the aides, and invited her to sit down. Belle Cassidy was in her early forties. There was something of the drill instructor in her demeanor. She stood ramrod straight, had short black hair, marble eyes, and wide shoulders. Rachel knew her, had even dined with her once when several of the astronauts had been passing through and the Skyport staff had given a dinner.

"Good to see you again, Rachel," she said, extending a hand. A gold chain tinkled on her wrist, a subtle flash of femininity in an otherwise masculine personality.

The office was big, as Skyport offices went. On the walls

were framed documents detailing its occupant's services to various federal agencies, to foreign governments, and to the Lunar Transport Authority, her current employer. Belle folded her arms and remained standing. "Rachel," she said, "we need your help."

"In what way?"

"Were you aware President Kolladner is dead?"

"Yes," she said. "I heard about it a little while ago."

"The new president is stranded out there." Belle waved her hand in the general direction of the overhead. "In about seven and a half hours he's going to sail past here, doing forty thousand-plus kilometers an hour. Unless we get something out there that has the juice to catch him, they might as well swear in whoever's next in line. That idiot Speaker, I guess it would be."

Rachel's eyes widened. "You're asking for the *Lowell*?"

"It's all we've got. The ferries can't handle it."

"Sure," she said. "I'll get the numbers from your people, and we'll be ready to go."

"I appreciate it."

"It's my pleasure."

Regret showed in Belle's face. "I'll be honest with you. We spent the last couple of hours trying to figure out how to do it with our ferries. I mean, how often does the LTA get a chance to rescue a president?"

"No way, huh?"

"Well . . . if we had to, we could give it a good run. But it's too close to take the chance." She shook Rachel's hand. "So NASA gets the glory. Again."

FRANK CRANDALL'S ALL-NIGHTER. 5:57 A.M.

For those of you tuning in late, and those who've been flooding our switchboard, let me say again, Frank's okay. He was slightly injured last night, but he's otherwise fine. As you know, the show is usually broadcast from Miami. But the storm knocked out our facility there. Frank twisted a knee, but it's nothing serious and he'll be back tonight. Meantime, this is Paul DiAngelo sitting in for the Old Trooper. Now we've got time for one more caller before we get out of here. And Llewellyn tells me we've got a live one. Hello, Margaret in Los Angeles.

Caller: Hi, Paul. Tell Frank all of us in L.A. wish him well.

DiAngelo: He'll be happy to hear that, Margaret. Why don't you tell our listeners where you are right now?

Caller: I'm in my office, on the third floor of the Warrior Warehouse on the waterfront.

DiAngelo: And what are you doing there?

Caller: Actually, I'm working late. I'm one of the partners at Warrior. But what I'm really doing is watching for the tidal wave. And I can tell you, the ocean is smooth as silk.

DiAngelo: Wait a minute, Margaret. You're sitting down at the waterfront watching for a tidal wave?

Caller: (Laughs.) I'm perfectly safe. These are high floors. I'm almost a hundred feet over the parking lot, and the building is concrete.

DiAngelo: Margaret, why are you doing this?

Caller: How many times do you get to see a tidal wave, Paul? Anyway, I've got my minicam up here, and if it comes I expect to get some good pictures.

DiAngelo: I hope so. Have you thought about the possibility you might get cut off up there?

Caller: The freezer's loaded. Listen, this isn't the reason I called, though.

DiAngelo: Okay, Margaret, but we're almost out of time. Make it quick.

Caller: How many people died last night?

DiAngelo: I don't know. The estimates are all over the place.

Caller:	*A lot.*
DiAngelo:	*Yeah.*
Caller:	*That's right, Paul. And we could have saved a lot of those people if those clowns in Washington hadn't just dismissed the whole thing.*
DiAngelo:	*Looks that way.*
Caller:	*I think we're ripe for an impeachment, don't you?*
DiAngelo:	*Margaret, the president is among the victims.*
Caller:	*I know. And I wish I could say I'm sorry he's dead. But they really screwed up this time. And somebody needs to pay.*
DiAngelo:	*Thanks for your thoughts, Margaret. We're out of time, folks. Don't forget, Frank'll be back tonight, at his regular time, live.*

3.

Micro. 6:22 A.M.

"I, Charles L. Haskell, do solemnly swear that I will faithfully execute the office of President of the United States, and will, to the best of my ability, preserve, protect, and defend the Constitution of the United States."

Justice Mary B. Longbridge administered the oath by radio. She was at Egmont Air Force Base. It was the first time in U.S. history that the presiding official and the incoming president were physically separated.

In fact, other than Haskell, no U.S. citizen was present at the inauguration.

Had Mr. Haskell been visible to the electorate, they would have noted that the new president looked as if he'd been mugged. His face was swollen and he was covered with bruises.

There was no physical Bible in the microbus. Therefore, Mr. Haskell brought up an appropriate biblical verse from the ship's library and placed his left hand on the display while he took the oath. The passage, recommended by Chaplain Mark Pinnacle, was from Numbers, Chapter VI, Verses 24–26.

At thirty-eight, Charlie Haskell became the youngest president in U.S. history, surpassing Theodore Roosevelt by three years. He was the ninth vice president to succeed to the presidency on the death of the incumbent, and the tenth over-all to assume the post (Gerald Ford having been inaugurated after the resignation of Richard Nixon).

His middle initial stood for Lionel, which was the name of an uncle he had met only once. He detested the name, and to the extent he was able, he never allowed it to be used or to appear in print.

He spoke for six minutes and eleven seconds, easily the shortest inauguration address on record. No other president, he said, had been sworn in at a darker moment. But he would do everything he could, with the united help of the American people, and their friends around the world, to ensure that the nation survived the event, to ease its burdens, to head off fur-ther disaster, and to begin the long process of recovery. "We will go on," he said. "We will learn from this, and we will not be turned aside. The broken Moon will remain in our skies, to remind us that we are not isolated on the Earth. There is a greater world beyond, and we must recognize we are part of that greater world. We must learn to apply our technologies to protect ourselves to the extent we are able; and we must also rethink who we are. Tonight we have arrived at a critical moment in our history. We must accept our losses, because we cannot do otherwise. But we will not accept defeat, we will go forward, because to fail to do so would be a betrayal of all who died during these last few hours."

When the ceremony ended, they drank a toast to his suc-cess. Evelyn had designed, and Saber printed, programs for the event, and everyone asked him to sign a copy.

"This isn't exactly the way I'd pictured my inauguration,"

he told them. "Usually the swearing-in includes a parade, ball-rooms, dignitaries, lots of press coverage." He smiled at Keith Morley, who'd agreed to shut the mike off momentarily. "This one is quieter than most. But I think no other president has been so fortunate in the persons who surrounded him during the rite of passage. Living and dead." He lifted his glass to toast *them*. "Thank you."

4.

<u>WPYX REPORTING.</u> 4:33 A.M. PDT (7:33 A.M. EDT).
(Helicopter in the background, rotors slowly turning.)
    "... atop the New County Courthouse in Los Angeles. From our perch up here we can see the Hall of Justice, the Federal Building, the Civic Center. Everywhere, frightened crowds are breaking into whatever buildings, whatever skyscrapers, they can, hoping to get up high." (*Crowd noises, explosions, gunfire audible in background.*)
    "We can see lights and people moving on the upper floors of police headquarters and at the Museum of Contemporary Art. As far as we can tell, there is no longer an organized police force left in the city. The streets are filled with people. I don't know where they keep coming from.
    "Our best information is that all highways out of the city remain hopelessly blocked. PacRail, of course, stopped operating earlier this evening, so right now the only salvation anyone has is to get above the water level. Whatever that might be. In fact, they're signaling me that we can hear people moving up in this building.
    "Okay, that's the story from Hill Street and Beverly Boulevard. We're going to switch over now to Linda Tellier, who's in our news copter at Redondo Beach. Linda?"
    "Thanks, Rod. We're about a half mile off shore, awaiting the first of the waves that the National Weather Service has been predicting for the last few hours. We're just over the water now, and while you can't see it in the dark, Redondo Beach is experiencing an extraordi-

narily low tide. That's one of the sure signs of an approaching wave.

"Looking east, we can see the lights of Torrance and Inglewood. Interstate 405 is almost dark, Rod. It's filled with abandoned cars. Police and military units were up there until about an hour ago, just pushing vehicles off the highway, but they're gone now too. And when we looked at it a few minutes ago, we saw only a few people wandering aimlessly, and some who were stripping cars.

"We were in touch with the Coast Guard—wait, I think I see something now. You're not getting this in your picture, but I can see what looks like a wall across the horizon. The ocean just seems to be rising up. And up." (*Long pause.*) "And up. God help us, Rod, it's hard to tell for sure, but that thing might be fifteen stories high.

"I hope everyone's out of Redondo."

Pacific Coast. 4:39 A.M. Pacific Daylight Time (7:39 A.M. EDT).

The first wave struck well before dawn. It roared ashore between Point Conception and Santa Barbara and boiled into the Santa Ynez Mountains. Forewarned, the population had scattered to high ground, and only a handful of casualties were recorded. The National Park Service estimated that the wave was one hundred fifty feet high.

Within minutes other tsunamis hit Seattle and Coos Bay. The Seattle wave was initially reported to have been a half-mile high when it struck the city, but videos taken from office buildings and aircraft put the crest at only a tenth of that figure. It was enough.

Between four thirty-five and five A.M., the Pacific rose from its bed and overwhelmed the coastline from Juneau to San Carlos. In the Los Angeles area, the city simply disappeared, save for a few downtown skyscrapers and the surrounding hilltops. Most of Santa Monica and Redondo, Inglewood and Long Beach went with it.

San Francisco also died. A wave estimated at six hundred fifty feet took down the Golden Gate Bridge, submerged the city from the Presidio on the north to San Andreas Lake on the south. It buried Oakland and Berkeley, and poured through the Simi Valley and the bays north of San Francisco into the California interior. The San Joaquin Valley became an inland sea.

Initial estimates put the death toll at two million in greater Los Angeles alone. Curiously, throughout the bombardment San Diego remained untouched. It reported lower than normal tides.

In Mexico the ocean surged over Baja California, spilled into the Gulf of California, and maintained enough power to impose severe damage on the eastern shore from Isla Del Tiburon to Mazatlán.

County Route 6, southeast of San Francisco.
4:59 A.M. PDT (7:59 A.M. EDT).

There were no emergency services. Phones were dead and the radio in the police car brought only a carrier wave. As the first gray light of dawn was appearing, a helicopter owned by Short Haul Airways arrived with a doctor and some medical supplies.

"Best I could do," said the pilot, whose name Marisa never caught. "It's pretty grim out there."

Among the group trapped by the landslide, there'd been only one physician, and he'd broken his back. Marisa and Jerry had taken charge of the rescue effort.

They had converted the restaurant into a makeshift hospital, and the antique shop into a morgue. She'd tried to treat the seriously injured where they fell, despite the threat presented by the cliff. But the ground had continued to shake, and eventually she'd bitten the bullet and ordered everyone away. Ten minutes later the mountain had collapsed.

Jerry had rounded up volunteers and they pitched in to help, cleaning wounds, setting bones, and applying tourniquets. The doctor who'd come in aboard the chopper had been vacationing at a mountain cabin when Short Haul found him.

They had about forty people who needed hospital treatment. "Not going to happen," said the doctor. His name was Hardacre and he was in his early thirties. He was a young, good-looking guy who complained that it was his first vacation in three years. He seemed to regard the disaster as a personal imposition. But he'd come, and he seemed competent, so Marisa wasn't complaining.

"What do you mean, it's not going to happen?" she demanded.

"You been watching the TV?" he asked.

"Not for the last hour or so."

"When you get a minute, take a look. Whatever hospitals are left will be swamped. It's likely to be a long time before anybody's going to have beds available."

She looked around at her patients. They had no cots, so the patients had all been placed on the floor and made as comfortable as conditions allowed. Hardacre had grabbed some painkillers and other supplies from the cache at the resort where he'd been staying, and they'd helped, had helped a lot. But these people needed serious treatment. What were they going to do?

As if to underscore the point, a distant murmur was becoming audible. Marisa's first thought was that the rest of the mountain was coming down. They were well across the road, far enough away to be safe, but the sound was different from the one she'd heard earlier. And it was coming from the opposite direction, from the San Joaquin. Maybe the part of the mountain they were sitting on was going to go this time.

She put it out of her mind and went back to changing a dressing. The patient was a middle-aged woman with a shattered leg and a sliced arm. Hardacre had put twenty stitches in the arm and supported the leg as best he could. The woman's husband, who'd come through untouched, was beside her.

Marisa's thoughts returned to Jerry. They'd set up a center for the lost kids wandering around. Jerry had seen that it was properly staffed. Now he was busy on the far side of the restaurant, changing bandages. It wasn't something he liked to do and, in fact, Jerry had never liked blood very much, but he was shining this morning.

When she finished with the woman, she went on to other patients. The distant sound was getting louder. It was nothing like the fearful roar of the avalanche, but it was disquieting all the same, as if something were coming.

She was changing a dressing when one of the volunteers charged through a door. "The valley's filling up!" she cried.

Marisa was almost immune to alarms by now. She finished what she was doing and strode to a back window that looked down into the San Joaquin.

It spread out before her, a vast basin rimmed by mountains lost in early-morning mist. Toward the west, a deluge was gushing out of a narrow defile and spreading out across the valley floor.

Later, when she took a break and went to see Erin and Jimmy, they hugged her and asked when they were going home. By then an inland sea, quiet and tranquil, stretched toward the morning sun as far as she could see.

"We *are* home," she said quietly.

Micro Passenger Cabin. 8:03 A.M.

"Say again, Al."

Charlie tried to keep his voice low so he couldn't be overheard. But the conversation among the other passengers always stopped as soon as he got on the phone. He knew they weren't trying to eavesdrop, except maybe Morley, whose job it was, but human nature was at work here. It was useless to try for privacy under these circumstances. Anyway, what did it matter?

"I said NASA tells us you'll be okay. They've figured out how to rescue you."

"I didn't know I needed to be rescued."

"My God, are you serious? You're on your way to Pluto or something. They're sending the *Lowell* after you."

Charlie waved it away. In the face of everything else that had landed on him, the news seemed almost anticlimactic. "Okay," he said.

He'd been off and on the phone with Al Kerr for the better part of two hours, getting updates on a series of increasingly desperate situations. The United States had literally millions of people on the road for whom there was neither shelter nor food, swamping efforts by relief agencies. Both coasts and the Hawaiian Islands had been heavily damaged by waves and storms. In some places earthquakes had been triggered. Property damage would be in the trillions. And God knew how much loss of life. Medical authorities were already warning about the possibility of infectious outbreaks; more tidal waves were reported in the Pacific.

Financial experts were pointing out that the functional loss of New York and Los Angeles would destroy the banking system, and were advising the government to move immediately.

"What do they suggest?" Charlie asked.

"I don't think they have any idea at this point, Mr. President. But they want us to know that action is of the essence."

What else?

There were major power outages in the Northeast and Northwest; tens of thousands of Mexican refugees for whom no provision could be made were streaming north; a freak electrical storm had virtually destroyed Tucson.

There were, however, some pieces of *genuine* good news: The heartland was still intact. The federal government was functioning well; early indications were that its agencies and the military were performing miracles. Europe and Asia had not been hit as hard as the Americas, and their allies, and even a few old enemies, were helping where they could. Best of all, the missiles were locked and loaded, and by nine A.M. the Possum would be history.

Charlie outlined his priorities. Foremost, they needed to concentrate on the refugee problem. "Do whatever's necessary to get food and services out. There's a potential here for even worse losses. We need to figure out what we can do for the people on the road, and we need to get it right the first time. And don't feel you have to wait for presidential authorization. Something needs to get done, do it. Just keep me informed. I'll support you."

"Or fire me," said Al, obviously uncomfortable. Kerr had never been a supporter of Charlie Haskell, and now he expected to pay the price.

Charlie had more important things to think about. "I want action plans waiting for me as soon as I get back. Assemble a working group to get ahead of the curve. I don't want to be just reacting to disasters. Put some people together to figure out what else might happen, what else we can do."

"What specifically did you have in mind, Mr. President?"

"Cholera and typhus, for one thing." He took a deep breath because he sensed the man's timidity. Anger flowed through him. There just wasn't time now for people who weren't ready to get things done. "Goddammit, Al," he said, "if I *knew*, I wouldn't need the working group. Keep it small. I want ideas, not ass-covering. What do we need to do to keep the country alive? Not just people, but the institutions. You got that?

"Get somebody from the military. CDC. FEMA. Some academics. Figure it out. We got blindsided this week, Al. And I think we've had all we can stand. No more surprises."

Was there anything else?

Yeah, there was. His voice softened: "I'm sorry about Henry and Emily. I know you and they were close."

"Thank you, Mr. President."

"I'll expect you to stay on as chief of staff. At least until we get through this."

"Yes, sir."

He broke the connection, wandered back into the passenger cabin, where everyone pretended to be busy reading. "Everything okay, Mr. President?" Evelyn asked.

They'd all gone formal on him again. And maybe it was just as well. He wondered how much Lincoln would have accomplished if everyone in the neighborhood had called him Abe.

"Fine," he said. "We're doing fine."

Which reminded him. He went up the ladder—he was getting good at zero-g moves now—and came in behind Saber. "Hello, pilot," he said.

She raised a hand without looking around. "Hello, Mr. President."

"I understand we're not going to Pluto after all," he said.

"Oh," she said. "You know about that. No, we'll be okay. We were never at risk."

He slid into the copilot's chair. "You're sure?"

"Yes, sir," she said.

"Anything I ought to know about?"

"No, Mr. President."

"If there's another problem, I'd like to be informed," he said.

"Yes, sir. I didn't think of it as a problem. I mean, I knew they had the *Lowell* in reserve." She smiled up at him. Saber was, he decided, a beautiful woman. Somehow, there hadn't been time to notice before. "I thought you had enough to worry about. Getting the Micro back was *my* job."

"Do we have any fuel left at all?"

"We've got a couple hundred pounds. Not very much. I'm trying to save it."

"Okay. What's the drill on the rescue?"

She relaxed a little. "*Lowell* will catch up with us around four. We'll transfer over and cut the Micro loose. They haven't sent me an ETA yet, but I'd guess we'll get back to the station by late evening. That's only a guess. I don't know what the capabilities of the *Lowell* are."

Charlie looked at the myriad blinking lights and telltales on the Micro's displays. "Can we see the Possum from here?"

She touched a key, and the rock appeared on a heads-up screen. "That's the view from one of the satellites."

The media descriptions said the Possum looked like something that had been cut in half. One side was flat, the other curved and rugged. It was more oblong than spherical, almost resembling a club. He was glad that idea hadn't occurred to anyone in the media. He watched it tumbling slowly across the display.

Saber's fingers moved over the keyboard. "Here's something to compare it with." An image of the Micro blinked on. It shrank until it was almost invisible against the object. "That's us." She pressed another key, and a series of micro-icons lined up along the length of the rock. "There are sixty-one of them," she said. "End to end."

"And how big are *we*?"

"Twenty-eight meters and change, blister to treads. We're pretty compact."

"We'll be well rid of the thing," he said.

The Possum exerted a near-hypnotic influence. He watched it turning, watched, on another screen, the blue globe of Earth.

The second image, Saber explained, was from the Micro's telescopes.

The distance between the vice presidency and the office of the chief executive, Charlie was discovering, is measured in light-years. It might be that no one really understands that who hasn't stood on both sides of the chasm. A few hours ago he was only worried about saving himself. That concern now seemed almost trivial.

The third decade of the twenty-first century had, until a few days earlier, been a good time for the planet. A hundred million Chinese were driving cars, almost everyone agreed that military incursions were in bad taste, the old economic cycle of boom and bust appeared to have been tamed, and the great powers had discovered that collaboration was more fruitful than competition. Technology was providing better lives for almost everybody. Science was forging ahead, and people now lived longer and stayed younger than ever before. Most cancers were curable; powersats supplied virtually unlimited energy; and the long struggle to reverse environmental damage had finally turned the corner. In the United States, racial tensions had been steadily easing, GNP was up every year, crime rates and population growth were down.

This is not to say there were no problems. There were far more people than the world's natural resources could comfortably support, and ancient traditions and religious groups fought every effort to reduce the numbers. There was still too much crime, and too much of it violent, particularly in Russia, the United States, and China. A recent survey of American adults by *USA Today* suggested that three-eighths of the population were functionally illiterate. This was the highest ratio of any industrialized society, and it continued to climb steadily. The advantages of participating in the global communications network were still not available to a quarter of the U.S. population, and to more than a third of those living in other Western nations. Every major government carried a staggering burden of debt.

These were the problems a Haskell administration would have reasonably expected to confront. Anticipating the possibility of victory in the fall, Charlie had already staffed out work and formulated some ideas on his own. He'd talked to the people on the front lines, teachers and parents and cops and emergency room physicians and first-line supervisors in a wide range of occupations. He thought he was ready to assume the burdens of the presidency with a series of initiatives to attack these problems across a broad front.

As things had turned out, he could hardly have been less prepared.

Saber frowned and touched her earphone. "Wait one," she said and looked at Charlie. "For you, Mr. President." But his lamp hadn't lit up, so the call wasn't coming in on his private channel. "Do you want to talk to a Wesley Feinberg?"

"I've got it." Charlie opened his cell phone. He'd never met Feinberg, but he knew him by reputation. And Al had briefed him on his part in the planning. Called him a troublemaker. "Good morning, Professor Feinberg. This is Charles Haskell."

"Mr. President." The voice was strained. "I've been trying to get through to you for hours. Are you still planning to execute the nuclear strike against the Possum?"

"Yes," said Charlie. "Of course."

"Don't."

Charlie's heart sank. "Why not?"

"We don't know enough to be able to change its trajectory. That's what we really need to do. But we don't know how."

"So we give it a try. What's to lose?"

"What's to *lose*? Mr. President, you blow it apart and you'll create a cloud of radioactive particles and debris that would be just as likely as the Possum to come back around and hit us later. Except that, if it were to happen, the consequences would be even worse."

"Worse how? My information is that the Possum would kill a few *more* millions. Maybe send us back to a dark age."

"Mr. President, a healthy radioactive cloud would have a good chance to kill *everybody* on the planet. I'm talking about an extinction event."

Charlie visualized a storm of hot pebbles ripping into the global landscape and the oceans, hot particles settling into the atmosphere, hot rain pouring down out of diseased clouds. "Why didn't you tell this to Henry?"

"I did. Or I tried to. I was talking to him when we got cut off. I think it was probably at the time his helicopter went down."

"What did he say?"

"He didn't have a chance to say anything." Saber was watching Charlie. "You *must* stop the attack," Feinberg went on. "It will gain nothing, but it raises the stakes dramatically for us if it comes down."

"But it might *not* come down. Is that right?"

"There's no way to be sure."

"For God's sake, Feinberg, isn't there a way to find out?"

"After it leaves the atmosphere, give us a few hours."

A few hours would put it out of range of the missiles. They'd have to wait, and hit it inbound. His own people had advised him that was a much more dangerous procedure. "Are you at all optimistic? Is there a chance it'll just go away?"

"Give me a few hours, Mr. President."

After the call, Charlie sat for almost ten minutes. He refused all calls and considered his options and the potential consequences. He thought about Feinberg's reputation, and he'd read enough between the lines of Al Kerr's account to understand the scientist had given Henry good advice.

But a lot of people thought the nukes were a good way to get rid of the goddam thing. If Charlie failed to pull the trigger and it came around and hit them, who was going to get the blame?

On the other hand, would it matter who got the blame?

He looked at his watch. The birds would fly in less than an hour. Beside him, Saber was very quiet. "You overheard all that?"

"I heard your end."

He punched in Al Kerr's number.

5.

Fax Received and Broadcast by C-Span. 8:26 A.M.

> We're all on a bus, the whole human race. The bus is tearing along a road that's mostly empty. But there are a few rocks on the road, and maybe once in a while another vehicle, and we've just discovered there's no driver.

—Dan White, Oklahoma City

Skyport Orbital Lab. 8:41 A.M.

Substantial pieces of the World Wide Web were missing. Whole networks had dropped out of sight; power companies had gone down; telephone systems had collapsed. Still, the redundancies and bypasses that had accreted over the years served it well, and it stayed up and running. If one's telephone company was still operational, access to the Web remained.

Skybolt's champions became especially visible on-line. There was a flood of I-told-you-so comments. And the names of congressmen who had been prominent in attacking the project were being posted for general consumption.

The Possum was still approaching, but it had passed behind the curve of the Earth and was consequently no longer directly visible from Skyport's onboard observatory. The best images now were coming in from ground-based telescopes. Tory and Windy watched the show on their main display.

POSIM-38's lack of symmetry, its resemblance to a flattened club, or possibly (as someone had suggested) a sliced squash, gave it a unique identity. The prevailing explanation for its shape was that one side had been more directly exposed to the blast and that combustible materials had boiled off, leaving a relatively smooth, cooling residue. The flat side was promptly dubbed the "Plain," as opposed to the rounded, heavily scored rear, which astronomers were calling the "Back Country." A ridge formed a kind of spine, running lengthwise through the Back Country. It was the *only* feature on the terrain that did not seem to have been smoothed by the melting of the rock. Someone called it "Solitary Ridge," and the name stuck.

It was six minutes away, approaching at 10.7 kilometers per second. Tory was relaying everything she had to her consumers, one of whom, she'd been informed, was the new president of the United States. "He's personally interested," the NASA higher-ups had told her with great solemnity.

Damned well he should be. She hoped he'd be smart enough to get the point.

A klaxon went off somewhere, signaling another penetration of the space station. Windy's eyes met hers. The prospect that a rock might rip through the bulkhead at any time tended to be distracting. She tried to push the thought into a corner of her mind and refocus on the Possum.

It was coming in over the western Pacific, where it would enter the atmosphere at an acute angle. The NASA Goddard Flying Observatory, positioned over the East China Sea, was sending them test pictures of clear, star-filled skies.

Ordinarily, the networks would have given the event extensive coverage, but on this Sunday morning it was all but preempted by the reports of continuing calamity from around the world. The scene of immediate disaster had moved well into the Pacific now, as Earth turned on its axis. Rock rained from the skies along Asian coasts, destroying Tokyo, and damaging Shanghai, Hong Kong, and Singapore.

Tory was tied into Feinberg's private channel on the AstroLab circuit. But the astrophysicist was off the line now. The BBC had interviewed him about an hour ago. The Possum would come very close, he said, but he assured the viewers it *would* miss.

Others were less certain. The Chinese had already announced their intention to register a complaint that their American allies were waiting until after it passed before using their missiles. They hinted darkly that the Americans secretly hoped it would fall on China. The secretary of state, in a predawn press conference, commented that he wasn't concerned, that if the Possum merely put on a fireworks display and continued on its way, as expected, the Chinese would have nothing to complain about; and that if it *did* hit China, and the scientists were correct that it was big enough to end civilization, then there'd be nobody around to listen to the complaint. He smiled at his remark.

A timer was keeping track: *Two minutes to atmospheric contact. Three minutes to closest approach.*

The station klaxons had stopped wailing. A voice over the intercom informed Tory that sections of D deck, the main promenade, had lost pressure and were temporarily closed.

A news bulletin appeared on the screen: the Americans were canceling the missile strike. No explanation given. Press conference at ten o'clock.

One minute.

The Possum was by no means the only big object out there. At last count, sixty-two others had been designated and tagged. But none constituted an immediate threat. The biggest, POSIM-55, was a true extinction rock. It was four times the size of the Possum. Enough to finish everyone except maybe the cockroaches. Fortunately, it was going into a relatively stable orbit. In fact, she thought, despite the terrible losses, we've lucky. It could have been far worse. And the rain of ejecta had noticably eased during the last couple of hours.

"There's still a lot of debris out there," said Windy. "When this is over we should recommend the airlines stay on the ground a few more days."

Ten seconds.

It was moving in quickly now, skimming across the face of the planet, the Pacific far below, the Asian mainland coming up fast. The virtual imager tracked it into the blue-black haze of the ionosphere. As she watched, the Possum began to redden, pieces fell away, and wisps of smoke formed contrails.

The screens dedicated to the Flying Observatory had not yet picked it up. Two of the displays showed enhanced telescopic images; the third was a naked-eye view. She watched intently and then saw it, a sharp white line drawn through the shimmering blue haze. Its closest approach to the surface would be at two hundred kilometers.

Other imagers on the ground tracked it. A CNN reporter, standing with a camera team on a hillside near Hainan, caught it as it burst into flame. People standing with him gaped and sighed. The long fireball streaked across their sky. Then the roar of its passage broke on them, deep and guttural. It took the witnesses by surprise and they covered their heads. A few shrieked and threw themselves to the ground.

It rumbled among the constellations, a celestial locomotive with the boiler ripped open and its fiery insides exposed. And then it disappeared in the west, toward Wuhan.

"Looks good so far," said Windy, his voice tense.

Mobile stations at Chengtu and in the Himalayas caught it as it began to dwindle. At Lahore, it became quieter, more sedate, and seemed smaller. The roar was gone. The Afghans saw only a long pink line in the sky, and somewhere over the land of the Mullah, it winked out.

Tory had a link open to the AstroLab and she heard their applause. "Bye-bye, baby," said a delighted female voice.

AstroLab. 8:58 A.M.

Feinberg was constitutionally unable to celebrate. He was by nature reticent, reserved, reclusive. For him, the local Wal-Mart was more remote than Cygnus X-1. Years before, Feinberg had had the good fortune to be at Palomar when Supernova 2017A exploded in the Lagoon Nebula, NGC6523. The Lagoon is in Sagittarius, less than five thousand light-years away. It had been so far the astrophysical event of the century. But while his colleagues celebrated, Feinberg had been forced to pretend. He understood his own personality well enough; he knew that he'd never learned to enjoy himself. Even this morning, when (at least in his own mind) he'd inter-vened to save the president from a potentially disastrous deci-sion, it would not have been his nature to take several of his colleagues out for a round of eggs and pancakes, and relish the moment.

Instead, when the dust settled, he simply went home.

He'd been up for the better part of five consecutive days, and he was exhausted. The sky was finally growing clear, and he didn't see that he could do any more. Cynthia Murray, his number two, would track the Possum, and when she knew what it was going to do, she'd call him.

Outside, the trees were full of birds and it was as if noth-ing had happened.

MEET THE PRESS, SPECIAL EDITION. 9:00 A.M.

In Atlanta with Judy Almayer, New York Times; Fred Chiles, Boston Globe; Karl Nishamura, Los Angeles Online; and moderator Pierce

Benjamin, NBC News; with special guest Julian Moore, director of the Minority Alliance.

NBC:	*Dr. Moore, your organization issued a demand an hour ago calling for the dissolution of the presidency and its replacement by a rotating executive council, subject to a parliamentary system providing quick recall.*
Moore:	*That's correct. And it isn't a position we've adopted lightly.*
NBC:	*What precisely do you propose? That we junk the Constitution?*
Moore:	*It's a rich man's constitution, Mr. Benjamin. Devised by the rich, for the rich.*
N.Y. Times:	*But wouldn't that be shooting yourself in the foot? After all, if you eliminate the Constitution, what's left to protect ordinary people? The people you claim to represent?*
Moore:	*The Constitution, I'm sorry to say, has always been an instrument of evasion. People who've been oppressed have to get on their feet and demand their rights.*
Boston Globe:	*But doesn't the Constitution provide the only real protection for those rights? To what other human document would you appeal?*
Moore:	*Maybe we need to write one. I'd remind you, Mr. Chiles, that the Constitution coexisted quite happily with slavery. Until the slaves just decided they weren't going to take it any more.*
L.A. Online:	*But the Constitution was the lever with which Lincoln worked.*
Moore:	*That's standard schoolboy history. The Union Army was the lever, and the spine of the Union Army, after 1863, was its black troops.*

NBC:	*Hold on a minute. Let's not wander off into a side street. Dr. Moore, if you abolished the present government, with what would you replace it?*
Moore:	*To begin with, we need an executive council that would be representative of all the people, not just the white majority.*
L.A. Online:	*But President Kolladner was an African-American. Surely—*
Moore:	*And he objected to the term. He didn't approve of hyphens, you remember. He claimed to be simply an American. The truth is, he was a lackey. I don't like to speak ill of the dead, but he was ashamed of his heritage. He was a classic Uncle Tom.*
N.Y. Times:	*Dr. Moore, the Minority Alliance has always been a reasonably conservative group in the past. You've been reasonably conservative. Tell us why the change in course.*
Moore:	*The poor people of this nation were left to die last night. When that happened, revolution became as inevitable as the sunrise.*
N.Y. Times:	*But there's no evidence it was deliberate. People of all socioeconomic groups died in large numbers last night.*
L.A. Online:	*You're obviously dissatisfied with Kolladner. Who do you think could have done better?*
Moore:	*I can think of no one who could have done worse. Moreover, when white America goes looking for a scapegoat, they won't forget that Henry Kolladner was a black man. Look, God only knows how many people have died during the last twelve hours. Are still dying. Millions. Mr. Nishamura, you don't even have a city to go back to.*
L.A. Online:	*Nobody could have done anything to save the city. The waves killed L.A. Period. Where would you have*

	put the Los Angeles population with a few days' notice?
Moore:	*I damned well wouldn't have left them at Gage Avenue and Avalon to be drowned. Listen: When we're finished counting our dead, we're going to discover there are upward of twenty million of them. Most will be people from the inner cities. Once again, the black man pays the bill for this country. Well, this is it. No more.*
NBC:	*You don't really expect the Congress to cave in to this demand, do you?*
Moore:	*They will if they want to save the nation.*
NBC:	*That sounds like an ultimatum.*
Moore:	*It's not, Mr. Pierce. It's a strong suggestion. The Alliance does not want to bring down the country. We really don't. But the survival of this nation is essential to our finding a way to lead people, especially black people, out of poverty. What we are saying to the Congress, and to the new president, is this: The old system doesn't work for us. It's time for radical surgery. I hope they'll see the wisdom of our suggestion. If not, then I have no doubt blood will run in the streets.*
Boston Globe:	*Dr. Moore, you must realize you're inciting rebellion.*
Moore:	*No such thing. I'm hoping to head it off.*

6.

Percival Lowell Flight Deck. 9:11 A.M.

Rachel completed her final check and switched over to internal power. Cochran, at the navigation plot, gave her a thumbs-up. Exit protocols locked.

"Lowell," said a voice in her earphones, "you are *go* for launch."

"Launch" from Skyport meant that the magnetic couplings would release the ship, and four sets of piston clusters would ease her out of her bay and give her a gentle push away from the orbiter. At about the same time, Rachel would fire up the engine and adjust attitude. She'd move out to six kilometers, rotate to her heading, and begin to accelerate.

It had not been an easy morning. Everyone at Skyport, it seemed, wanted to be on board *Lowell* when she made her rendezvous with the Micro. The phones had rung constantly. People identifying themselves as engineers and communications specialists and every sort of professional in the book thought it would be a good idea if they were present in case of one emergency or another. The truth was, of course, they wanted to meet the new president. There had even been a couple of station bureaucrats who tried to suggest that a high-ranking Skyport representative should be present.

In fact, the only crew she needed was Lee Cochran. She was sorry, she explained patiently time and again, but anyone else would only be taking up space. And, more important, air. They would be at eight people for the return trip, which was already thirty-three percent over life-support design capacity. When some persisted, she simply explained it was against the rules. Even the most determined seemed to understand that.

Belle sent a physician. Just in case. The head man had been on leave when the emergency broke out, so the assignment went to the station's assistant chief medical officer, Dr. Arthur Elkhart. He came from the shy end of the bureaucratic spectrum. He was clearly unnerved at the possibility of acquiring a presidential patient, and would have preferred to stay home. But his position didn't allow it. Still, when Belle was gone, he openly admitted his jitters to Rachel and thereby won her respect. He was middle-aged, prematurely gray, built low to the ground. "I hope they're all okay," he said.

"This is *Lowell*," she told Control. "Ready to go."

There was a mild shove as the pistons started the ship out of the bay. The long viewport that looked out from Control passed on her left. She hit the intercom. "Moving out, Doc. Buckle in."

She got no answer and tried again: "Hit the yellow button to talk."

A moment. And then a click: "Thanks," he said. "I'm all set."

Twenty thousand miles below, the coastline of Ecuador and Peru emerged from cloud banks. The Pacific stretched away to the west, bright and calm in the midday sun. Like everyone else, she'd been dismayed at the reports of wholesale death and destruction coming in from around the globe. She'd been unable to reach her own family, who lived in Charleston. Looking down on the vast serenity, she thought about the tendency of people to transfer their troubles to the world around them. Whatever damage might be visited on homes, temples, and city halls around the Earth as a result of Tomiko, the planet itself would continue calmly on as though nothing had happened.

She lit the engine.

It came on-line quietly, a liquid rumble, utterly unlike the chemical power plants of the moonbuses and space planes, which roared furiously and shook bulkheads.

"All go," said Cochran.

She acknowledged, and gave the ship to the autopilot, which adjusted attitude and began to accelerate.

Lowell would do a three-quarters orbit and come out on a course parallel to, but well ahead of, the Micro. From that point they'd boost speed gradually and allow the bus to overtake them.

Rachel did not like going out into this sky. At first she'd thought it was because there were still too many rocks in it. But she gradually came to realize that she shared Doc Elkhart's nervousness about welcoming the president of the United States on board. She glanced over at Cochran, whose prime duty during the flight was to monitor internal power and life support. In other words, to stay awake in case of emergency. "Lee?"

"Yo?"

"How do you feel?"

"Fine. Why do you ask?"

She let it go. The astronauts were, with one or two exceptions, all former military air jocks. And the code of the brotherhood of combat pilots, *admit no fear*, was alive and well.

Rachel had mastered whatever uncertainties she might have had the first time she'd sat on top of a rocket and touched a match to it. She'd done well and come through it better than some of her male counterparts. She'd never backed down in her life from anybody or anything. But today she could feel her hands shake.

Below, the world turned green. They were eastbound, running above Brazil. Ahead, stars shone through portions of the pale cloud that had replaced the Moon.

The lunar cloud was already growing thin, drifting apart. The ancient sphere, mathematically perfect, reassuring in its promise of universal harmony, was gone.

Micro Passenger Cabin. 10:15 A.M.

"Al, we're going to nationalize everything. Airlines, trucks, the power companies, you name it. Get Tierney to head up the effort." Tierney was respected by the major CEOs. Having him on board would deflect a lot of resistance.

"Okay, Charlie." They had by now gotten back to their old first-name basis. "Let me run it past counsel—"

"Forget counsel. Just do it."

"I'm not sure about the constitutionality—"

"Al, we've declared a national emergency. By definition

anything I do is constitutional. People are dying in large numbers out there. We will do what we have to." He spelled out a long list of precisely what he wanted, leaving the details to Kerr.

"Something else, Charlie," Kerr said when he'd finished. "The Latin countries have been hit pretty hard. They're asking for help."

"We've none to give. Tell them they're on their own. Pass our regrets, but point out to them we've taken substantial losses. Ask whether they can help *us*. Tell them we need whatever they can spare. Get it coordinated. We'll take help from anyone who offers it. Oh, and Harmon was making jokes last night about the Chinese protest." Harmon was the secretary of state. "I have to wonder about the diplomatic skills of a man who finds anything funny about this kind of disaster. He's fired. Tell him."

"But Charlie—"

"I'd tell him myself but I'm busy. If he insists on hearing it from me, I'll do it, but warn him it won't be pretty."

Charlie had been on the phone all morning with Kerr, with cabinet members, with heads of state around the world, trying to coordinate a global response. But it wasn't enough. Talking to people here and there wasn't going to get the job done. They needed a global executive during the emergency. Ordinarily, the logical person for the choice would probably have been the U.S. president. But the U.S. was among the hardest-hit nations. That changed the chemical mix. Several candidates had already been put forward. One was the Belgian chief of state, whom Charlie knew to be able and honest. "Throw our weight behind him," he said.

Good news was still coming in. Other Possums were on the loose, but none constituted an immediate threat. The frequency and intensity of meteor strikes had declined precipitously. The storm seemed to be passing, and within a few more hours it might be possible to reduce the state of alert.

Everyone had been hit. But the Americas had suffered maximum damage. Offers of assistance had come from all major, and many minor, nations. *Yes,* Charlie had told them. *We need food, clothing, medical supplies, transportation, and communication equipment. Whatever and whomever you can send.* Multinational corporations were also mobilizing help. "Goddam selfish bastards," Kerr had said. "They're only in it because they know they have to keep their customers alive."

Charlie didn't care much about motivation.

By late morning he was emotionally exhausted. There'd been a sea change in the way people thought about their lives and their world. They were, he thought, closer together than they'd ever been before during his lifetime. Maybe than they'd been since people started keeping records.

Nevertheless, Charlie's position wasn't enviable. Virtually every political leader in the world was in difficulty, expected to head off further disaster. And no one more than he, who represented an administration that was widely held responsible for having failed even to warn its citizens.

His cell phone chimed.

"Pilot, Mr. President."

"Yes, Saber?"

"I just wanted to let you know. *Lowell's* on schedule. She'll be alongside in about five and a half hours."

"Thanks." He looked over at Evelyn, who was reading. The chaplain was asleep, and Morley was writing, listlessly punching the keys on his notepad. Probably recording everything for a book. The cabin was undoubtedly the most public setting from which any president had ever conducted business. His runaway White House.

Well, if he accomplished nothing else, he'd be a natural for future trivia questions.

•   •   •

Hilltop west of Staunton, Virginia. 11:47 A.M.

Lieutenant Colonel Steven R. Gallagher lowered his field glasses. He didn't like working his troops Sunday morning, when they should be at church, but he knew that the critical moment was drawing close and he wanted to ensure that the Legion was ready.

He was with the Blue Star Company, Third Freedom Battalion, Thomas Jefferson Legion. The exercise was in its fourth hour. He leaned his hefty frame against the Ford van that served as his command vehicle, and looked at his watch. "They're about out of time, Jack," he told his brother, who was wearing a major's oak leaves.

"Tad reports he's in position to take out a few more," said the major.

They were running a security exercise. Tad Wickett, with six men, had blown up a simulated arsenal. The security forces, charged with defending the target, could now hope for nothing better than to apprehend the strike force. But it was apparent they weren't going to do that either. "It's not entirely their fault, Colonel," said Jack, reluctantly. "Tad is *very* good."

Steve knew security assignments bored his people. They wanted to blow things up, not protect them. But the day was coming soon when they would have to defend installations against guerrillas. His accession to power in Virginia would be resisted. Not least of all by surviving government loyalists. But he understood he'd also have to face a lawless element that had simply been waiting for something like the Tomiko affair to seize power. And in the days to come, the only protection civilized life would have against the inevitable wilderness thugs was going to be the Jefferson Legion.

Tad was still pinned within the six-square-mile training area. There were two roads and two bridges by which he could leave, and all had been sealed off. But the security forces had failed to bring him to ground, losing several more people in the effort. Not a particularly good demonstration. "Did I explain about *methodical*?" he asked Jack. "Did we talk about how important it was that operations be *systematic*?"

His brother nodded. "Doesn't look like it took, Steve."

"No, it doesn't." The colonel looked at his watch. It was twelve o'clock. "Okay. Let's call it a day. Send the troops home and we'll get the officers in. We need to talk for a bit."

Legion headquarters was located in the east wing of the colonel's rambling frame house. There were seven officers all told, not counting himself. They were good, well trained, intelligent, loyal. A hell of a lot better than his critics knew.

A large family room in back served as his conference area. When Jack signaled that everyone had arrived, Colonel Gallagher entered from the side. They jumped to attention. "As you were, men," he said, and took his place at the lectern. (Actually, one of the captains was a woman, but no distinction in gender was ever noted, nor did she seem to object.)

The aroma of coffee filled the room. Someone handed the colonel a cup, and he began the proceedings by inviting Tad to explain how he'd evaded the security forces all morning. Wickett, who was only a captain, irritated his colleagues by observing it had been simple, that the security units hadn't been coordinated. He showed why, drew arrows on maps, and suggested alternate strategies. Wickett was one of the two people in the room with actual military experience. The colonel himself had never worn the uniform of his country. But no one other than his brother Jack knew that. To the rest, Steve Gallagher had served a dozen years with combat infantry and the Rangers. That he was able to carry off this imposture was a tribute to his extensive interest in, and ability for, military techniques and technology.

There was something cold and vaguely reptilian about Tad Wickett. Jack listened to him speak, watched his eyes move smoothly around the room, saw his tongue occasionally brush his upper lip, noted the sense of ongoing calculation about the man. He never missed a chance to make his colleagues look incompetent.

When Wickett finished, Steve invited comments, listened dutifully, and then added his own observations. Peterson's unit had been slow to react when their planning went awry; Barber had failed to anticipate several possibilities; as a result, the terrorist force had been completely successful and had escaped with only one casualty. It was, he implied, a pathetic demonstration by the security force.

If Steve Gallagher had never served, it hadn't been for lack of desire. He'd struggled with asthma and a multitude of allergies, and they'd kept him from the colors. The asthma was gone now, long since outgrown. He'd learned a lot since those early days when he wanted nothing so much as to qualify for the Rangers. Mostly he'd learned that the United States was governed by a small cabal of families who pretended to squabble but who kept power in their own hands and milked the nation's working people dry. Today he would never have considered defending the dictators.

He'd found a better way to serve the American Ideal. He'd founded the Thomas Jefferson Legion, a group of God-fearing, country-loving men and women dedicated to preserving liberty at home against the assorted shadowy manifestations of an oppressive government that was itself an arm of a world body whose only interest was to maintain its grip on power.

The colonel owned the Potluck Restaurant in downtown Staunton. The Potluck, founded by his grandfather, had been in the family thirty-eight years, and had thrown off a sister establishment in nearby Harrisonburg.

But the Potluck was not as profitable as it should have been. Unlike most Americans, whose tax money vanishes without their ever seeing it, the colonel was burdened with actually paying out substantial sums each month to an increasingly onerous and corrupt government. But that wasn't the worst of it. Regulators were everywhere. Inspectors from all levels of government, following the example set by the feds, harassed him continually with safety and health inspections, demanded licenses, controlled how much he paid his help, dictated whom he should hire and what medical plan he should provide. All the money went to support the vicious practices of a decadent nation, a nation that forbade God to enter the schoolroom, that allowed women to murder their children, that had so distorted the reproductive process that men were no longer necessary.

He had become over the years a fiery enemy of the invisible hand that weighed so heavily on his fortunes and on those of his countrymen. Right-thinking men and women across the state of Virginia had flocked to him, and the Jefferson Legion now had units in a dozen counties.

It wasn't only the godlessness and the corruption that enraged Steve Gallagher, much less the money or even the inspections. Rather, it was the condescension of the official agents, their obvious belief that he was not a man of honor, that he could not be trusted, that it was necessary to keep him on a leash.

. . . In order to . . . secure the Blessings of Liberty to ourselves and our Posterity . . .

It hadn't happened.

Tom Jefferson had lost to the federalists, and his ideals had been sacrificed to Hamilton's notion of an oppressive central government. The colonials had exchanged one set of chains for another. But because the second set was emblazoned with an eagle, they hadn't noticed.

"Gentlemen," said the colonel, winding down his remarks and wanting to send them home with something to think about, "I'd like to talk with you for a moment about something other than the exercise." He drew himself to his full height. "As you're aware, last night was a disaster for the dictators. The people of this nation have finally seen their government for what it is, and the potential for revolt is everywhere. All that's needed now is a spark.

"Be aware that I've been in touch with our brothers-in-arms around the state and in other parts of the country. We're almost ready to move. When the moment comes, and I can tell you that it's very close, we'll be ready to seize the power brokers and give the nation back to the real Americans."

They applauded, assured him they were with him, and went home. Afterward he sat alone in his kitchen and listened to the lazy hum of insects.

The horse is prepared against the day of battle. But when, O Lord? When?

7.

NEWSNET. 12:30 P.M. UPDATE.
(Click for details.)

POPULATIONS IN FLIGHT AROUND WORLD
Did Experts Underestimate Comet Fallout?
Refugees Overwhelm Resources Everywhere

AMERICAS HIT HARD
Western Hemisphere In Direct Line Of Explosion
Fatalities Expected To Reach Three Million
Scientists Say Worst May Be Over
But Some Still Fret About "Possum"

X-RAY SURVEY: MOON HAS BROKEN UP
Astronomers: Most Large Fragments Pose No Danger
Will Earth Eventually Get Rings?

TOMIKO HARRINGTON REPORTED IN HIDING
> Drive-By Shootings, Death Threats For Comet's Discoverer

HASKELL SWORN IN AS 47TH PRESIDENT
> New Chief Executive Adrift In Space
> But Not In Danger, Says Administration

CHILE SAVES MANY BY MOVING THEM TO MOUNTAINS
> Anderos: "Never Believed Happy Talk From U.S."

POPE LEADS THOUSANDS IN PRAYER AT ST. PETER'S
> Calls For Unified Relief Effort

GUNMAN KILLS ELEVEN IN MACAO SCHOOLYARD, THEN SHOOTS SELF
> Left Note: Wanted To Save Children From "End Of World"
> "Everybody Liked Him," Say Neighbors

REPORTS OF DAMAGE BY MOON "PEBBLES"
> Golfball-Sized Objects Still Pack Wallop
> Several Killed, Cars And Houses Wrecked

GIANT WAVES DECIMATE CARIBBEAN
> Few Survivors At Nassau, St. Lucia

PRESIDENT DOES SPACEWALK TO RESCUE MOONBUS
> Haskell Wears Home-Made Suit Outside

IRS WILL EXTEND TAX DEADLINE ONE WEEK
> Transportation, Communication Difficulties Cited

Micro Passenger Cabin. 12:38 P.M.

Saber's voice, speaking through the intercom, was cool and detached: "We've used the last of our fuel," she said. "Tank's empty."

Morley looked across at the chaplain. "What happens if we have to get out of the way of one of those rocks?"

"Splat, I guess," said Pinnacle.

Morley got up and looked down at Charlie. "I'm going to file a report," he said. He and the president had reached agreement on what might be broadcast and what demanded discretion. All of the president's calls, for example, were off-limits.

"Okay," said Charlie. "Go ahead. But add that there's no immediate danger."

"Mr. President, that takes the bite out of the story."

"Not at all, Keith. I wouldn't want to be the one to tell you how to do your job, but understatement will jack up the drama."

Keith grinned. "You're a good politician. But I don't think you'd make it in my profession."

C-SPAN SUNDAY JOURNAL. 1:07 P.M.
Host: Cleveland Somers; Guest: Senator Audrey Belmont (R-NJ).

Somers:	*Go ahead, Caller.*
First Caller:	*I live in Kokomo. North of Indianapolis. And I have a question for Senator Belmont.*
Somers:	*Okay.*
First Caller:	*They were saying on the television this morning that the damage in your state, Senator, is going to be up in the billions.*
Belmont:	*That appears to be true, Caller.*
First Caller:	*And that's only New Jersey. The whole East Coast is wrecked. For that matter, most of both coasts is wrecked. Did you see California? It's just a bunch of islands.*
Somers:	*I saw California. My understanding is that the water will go away on its own.*
First Caller:	*Well, the damage sure as hell isn't going to go away*

	on its own. We're talking about rebuilding. My question is, where's the money going to come from? Because I can just see what's going to happen. The president's going to declare both coasts emergency areas and the government's going to pay for it. Which is to say, the taxpayers will pick up the tab. Like always.
Somers:	Okay, Caller. We've got the question. Thanks. Senator?
Belmont:	I think the caller means the stricken areas will be declared disaster areas. But yes, of course, federal funds will be used to help stave off the worst effects of what happened last night. I'm sure the caller doesn't think we should just leave several million people on the road with no place to turn for help.
Somers:	We have another caller. Go ahead, please.
Second Caller:	Hello?
Somers:	Yes? You're on.
Second Caller:	Am I on?
Somers:	Yes, you are.
Second Caller:	I was listening to the last caller. And he's absolutely right. I live in Grand Island. In Nebraska. Why should my taxes go up to rebuild New York and Miami? I think we should secede, that's what I think. It's the only way to save the country.
Somers:	Senator?
Belmont:	I don't want to offend anyone, Cleveland, but if there's an attitude that guarantees this nation will go down the drain, I think we've just heard it.

Micro Passenger Cabin. 1:32 P.M.

The passengers heard the PA system click on, and heard their pilot's voice. "This is Saber. We are now at our closest approach to Earth, traveling at 11.7 kilometers per second.

The *Lowell* is ahead of us, gradually accelerating to our velocity. We will rendezvous with them at about four."

109th Airlift Group, Scotia, New York. 1:31 P.M.

The big army chopper that had brought them from Manhattan skirted the airfield and descended on a bare field behind a hangar. It blew up a cloud of dust and the pilot cut the engine. The blades slowed and drooped. Marilyn, who'd never been in a helicopter before and didn't like planes all that much anyhow, was grateful they were on the ground.

Almost all of the people on the aircraft were from Louise's party. They looked sodden and tired and lost. Larry sat beside her and squeezed her hand while they waited for the hatch to open. "When do you think we'll get home again?" she asked him.

He shrugged. "Probably only a few days. The water should go down pretty quick. And our stuff'll be okay, as long as they keep the looters out. That's what worries me."

Louise was sitting directly across from them. She'd changed into a woolen shirt and jeans, and had contributed clothes to several of the women. "I doubt there are many live looters left," she said. "But I don't think we'll be going back for a while. Place like Manhattan. . . ." She shook her head. "I don't want to be downbeat or anything, but there're going to be major health problems. We'll be lucky if we're home by the fourth of July."

"Goddam, Louise," said a balding little economist near the door, "you sure know how to give a party."

That brought some hollow laughs. Marilyn didn't join in.

She'd changed. She wondered what the little boy's name was. What his mother had thought when Marilyn closed the door.

Something else had happened: She felt closer to Larry than she had at any time during, or before, their marriage. He'd been taking her for granted for a long time, but that had stopped last night. Maybe it wouldn't last, but she felt as if she had her husband—her old boyfriend—back again.

The hatch opened to reveal two female soldiers in neatly pressed khakis. Marilyn looked past them and saw crowds of dazed people being shepherded between vehicles and buildings. Some were sitting on the ground.

One of the women wore a sergeant's stripes and carried a clipboard. The other was barely eighteen.

"Welcome to Scotia," said the sergeant. "The pilot tells us that nobody here has any injuries. Is that correct? Anybody hurt? No? Good.

"We'll start unloading over here on my left. Please be careful; it's a long step down. And I'd appreciate it if you'd give your card to Private Turner here." The pilot had distributed yellow data cards on which they'd printed their names and other personal information. "Please note the long gray building behind me. We'll go over there. You'll be able to get a sandwich and some soft drinks or coffee. I wish we could provide a hot meal but we just don't have the capability. Not for so many people.

"You've got about an hour before your next flight leaves. We'll make an announcement. This is the seven-fourteen group. Can you remember that?"

"Excuse me," one of the passengers broke in. "You're putting us on *another* plane?"

Several people now began to talk at once. The sergeant held up a hand and waited. When they'd quieted, she continued: "I'm sorry, folks. Truth is, we're a little crowded here right now. We're asking for your cooperation. And your patience. We'll move you out and get you to a permanent relocation facility as quickly as we can."

"Where's that?" asked one of the women. "Where are we going?"

She consulted her clipboard. "Bismarck."

"Bismarck?" whispered Larry. "Where's *Bismarck?"*

"North Dakota," said Marilyn. She got up and started for the exit. "That might not be so bad. It's a long way from the ocean."

8.

SSTO *Arlington* Passenger Cabin. 2:28 P.M.

In its headlong flight, the Micro had caught up with and passed *Arlington*. Andrea had not been aware of it when it happened. But she was delighted, a few hours later, to see the gleaming, counter-rotating wheels of Skyport. Like virtually everyone else on the spacecraft, she felt lucky to be alive. Nevertheless, the overall mood was somber. The death of friends and colleagues on the lost flight, and fears for family and friends at home, weighed heavily on the passengers. They were also tired, sweaty, weary of plastic food, still frightened. It was, after all, no small thing to look out the window and see a rock the size of a small garage whistle past.

Debris now might come from any angle. The pilot explained that much of the material that had been blasted off the surface of the Moon had gone into orbit. It would, he added, probably constitute a navigational hazard for a long time to come. The unspoken implication, in Andrea's mind, was that transatmospheric flights might be discontinued.

Among those who'd been on the missing spacecraft were several close friends, a former lover, her favorite bridge partner, most of her work crew, and God knew who else. She'd find out when they were off the plane and she could get a look at the passenger manifest. Right now nobody was saying anything official.

They slipped nose-first into their cradle. The bulkheads moved past and steam leaked out of gargantuan fittings.

People behind long observation panels bent over consoles and talked into microphones. The bulkheads slowed, and there was a mild bump.

"This is Captain Culver." The pilot sounded as if he'd just concluded a routine flight. "Please remain in your seats until the light has gone off." He paused. "We were glad to be able to assist you, and I want to thank you for your cooperation during a difficult flight." The cabin lights blinked. "There'll be representatives of the Lunar Transport Authority waiting in the deplaning section to answer any questions you might have."

A minute later the warning sign went out. Andrea unbuckled and watched her fellow passengers get up.

They took her name as she went down the ramp, gave her some clothes, and assigned a room. She asked if it would be possible to get a passenger manifest for the lost flight. "Sorry," a woman in an emerald LTA jacket said. "They're not available yet." Then they asked whether she felt all right and did she want to talk to a counselor?

Andrea declined and went looking for her room. It was on B deck in an area usually reserved for flight crews. It had a gorgeous view of Earth, which was sunlit and peaceful and moving gradually from right to left across her picture window. She studied it for a minute or so, taking strength from it. Then she stepped out of her clothes and turned on the scrubbers. Ten minutes later, feeling clean again, she collapsed naked on the bed, grateful for the chance to stretch out. But despite her weariness, sleep wouldn't come.

She gave up after a while and went down to the main promenade to look for food. Almost all the shops were shut down. But there were a couple of restaurants. She selected Mo's, which was decorated heavily with a Three Stooges motif.

It was crowded. She looked around for familiar faces, saw a few from the plane, but settled alone into the only available table. A television mounted over a central bar carried news reports from groundside. Someone was talking about a memorial service for Henry Kolladner. It struck her that the president of the U.S. had died and she'd scarcely noticed.

She studied the menu, decided she wasn't really hungry but just wanted to chew on something that wasn't space-plane fare. Toast and coffee looked good. She punched in her selection and propped her chin in her hands. The tears she'd kept at bay for so many hours dribbled down her cheeks.

Mo's was too public a place to come apart, so she fought down the crying jag that threatened to erupt. Then a woman in a NASA jumpsuit was looking down at her.

"Hi," she said. "Mind if we share?"

She had dark hair, alert brown eyes, and an amiable expression that immediately changed to concern when she got a good look at Andrea. "You okay?" she asked.

Andrea sniffled, wiped her nose, and smiled. "I'm sorry. Yes, please. Of course, sit down."

The woman eased into a chair. "Lose somebody?" she asked carefully.

Andrea nodded and felt the tears come with a rush.

"Let it go," the woman said. "It's okay." She took Andrea's wrist, squeezed it reassuringly. "I'm Tory Clark," she said when the storm subsided. "I work at the Orbital Lab."

"Physics?"

"Astronomy."

Andrea nodded. "Must be an exciting time for you." She saw the sudden bleakness in the other woman's expression. "Sorry," she said. "I didn't mean that."

"It's all right. It's been hard on everybody."

Andrea felt as if she were moving through a dream. "I'm Andrea Bellwether." She extended her hand and smiled.

"Famous name." Tory smiled back.

Andrea nodded. "He was my father."

"Oh." Tory bit down her embarrassment. "Open mouth, insert," she said. "I'm sorry."

"It's okay. It was a long time ago."

They sat watching while an attendant brought two glasses and filled them with water. "Listen," Tory said, looking at the menu, "I think I need a real drink. How about you? My treat."

AstroLab. 3:11 P.M.

Cynthia Murray had been the director at Kitt Peak for six years. She'd taken a leave of absence and come to the AstroLab to work with Feinberg on the effort to map cosmic directionality. And, more significantly, to understand it. She'd already established a reputation for her work in macrogalactic structures, and now, like everyone else in the field, had been diverted by events into the Possum watch. And specifically into tracking POSIM-38.

Cynthia had gone through five husbands. One had died; the others had grown wearisome for one reason or another. The only passions Cynthia had were for her two daughters (by the second and fourth spouses) and for the galaxies. That was, of course, a shortcoming in the eyes of most men, even other astronomers. But she couldn't help it, didn't want to help it, and had finally accepted the fact that she was simply not meant to be somebody's wife.

She recognized a mirror image of sorts in Feinberg except that he was lonely, although he'd never admit it. She, on the other hand, had felt alone only during those hours she was forced to spend in domestic harness, away from the telescopes.

Cynthia had been drinking coffee and watching the Possum after it struggled out of the atmosphere. Its velocity had diminished considerably, and of course it had emerged with a new heading. It had lost about five percent of its mass during passage.

Her display extended Possum's trajectory out over a long narrow arc, and then brought it back.

It was still too early to be sure. But her instincts told her that Feinberg was going to be right. Again.

She finished her coffee, sighed, and reached for the phone.

AstroLab. 3:36 P.M.

Feinberg sat in his white Fleetwood under some trees (a contractor was pouring blacktop in the parking lot), looking up at the AstroLab. The building was a flat swirl of steel and glass, two encircling wings emanating from a crosspiece. At night, when the light was favorable, it resembled an *SBa*, a barred spiral galaxy. Now, in the middle of the afternoon, *this* afternoon, it looked vaguely like an oversized bat hiding from the daylight. He did not want to go inside. He'd hoped the Possum would just go away, had hoped the run through the atmosphere would not slow it down excessively, would give it a decent trajectory. So he'd pushed it away from his thoughts, much as he'd have liked to push it away from the planet, and gone home to sleep. To hide from it, knowing that if things *did* go as he expected, Cynthia would call.

And Cynthia had called.

The jangle of the phone had been enough. He'd looked at his watch and known before he picked it up, before Cynthia had simply breathed his name. It was all she'd said.

"Apogee?" he'd asked.

"Two hundred thirty-seven thousand k."

No surprise there.

"Perigee?"

"Close."

How close?

"Looks like a bell-ringer."

Two hundred thirty-seven thousand kilometers. That

sounded like Tuesday. They weren't going to get much of a breather.

He climbed out of the car and started walking toward the lab.

It was a brilliant April afternoon, lazy and cool, the wind whispering in the trees, the Sun high and bright. The acrid smell of blacktop brought back memories of his boyhood in south Boston, where the streets were eternally being repaved. And where the future stretched on forever.

He trudged up the long, curving gravel walkway, mounted the wide stone steps, and pushed in through the glass doors. The security guard in the lobby looked up and smiled. "Good morning, Professor Feinberg," she said. She was about twenty-five, pretty in the way all women of that age are pretty. Her eyes lingered on him a moment too long, almost flirtatious but not quite. Her name was Amy, and she was, he had heard, recently engaged.

She looked at him, frowning. "Are you okay, Professor?" she asked.

Her pleasant air-conditioned world, with its automatic dishwashers and its video call-ups and its relative security, was crashing in on her. He wondered whether she understood that. "Yes," he said. "Everything's fine."

Cynthia was waiting for him. "I'm sorry, Wes," she said.

"Well, we knew it was going to happen, didn't we?" He pulled off his sweater and threw it across the back of a chair. Half a dozen of their associates were already there, gathered around the displays, talking in low voices.

He took time to go over the numbers, hoping to find a mistake somewhere. When he didn't, he sat back and massaged his forehead. Four fifty-six A.M. Tuesday. "We'd better let the president know," he said.

•   •   •

9.

Micro Passenger Cabin. 3:47 P.M.

CNN was covering a press conference conducted by the senior senator from Idaho. She was the mouthpiece for Tom Clay, the majority leader and Charlie's probable opponent in November. Even Clay, he thought, should be willing to get behind the White House now.

But that wasn't the way it was going. ". . . should step down," she was saying, looking directly out of the screen. "Don't misunderstand me. I have no wish to attack Charlie Haskell. I saw some electronic bumper stickers already this morning saying that Haskell's a rascal, and I don't much like that kind of mindless mudslinging. But I can understand why people are outraged. We all know the president would like to dissociate himself from the policies of Henry Kolladner. But he can't. The country no longer trusts his party, it no longer trusts *him*, and we just can't go on this way. The life of the nation's at stake. We need to move forward and to move forward fast. Consequently, it would be in everybody's best interest—"

Charlie killed the sound and stared at the woman. Pompous, arrogant old bitch, willing to take a chance with national survival to accrue immediate political advantage. Evelyn had been watching from her seat.

"I wonder how these people ever manage to get elected," he said.

She looked at him oddly.

"What?" he asked. "What's so amusing?"

"Your friend Rick Hailey specialized in getting people like that elected."

"Including *me*?" he demanded.

Her eyes narrowed as she appraised him. Charlie had been in the arena too long to be concerned by blatant political attacks, but Evelyn's opinion seemed unduly important.

"No, Charlie, not including you. You were something of an anomaly in his career. You must explain it to me sometime."

Charlie was getting reports of isolated uprisings in the heartland. The crazies, spurred by the national crisis, were swarming out of their nests and proclaiming independent sovereignties, threatening local law enforcement officials, and in some cases committing murder and taking hostages. Several towns in Montana and Idaho had been seized and were broadcasting claims they had seceded from the United States.

He wished there were a way to get some privacy other than by retreating to the washroom. He found himself phrasing his remarks to Al Kerr, and to the others with whom he spoke, with an eye to their effect on the other passengers. When, for example, he advised the governor of Idaho to act against the rebels, to be assured of full presidential support, he found himself toning down the message. *We don't have time or resources for sieges,* he'd wanted to say. *Send in the Guard and shoot their asses off if they don't cave.* Instead, he'd delivered some mealy-mouthed comments urging appropriate state action and promising it would have the full support of the government.

Saber's voice came over the PA: "You folks might want to look out to port."

"Which way's port?" asked the chaplain.

A set of lights was moving among the stars. The cavalry had arrived.

They shook hands all around and congratulated one another. Morley went live, captured the celebratory mood, and noted for his audience that there was only a two-hour air supply left. It struck Charlie that the journalist would have been happier had it been more of a close thing, with people passing out as the *Lowell* drew alongside for a last-minute rescue. Well, Transglobal couldn't have everything.

He made a final trip up to the flight deck, where Saber

greeted him with a broad smile. "Thanks," Charlie said. "For everything."

She shrugged, suggesting it had all been in a day's work. "Glad to help, Mr. President."

It had been, to say the least, a harrowing flight. Charlie Haskell, in a way, had been no more than one among equals. He'd grown accustomed to traveling with aides at his side, like Rick, or foreign dignitaries, or journalists. And security people. He was always the vice president, and never Charlie Haskell. Haskell had gotten lost somewhere, but during the last seventeen hours he'd come back.

The chasm had opened again when he'd been sworn in. Even Evelyn had withdrawn after the ceremony. The sense of camaraderie that he'd shared with them at Moonbase and during the early hours of the flight had receded. Why? His mere accession to the top job should not have replaced the barrier that had been breached by the fire of common danger. Yet it had happened, and he knew that he was partially responsible. He spent most of his time now squirreled away with his cell phone, talking to the makers and shakers. The affection in his fellow passengers' eyes had been replaced by respect. He wondered whether he wasn't paying too high a price for political power.

Saber was listening to her headset. She swung the mouthpiece forward and nodded. "He's standing right beside me, *Lowell*," she said. "Wait one." She pointed Charlie into the right-hand seat.

"Charles Haskell," said Charlie.

"Mr. President, the *Percival Lowell* sends greetings. We're pleased to have the opportunity to provide transportation for you, sir."

Charlie stared at the communication console. Even out here, under these circumstances, it was all politics. And he understood immediately what Rachel Quinn—he'd met her once—wanted. *Don't forget Mars.* "Thank you," he said, keeping the resentment out of his voice. "We're all delighted to see you."

Something banged against the hull, one last rock for the Micro. They paused, listening for alarms. But no klaxons sounded and no red lights blinked on.

Sensing his discomfort, Saber rescued him: "*Lowell*, are we ready to make the transfer?"

"At your pleasure. Do you have any power at all?"

"Negative."

"Okay. Just sit tight. We'll take care of everything."

The interplanetary ship acquired definition. It was a long, elegant vessel, spare and utilitarian, lights glowing warmly. The civilization that could build such a vehicle and send it off into the dark certainly had a future. Charlie resolved that he would not stand by and allow that future to be sidetracked.

His cell phone chimed. "Yes, Al?"

"Bad news, Charlie. The Possum's coming back."

He was so numbed by the litany of disaster stories that it seemed like just one more, an extra statistic in a train wreck.

"You mean coming *down?*" he said at last.

"Yeah."

His eyes closed, trying to shut out the sense of the vast emptiness beyond the bulkhead.

"When? How long?"

"Tuesday morning. Around five."

Charlie pulled a headset on. "Are they sure?"

"Yeah. Well, they're saying it's too early to be absolutely certain, but they want us to assume the worst."

"Okay. Get back to Feinberg, get NASA, and get the facts. There's no room here for guesswork."

"Okay, Mr. President."

Charlie didn't miss the switch back to formality. "Where?" he asked. "Where's it going to hit?"

"Looks like the middle of Kansas."

"My God. We don't get a break, do we? Okay, Al, we'll have to go back to the nukes."

"That's what we thought. We can't just stand by—"

"Absolutely. Let me know what you come up with. Everything else goes to the back burner. We need to get rid of this son of a bitch. Don't just talk to the military. Talk to Feinberg and anybody else out there who might have an idea what we can do. Have them double-check the numbers." He watched the lights of the *Lowell* getting brighter. "What else have you got?"

"I'm not sure what to do about Henry. We've announced a joint memorial service Wednesday for him and Emily. But there's some disagreement about how to do it. Anything elaborate might not look good with the way things are now. His family thinks, under the circumstances, we should keep it modest."

Thank God. There at least was a problem that was manageable. "Listen, Al, if you're right about the Possum on Tuesday, there might not *be* a Wednesday."

Kerr did not respond.

"The family's right," Charlie continued. "Keep it small. Tasteful but small. The country doesn't need a parade right now. After we get through this, maybe we can do something more. Any chance of getting back into Washington by Tuesday or so?"

"The city's still under water."

"Okay. Look, Henry was a vet. A Marine. If the families agree, let's run the memorial at Arlington. That's high ground. They're okay over there, right?"

"I suppose so."

"Do it. Bring in the Marine band. He'd like that. Fire the weapons, fly some jets overhead. The missing man, right? Just keep it modest."

"Yes, sir. What about the government offices? We need to get running again."

"Al, you're on the spot. Figure out what needs to be done and do it. Close up and give the hordes a few days off. Find some temporary space somewhere. But keep a presence. Understand?"

"Sure. But—"

"Take care of the details. I'm about to be rescued and I want to enjoy it."

"Okay, Charlie. By the way, I'm glad to hear it. We've been worried."

Charlie disconnected, returned to the passenger cabin, and took a window seat beside Evelyn. *Lowell* was running parallel with them now. It drew closer and he could see into the interior, see someone moving.

"Unforgettable moment, Charlie," Evelyn whispered. "This'll be a major TV movie next year."

"I hope so," he said.

The *Percival Lowell* had been described as the principal engineering marvel to date of the century. Its proponents maintained that it was the key to opening the solar system to exploration and development. With the technology that had been employed on this vehicle, no one knew what the limits might be.

The *Lowell* moved in close and Charlie could count the rivets. "Everybody please belt down." Saber's voice.

Morley was speaking quietly into his mike. Charlie didn't know whether he was broadcasting or recording impressions until he saw the journalist's picture—a still—on one of the displays, with the legend: *LIVE FROM THE PRESIDENT'S MOONBUS.*

There was a heaviness in the air, compounded by the sweaty pungency of human bodies that had lived too long with fear and without showers. The chaplain was seated behind him. He leaned forward. "Mr. President, I'm happy to have had the chance to get to know you." He spoke in a tone that sounded like good-bye.

Charlie understood. Once they got safely across to *Lowell*, the last hazard would have been passed and the last intimacy would drain away. "Me, too," he said. "Maybe you can come over for lunch when we get home." Halfway through the remark, he realized it was the wrong thing to say, simultaneously pretentious and mindless. But he was committed, so he blundered ahead.

"That would be nice," said the chaplain with a straight face.

Lowell was now within about twenty meters. One of its hatches swung wide, and someone in a p-suit emerged. The astronaut looked up, saw Charlie and the others watching him, and waved.

Propelled by a jetpack, he pushed away from *Lowell*.

"They're going to take Bigfoot and Tony aboard first," Saber told them. "It'll take a while before they get to us."

Forty minutes later they were ready to go. The airlock opened and Charlie took a last look around the passenger cabin. The chaplain caught his glance and nodded. "What'll happen to it, do you think?" he asked.

"It'll make Jupiter eventually," said Saber. "There won't be any effort to retrieve it. It's not practical."

"I don't know," said Morley, speaking simultaneously to them and to his audience. "I suspect this rig'll have real historical value eventually."

"If the historians want it," said Saber, "I think they're going to have to get it for themselves."

But Morley was right. And Charlie suspected that if they all came through this, if the nation survived, and the world went on, there'd eventually be an attempt to recover the Micro. He could visualize it standing one day in the Smithsonian. Of course, the prospects for that might depend on what kind of president it had rescued. Nobody would have gone far to recover a James Buchanan artifact.

10.

TRANSGLOBAL SPECIAL REPORT. 3:53 P.M.

"White House Press Secretary Pat Russell, at a televised news conference from Camp David a few minutes ago, announced that the mile-long, club-shaped piece of moonrock known as the Possum is coming back and is expected to fall on central Kansas early Tuesday morning. A major evacuation effort is currently under way. Experts have conjectured that no one within seven hundred miles of the impact site will be safe from the immediate blast effect. Chicago, St. Louis, Kansas City, and numerous other Midwestern cities will be affected."

TRANSGLOBAL SPECIAL REPORT. 3:58 P.M.

". . . the panic in the Midwest. Federal and local authorities this afternoon are struggling to maintain a semblance of control over a terrified population. . . ."

Percival Lowell Utility Deck. 4:11 P.M.

Major Lee Cochran, in a white dress uniform, was waiting when Charlie stepped through the hatch. He snapped a salute. "Welcome aboard *Percival Lowell*, Mr. President." A full-throated version of "Hail to the Chief" roared out of the sound system. Charlie had to make a conscious effort not to show his dismay, but everything froze while the march went on, until he signaled that he was gratified and that it could be turned down or off. Someone reduced the volume. "I'm Major Cochran, sir," he snapped. "The captain asked me to present her regrets that she could not be here personally, but the situation requires her presence on the flight deck."

Charlie nodded and smiled. "Thanks, Lee," he said. He'd been introduced to both astronauts a week before on L1.

Cochran glowed at the use of his first name. "I didn't expect to see you again quite so soon," the president continued. They were standing in a small chamber lined with lockers and storage bins.

The others came through the airlock: Evelyn, who'd regained some of her imperious manner; Morley, talking into his microphone, his voice low; the chaplain, withdrawn and silent.

The major threw a disapproving glance in the journalist's direction, but said nothing. Saber brought up the rear, looking pleased to have responsibility shifted to other shoulders. Cochran peered through the connecting port. "Is that everybody?" he asked.

"Yes," said Saber.

He nodded, closed the hatch, and hit a couple of press-pads. *Lowell* rolled slightly and lamps changed color. "Everybody get hold of something," he said. He spoke into a commboard: "Rachel, pickup's complete. We're clear."

Charlie felt the ship change direction. "Mr. President," said Cochran, "you'll have the mission commander's quarters. If you and your . . ." he paused, looking for the right word, "associates will follow me, please."

Lowell seemed smaller now to Charlie than it had during his L1 inspection. The passageways were narrow, the spaces jammed with equipment, the appointments utilitarian. The mission commander's quarters, which might have appeared cramped under other conditions, seemed almost spacious in comparison. The bunk was drawn up into the bulkhead. There was a chair and a desk with an overhead display. Drawers and closet space were built into the walls. Two towels, a comb, a cup, and a tube of toothpaste were secured to the chair. An extra-large *Percival Lowell* jumpsuit was laid out for him. It was complete with a mission insignia and a HASKELL label across the left breast pocket.

Cochran invited him to call if he needed anything, showed him how to use the intercom, and how to tie into ship's communications. "We have two-way visual from the flight deck, Mr. President, should you have need."

"Thanks," said Charlie.

He pointed to a pair of doors at the end of the passageway. "I'm afraid we don't have private bath facilities," he said. "Use either."

After Cochran withdrew, Charlie pushed his bag into a cabinet, picked up the jumpsuit, his electric razor, and a few toiletries, and made his way to the washrooms. One was occupied.

He opened the other and squeezed inside. He stood for a moment, contemplating the compartment, with its clumsy zero-g toilet and its ultrasonic scrubbers. When he'd looked at *Lowell* before, he'd wondered what would possess anyone to commit to live two or three years cooped up inside her claustrophobic spaces. His first thought had been that humans probably shouldn't go to Mars until they could go in style.

His second thought had been that TR would have disapproved roundly of such a notion. Still, the first President Roosevelt hadn't been put to the test. Charlie himself enjoyed living in the wilderness, as TR had. That wasn't at all the same as walling oneself up in the high-tech equivalent of a cheap hotel with no exit.

He stripped, pushed his used clothing into a plastic bag, and turned on the scrubber. His flesh tingled, although not the way it would have under a hot shower. The grime flaked away and he rubbed off the residue with one of the towels. When he'd finished, he was clean, but he didn't really *feel* clean. He would gladly, he decided, leave space flight to others.

His phone was chiming when he arrived back at his quarters. "Haskell."

It was Al. "It's confirmed. The Possum's going to hit Kansas."

"Okay." Charlie had expected no less.

"I'm sorry." Kerr paused, maybe feeling a need to change the subject. "I see you got on board *Lowell*. We've been following the whole thing. You're getting great press. What did you do, buy off this guy Morley?"

"He's doing a good job, isn't he? Rick'd be proud."

Charlie was trying to decide what to do about the Possum. He wished now he'd taken his chances with the nukes. Maybe they'd have knocked it onto a different course. He'd still have to try to blow it apart, but now it would be *in*bound.

"Feinberg wants to talk to you again," said Al.

"What's he saying?"

"He won't tell any of us."

"Okay. Get him for me. Make sure he's got a scrambler." Charlie disconnected and watched the walls close in. He was deathly afraid they'd spotted another rock. His stomach began to twist, and he thought about Henry during the early days of the crisis, responsible for all those lives, and then knowing before he died that he'd made the wrong call.

The phone chimed again. "Mr. President." Female voice. He'd expected to hear Kerr saying he was about to switch him to Feinberg. But this was Rachel Quinn.

"Yes, Captain?"

"Sir, two things. We grabbed some prepared meals from Skyport's galley before we launched. I'd like to invite you and the other passengers to join us at my table for dinner."

"I'd be delighted, Rachel."

Her voice softened, became less formal. "Is seven o'clock suitable, sir? Or would you rather eat earlier?"

"No, that's good."

"Also, we're going to be starting a long turn back toward home, so you'll be feeling the g-forces a little. It won't be severe. We're taking it easy. That means it'll go on for a couple of hours. If it presents a problem in any way, please let me know. We can make a wider turn if we have to, but it would take longer to get back to base if we do."

"I'm sure it'll be okay, Rachel."

"You should also be aware we have a doctor on board. He'd like to take a look at you. At your convenience. And it looks as if you're getting another call, sir." She paused, and Charlie told her to patch it through.

"Mr. President." Feinberg's voice was precise, tired, ominous. "How are you? I see you've had quite a ride."

"Tell me about the Possum," said Charlie.

"Kansas. Four fifty-six A.M., Tuesday."

All Charlie could think of was using the nukes. "Wesley, we can't just sit here and let that thing come down on our heads. Do you still dislike the missile option?"

"Very much. It would be better to do nothing."

"No. I will not sit by and do *nothing*. Give me an option."

"Actually," the scientist said, "I *do* have a suggestion. We can try to lift the Possum into a higher orbit. A more stable orbit, where we can deal with it at our leisure."

"How do we that? With bombs?"

"You have to stop thinking *weapons*, Mr. President. Get outside the box. Use the space planes."

Charlie tried to visualize it. What would they do? Get under and *lift*? "In what way?"

"The world currently has a fleet of ten SSTOs. If my math is right, seven of them, working in unison, should be adequate to accelerate the Possum and move it past the collision point before the Earth gets there."

"We can really *do* that?"

"We can do it. *If* the planes can be deployed in time, if they are properly distributed, and if we coordinate the operation properly."

Charlie began to breathe a little more easily. "Great," he said. "Thank God." It seemed too good to be true. "Are you sure?"

"Of course I'm not *sure*, Mr. President. At this point, very little's certain. There are too many intangibles. For one thing, we don't know enough about the Possum. For another, I'm not certain how much fuel your planes will have left when they reach the Possum. But I'm reasonably confident."

"Okay. I'll run it by our people."

"Time is of the essence, Mr. President. This is not one of those issues you can allow to get caught up in bureaucratic wrangling. If you're going to do it, I think you have to simply make the decision now and get started."

Charlie needed a minute to think. He wasn't accustomed to making major decisions without staff work. "All right," he said. "I'll put Orly Carpenter in touch with you. He can get things started. Anything else?"

"Yes. We need more information about the Possum. Somebody needs to go out forthwith and take a closer look. Take pictures. Land on it. Punch holes in it. We need to determine its mass and mass distribution very precisely. We need to locate places on the surface where we can anchor the planes. We need whatever data we can get.

"I suggest you use every available SSTO," continued Feinberg. "All ten, if you can get them. The more you have, the better our chances. But no less than *seven*, under any circumstances. We'll need a minimum of seventeen minutes' burn at full throttle by at least seven vehicles. Provided everything's in place on the POSIM by no later than four A.M."

"Okay, Wesley. Tell Orly Carpenter what you told me." He paused, thinking about options, deciding this was really all he had.

"Is something wrong, Mr. President?" asked Feinberg.

"I don't see an easy way to get a look at the Possum."

"That's simple. *You're* already out there."

•   •   •

Downtown Indianapolis. 4:27 p.m.

Harold K. Stratemeyer settled into the back of his limousine and let his head drift onto the cushions, wondering whether everything he'd struggled to build over the last few years was going to come crashing down. He was commissioner of the Lunar Transport Authority and a few days before he had seen no major obstacles whatever to a brilliant corporate future. Now, literally overnight, Moonbase International and Hampton were out of business, and he suspected the LTA and Stratemeyer were close behind.

Private enterprise was not quite ready to take over manned space flight without substantial government assistance. Enormous potential was lying out there, but they were still several years from being able to exploit it. Meantime, capital expenditures were astronomical. (He no longer grinned at his old joke.) And so was the need for confidence that the program would be seen to its conclusion. If governments withdrew their support now, there'd be a meltdown. LTA, Moonbase International, and several hundred other, smaller, corporations, were developing ever more sophisticated technology.

Stratemeyer had spent a long, gloomy day in hastily arranged conferences, trying to devise a strategy to keep the industry alive. But the consensus was that space travel was dead for the foreseeable future. The client governments could be expected to go into a survival mode and the industry could not hope to shoulder the burden alone. And what would be the condition of the world economy in another week? Some had argued that the products of the space age, even if they could be delivered, would no longer find a market.

His cell phone trilled. He looked at the display: incoming from Camp David. "Stratemeyer," he said.

A woman's voice on the other end: "Please stand by for the president of the United States." Stratemeyer felt his heart speed up a little. Despite all his years dealing with the men and women who controlled the direction and momentum of Western civilization, he'd actually spoken with a sitting president only once before. That had been Culpepper, when Stratemeyer had joined a group of other executives to push for White House support in space technology. He'd been younger then, more impressionable. It irritated him that he once again felt a rush of blood.

He heard a series of clicks and a change in tone. Then another voice: "You're connected, Mr. President."

"Mr. Stratemeyer?" He recognized Haskell's rolling tone, somewhat distant, relayed presumably from the *Percival Lowell*.

"Good afternoon, Mr. President. I'm happy to see you've been rescued."

"Thanks. We seem to be in good shape now." He paused. "Harold—it's okay if I call you 'Harold'?—You know the Possum's on its way back."

"I know, Mr. President." The whole world knows. "What's going to happen?"

"That's why I called. Harold, we need the space planes."

"The *fleet*? All of them?"

"Yes."

"Why?"

"We're going to try to steer, to *lift*, the Possum into a higher orbit."

The limousine swung north onto Arlington Avenue. Stratemeyer looked out at the broad manicured lawns of the Naval Avionics Center. Traffic was light; downtown had been deserted. Unusual for a Sunday afternoon. Indianapolis seemed somehow ghostly, as if its reality were slipping away. As if it were becoming part of the past.

"With my planes?" he asked.

"Harold, you're all that stands between the world and a major catastrophe."

"Mr. President, I think we've already had the catastrophe." He looked out at the empty streets. "Why don't you describe precisely what you intend to do?" He listened while Haskell explained the plan. They wanted to fly all the planes to Atlanta tonight, where they'd be fitted with devices that would allow them to anchor themselves to the Possum. Then they'd launch to Skyport, where they'd be refueled. By Tuesday morning they'd be in position to move the rock.

"It's a *big* rock," said Stratemeyer.

"I know."

"What kind of guarantee do I have that I'll get my planes and crews back?"

"Harold, we're sending ferries out to bring the crews back. We don't anticipate we'll be able to recover the planes immediately. They'll probably expend their fuel during the operation."

Which meant, reading between the lines, he'd lose the planes. Insurance would never pay for them. Not under these circumstances. "Mr. President, I'd really like to help, but I have shareholders to consider. As I'm sure you know, a substantial portion of the LTA's assets are tied up in the fleet. I can't just allow you to fly off with it."

"I understand, Harold. But the government will underwrite any losses."

Hell, the government was already broke. Where would the Treasury get the money to make good the losses he'd take? Who said the Possum was that big a deal, anyway? A lot of rocks had come down during the last eighteen hours and the planet was still here. Moreover, it was Charlie Haskell making the promise; and Haskell was just one more politician. Stratemeyer knew better than to trust him. Not with the fleet. Hell, the way things were going, the president would be damned lucky to get reelected.

Best to ride it out.

"I'm sorry, Mr. President. I don't have the authority to authorize this on my own. Wish I could. But I tell you what: I'll track down the board members. Get them to okay it. And I'll get back to you."

"When?"

"Soon as I can."

11.

Percival Lowell Main Deck. 4:38 P.M.

"It's a stall," said Evelyn. "He doesn't intend to do anything."

"I know."

Rachel's voice broke in over the PA: "Mr. President, we've laid in a course for the Possum. But we're going to need about thirteen hours to catch it."

Charlie nodded. "That's the best we can do, huh?"

"Yes, sir. It has a long start on us."

"Okay."

"By the way, we'll be arriving almost immediately after apogee."

Charlie frowned. "Inform Feinberg. Let him know when he can start expecting his data."

"Will do," she said.

"What about *you*?" asked Evelyn. "What are *you* going to do?"

"I've already done it. We'll seize the planes."

"Most of them are outside the United States."

"It complicates things. But we can get international cooperation. Especially in a case like this."

"Won't it take time?"

"Sure. And it's time we don't have. In case you have a better suggestion?" He knew she would.

•   •   •

Indianapolis. 4:43 P.M.

Stratemeyer had just stepped out of the limo onto his gravel walkway when his cell phone sounded again. Not from Camp David this time, he saw, but from Moonbase corporate. That was odd. There was only one person there who had his private number.

"Stratemeyer," he said into the instrument. "Is that you, Evelyn?"

"Yes, Harold. Good to hear your voice again."

"You've been through something of an ordeal."

"We all have. Listen, time is short so I'll get right to the point. You can trust Charlie Haskell."

"Oh, I'm sure I can, Evelyn. I hope I didn't give him the idea I don't *trust* him. I'm just not free to do what he wants me to."

"Harold, it's your call and we both know it. The board will go along with whatever you decide."

"Unless the planes don't come back. And they won't. They aren't going to be happy with that, Evelyn." His front door had opened. His butler stood politely to one side. But Stratemeyer hesitated, standing on the third and fourth stone steps.

Evelyn also hesitated, and time seemed to stand still. A cool breeze lifted the flaps of his jacket. "I meant what I said about him," she said. "You can trust him. Not only to keep his word, but you can rely on his judgment. I've been close to what's happening. If we don't stop the rock, your planes won't be worth a damn anyhow. You've got a chance to use them and save everything we've ever worked for. Maybe everything *anybody's* worked for. Charlie says he'll see that you get reimbursed. Okay, that may be a promise he can't keep. But he'll *try*. And that's a better shot than you'll have if you just stand aside and let this thing happen."

"It's exaggerated," he said. "I've made phone calls, too. Everybody doesn't see this the way Haskell does."

"Come on, Harold. People like us can always find experts to tell us what we want to hear. It's the biggest problem we have. Everybody lies to us because they want things from us. Okay, the truth is, Feinberg thinks it'll kill millions if it impacts. It'll trigger a nuclear winter. It'll send us back into a dark age. You think there's a payoff for *anybody* in that?"

Skyport, Mo's Restaurant. 6:00 P.M.

The passenger list for the lost plane was still unavailable. Relatives were being notified, according to the transportation office. Andrea tried calling her friends, but most of the calls simply returned the monotonic recording announcing that the number was unknown. *Unknown.* That could mean they'd been on the plane. Or they simply hadn't tied in yet with the Skyport relay center. It was possible they'd forgotten, hadn't bothered, whatever.

Some answered, had been relieved to hear her voice, and they'd talked, exchanging what information they had (*"Yeah, I'm sorry, Hanlon was on the flight, he went with the others. . . ."*), indulging their mutual pleasure at finding each other alive. By late afternoon, Skyport had posted a list of persons from Moonbase to whom quarters had been assigned. She looked through the list and found a few more names. But most of the people she'd known and worked with over the last two years were gone.

She saw Tory Clark again at dinner. The astronomer was sitting with friends, and invited Andrea over. They were talking mostly about the Possum, about the effect it would have if it crashed. They were, to a person, furious with the politicians who had laughed at Skybolt and campaigned against it.

After dinner she and Tory wandered off together. They paused in one of the lobbies and looked at the Moon-cloud. It had flattened and begun to spread out along the orbital arc. "You doing okay?" asked Tory.

Andrea felt empty. Almost guilty. Survivor's guilt, she supposed. Well, what the hell, it had been luck of the draw, hadn't it? "I wonder how long it'll be before they let us go," she said.

"*Go?* You mean groundside?" Tory shook her head. "Not for a while, I don't think."

"They told us a day or two on the plane."

"Yeah. I just don't know. It's still pretty bad out there. I doubt they'll want to launch anything they don't have to." She looked at her watch. "Got to go. We're busy and the damned fools sent everyone home."

"Anything I can do?" Andrea asked. "I don't care much for just sitting around."

Tory shrugged. "I don't think so. The work's pretty technical. What's your specialty?"

"Communication. You must need somebody to handle traffic, right?"

Tory thought about it. "Sure," she said. "Maybe we could use you at that."

The Moon-cluster was passing out of sight, below the window. "Good. When can I start?"

"Why don't you come over and talk to Windy Cross? He's my boss. I can't make any promises, but who knows?"

Camp David. 6:28 P.M.

Stratemeyer glared down from the screen. "Let me try it again, Al. Feinberg thinks there are *ten* planes. But one's in maintenance and can't be made ready in time to participate. We lost another coming back from the Moon. Or doesn't anybody remember? And we've got another one at Skyport that's too damaged to get home. So we're down to *seven*. That's what you're going to have to settle for."

"The president wanted eight or nine, minimum."

"They don't *exist*, Al."

• • •

TRANSGLOBAL SPECIAL REPORT. 7:02 P.M.

"This is Peggy Bitmauer at LTA headquarters in Indianapolis. A fleet of space planes will blast off from Atlanta tomorrow morning in an effort to head off the Possum, a large chunk of moonrock which scientists expect to fall in Kansas Tuesday morning. Lunar Transport Authority Commissioner Harold Stratemeyer, a few moments ago, said that the LTA's entire fleet of Single-Stage-To-Orbit spacecraft have been placed at the disposal of the Government...."

Atlanta. 7:09 P.M.

Pete Telliard and his wife were celebrating their twenty-second anniversary at Horatio's, where no prices were printed on the menu and the meals were a hundred sixty per. Reservations were usually required weeks in advance; but tonight, like the city it served, Horatio's was three-quarters empty.

Pete squirmed in his jacket, uncomfortable with the formality of the waiters, trying to look as if he ate in establishments like this all the time. His wife smiled at him. "Next year," she said, "we'll go to the Steak and Ale."

His phone beeped. He pressed the face of the device and watched the antenna rise. "Telliard," he said.

"Pete." His boss's voice. From the shop. "We need you. Right away."

He stared at the instrument. "I can't make it," he said. "I'm with my wife. At Horatio's. Anniversary."

"I'm sorry, Pete. I really am. But we have to have you. They're bringing in the SSTOs for some refitting. It has to be done yesterday and there's no wriggle room."

Skyport, Flight Control. 8:17 P.M.

George Culver gazed at a close-up of the ruined tail assembly. The hull was battered and scorched, most of his sensors were gone, the port wing was jammed shut.

"We just don't have the facilities to do the kind of repairs it needs, George." The speaker was Skyport's maintenance chief, a quiet, intense man in his fifties. "I can't certify it. It wouldn't hold together if you tried to take it down."

"So what happens now?"

He shrugged. "Not my department. But if they ask me, I'll recommend they salvage the parts and junk the rest."

"You might not have a choice about certification," George said. "They need all the SSTOs."

The eyes narrowed. "They already tried to pressure me, George. Look, if you try to take that thing down, odds are you're not going to make it. I told that to management and I told it to NASA. If my boss wants to override me and sign the paper, he's free to do so. *I won't do it.* And if I were you and they *do* certify the plane, I'd refuse to fly it. Quote me if you want."

Skyport, *Copenhagen* Flight Deck. 8:36 P.M.

The engines were running.

Nora Ehrlich was an accomplished woman. Aside from flying the big space plane, she played a competent organ, had twice served on her school board, and had published two books of humorous aphorisms. She knew an *event* when she saw one, and she was taking notes for a third book, which would be an account of the rescue at Moonbase, followed by the pursuit of the Possum. The thing couldn't miss, and she already had the title: *Blindside*. She'd considered *The Doomsday Rock* and *Moonwreck*. But *Blindside* had a nice ring to it. Her first two volumes, *Nude in the Fast Lane* and *Scatter My Ashes at Lord & Taylor*, had been written under a pseudonym and had been modestly successful; *Blindside* would appear with her own name on the jacket. And she expected to make the best-seller lists.

Nora was a Londoner. She was tall, model-attractive, red-headed, a widow. She'd never lacked for dates, had married a wealthy Dane, moved to Copenhagen, had two daughters, and been successful at everything she touched. In the fall, her older daughter would be starting at the University of Zurich. Her husband had died three years earlier in a plane crash. She missed him, and had formed the unfortunate habit of contrasting everyone else against him. They all came up short.

But life without a steady man wasn't as bad as she'd imagined, and she was reasonably content. And the Tomiko Event, which was a disaster for everyone else, was developing into a godsend for her. She was at the center of the action. She knew that Keith Morley was riding out to the Possum now, and she expected to persuade him to do an interview with her. She expected to become an overnight celebrity, and that wouldn't hurt the book at all.

"*Copenhagen.*" The voice was from Skyport flight control. "Ready to launch."

"Roger. On your count."

"Sixty seconds."

Her copilot, Johann Blakeslee, nodded. Boards green. The flight engineer was Wendy Carpenter, a friend since college days, and a niece of Orly Carpenter, NASA's director of operations at Houston.

"We're *go*," said Wendy.

Thirty seconds.

Blakeslee was tall and blond. Chiseled chin, clear blue eyes, butter-wouldn't-melt smile. He was one of the few really good-looking guys Nora had met who was worth a damn. "Did you hear they got some complaints?" he asked. "Some people are upset because we're going back empty and they can't get home. I understand they were raising hell with the scheduling desk."

"Nothing surprises me anymore, Blakes," she said.

They launched precisely on schedule. The standard flight

plan to Atlanta called for the spacecraft to complete almost three-quarters of an orbit before starting its descent. But they were barely away from the station when they were overtaken without warning by a storm of pebbles and dust. It tore at the plane, broke off antennas, smashed the radome, and cracked a passenger window in the rear. The window blew out and air pressure plummeted. Nora cut the engines, but that was a mistake. The debris, moving faster than the SSTO and coming at it from almost directly behind, penetrated the rockets and coated fuel pumps and the combustion chamber, and all but blocked the exhaust ports. Warning lights for both engines glowed blood red.

Rocks clattered against the hull. Klaxons sounded in the passenger compartment.

Nora opened a channel to Skyport. "This is *Copenhagen*," she said. "Mayday."

"I see it. Sit tight, *Copenhagen*. Wait one."

Abruptly the storm was gone.

Skyport came back: "Stay with it for one orbit. Then we'll abandon. *Kordeshev* will rendezvous."

"You can't do that," said Ehrlich. "They need the plane."

"Forget it."

"Yeah, I can save it," she said. "I'm going to restart, and we'll bring her back."

"Negative, *Copenhagen*. Restart is not authorized."

Blakeslee's eyes had gone wide. "They're right. You can't take this kind of chance."

"We start *one*," she said. "We only need one."

Blakeslee shook his head. Not a good idea. Wendy caught Ehrlich's eye and nodded. *Do it.*

"Do not try to return," said flight control. "*Copenhagen*, acknowledge."

Nora used the thrusters to adjust attitude. All she needed to do was get a little lift. A little acceleration. "You're break-

ing up, Skyport," she said. "We cannot hear you." She glanced
at Blakeslee. "Ready?"

He nodded.

The starboard engine misfired and ignited the fuel tank,
which erupted. The blast broke the plane in half and set off a
series of secondary explosions. A nearby satellite recorded the
event.

It was almost a minute before the blinding light died.

12.

FOX MEDIA SPECIAL REPORT. 9:18 P.M.
Excerpt of an interview with Physicist J. Robert Collins of Princeton
by Harmon McMichael.

Collins:	*. . . three hundred thousand megatons. It's my opinion that, under these conditions, no one in North America would be safe.*
McMichael:	*Then we'd better hope they succeed in getting rid of the thing.*
Collins:	*Oh, yes. I don't think there's much question about that.*
McMichael:	*What do you think of their chances?*
Collins:	*You might say I'm cautiously optimistic.*

Skyport, Office of the Director of Operations. 9:32 P.M.

Belle escorted him in from the outer office. "George, I'm
glad you came by," she said. She looked rumpled, worried,
worn.

George found his way to a chair. "You're a plane short," he
said, coming right to the point.

"Yes. That's why we need you."

He nodded. He couldn't take his plane into the atmosphere, but there was no reason he couldn't help chase down

the Possum. "We'll have to find a way to anchor it," he said.

"We've been thinking about that. We should be able to tie you down with cable. We've got plenty of it." Her eyes were rimmed with worry. "George, you understand it's going to be makeshift. We'll get you secured as best we can, but there's a risk. If it tears loose while you're at full throttle. . . ."

He knew. "It shouldn't be hard to make sure that doesn't happen." He knew damned well how optimistic that statement was. "Do we have some engineers on call?"

"Not anybody who has experience with this kind of situation." (Who, wondered George, might have *that* kind of experience.) "But we'll get you some help." She drummed her fingernails on the desk. "We'll want you and your people in p-suits once the operation gets under way."

In case the plane cracks open. "Yeah," said George. "I think that's a good idea."

13.

Jack Gallagher was in bed, thumbing through the current edition of *The Patriot*, when the phone rang. Ann glanced up from the CNN newscast, which was detailing movements of the space planes to Atlanta for refitting.

His teenage son was away at school, so late-night calls were down to almost nothing. "Hello?"

"Jack." Steve's voice. "Can you get over here?"

Jack was a cook at his brother's restaurant. It was a job he detested. No particular reason. Steve treated him well enough, it paid all right, and the hours weren't bad. But it was a dead end, and he knew that thirty years from now he'd still be a cook. That was what he liked about the Legion: He was a *major.* People saluted him. Took him seriously. "What's going on?" he asked. (He tried to avoid using Steve's rank when Ann was in the room. She never said anything, never showed any disapproval. But it sounded ridiculous in her presence.)

"Just come down, okay? We've got ducks on the pond."

The remark meant to come armed. It meant that the Legion was threatened. Or that it was going to take the offensive. But what the hell was it all about? Despite his inclination to join in on the general criticism of the government, Jack Gallagher never thought it would come to shots actually being fired. It was all just *talk*.

"I'll be waiting." Steve paused. "No uniform."

Ann looked at him. "It's late, Jack."

"Legion business, hon," he said. "I'll be back in an hour or so."

She was used to late-night exercises and she didn't complain. "Try to get home at a decent hour," she said.

Ten minutes later, Jack backed out of the driveway that circled his mobile home, slipped onto Banner Street, and headed west on Route 250. Steve's home was located a couple miles outside town on the Middle River. It was a ranch really, a nice place, spread out over eight acres.

Jack saw Tad Wickett's Chevy pickup parked in the driveway. He pulled in beside it, and the front door opened. The colonel stood silhouetted against the light. "Hello, Jack," he said. "This looks like our night."

He was wearing a pair of dark, neatly pressed slacks and a pullover shirt with the manufacturer's logo stenciled across the breast pocket.

Tad was seated in the living room, fondling a cold can of Coke, his eyes expressionless. (He was a beer drinker. But Steve never allowed his people to combine alcohol with duty. They were clearly in an operational status.) His glance touched Jack and moved on to one of the colonel's bowling trophies. Tad didn't entirely approve of Jack Gallagher.

Tad had spent five years with the Corps. He'd been cited

for valor when the Marines went ashore to rescue Western hostages at Benghazi. He'd made sergeant first class, and been busted for fighting and insubordination, and court-martialed for assaulting a lieutenant. But he'd matured since then. He was an ideal officer now. Steve had been so impressed, he'd commissioned Tad after only three years.

In civilian life Tad worked in a lumberyard. He was a solid, churchgoing man with a proclaimed passion for the United States, and a streak of cruelty wide enough to accommodate a tractor-trailer. He didn't know where his family was. His wife had abandoned her duties and left him two years before, taking both their sons. Like so many others, he'd been watching with dismay the disintegration of civil society, the erosion of rights, the continuing encroachments by the federal government and its agents around the country, the gradual sellout to the United Nations and the inferior races. Getting worse all the time, he'd once told Jack. Today a free man can get away from oppression if he has to. He can go to Argentina, Sri Lanka, wherever. Soon, though, there'll be a world government and there'll be no escape anywhere.

"You've seen the reports?" the colonel asked, offering Jack a chair. "About the SSTOs?"

He sat down and accepted a glass of apple juice. "Yes, Steve. I've seen them."

"What do you think?"

"That's a big rock coming down. I hope they can stop it."

Steve relaxed on the sofa and crossed one leg over the other. "Jack, you know they lost one of the planes earlier this evening."

"I heard."

"They've found a substitute somewhere. They're saying they've still got enough to push the rock aside."

"I don't think I understand where this is headed," Jack said. He wished Tad were not there. The ex-Marine was somehow a defining presence. Tad was still young, barely thirty, trim, muscular, vaguely hostile. His eyes were hard and lines of cruelty had already formed at the corners of his mouth.

Tad smiled, as if that was exactly what he'd expected Jack to say, as if Jack were reading from a script. Tad was emotionless, save when he was enjoying himself, as he seemed to be doing now. It seemed to Jack that he had no real connection to life outside the militia.

Steve leaned forward, his gaze narrowing. "Think it through. What happens if the Possum hits?"

"A lot of people die," Jack said. "And the media are saying the country wouldn't survive."

Tad raised his glass in silent approval. "The *government* wouldn't survive," he said. "The *institutions* would go under; that's what they're really saying. And the question we have to decide is, is that a bad thing?"

"It's a bad thing if it takes out the whole Midwest, and maybe the rest of us as well, which is what they're saying it'll do."

"Hell, Jack," said the colonel. "Tad's right. It's the media who're talking. When did you start believing *them*? They're part of the establishment, too. You don't think they want to save their asses?" He drew a window curtain aside and looked out. A distant streetlight illuminated the egress road. "Isn't this what we've been looking for all along?"

Jack's stomach began to tighten. He'd been loyal to the Legion. Loyal to Steve. And he'd played his end of the game. Us against the government. One day we'll show them. But the weapons had never been loaded. Never *would* be loaded. Not really. That was part of the unspoken understanding. "What do you intend to do?" he asked.

"It's simple. We're going to Atlanta. You and Tad and I are going to take out one of the SSTOs. That's all we have to do: take out *one*. If we do that, it's *over*. The Possum hits, and the government will be gone within weeks. Maybe days."

"My God," said Jack. "How many people would we kill?"

Steve nodded sadly. "Too many," he said. "But the price of freedom is always high. Fortunately, it's a price free men have been willing to pay." He refilled his glass. His eyes gleamed in the light. "Jack, don't you think I'd use another way if I could? But this is all we have. This is *it*. It's a God-sent opportunity, and it'd be criminal not to take advantage of it just because we have weak stomachs."

"*Weak stomachs?* Steve—" The words wouldn't come. Jack had always looked up to his brother, had never known him to be wrong about *anything*. Steve Gallagher was the soul of courage and integrity. That he'd lied about his Ranger status was of no significance because he'd needed that extra bit of prestige to ensure control over the Legion. Jack understood completely. But this was *horribly wrong*. It occurred to Jack that his brother had read too many manuals, had begun to believe all the things he said, all the things that gave him power.

The colonel's eyes slid shut. "I know," he said soothingly. "I know everything you're going to say. And I've thought about it. But won't we be better off in the long run if we populate this country with a few thousand free men rather than three hundred million slaves? That's what we've got now, Jack. You know that as well as I do."

Tad was watching Jack carefully.

Steve leaned forward. "So what's your answer, Jack?"

"No." Jack's voice shook because he *never* said no to Steve. "I don't want any part of it."

"Okay." The colonel nodded. "I understand your feeling on this. And I respect it."

Thank God. "Then we'll look for another way?"

"We've *looked* for another way. We've been looking *years* for another way. Jack: Tad and I are going to complete the mission." He looked over at Tad, and Tad's eyes were amused. "But

I understand you have a moral reservation that will not allow you to participate."

"Colonel—"

"It's okay."

Tad's jacket had been thrown carelessly across a coffee table. Now he picked it up and his right hand went into a pocket. The colonel signaled *no* and the hand came out. "I'm disappointed, Jack," he said. "I thought you'd want to be with us on this."

"No. I don't know how you could say that. I've never wanted to kill anybody."

"Then I have to ask what you've been doing all these years in a military unit. What was this? Some kind of joke to you?"

"This isn't a military action, Steve. It'll be mass murder. Is that what you want?"

Steve's eyes slid shut. "Okay. I'm sorry you see it that way, Jack." He looked at Tad. "You were right. We should have left him out of it."

Tad nodded almost imperceptibly.

"I can't turn you loose," he said to Jack with a mixture of regret and irritation. "You're going to *have* to come with us."

"With your permission, Colonel," said Tad, "he'll be in the way. We'll have to watch him constantly."

"I understand the problem," Steve said. "But I don't have a lot of choices here. And I won't have my brother's blood on my hands." He stared at Jack, who was having trouble comprehending what was happening to him. "But fortunately, I'm not entirely unprepared." He produced a pair of handcuffs.

BBC WORLDNET 11:55 P.M.
Dr. Alice Finizio at the Jet Propulsion Laboratory, Interviewed by Connie Hasting

Finizio: (Finizio and Hasting stand in front of a map of the United States.) *We're projecting ground zero right about here,*

Connie, near Interstate 35 in Chase County, roughly mid-way between Wichita and Topeka. (A circle appears in the center of the map, in Kansas. It expands until it touches Canada and Mexico, extending roughly from eastern Utah in the west to Columbus, Ohio.) This is the primary blast zone. We would expect very few survivors in this area.

Hasting: (Breathless) *It includes Chicago, St. Louis, Dallas. . . .*

Finizio: *. . . Minneapolis, Lansing, Fort Wayne. The entire heartland, I'm afraid. I wish we could be more optimistic. (A second, shaded circle rolls out from the first through large sections of Canada and Mexico, absorbing the entire United States, with the exceptions of Oregon, Washington and northern California in the west, and Florida and northern New England in the east.) This represents a heavy-to-moderate destruction zone. People living in this section, if they take precautions, should survive the immediate impact.*

Hasting: *Immediate?*

Finizio: *The long range prognosis is not good. The blast will throw up a cloud of dust that will spread around the globe. The skies will be dark for decades. It's going to get cold, and it's going to stay cold, Connie—*

(Picture flutters and vanishes. A BBC anchorwoman appears.)

Anchor: *We are having technical difficulties at the source. We'll return to the Jet Propulsion Laboratory as soon as we are able. Meantime, we have a report from the Federal Emergency Management Agency on how to prepare for the impact. . . .*

CHAPTER NINE

PHYSICS AND POLITICS

Monday, April 15

1.

Hartsfield SSTO Maintenance Facility, Atlanta. 2:55 A.M.

A pair of SSTOs were berthed in the hangar; another waited outside. Work crews swarmed over all three vehicles. Sparks flew from welding torches. Exterior panels were removed while technicians poked at the planes' circuits.

The crew chief was satisfied that they were getting all the preliminary work done. There was still a question about the type of piton that would be installed. And that couldn't be resolved until whoever was doing the analyses of the Possum's surface made up his, or her, mind about specs. But once they knew, it would just be a matter of slapping in junction boxes, bolting on the mounts, and inserting the units.

"Four hours," the crew chief told his department head. "Minimum."

"Four hours?" The department head wiped his mouth with the back of his hand. "Look, Arvy, we've got the goddam president of the United States personally taking soil samples—"

"Well, that sure as hell makes me confident."

"Just have everything ready to go, okay?"

AstroLab. 4:11 A.M.

Feinberg was sleeping on a couch in his office when the call came in. It was Al Kerr: the president would be grateful if the professor could see his way clear to *accompanying* the Possum mission.

He hesitated. Feinberg didn't like planes all that much,

much less rockets. He argued that he was better placed to help at the AstroLab, but Kerr insisted. The president thought his presence might make the difference if problems developed. "Besides," Kerr said conspiratorially, "the country's in a panic right now. If you're there, people are going to feel better."

"They need me to hold their hand," he told Cynthia a few minutes later. "But I want you available. Stay here. Sleep in your office if you have to, but stay near the action."

A military escort had a helicopter waiting to take him to Atlanta. Cynthia Murray was therefore directing operations at the AstroLab when POSIM-38 reached its apogee, a little more than an hour later, and began to fall back toward Earth.

Percival Lowell Flight Deck. 5:42 A.M.

Rachel Quinn moved into a parallel trajectory with POSIM-38. They circled the object and began mapping its surface. They made extensive and detailed images, concentrating on areas suggested by Feinberg, who was in communication from a military transport flying over Pennsylvania.

The chaplain had asked what he could do to help, and Rachel showed him how to operate the imaging equipment. It was really quite simple. When Feinberg, watching on his notebook, asked that the image be shifted, or rotated, or that they simply move on, the chaplain pushed the appropriate button.

When they were satisfied they had enough, Rachel laid in alongside the Possum and matched its tumbling motion, so that its rocky walls stabilized in *Lowell*'s viewports while the stars and the Earth began to tumble. Feinberg had suggested a number of touchdown sites, and she began now to ease toward the first of these. The ship rotated and corrected.

In the right-hand seat, Charlie watched the cliff wall approach, tilt, move up past the window, become a plain. His stomach began to feel queasy. The chaplain smiled and told him it'd be over in a minute. "Try to think about something else," he said.

Charlie was looking out over a stretch of unearthly terrain. Not a moonscape; this was rather a profusion of rolling hills and flowing valleys, a spectral panorama possessing a dormant liquidity. This section of the Possum reminded him of the Dakota Black Hills, which he'd visited as a boy on one of his family's sight-seeing vacations. It had, like that bleak place, erupted and quickly cooled. This was the Back Country, the spheric area that made up three-quarters of the Possum's surface. It was dark, probably seared in the fireball. In the distance he saw Solitary Ridge, a long, ramrod-vertical cliff, distinctive by its angularity in this relatively uniform area.

Morley was once again equipped with a microcam, delivered at his request by Rachel. Now he used it to send close-ups back to his television audience while he described the mission. Samples, he explained, would be drawn and analyzed to provide data on density and to allow the analysts to estimate the Possum's mass. They were starting here because it was smooth and they could gain some experience before tackling the rougher sections.

But even Morley couldn't make the preparations for taking rock samples look exciting, so he signed off after ten minutes, promising to return if anything happened. There was a breathlessness in his tone, as if he thought something *would* happen, *had* to happen.

Getting the samples was Cochran's job, and when he announced the equipment was almost ready, the other two members of the "rock team"—Saber and Evelyn—retreated below and began changing into their gear.

Charlie had argued that Evelyn's EVA experience didn't compensate for her lack of strength, and that *he* should be the third member of the party, but Rachel was adamant that she wasn't going to risk a president. She was captain and she'd

damned well make the call. Charlie saw that she was uncomfortable, and backed off. She was right anyway, he realized. The
last thing the country needed just now would be to lose
another chief executive.

Rachel laid the *Lowell* gently on the surface. Since there
was no gravity to speak of, she had to use her thrusters to keep
it in place. The flight deck was high enough to see over most
of the mounds, and Charlie studied the horizon, which looked
about as far away as the other end of a football field. It was hor-
izontal rather than curved, and he had the sense of being atop
a plateau.

When Rachel suggested, with considerable reluctance,
that they could use his help with the laser drill, he readily complied. She added that she'd look forward to telling her grandchildren she'd once given direction to a U.S. president.

The drill was about the size of a large farm tractor. A
spherical reflector was mounted on its hood, from which the
laser beam would be transmitted. A pair of flex-jointed extrac-
tor rods, of different diameters, rose on either side.

The operator, seated on a saddle, could raise, lower, or
extend the reflector in its manual mode, or he could turn the
entire operation over to onboard computers. The semiconduc-
tor heart of the system was located inside a black box forward
of the operator's position.

The unit normally traveled on six independently suspended wheels, which were obviously not going to be of much
use in the Possum's zero-g environment. Wrestling it around
wasn't going to be easy.

The drill was big and awkward and tended to want to stay
where it was. When they got it moving, it was difficult to steer
or stop. Cochran warned that, once outside, they'd have to be
careful not to lose it.

Charlie's physics weren't good, but he could visualize the
situation: The Possum was turning at a pretty fast clip and it

would try to throw the laser drill into space, along with the three astronauts. Consequently, once clear of the ship, they'd have to bolt the unit to the ground. The situation was complicated by the fact that the *Lowell*'s p-suits weren't equipped with grab shoes, so the astronauts would have to anchor themselves first. They'd cannibalized the modules that were to have served as living quarters on Mars to find cables and spikes from which to fashion anchors. In all, it was going to be a clumsy operation. Charlie suited up so he'd be ready to go outside in the event of trouble.

Morley came down and caught everything live as they loaded the unit into the airlock. Then they followed it in, closed the hatch, and minutes later emerged on the surface of the Possum.

Charlie listened on a headset and watched the action through cameras mounted on the hull.

The rock team, tethers attached, pulled the drill out onto the surface.

"Over there looks good," said Cochran. "Lift easy. No sudden jerks, okay?"

"I got it," said Evelyn. Then: "Look out; it's drifting."

"Hell, Evelyn, you're the one's drifting. Take in some of the tether."

"It's like trying to stop an elephant."

"You guys need help out there?" asked Rachel. "Want me to send the president?"

"Negative."

They tugged the unit into place and secured it with cables.

When that was done, Cochran swung a leg over the saddle. "Set for one meter. Power up."

Moments later the black box produced a ruby beam that bounced off a mirror, penetrated a lens, and was turned ninety degrees toward the ground by the reflector. After a wait of several seconds, the ground began to bubble. A wisp of smoke rose, and at Cochran's direction, one of the mantis arms telescoped into the rock, rotating at high speed. When he was satisfied, he withdrew it and deposited its contents into a gleaming plastic case. Then he reset for four meters, and they repeated the process.

They took samples down to depths of twelve meters. Then they came back inside, turned them over to Charlie, and Rachel made for a new location.

Charlie labeled the samples and delivered them to Morley. Morley and Doc Elkhart had received a quick course in using *Lowell*'s geological lab. They ran the rocks through a series of simple procedures while Cynthia Murray monitored the results from the AstroLab and passed the data on to Feinberg.

The chaplain wondered aloud whether they might be taking another risk in attempting to lift the Possum to a more stable orbit. "Once the space planes start to work on that rock," he told Charlie, "I would think they'd *have* to succeed. Because if they don't, they'll change the impact point, won't they? Nobody'll know *where* it's coming down."

Charlie didn't press his own thoughts, that if things went that far it wouldn't much matter.

Relocation Station, Bismarck, North Dakota. 5:11 A.M.
Central Daylight Time (6:11 A.M. EDT).

Marilyn heard distant voices, commotion, the sound of trucks. It was cold in the army tent they shared with twenty others. Some were refugees from Louise's party, though Louise herself was gone, swallowed in the vast hordes arriving hourly by bus and plane from around the nation.

People were on their feet in the tent, dazed, frightened, discovering how much they missed the daily amenities of private shower and breakfast at leisure. There was no privacy, of course. She'd come to realize that was a civilized luxury.

"Let's go, everybody," said a shrill voice. Marilyn needed a moment to locate the speaker—a small, white-haired woman dressed in frumpy brown with a red and green arm patch identifying her as a Civil Emergency Corps volunteer. "We're moving out. Buses will be here in twenty minutes."

Larry rolled over on his cot and looked up at her. The early-morning air was cold and damp. "What's going on?" he asked. "Are we going someplace else *again*?"

An elderly man sat, trying to pull on his trousers while shielding himself with his blanket. "We're too close to Kansas," he said. "I heard somebody say we're going to Saskatoon."

Larry's eyes rolled. "Where the hell's Saskatoon?"

"Canada somewhere."

Somebody pulled a tent flap aside and a cold wind blew in. "North," Marilyn said. "We're headed north again."

AstroLab. 7:17 A.M.

The Possum was composed primarily of crystals: plagioclase, pyroxene, ilmenite, olivine, and other minerals. Their size and arrangement suggested they'd crystallized as fluid lavas. Of course, considering the circumstances, that could hardly be news. But the terrain should be firm enough, Feinberg thought, to hold the anchors. He passed his conclusions, with recommended specifications for the equipment, along to the Johnson Space Center. Johnson relayed the specs to the primary contractor, and to LTA at Hartsfield. The contractor responded that they'd already shipped two dozen units of each of the potentially applicable models, so the pitons were already at the Atlanta airport awaiting installation.

This news was passed back to Feinberg, who was at that moment landing at Hartsfield.

He'd been keeping abreast of the varying fortunes regarding the SSTOs. Last night, when one of the planes had been destroyed trying to return from Skyport, he'd been informed that they were down to *six*, and that he'd have to find a way to make do. When he'd explained to Orly Carpenter at NASA that it simply wasn't possible, they'd found another one some-place.

Damned bureaucrats. Playing their games even when the life of the world was at stake.

Carpenter was waiting for him when he landed. The imaging data from *Lowell* had arrived and they retreated to a virtual tank to begin picking landing sites. Feinberg stared at the Possum, tumbling, rotating around its long axis once every fifty-three minutes and eleven seconds.

He was, in a way, gratified. His life had been devoted to the quiet collection of knowledge that should have had no practical value. Yet here he was, able to engage his specialty to save the United States of America, for God's sake, and maybe civilization itself. Not bad for an astrophysicist. It would be a rousing climax to a life lived, despite his awards, in relative obscurity. Knowledge was its own justification, of course. To discern how the solar engine worked, why galaxies formed, how long a given star could be expected to live. These kinds of issues were the proper pursuit of humanity. No matter that they might not provide a blueprint for how to build a better house or make the economy behave. (The issue of practical applications had driven him to fury last year when yet another effort to fund the supercollider had failed. The Congress had asked what benefit could be derived from understanding how creation had happened; and the physicists, to their eternal dis-credit, had no answer.)

Still, it felt *good* to apply his knowledge. To know that, because the astronomers had been here, this civilization would live.

"Here," he said, illuminating a point toward the rear, high in the Back Country. "And here." Toward the front of the

Plain. "The real problem is that a lot of the ground's just too rough. They wouldn't be able to get close enough to lock the planes down. And in some places, the lava base is too weak. But we can make do." Eventually they agreed on the seven sites.

TRANSGLOBAL SPECIAL REPORT. 7:20 A.M.

"This is Shannon Gardner in downtown St. Louis. I'm only a few miles from where it all started, in Valley Park, one week ago today when a young woman spotted a comet during a solar eclipse. Since that momentous afternoon, countless people have died, the nations of the world have been ravaged, there are trillions of dollars in property damage, and the worst threat of all still hangs over our heads. In the background, you can see looters. There are few police left here now to stop them. With less than twenty-four hours to go before the Possum is scheduled to impact in Kansas, everyone who can get out of the city has done so, and the only ones left are those who have no money, or no hope.

"The buses that were brought in by the city, and by various civic organizations, are gone now. The highways around this abandoned metropolis are locked tight with dead vehicles. The only way in or out is by air. Or on foot. We'll be abandoning our sound truck when we go to the airport. Maybe, if we're lucky, and the president's task force of space planes does what they're saying it can do, we'll be able to come back and get our truck. Maybe—

"Hey, what are you doing—?"

(*Harsh voice off-camera.*) "Up yours, bitch—"

(*The camera image leaps skyward, but viewers hear sounds of struggle, screams from reporter.*)

(*Cut to Bruce Kendrick.*) "We seem to have developed technical problems with our mobile unit in St. Louis. We'll be going back there as soon as we reestablish contact. Meantime, let's switch over to Jay Hardin, who's standing by at ground zero, in Chase County, Kansas."

2.

Hartsfield SSTO Maintenance Facility. 8:14 A.M.

There were now five SSTOs at Hartsfield. The shipment of pitons lay gleaming in their crates while teams of technicians proceeded with installation.

In an adjoining building, the flight crews were receiving instructions on their new equipment from Orly Carpenter. Carpenter was tall and angular, with a full head of silvery hair that in his astronaut days was such a fiery color it had earned him the nickname "Red." His usual high-energy delivery was subdued that evening, probably because of the nature of the mission, possibly because he was still trying to put the loss of *Copenhagen* and his niece Wendy's death out of his mind.

They sat in a crowded conference room around a long table designed for half the actual number of attendees. "Ladies and gentlemen," he said, speaking from a lectern in front of a video screen, "welcome to Operation Rainbow." He saw the smiles, some skeptical, some in the best can-do military tradition. "The media have been saying we're going to attempt to *lift* the Possum into a higher orbit. That's true as far as it goes. We *will* change its course somewhat. More important, we are going to accelerate it. We are going to speed it up and we are going to move it across Earth's orbit before Earth arrives.

"After your planes have been equipped, we'll take them to Skyport, refuel, and rendezvous with the Possum. We estimate that all seven vehicles will be in position on the rock between three-thirty and four A.M. Since this thing is due to come down at four minutes to five, we won't be much ahead of the curve.

"The SSTOs should have eighteen to twenty minutes burn time left at full throttle when they arrive at the Possum. That's not much. But it *will be* enough. What's essential is that no fuel be wasted. When we arrive, we'll lock down at our desig-nated spots, and at the designated angles, and shut off the engines. From that point, do nothing without instructions. Questions so far?"

A hand went up, from Ben West, the pilot of the L.A.-based plane. "If I understand this, we're going to burn up most, or maybe all, of our fuel during the operation. Is that right?"

"That's correct, Ben."

"How do we get home?"

Carpenter nodded. "That's a fair question. We'll have ferries standing by. When the mission's been completed, if planes are unable to leave the Possum under their own power, which will likely be the case, the ferries will pick up the crews."

"Orly." Willem Stephan, who had just come back from the Moon. "What happens then? To the SSTOs?" The pilots had a traditional affection for their spacecraft. Casting them loose wasn't entirely appealing.

"Unfortunately," Carpenter said, "we've no immediate way to refuel them. We *do* expect to get them back eventually. But we're taking this one thing at a time. The objective is to stop the rock, not to save the planes. Anyone else?"

No hands went up.

"Okay. Once you're in place, the pitons will anchor you to the Possum. You'll be able to release from them any time you want, but if you do so the pitons will remain in the ground. You *won't* be able to reattach. So we only get one shot at this. Everything has to work right the first time.

"The pitons will be handled from the flight engineer's station. You'll need relatively flat ground, and we've tried to pick sites accordingly. If when you get there you don't like the terrain assigned to you, let me know. Don't try anything that looks unduly risky. But tell me *before* you lock down. Afterward, it's too late. Is that clear to everyone? Please be careful about all this. We're at a point now, if we lose a single vehicle we're in deep trouble.

"I'll be aboard the ferry *Antonia Mabry*, which'll serve as our command center. We'll have another passenger and I'd like to take a moment to introduce him." He looked down at a short, stocky, bearded man who'd been sitting up front. "Professor, can I ask you to stand, please?"

The bearded man, obviously reluctant, did so.

"This is Professor Wesley Feinberg, who's done much of the planning behind the mission."

"Good morning, everybody," Feinberg said. "I'm pleased to be with you." And with that he sat down.

Carpenter resumed his place, looking somewhat startled at the brevity of Feinberg's remarks. "Thank you, Professor Feinberg," he said. "And I'd like to express our appreciation to the flight crews as well. I know you're all volunteers, and I won't try to downplay the dangers inherent in the operation we're undertaking. Nobody's ever tried anything like this before. But I see no reason we can't bring it off."

Percival Lowell, Presidential Quarters. 8:28 A.M.

"Charlie, you've got to do something or it's not going to matter whether you push that rock aside."

"What do you need, Al?"

"We've got too many dead people. And that makes the survivors goddam nervous. When they hear the sky's coming down, they believe it. Hell, Charlie, we're telling 'em everybody between Canada and Mexico, from Ohio to Utah's at risk. What do you think they're feeling out there today?"

"You want me to talk to them?"

"Yes."

"But I don't know how reassuring I can be. We think we can do this, the experts are confident. But that's not exactly a sentiment that's going to send people to the barricades."

Someone was knocking. Charlie opened the door and saw

Evelyn. She was loaded up with coffee and eggs. She mouthed the word *breakfast*?

"Then *lie*," said Al.

"Haven't they had enough of that?"

"Goddammit, Charlie, the middle of the country's in a panic. Everybody's running for cover."

He nodded. "I've been watching the reports."

"Then you know you need to do something. Sir." Evelyn was setting a place for him, locking the coffee and food containers in place on a small table. "We've arranged to set aside a block of time with the networks. At ten A.M."

"Ten o'clock? Have you lost your mind, Al? It's, what, eight-thirty now."

"The sooner the better, Charlie. We've got to calm things down."

He felt his stomach tightening. "I'll get back to you," he said.

He disconnected. Evelyn maintained the silence for several seconds, but he knew she was watching him.

He shrugged. "I thought you were outside, working with Lee."

"We're between sites. Taking a break." Then her tone changed: "What are you going to do?"

She was a lovely woman. He'd have liked to retreat with her to a lonely island. Get away from all this. "What *can* I do? I'll make the broadcast."

"I mean, what will you say?"

That was a good question. "I'll tell them it's under control. I'll ask them to keep calm and stay home and remind them it's more dangerous on the road than it is under their own roofs."

She frowned, and her dark eyes hardened. "Isn't that the same thing Kolladner told them?"

"Son of a bitch, Evelyn. What do you *want* from me? What am I *supposed* to tell them?"

"The truth?" she asked.

"What's the truth? That I'm up here looking out the window at that goddammed flying Everest and when Feinberg tells me a few planes can make it go away I want to believe him but in my heart I just can't see it. That I think the whole goddammed thing is going to fall in the middle of Kansas and break the country's back?"

"Oh," she said.

"No. My job right now is to keep a lid on. And give Carpenter and Feinberg a chance to do their work."

"If you lie to them," she said, "they'll know. I don't think you're a good liar, Charlie." And then, without warning, she looked at him and he understood the invitation. He hesitated, decided why the hell not, and embraced her. Her lips touched his cheek and then pressed against his mouth. She was warm and yielding and her breasts and hips melted into him. "Stay with the truth," she said. "It's who you are." Her cheeks were wet.

He found the nape of her neck and held her. They rocked gently.

"Stay with the truth," she repeated. "But don't give your opinion."

Route 411, west of the Cherokee National Forest, Tennessee.
8:42 A.M.

They'd taken his revolver and cuffed his hands behind his back and put him in the rear of the colonel's white Ford van. There were no windows, save those atop the rear doors. He sat on the floor with the launcher and a spread of AN/415 Cobra heatseekers.

Up front, Tad and Steve didn't talk much. The radio was filled with the voices of disaster, people mourning friends and relatives, others predicting the end of the world. A tidal wave had struck Anchorage; and a rock had landed in China, triggering an earthquake that had swallowed several towns. Jack knew, *had* known, people in Los Angeles and Seattle, on Cape Cod and in Miami. His uncle Frank, who'd remembered him every Christmas when he was a kid, lived in Anchorage. Who was alive and who dead? And Jack had two children at home. What would happen to them and to Ann if his brother actually succeeded in downing one of the planes?

He'd pleaded with his brother as they rolled along the Blue Ridge Parkway. After a while he'd begun to scream at the men in the front seat until Tad had climbed back and gagged him.

Eventually they stopped, and Steve grumbled that the parkway was blocked, and Tad noted there were no cops visible anywhere, and it was just another demonstration of how quickly the government abandoned its responsibilities under pressure.

They exited onto a mountain road and drove through the night. Occasionally they stopped, once to get a charge, a couple of times to get snacks and ask directions. At one point Steve removed his gag, said how disappointed he was at Jack's behavior, but asked whether he wanted something to eat. Jack screamed for help and the gag went back on.

In spite of everything, Jack hated seeing the contempt in his brother's eyes. He'd made a lifelong effort to earn and keep Steve's respect. It was, in fact, the reason he'd joined the Jefferson Legion. The truth was, he thought life was not that bad under the government everybody else wanted to bring down. Although he'd never have said that to any of his compatriots. Least of all Steve.

They spent several hours somewhere, blocked by traffic.

After the Sun came up and he could see, he tried to load one of the heatseekers into the launcher, with a view to firing it through the front of the vehicle. But it wasn't possible with his hands cuffed, and he made so much noise he attracted attention and Tad came back and told him to stop or he'd put out Jack's lights.

By midmorning they were moving again and at noon Tad announced they'd crossed the Georgia line. The first of the space planes was scheduled to depart at about one. The media were on the scene and they were making an event of it. Crowds had lined up at Rico, Georgia, near the mouth of the underground launchway. The networks were giving it full coverage, interviewing people as far away as Chattanooga. Witnesses were on rooftops with binoculars and telescopes. Night launchings were best, one old man said. *They really put on a show.*

"So will we," said Steve.

The colonel had Interior Department maps, which he studied for the best attack site. Jack knew it had to be west of Rico, in the direction of the launch, but Tad commented that the area was built up and looked unlikely to provide, say, a covering patch of forest.

Tad remarked they didn't really have much choice, and that he'd stand out in the middle of the street and launch the missile if that's what the colonel thought they should do.

"I think we can improve on that," said Steve. "Here's the Chattahoochee. Somewhere along its banks there has to be shelter of some sort."

Jack saw blinkers ahead and they slowed down again. Accident, probably. He started to move toward the rear doors, hoping to throw them open and jump out, hoping for police. But Tad climbed back and stayed with him until they'd gotten past and were moving along again at a steady clip.

There were other slowdowns, and Tad complained they wouldn't make it by one.

Gallagher glanced at his watch. They'd switched places several times and Tad was driving now. "It's okay," he said soothingly. "We can take our time. All we have to do is knock down one plane. Doesn't matter which one it is." He looked at peace with the world. It was odd. He seemed to discount the risks they were taking. As if they were destiny's favorites.

STATEMENT FROM THE PRESIDENT. 10:00 A.M.

President Charles L. Haskell, speaking from the Percival Lowell.

"This morning I'd like to address, not only the American people, but our friends around the globe. The world community is currently going through an experience unlike any ever faced before in our collective history. Coasts everywhere have been inundated, cities battered, whole populations turned out of their homes. Millions have died. In the United States, we have lost a president, the government is scattered, casualties are terrifyingly high. And an even greater danger hangs over our heads.

"I'm on board the *Percival Lowell*, a nuclear-powered ship designed and built by us, by the human race, to carry our representatives, and eventually our civilization, outward. To Mars and beyond. Now, instead, it is being used to scout an enemy of that civilization. It's a technological marvel and it stands as a symbol of what we can accomplish when we put aside our differences, and our fears, and act in our common interest.

"During the last two days, the United States has received massive aid from its friends, and even from some longtime rivals, around the world. Italian surgical units, Canadian wheat, Mexican disaster teams, Chinese helicopter and transport services, have arrived on our shores and have helped save the lives of thousands of our people. Japanese technicians freed Americans trapped in collapsed buildings in Seattle and Anchorage; Russian ships rescued sailors from capsized vessels in the North Atlantic; Israeli and Egyptian army engineers, working in concert, have shored up dozens of damaged buildings, bridges, and dams. Our own armed forces have reacted with courage and determination.

"We've begun to hear of individual acts of heroism, people throwing themselves into the path of torrents to rescue others from overturned automobiles, a young woman in Tallahassee who lifted an automobile off a child's chest amid rising waters, a helicopter pilot in Hawaii who snatched three teenagers from a roadway and had to outrun a tidal wave.

"The world is drawing together. We're putting aside politics and ancient rivalries and all the other causes that divide us, and we're acting, for the first time in our history, as a single family. It is this fact that gives me great hope for the future. That persuades me we can come back from all the damage we've sustained over the last two nights, from the terrible losses we've taken, that we will rise from this calamity stronger and better than we have ever been before. That we will memorialize those who have died by rebuilding their world. That we will do it together, and that when we have finished, we will have created a civilization that will give pride to men and women as long as we inhabit this globe.

"Unfortunately, none of this will be possible if we don't turn aside the Possum. So let me tell you what the situation is: You already know that, if left on its present course, the Possum will come down in Kansas at four-fifty-six A.M. tomorrow.

"We don't intend to let that happen. With the cooperation of the Lunar Transport Authority, we're going to put the entire fleet of space planes on the rock. We're going to anchor them down and then we're going to fire their engines, and we're going to accelerate the Possum so that it crosses Earth's orbit early. That will get it out of the way. We expect it'll remain a neighborhood nuisance for a while after that, but we'll be able to deal with it at our leisure.

"Will it work?

"I've seen the same interviews you have. Some experts say no. Furthermore, a lot of people don't trust the government very much. They think it's either dishonest or incompetent or both. Okay, I'm not going to argue that point tonight. We can address it later after we've solved the more pressing problem of our survival.

"Will it work?

"I can't guarantee success. But I've been close to the effort to detour the Possum right from the beginning. I suppose you could say no one's closer. In fact, I can look out my window here and you'll notice it's only a few hundred feet away.

"I'm not a mathematician. The physicists who've planned this mission are confident. We've assembled the best people from around the world to make it happen. So I'll tell you this: If it's humanly possible, we'll get it done. Meantime, I ask you to keep calm, trust us to persevere, and we'll come through this together.

"Thank you. We'll keep you informed."

3.

NEWSNET

WE REGRET _NEWSNET_ SERVICE IS TEMPORARILY OFF-LINE DUE TO RELOCATION OF NEWS AND PROCESSING CENTER FROM CHICAGO TO TORONTO. CHECK THIS SITE TOMORROW.

Skyport Orbital Lab. 1:10 P.M.

Andrea was a useful addition. She took over the communication systems without undue delay, learned to monitor the data feeds that provided information from hundreds of remote and manned facilities and relay it to appropriate consumers, and showed a natural talent for mollifying researchers who weren't satisfied with the quality or alacrity of responses.

The lab, and the various facilities it served, were now almost exclusively concerned with the fallout from the collision between Tomiko and the Moon. A subsidiary branch of specialization had appeared almost overnight: an interest in Tomiko itself, and the suspicion that it was something more than simply a comet. That notion was rapidly developing into a full-scale argument. But like philosophical and religious debates, it appeared to be an argument that would lead nowhere. The comet had vaporized, and if anything unusual had lain within its frozen exterior, it was hard to see how any of it could have survived.

Meantime, the return of POSIM-38 had claimed primary attention. People who wanted details, say, on energy release or gravity fluctuations during the collision were being put on hold. Virtually every instrument under the lab's auspices was aimed at the Possum.

For her part, Andrea was delighted to be back at work. Windy had even signed papers to grant her status as a temporary employee. (It turned out the government had rules against using volunteer professionals without paying them.)

By this time a small network of stations directly involved in the effort to get rid of the Possum were linked directly to the *Lowell*. These stations included the Lyndon Johnson Space Center in Houston, Feinberg's temporary location at Hartsfield, the Mauna Kea Observatory in Hawaii, Palomar in California, an advisory post at Cambridge University, and the AstroLab. All other communications to the *Lowell* were funneled through the Orbital Lab.

Most of these were either for Keith Morley from his producers, or for the president. The latter were, for the most part, scrambled.

Andrea was a professional. She did not try to eavesdrop, but it was her duty to stay on the circuit until she was sure connections had been made. In so doing she'd learned that Evelyn Hampton, the chaplain, and Rachel Quinn had all received book and movie offers. She also knew that the president had spoken to the families of Tony Casaway and Bigfoot Caparatti; that Hampton had called Jack Chandler's son.

She wondered about Chandler. He hadn't been on the microbus, but she knew he'd volunteered to stay behind. What had happened?

A new *Lowell* radio operator had appeared. The voice was

familiar, but she couldn't place it. "This is Andrea Bellwether," she said. "Do I know you?"

"Yes you do, Andrea," the voice said. "This is Mark."

"Chaplain, hello." They'd been only casual acquaintances at Moonbase, but now he seemed like an old friend. "You're the comm officer now?"

"Yes. Bottom of the barrel, you know. I'm glad you got back all right."

"Thanks," she said. "I think you had a rougher ride than I did. Tell me, are you going to get rid of that thing?"

"I hope so. I think Charlie Haskell will go after it with a pickax if he has to."

Percival Lowell Utility Deck. 1:19 P.M.

Evelyn and Saber stripped off their p-suits. Lee Cochran was gracious enough to keep his back turned. "I think we did pretty well," he said.

They had. They'd established that four of Feinberg's preferred sites were located on solid ground, and eliminated two others. Three to go.

Evelyn was stiff and sweaty, but she felt good. She'd come through the most desperate crisis of her life and had been nothing but extra weight the whole time. Until today. Today she'd gone out with Lee and Saber and they'd wrestled the laser drill around, bored holes, collected samples, gotten back inside, and waited while Rachel moved the ship to another niche on the rock's surface, where they got out and did it all again.

They were accomplishing what they needed to and they were running ahead of schedule.

She cleaned off in the scrubber, changed back into her blouse and slacks, and went to the galley for a quick lunch. Mark Pinnacle looked up as she walked in. "Hail the conqueror," he said. "We've got some great videos of you and Lee with the tractor."

"Thanks." She opened the refrigerator door and pulled out a QuikPack. Turkey sandwich with cranberries. "Save me one to put over my desk."

Lee walked in. "That is a very big boulder out there," he said. "Seven pairs of rockets don't seem like much against it."

"Seven is historically a sacred number," said the chaplain. "Seven sacraments, seven sins against the Holy Spirit, Japan's seven gods of happiness, the Seven Against Thebes. Maybe we'll add to the canon."

"Let's hope so," said Evelyn.

The chaplain had been munching a piece of meat loaf. He swallowed it, finished off a container of apple juice, and got up to go. "Got to get back to my work station," he said, looking pleased with himself. "By the way, they've got one of the Moonbase people manning communications at the Orbital Lab."

"Really?" asked Evelyn. "Who?"

"Andrea Bellwether."

"I don't think I know her," said Evelyn.

"Is she by any chance related to *Frank* Bellwether?" asked Cochran.

"His daughter," said the chaplain.

"If we're going to talk about omens," said Cochran, "that's not a good one."

Frank Bellwether, the pilot who'd *bounced*. Who had come in with damaged instruments and a damaged *Ranger*, and who had tried to insert himself into the atmosphere at the precise angle needed to maneuver between a ricochet and a burn-up, and who had ricocheted. Beyond any hope of rescue.

There'd been talk about the incident recently, of using a *Lowell*-type vessel to recover the *Ranger*, which in its lonely solar orbit was still visible on the world's radar screens. But the consensus seemed to be that it was better to leave the ship where it was. Evelyn shared that view.

"Nobody's talking omens," the chaplain said, a surprising edge to his voice. Out of character. Evelyn wondered if he was beginning to feel the pressure.

SSTO *Berlin* Flight Deck, Hartsfield Maintenance Facility.
1:43 P.M.

"Try it now, Gruder."

The flight engineer looked down at the yellow box they'd mounted on the bulkhead by his hip, and pressed the black button. This time, lamps lit up and machinery moved beneath the deck. The engineers who were crowded together on the hangar floor, where they could see the undercarriage, jabbed fists upward and shook hands with each other. "That's good, Gruder," said Kathleen's voice in his earphones. Kathleen was down below with the engineers. "It was a loose cable. We'll put the panels back, try it one more time, and we should be ready to go."

The SSTO was on a cradle so the pitons wouldn't dig up the hangar floor.

Gruder nodded to his captain.

Willem finished going over his preliminaries and glanced out at the engineers. One of them was a deliciously attractive blonde.

"When we come back," said Gruder, "we will be heroes. Women like that will be our oyster. They will open to us on request." He grinned and the captain grinned back. It was, of course, quite true.

The ground crews brought in three flatbeds of brown earth. They drove them under the spacecraft, positioning one beneath each of the three pitons.

Kathleen spoke to him: "Okay, Gruder, try it again."

He hit the button and felt the spikes come down. Felt them dig into the dirt, felt the spacecraft lift slightly as weight was transferred from the landing gear, watched the lamps stay amber until a string of lights indicated the pitons were fully extended. Gruder touched a presspad and flanges pushed out in three directions from the head of each piton, anchoring it. If necessary, he had a break switch that would jettison the units and allow the SSTO to lift away from the surface. The break switch was hidden inside the box to prevent its being accidentally activated.

"Retract," said Kathleen.

They would not be able to retract on the Possum, where the pitons would be anchored in rock. But here, it was no problem. Gruder keyed the command. The flanges released their grip and the pitons withdrew into the mounts. The undercarriage creaked.

They went through the exercise a second time, after which the pitons received a thorough cleaning and lubrication. The engineers, satisfied, walked away, and Kathleen, after shaking hands with a couple of them, left the group and returned to the plane.

"*Berlin*," said a voice in Gruder's earphones, "installation is complete. We are ready to move you out."

Kathleen came onto the flight deck and took her seat. "You know," she said, "I wish they'd come up with something more appropriate than 'Operation Rainbow.'"

"Why?" said Willem. "It's a reference to the aftermath of the flood. Everything turned out all right."

"Only for Noah and his family. Everybody else drowned."

Kathleen was a distant cousin of Gruder's, although he hadn't known that until they began working together. Both were from the Bremerhaven area, both had flown combat jets, and both had the same birthday, although Gruder was a year younger. They were fond of thinking their lives were linked, and that time would either uncover or produce other parallels.

They already had one: They were both on the same historic mission.

The earth-haulers reappeared and left the hangar. Now a pair of tractors tied onto the spacecraft and began to draw her outside into the bright afternoon daylight.

"Tower," said Willem, "*Berlin* is ready for departure."

"Roger, *Berlin*."

The tractors connected them to the SSTO track, which hauled them inside the Transatmospheric Terminal and began moving them slowly toward the launch tunnel. They passed the boarding plaforms, which ordinarily would have been crowded with passengers.

Willem started the engines.

"*Berlin*," said the tower, "you are locked and loaded. Go in sixty seconds."

Gruder looked at his watch, but failed to note the time. *All the women you could possibly want.* He wondered what Kathleen was thinking.

CNN NEWSBREAK SPECIAL REPORT. 2:05 P.M.

"This is Mark Able reporting from the mouth of the Transatmospheric Tunnel outside Rico, Georgia, where the first space plane is ready to launch...."

4.

Along the Chattahoochee River, west of Rico, Georgia.
2:11 P.M.

Steve Gallagher had pulled over to the side of the road to watch the launch. He liked space hardware as much as he liked military hardware. There was something in the cold, gray, utilitarian vehicles moving between Earth and Moon that stirred the depths of his soul in a way that no woman, no *cause*, ever could. And among the LTA's assorted buses, trucks, and ferries, nothing made his blood race like the Single Stage To Orbit space plane, the rocket-powered vessel with its sleek wings folding back while it raced into a moonrise. It genuinely hurt him to contemplate destroying one of them. He hoped that the free men and women of the future would appreciate the sacrifice he was making in their name.

The radio was saying launch was imminent. Tad opened his door, got out, and turned toward the east. "Should come right up over those trees," he said.

The trees were about fifty yards away, lining one side of a schoolyard. There were kids running around a circular track, others simply chasing one another, skipping rope, playing games. The colonel could see movement in the classrooms. "You'd think they'd bring everybody out here to watch," he said. "The government claims it's saving the world, and they don't even care enough to inspire the kids to watch." He'd always understood that the people who worked for the government weren't individually vindictive. It was the institution that corrupted them, the institution that was mindless and overbearing. He'd seen enough TV interviews to know that the feds really believed the propaganda they put out, really believed they were on the side of the angels. But sometimes that faith in human nature was shaken, and he wondered whether they were not individually malignant and knew exactly what they were doing. How else did you explain the fact that they claimed the spacecraft of Operation Rainbow were going to save the world and then failed to rally the kids to watch the effort?

Maybe *everyone* knew it was a facade. They knew, but they went along because they saw no other course. It was like Orwell, except that Big Brother had turned out to be a lot more subtle, a lot more insidious, than anyone had expected.

"There it is," said Tad.

The space plane sailed out over the trees, riding twin contrails, ascending sharply toward a bank of glistening white clouds. Then they heard the sound of its passing, a distant rumble, like the sea breaking on a remote shore, its volume descending and then rising again. A few of the kids turned to watch.

Steve stood a long time after it had vanished, his anger growing against the men—and women too, God damn them—who forced him to take military measures.

The Chattahoochee wasn't much more than a narrow stream, nor did it harbor, as he'd hoped, any patches of forest. But at one point it ran behind the Golden Apple Health Spa. The spa looked closed, and heavy shrubbery partially shielded it from the view of neighbors. A Little League field lay on the far side of the river. "Looks ideal," said Steve.

Tad nodded. There were no vehicles anywhere on the grounds, and no sign of life in the neighborhood, save for a black Labrador retriever barking at them from the porch of a frame house across the street.

"We ought to shoot him," said Tad. "I brought a silencer."

Steve looked at him reprovingly. "Dogs bark," he said. "Forget it."

The Golden Apple was a long brick building with a row of glass doors opening into a lobby. Its rear rose to two stories. A row of windows lined an Olympic-sized pool from which the water had been drained. An oval driveway circled the front.

The radio reported that another launch was only minutes away.

"I'd feel better if we could get the van out of sight," said Steve. "Neighborhoods like this, they remember strange vehicles. Somebody might even copy down the license number."

Tad surveyed the street. "I don't think anybody's even home."

Steve considered this. "Okay," he said. "Let's do it."

The radio announced that a second space plane was being towed out of the hangar toward the launch ramp.

"Timing's perfect, Colonel," said Tad. Steve nodded. He liked Wickett's enthusiasm.

He was saddened and disappointed that, in the hour when the Legion was taking the high ground, his brother had proved wanting. "We'll have to restrain him," he told Tad, glancing back over his shoulder. Jack sat propped against the wheel well, glaring at him. His feet were pressed against the launcher. "Secure him to the seat anchors."

Both sides of the spa's grounds were lined with enormous hedges that hadn't been trimmed in several weeks. Steve parked as close to the shrubbery as he could. Tad slipped out his side, went around to the back of the van, and opened up.

Minot, North Dakota. 1:17 P.M. Central Daylight Time (2:17 P.M. EDT).

The army bus in which Marilyn and Larry had been riding pulled onto a football field saturated with other buses. They'd now been in the vehicle almost seven hours, and they were still in North Dakota.

The driver, a portly little man who was trying hard to remain cheerful, maneuvered into a line of parked vehicles in an open space beside a football stadium, and then got up and turned to face his passengers. "I'm sorry, folks," he said. "Our traffic control is telling us the road ahead just isn't moving very much. There're a couple of rest rooms here we can use, and the Red Cross is supposed to be in the area somewhere. We're going to take a forty-minute break. Take care of yourselves, do whatever you have to, and we'll meet back here at, uh, three."

"We're not gonna get out of here, are we?" demanded a big man with a thick curly beard and a childish pout.

"We'll be fine," said the driver. "The cops are trying to clear the traffic up ahead."

"The cops all took off." The bearded man turned to the woman behind him. "Wouldn't you?" he demanded.

Maybe they were too weary to be terrified. Marilyn stood up and tugged at Larry. Live or die, she wanted something to put in her belly. "You coming?" she asked.

Larry nodded, and they headed for the door. The bus emptied out.

The washrooms were located under the stands. There were long lines, and it was here that they finally separated from the last of the people from Louise's party.

The Red Cross wasn't visible. Marilyn hadn't eaten for hours. They wandered back to the bus to see if anyone had located food. Nobody had.

"I think I've had enough," Larry said. "Why don't we stay here until it's over."

"We're still inside the red zone," said Marilyn.

"We aren't going to get out of it on *this* thing," he said, looking at the bus.

She thought about it. By this time tomorrow, one way or the other, it would be over. And he was right: The bus was going nowhere. It reeked of sweat and bodies and she didn't think that she wanted to be on it when she died.

"Okay," she said. "Let's go have a look at the town."

The driver overheard and frowned. "You're not coming back?" he asked.

"No," said Larry.

"I can't be responsible," he warned them.

"Nobody's *ever* responsible," said a harsh voice in back. "That's what's wrong with this country."

TRANSGLOBAL SPECIAL REPORT. 2:18 P.M.

"St. Louis. Transglobal correspondent Shannon Gardner was seriously injured and her cameraman was killed when he tried to come to her assistance this morning. During on-air coverage. . . . "

•   •   •

5.

**SSTO *Tokyo* Passenger Cabin, Transatmospheric Terminal,
Hartsfield Airport, Atlanta. 2:31 P.M.**

Orly Carpenter sat across the aisle from Wes Feinberg. The physicist looked drawn. "First time into orbit?" Carpenter asked.

Feinberg managed a smile. He looked out at the tarmac, which was moving slowly past the windows, and back at Carpenter. "Yes," he admitted.

"Nothing to be afraid of, Doc."

"Don't be ridiculous," he said. "I'm not afraid of these things. Truth is, I have a touch of indigestion."

"Good. It's not much different from an ordinary airplane."

Feinberg nodded. His position required him to fly occasionally, and he knew the statistics, that he could fly around the world a hundred thousand times or so before he would become due for a crash. But he also remembered the story of the man who'd drowned in a stream that averaged only eight inches in depth. Numbers were funny, and he preferred being able to keep his feet on the ground.

The forward motion stopped. The spacecraft seemed to rise slightly and then settle back down again. "What was that?" asked Feinberg.

"We got loaded onto the launch ramp."

Carpenter was at the apex of a long and distinguished career. He'd been a fighter pilot, a test pilot, a trainer at the Navy's Top Gun school, and he'd become an astronaut at precisely the right moment to participate in the return to the Moon.

The week's events had shaken him, and he'd heard all the talk about closing NASA down, about cutting losses with Moonbase International and the LTA, about returning to the ground and rebuilding the cities and letting future generations worry about space. But he was by God not going to let that happen. What we had here was an object lesson in what could occur when defenses weren't in place. The next big comet could come down on North America. In fact, they had a big rock trying to do precisely that.

But with the new president in the thick of the action, Carpenter recognized a historic opportunity. And it wasn't simply a matter of selling him on Skybolt. The reality was that humans had to get off-world. They needed the resources the solar system could provide, and they now had the technology to make it happen. All that was necessary was will.

After they turned the Possum aside, Carpenter knew he could find a way to reach *this* president. And consequently touch the future. "We *are* going to make this happen, aren't we, Doc?" he asked.

Feinberg nodded. "If everybody gets there, if nobody burns too much fuel, if the pitons hold, *yes*. If everything goes according to schedule, we will most certainly make it happen."

The pilot's voice sounded over the intercom: "Buckle in, gentlemen. We are one minute to launch."

"Doc," said Carpenter, "sit back and enjoy the ride. You and I are going to make history tonight."

Chattahoochee River. 2:34 P.M.

Very carefully, they removed the launcher and two heat-seekers from the van and laid them on a strip of canvas. Then, while the colonel inspected the weapons, Tad climbed in and pushed Jack onto his back. "You're goddam worthless, you know that?" he said in a voice pitched too low for Steve to hear. Jack's eyes were yellow around the edges.

Tad got Jack's belt off, looped it around the rear stanchion of the front seat, and dragged him forward. When Jack tried to resist, Tad twisted his arm until his face grew white.

But it was an awkward business. And when Tad bent over him, trying to secure the belt to the handcuffs, sudden agony exploded in his groin. He rolled over and Jack scrambled out of the van.

Tad shut down the pain, lay breathing steadily for a few moments while his mind cleared. Somewhere far off he heard a door open. He could see Jack, hands cuffed behind him, stumbling toward the street. A U-haul rounded a corner and moved slowly past. Its driver looked but didn't stop.

Tad pulled his Smith & Wesson out of his pocket, and dropped slowly, and very tentatively, onto the asphalt. His legs were wobbly. He kept thinking what a clumsy son-of-a-bitch operation this was turning into.

The door he'd heard opening belonged to the house with the dog. A woman had come out onto the lawn and was watching. Tad raised the weapon and caught her in the sights. She suddenly became aware of the gun. She tried to get back inside, but he pulled the trigger, heard the explosion, watched her go down.

Jack's movements became even more frantic. He'd reached the street and was running for the cover of a group of trees at the corner. Tad tracked him with the weapon, leading him slightly. But the colonel stepped in, covering Tad's gun hand with his palm. "He's *my* brother, Tad," he said quietly. "My responsibility."

He raised his own pistol, a .45, and fired once. Jack lurched forward and fell.

"We'll have to find someplace else," Steve said, pushing the weapon back into a shoulder holster. They put the missiles back in the van, rolled out onto the street, and as they passed Jack's crumpled body, the colonel fired three more rounds into it. "God forgive me," he said quietly.

•   •   •

6.

SSTO _Tokyo_ Passenger Cabin. 2:38 P.M.

"You okay, Doc?" Carpenter leaned across the aisle and looked with concern at Feinberg, whose color was slowly coming back.

"Yes." His head sagged against the back of the seat, his eyes closed. "I'm fine."

"Good. We'll be leveling off in a bit now. The worst is over."

"Not a problem." He didn't once open his eyes.

Chattahoochee River. 2:41 P.M.

The Atlanta area had escaped the general devastation almost without a scratch. Here, the disaster was something seen on television screens, impinging on personal lives only to the extent that the inhabitants had friends or family in danger, or that telephone and computer links had broken down. Consequently, when Frieda Harmon heard the shooting, there were still people manning the 911 lines. Her neighbor Harriet was lying outside her front door, bleeding severely, and there was another man in the street who looked dead, and please send the ambulance right away. Yes, she'd seen who did it, two men in a white van parked outside the Golden Apple Spa, which has been closed the last two months. Please hurry.

And no, the van wasn't still here.

Ambulance and police arrived within minutes. They whisked Harriet away to the hospital and cordoned off the street. And they took a statement from Frieda.

What had the killers looked like?

She gave them a reasonably complete description. The one who shot the man in the street was tall, about forty, very imposing, walked like he owned the place. The other was trim, wiry, maybe thirty years old, hard to tell, wearing a dark blue jacket. He had receding black hair. Looked like a thug.

She wasn't sure which had shot Harriet, but assumed it was the big man. And, oh, they were wearing army helmets. No, not uniforms, just helmets.

They'd had something with them that might have been rockets. Or shells. Looked like shells. The shells were on the ground when she first saw them. After the shootings, the men gathered them up and put them in the back of the van.

No, she was sorry, but she didn't get the license number. Her eyes weren't that good and she hadn't been wearing her glasses and everything happened so fast.

Police identified the body of Jack Gallagher, ran his name through NCIC. It came out negative. He had no criminal record.

Gallagher lived in Staunton, Virginia, they learned. They arranged to have a Staunton detective visit his home and inform the widow. Staunton police informed Georgia law enforcement that Gallagher had been a militiaman.

Steve Gallagher's name surfaced within minutes. They showed his picture to Frieda, who couldn't identify him. "He was too far away," she said.

The Atlanta area detective was Joe Calkins. He made some calls to ask questions about the militia unit, and he ran a check on Steve Gallagher, who also had no priors. While he sat in his unmarked car, pondering the killing, another SSTO soared into the sky.

He flipped a switch on the radio: "Request APB: two Caucasian males in white, late-model Ford van, probably Virginia plates. . . ." He gave everything he had to the dispatcher, thought a minute, and then added: "Better call Hartsfield. Tell them somebody might be trying to shoot down one of their planes."

•   •   •

Skyport Flight Terminal. 3:27 P.M.

"That's it." Carpenter paused by a viewport and pointed at a boxy vehicle docked beside the *Tokyo*. It was dwarfed by the SSTO.

"I still think we'd be safer if we stayed on the plane," said Feinberg.

"Trust me, Wes," Carpenter said. "The plane's going to be pulling against its mooring. At full thrust. If it breaks loose. . . ." He shrugged. "The *Mabry* isn't very pretty, but it's a lot more likely to come back."

Chattahoochee River. 4:01 P.M.

What had started out as a lark had developed into grim necessity. Steve knew it wouldn't be hard to connect Jack with the Legion, and subsequently with himself. The only real protection for him lay in obliterating the police, in demolishing the state that sent these goons out to hound innocent citizens. Actually, he recognized he might not be so innocent in this case. But he had only done what he had to do.

The way to bring down the state was to bring down one of the space planes.

He'd counted three launches so far. Still plenty of time to get the job done.

They were several miles southwest of the river now, starting to stretch the range of the Cobra, and still looking for a launch site. Steve had begun to think maybe they should just park, wait their chance, and take the spacecraft down from the middle of the street. Who'd try to stop two armed men anyway? Then he saw the Munson Funeral Home.

It stood on a mild rise about fifty yards back from the road. Thirty or so cars were parked in the adjoining lot, and a few people were standing near the front door. A secondary lot in the rear was empty save for a station wagon and a black limo. The property was lined by a thin screen of trees. Just enough to shield them.

Hartsfield Airport, Security. 4:03 P.M.

"Police on line three, Mr. Martin."

Rob Martin frowned and picked up the phone. "Security. Can I help you?"

"Hello, Rob."

He knew the voice immediately. It belonged to Oscar Tate, a former FBI agent who was now the Fulton County chief of detectives. "Yeah, Oscar, what have you got?"

"A couple of militia types, we think with a missile launcher. They might be trying to bring down one of your planes."

"They picked a hell of a time to do it."

Martin could almost hear the shrug. "There's no accounting for loonies. Anyway, for what it's worth. . . ." His voice trailed off.

"Yeah. Thanks, Oscar. Let us know when you catch these guys, okay?"

He looked up at the photo of the Delta 787 hanging over his couch. Then he changed to another line. "Janet," he said, "get me Wolfy over at the LTA."

Hartsfield SSTO Launch Tunnel Control, Atlanta. 4:05 P.M.

Wolfgang Bracken picked the phone up on the first ring. "Support Services," he said.

"Wolfy?" Rob Martin's voice. "We got a call from the police that there might be somebody out there with a ground-to-air missile trying to take down the SSTOs."

Bracken delivered an obscenity. "How sure are you?"

"The cops don't know. But I think you ought to put a hold on the operation until they have a chance to look around."

"Thanks, Rob." Bracken was a squat little man with huge black eyebrows, bulldog jowls, and an absolutely hairless skull. "We just launched one."

•   •   •

SSTO *Los Angeles* Flight Deck. 4:06 P.M.

Ben West was the only one of the LTA pilots who had not gotten his early experience in military jets. He had begun flying with his father's air cargo service in the Southwest, and had shown an affinity for the cockpit that eventually landed him a job as a test pilot for Allied, where he'd flown the first SSTO prototype, the Alpha-6. He was also the only SSTO pilot who had been *invited* into his job.

Ben was an African-American, divorced, with two teenagers. He was a bridge player of extraordinary ability, and had twice represented the United States in world competition. His kids were doing well in school, and after six years he'd finally found a woman who could engage his emotions and fill his life. Like the other volunteers of the Rainbow mission, he knew in very personal terms what he was trying to save.

His flight engineer was Tina Hoskin, who came equipped with a Jekyll-and-Hyde personality, a woman who was all quiet efficiency and decorum on the spacecraft, but whose off-duty bluntness alienated friends and occasionally offended management. She'd made too many enemies at higher levels, and Ben knew she'd never rise any higher than where she was at that moment. He occasionally wondered about the wisdom of flying with her, knowing that a lot of people were praying the plane would go down.

His copilot was Harmony Smith, attractive, cold, single-minded. If Ben was the only non-jet-jock among the flight crews, Harmony was the only one who'd done jail time. She'd once been a gunrunner. That was after six years as an air force pilot. But Harmony had come back, and the Lunar Transport Authority had thought enough of her skills to give her a chance. They hadn't been disappointed.

My two desperados. It stood to reason that when the crunch came, they hadn't hesitated to help chase down the Possum. The nature of this flight necessarily rendered it an emotional experience, and Ben was thinking just how much affection he had for the two women when Harmony mentioned almost matter-of-factly that there was something coming up behind them. Fast.

"I think it's a missile," she said, a hush in her voice.

The SSTO was too big to jink.

"Range ten miles," she said. "Closing at mach two. We've got maybe thirty seconds."

"Heatseeker?"

"Can't tell."

He'd have preferred to wait until the object got closer and then turn as sharply as he could and shut down the engines. But the spacecraft was too big and just not sufficiently maneuverable to wait. "Hang on," he said, and cut hard to port.

"Ben," said Tina, "we're getting a warning from the tower. They're telling us to look out for a missile."

"Good," said Ben. He counted to five and killed the engines.

"Twenty seconds," said Harmony. "It's turning with us."

"We need some chaff," said Tina. Chaff was routinely used by military aircraft to decoy missiles.

Ben opened his mike. "Tower," he said, "this is *L.A.* We've found your missile."

"We see it, Ben. We've been alerted there are a couple of loonies down there with a launcher."

"Five seconds," said Tina.

"It's on us," he told them.

The heatseeker exploded just aft of their starboard engine. The plane rocked hard to port. On the flight deck, trouble lights blinked on all over the board. Ben fought for control, expecting the fuel lines to rupture and the tanks to let go. But it didn't happen.

The tower was still talking to him.

"We're still in the air," he told the mike. And to Tina: "Any more?"

"Affirmative," she said. "Another one coming. But it's off-target. Don't restart."

Ben set the wings to manual and extended them to their full thirty-eight degrees for maximum lift.

"Starboard engine's off-line," said Harmony. "And we've got some hydraulic problems."

Tina raised a fist. "Missile's past," she said. "Sky's clear."

"Stand by to start portside." He opened the fuel line and hit the ignition. The engine roared into life.

Thank God for that.

"L.A., what's happening?"

The controls were stiff. "Tower, we have one engine off-line, hydraulics. Not sure what else. But we have control."

The relief in the voice was audible. "Can you make it back?"

"Wait one." They were still losing altitude. Tina did a quick calculation and held up her thumb. "Affirmative," he said. "But we'll have to make it on the first pass."

"We'll have it wide open for you, Ben."

The plane felt heavy, awkward, slow. He had to compensate for the constant drift to starboard. And he was losing fuel from somewhere.

He checked the landing gear and was relieved to get a green light. "We'll be okay," he said.

"Maybe." Harmony's dark eyes were fixed on a point somewhere over his shoulder. "Maybe *we* will."

7.

***Percival Lowell*, Presidential Quarters. 4:17 P.M.**

Kerr gave him the news. Charlie's eyes closed and he fought to contain his rage. He was beginning to suspect there *was* a malevolent force loose, a white whale determined to bring everything down. "They can't repair it?" he demanded.

"Not in twelve hours."

"Then we need to find another one. There must be one squirreled away somewhere. How about the manufacturers? Goddammit, Al, *somebody* must have one."

"We've been looking. Allied has two of them on display in Paris and Berlin, but neither one can be gotten ready to fly in time."

"You're *sure*?"

"Yes, I'm sure, Charlie. Hell, they couldn't even get them to the airport by tomorrow morning."

Charlie wanted to sit down, but wasn't able to make himself comfortable in the zero-g. He'd come to *hate* the weightless environment. It seemed to him that nothing had gone well since his stomach tried to crawl up his esophagus right after he left Washington last week. "All right, Al," he said.

"What do you mean, 'All right, Al'? Do you want to cancel Rainbow?"

"*Cancel* it? It's all we have."

"No, it isn't all we have. We've still got the nukes."

The nukes. Here, as always, they were the weapon you didn't dare use. "All right," he said. "Do this: Have them target the damned thing. Be ready to fire on my command. But we aren't going to use them except as a last resort."

"Charlie, I think that's where we are now."

"No," he said. "Not yet."

TRANSGLOBAL SPECIAL REPORT. 4:21 P.M.

"Two men were apprehended this afternoon minutes after they allegedly fired two ground-to-air missiles at one of the space planes being launched from Hartsfield Airport. At least one of the missiles was reported to have struck its target. The plane landed safely shortly afterward. There were no casualties on board, but the spacecraft is said to have been severely damaged. Two persons, a man and a woman, were reported dead on the ground, and murder charges are being considered.

"Police identified the two men as Steven Gallagher and Thaddeus Wickett, both of Staunton, Virginia, and both associated with right-wing militia groups. Gallagher has been seen numerous times on television in support of ultra-right-wing causes. No motive was given for the attack.

"Meanwhile, Canadian authorities are bracing for an avalanche of refugees fleeing the anticipated impact of the Possum early tomorrow morning. Border stations are already overwhelmed. Sources close to the government are continuing to deny persistent rumors that the Canadians will suspend inspections for the duration of the emergency."

Percival Lowell Flight Deck. 4:27 P.M.

"You heard, Mr. President?" Feinberg sounded shrill.

"I heard. We'll just have to make do with six."

"If you'll forgive me, sir, physics is not politics. You can't make things happen by trying harder."

Charlie was seated up front with Rachel Quinn. Outside, the Possum's terrain rolled slowly past. "Wes, we're not going to give up."

"It doesn't matter whether you give up or not. It won't work without a seventh ship. But, I should point out, you're *sitting* in one."

That fact hadn't escaped Charlie. Like Feinberg, he was beginning to wonder if the *Percival Lowell* could substitute for the damaged space plane. But the *Lowell* was dwarfed by the giant SSTOs. He covered the mike and glanced at Rachel. "Will this thing put out the kind of horsepower the space planes do?"

"We don't call it horsepower, Mr. President," she said. "But no, it won't. It doesn't need that much thrust."

"It's close enough," said Feinberg, when Charlie repeated her comment.

"Okay," said Charlie. "Why don't you hang on a minute and let me put you on the speaker so the pilot can get into this conversation."

He flipped a switch and Feinberg's voice filled the cabin: "You need to find a way to anchor the *Lowell* to the Possum. Actually, the *Lowell* makes a more effective engine anyway than the SSTOs, because you won't run out of fuel in twenty minutes. If we had a handful of ships like yours, we wouldn't have a problem."

Rachel made a slicing motion across her throat. Charlie nodded. "Give us a chance to talk about it, Wes. We'll get back to you." He cut the connection and turned to the pilot. "What?" he said.

"You remember the damaged SSTO? They're sending *it* over with some equipment to try to lash it down. I don't think they've left Skyport yet. Why don't we suggest they send extra gear for us?"

"Do it," said Charlie.

She put in the request and then turned back to him. "There's a downside, you know."

"What's that?"

"There won't be any easy way to *un*anchor us. My understanding is that the pitons they're putting on the SSTOs can be jettisoned. If things get hairy, they push a button and they're gone. In case, say, the rock goes down."

"You're saying—"

"In our case, we'll just get fastened to the rock. If Plan A doesn't work, there'll be no way to get *Lowell* clear."

Skyport Flight Terminal. 4:36 P.M.

The maintenance people had patched the holes, cleaned and lubricated the engines, and replaced *Arlington*'s broken antennas. There'd been some talk about removing tail and wings to cut down on drag, but apparently they'd decided it was just too big a job. The external damage, a shattered tail assembly, assorted dents and chips, and a bent undercarriage had been left alone. All that could be taken care of later. If necessary.

With flight engineer Curt Greenberg and copilot Mary Casey in tow, George met with Belle Cassidy and a couple of her people in operations to discuss the mission profile. They went over flight data and were shown their assigned place on the Possum. While they talked, George watched one of the SSTOs arrive from Atlanta and glide gently into its bay.

Belle introduced Jonathan Porter, an engineer, who would help anchor the plane. Porter was a dark-haired, middle-aged man of remarkably passive appearance. He looked uncomfortable in Belle's presence, and smiled too much. His voice was reedy. This, George thought, was the kid they always picked last when they were choosing up sides. Not the man he'd have wanted on board during an emergency. But Belle didn't seem to have any qualms.

"We're lucky Jonathan didn't leave with the rest," she said smoothly. "We've given you plenty of cable and spikes. Jonathan will see that you're securely bolted down. When that's done, he's going to do the same thing for *Lowell*."

"*Lowell?*"

"Yep. I guess we're throwing everything we've got into this little tug of war."

Skyport Flight Terminal. 9:45 P.M.

Everything went like clockwork. Five planes arrived from Hartsfield, the last three only slightly delayed by the terrorist incident. They refueled and got a final inspection while they waited for their window to open.

Although all were owned by the Lunar Transport Authority, they were based around the world. SSTO 702 was from Atlanta, 703 from Berlin, 704 from London, 705 from Tokyo, 708 from Moscow.

The journalists at Skyport, most of whom had been on the Moon for the opening ceremonies, had a field day. The networks were filled with interviews of crewmembers, all of whom seemed calm and confident. Feinberg predicted success. "The numbers are there," he said. "Barring another crazed act by terrorists, we should see the Sun rise tomorrow on a happy Kansas."

FRANK CRANDALL'S ALL-NIGHTER. 10:53 P.M.

"I'll tell you, Frank, I'm with the woman who said the whole thing's just a con game to free up money for the aerospace people. That's all it is. That rock isn't coming down tonight, never was gonna come down. But Haskell will claim credit and a lot of taxpayer money'll go to Lockheed and the LTA. Mark my words."

TRANSGLOBAL SPECIAL REPORT. 11:43 P.M.

With Bruce Kendrick.

"The entire world appears to be kneeling in prayer tonight. . . ."

Skyport Flight Terminal. Midnight.

The last of the SSTOs, 708 from Moscow, broke away from Skyport with measured speed. Almost everyone on the station was standing along the flight terminal's Apollo Deck, which had the best view of the launch. For a long time after *Moscow*'s lights vanished into the night, almost no one moved.

Chapter Ten

BELLWETHER
Tuesday, April 16

1.

Percival Lowell **Flight Deck. 12:03 A.M.**

"*Arlington's* here, Mr. President." Rachel pointed to the scope over the heads-up display, where three blips had appeared. The objects were approaching from the rear, after having completed a long, looping orbit to allow them to match the Possum's trajectory. Dead ahead, Earth looked very big and very vulnerable.

Thank God. Charlie felt the weight shift on his shoulders. It was too easy to visualize this thing ripping through the planet's pink skies, blasting the lush brown soil of Kansas into the upper atmosphere, melting the underlying bedrock.

"*Arlington's* damaged," she continued. "It got hammered coming back from the Moon."

"I hope it holds together."

"I don't think there're any fears about that."

"Who are the others?"

"Ferries, Mr. President. The *Alexei Kordeshev* and the *Christopher Talley.*"

Charlie raised his coffee in silent salute. They had been crew members on the *Ranger.*

Rachel was getting another transmission. She touched her earphones, nodded, and switched on the speaker.

"This is *Arlington*," said the radio.

"Good to see you, *Arlington.*"

"Roger that. It's a *big* son of a bitch, isn't it?"

"Yes it is."

"Okay, I guess we're a little pressed for time. We've got the engineer and the equipment. We're going to set down and get locked in. You'll follow us, right?"

"*Arlington*, we'll be right behind you."

"Why are we going down with them?" asked Charlie.

"They need to use the laser drill. After they're set, we'll pick up some of *their* gear and their engineer and go tie down on *our* site." She flipped a switch on the PA. "Lee, are you ready?"

"Roger."

They watched *Arlington* make its approach. Feinberg had assigned it a site in the Plain. Its pilot moved in and turned control over to the navigational computers, which matched course and speed with the Possum, then duplicated rotation and tumble.

It touched down in the zero-g equivalent of a landing.

Lowell descended nearby, and Rachel told Cochran he was clear to go.

Arlington's airlock opened and two figures in p-suits emerged. One climbed down the ladder. The other, their engineer, began pushing out a series of large drums that had to be hauled to the surface by tether. The drums were followed by loops of heavy cable and spikes about two meters long. Cochran, assisted by Saber and Evelyn, moved the drill outside.

Cochran and the engineer examined the ground, conferred, and selected their sites. They used the drill to cut four sets of holes in the ground. Then they inserted the spikes, which telescoped out to twelve meters, into the rock.

"What's in the drums?" asked Charlie.

"Polycrete." Polycrete was a concrete derivative that had been used extensively in lunar construction.

While the teams worked, Charlie took a call from the British prime minister. The PM was preparing a public statement and wanted to know whether there was any good news he could pass on. Charlie switched off the speaker, but the subject of the conversation had to be obvious to Rachel, who watched him sympathetically. *She's thinking she wouldn't have my job on a bet.* "Nothing yet, Phil," he said. "But you can say the operation's on schedule and we're cautiously optimistic." He thought about it. "No, make it just plain *optimistic.*"

"Yes," the PM said. "My thought entirely."

Kerr called moments later. There were more problems, mostly having to do with banks.

"Not now," Charlie said. "I don't have time to deal with *banks.*"

"I think you better make time, Mr. President." Kerr's resort to formality irritated Charlie. "You don't want to save the planet, and then have to deal with a depression."

The problem was the loss of the financial centers along both seaboards, primarily in Los Angeles and New York. Mechanisms had to be put in place to keep the monetary system functioning through the crisis. Would the president agree to a few short-term measures? Would he support a new National Recovery Act? ("We should do so," Kerr advised.) There was a draft copy of one floating through the Senate, said the chief of staff, with provisions that were unworkable. "We need to put together our own version."

Disaster funds had been appropriated by the House and approved by the Senate in a late-night session. It would be a good idea to provide the presidential signature forthwith, Kerr said. Everybody in the country who still had access to a TV or a computer was watching it. "We need to do what we can to encourage the belief that there *will* be a tomorrow."

"Fax me a copy," said Charlie. "Along with your reaction, and Bert's in Commerce. And anybody else's you think I should see. If I like it, I'll sign it and get it right back to you."

Other calls came in, and by the time he got off the phone,

more than two hours had passed. By that time four large cables, one forward, one aft, two amidships, restrained the space plane.

The Earth rose and set twice during that time, at widely divergent points on the horizon. It was growing rapidly larger.

He heard hatches open and shut.

"Clear," came Cochran's voice. "We've got our passenger."

Rachel nodded. "The engineer from *Arlington* is on board," she told Charlie. Then: "Lifting off."

The surface dropped away, and the rock began to spin again.

"*Tokyo* and *Berlin* are on approach, Mr. President," she said. "The cavalry's starting to arrive. And there's another ferry. Your Professor Feinberg's on it."

Good. The sense that he was alone in all this began to ebb. Charlie looked at the blinking lights on the display and asked which one.

Rachel tapped the screen with an index finger. "The *Mabry*," she said. "And it looks like time to tie down our own bronco." She withdrew the *Lowell* to about a kilometer and then took it around to the Back Country, gliding low over the melted terrain until her sensors told her she'd arrived. They settled toward a plateau.

Ferry *Antonia Mabry*. 2:27 A.M.

Sitting in the passenger cabin, which was serving as Mission Control, Feinberg seemed to have forgotten his queasiness. He stared out at the rock. "It would be a much easier problem were it not tumbling," he said. "Our first objective will be to impose a degree of stability."

Carpenter knew the plan, but he understood that Feinberg was speaking for his own benefit, reviewing the operation to reassure himself he'd overlooked nothing.

The procedure would be too complicated to handle by

voice command and manual control on the individual flight decks. Instead, the *Mabry* would serve as a command center, accepting readout data from the seven onboard navigational computers and returning firing instructions directly to the engines.

Because of the need to align the Possum's flight path with its long axis, the ships had to be placed to allow lateral thrust well beyond that provided by attitude clusters. This meant that, while all seven vehicles would face more or less in the same direction, which is to say pointed forward, they would be sited not quite in parallel.

Feinberg talked at length with Rachel Quinn in *Lowell*, to ensure the systems were in sync. Then he repeated the process with George Culver in *Arlington*. He'd already gone through the setup routine in detail at Skyport with the other pilots.

"The one thing that worries me," he said at last, looking across at Carpenter, "is fuel expenditure. We have none whatever to spare." He shook his head. "If we get through this, the president might be advised to think seriously about assembling a fleet of nuclear-powered vessels. The research is done. We know how to do it. Now it would be just a matter of building the ships."

"The president's out here," said Carpenter. "You can tell him yourself."

"I already have," he said. "I hope he's getting the message."

The pilot's voice came over the PA: "Mr. Carpenter?"

"Go ahead, Rita." To Feinberg, Rita seemed too young and too relaxed to be piloting a spacecraft.

"The other spacecraft have all checked in. The Russian plane is last in line. They're giving us an ETA of four A.M."

Carpenter acknowledged.

Feinberg looked out at the Possum. His expression seemed to reflect a degree of melancholy. But he said nothing.

• • •

Percival Lowell **Flight Deck. 2:29 A.M.**

"For you, Mr. President. From the *Mabry*." Rachel relayed the call and Charlie felt the tingle of his handset.

"This is Orly Carpenter, sir." Charlie knew Carpenter, had spoken with him before on occasion.

"Hello, Orly," he said. "Nice to have you and Wesley with us." The problem throughout had been that this situation was essentially nonpolitical, Charlie had been in charge, and Charlie had no idea what he was doing. He hoped that Carpenter *did*.

"Good to be here, Mr. President. We're going to be running things from the *Mabry*. I thought you might want to join us. You'll have a better view of the overall operation from here."

The *Lowell* had just arrived at its own assigned site, and Jonathan Porter and the rest of the anchor team were preparing to go outside. Charlie glanced through the window at the softened mounds rising around the ship. The Sun was on the horizon, and they cast long shadows.

"Okay," he said. "How do you pick me up?"

"We can take you right out through the airlock."

"When?"

"Twenty minutes. We're on our way."

Charlie noted a strange expression, a flicker of contempt, on Rachel's features. And then it was gone.

"Orly?"

"Yes, Mr. President."

"I assume I'll be safer with you too, won't I?"

Carpenter hesitated. "Yes," he said. "You will."

He nodded. "I'll stay where I am," he said.

"Not a good idea, sir."

"Thanks anyhow. I'll stay put."

Carpenter's tone changed, acquired a hint of irritation.

"Mr. President, I really wish you'd reconsider. I have my orders . . ."

"Forget them," said Charlie.

Rachel glanced at him quizzically.

"Anything I can do from up there," he said, "I can do from here."

2.

On the Possum. 2:34 A.M.

George Culver's instincts had been right about Jonathan Porter: He *had* always been the last kid picked, he *had* been put in right field, and he *did* bat ninth. Everything in his life had been like that. There was something in his manner that inevitably induced low expectations, that generated surprise when he performed well. Whatever it was, it had followed him into adulthood.

Jonathan was single, but not by choice. He seemed to be invisible to women. His acute intelligence did not lend itself to a sharp wit, and he had almost no sense of humor. He bored people, knew it, and so had never overcome his childhood shyness. But he had the respect of those in his immediate chain of command, and that was the reason they'd kept him at Skyport when they sent everyone else home. If something happened, he was the best they had, and they knew it.

Now he was being called on to use his skills to do far more than seal off puncture wounds around the station. He had suddenly become an integral part of the most significant engineering operation of all time. It was heady stuff. Jonathan was delighted to have the opportunity, and it was all he could do to keep himself from leaping off the melted surface of the Possum.

He'd inspected the images of the terrain before they came out, looked at the results of the sampling studies, and concluded the task would not be unreasonably difficult. He'd been satisfied with the composition of the rock into which he'd anchored *Arlington*. But *here*, standing at the site chosen for *Lowell*, he was not so sure. The texture was almost spongy. It had melted during the impact, had turned to lava and possibly plasma, and then cooled. A bare hand would still have found it warm.

But this was where they wanted the ship. Another engineer might have protested, but Jonathan accepted the challenge, looked around, chose where to sink his spikes, and decided what sections of the hull would best accept the cables.

Unlike the planes, the *Percival Lowell* had never been intended to enter an atmosphere. But the designers had expected there would be EVA activity, and they had consequently equipped her with guard rails, ladders, and a multitude of extrusions to expedite getting around on the ship's outer skin. She'd be much easier to secure than the space plane had been. His only reservation was whether the rock itself would hold.

He used chalk to mark the places where they'd sink the spikes. There would be eleven in all. He knew everyone was worried about the jury-rigged anchors, fearful that either *Lowell* or the *Arlington* would break loose from its moorings and hurl itself across the ground, killing its occupants and crippling the mission. And they were right to worry: Jonathan's portion of the operation was critical, though by necessity it had been put together almost haphazardly at the last minute with spare parts and rubber bands.

He'd been irritated by George Culver's reaction. The pilot, in private conversation with him, made no secret of his conviction that his plane would tear loose from Jonathan's restraints when he went to full thrust, would erupt into a fireball and spiral across the rockscape. But Jonathan knew that the cables could withstand a dozen times as much power as the plane's twin engines could generate, and they were securely locked to the spacecraft. What he knew for damned sure was that his cables and anchors would hold together. If the ground stayed firm, neither the *Arlington* nor the *Lowell* would be going anywhere.

They started at the rear of the *Lowell*, using the laser drill. When the rock had been softened to a sufficient depth, they inserted a polycrete-coated spike. At a signal from his remote, flanges sliced out all along the central core, locking the spike in place. "It'll take about an hour to cool," he said. "Then you'd need a bomb to move it."

When they finished planting the spikes, they attached the cables, looped them over the hull, and used a series of clips, clamps, and connectors to lock them in place. When they were finished, Jonathan stepped back to admire the work.

He watched as the woman they called Saber walked around, tugging on the lines, as if that could possibly tell her anything worth knowing. It was the equivalent of kicking the tires.

Percival Lowell Utility Deck. 3:58 A.M.

"*Kordeshev*'s approaching. Time to go, folks." It was Rachel's voice on the PA.

Jonathan, Doc Elkhart, the chaplain, and Evelyn gathered by the main airlock, awaiting transfer to the ferry. They were being moved out for several reasons: They'd be less at risk; there were more people than p-suits on board *Lowell*, and everyone would be required to wear a p-suit during the upcoming operation; they were a strain on the life-support system; and finally, if things went wrong, it would be easier to evacuate five people than nine.

Charlie, Saber, and Morley shook their hands and wished them well. "This has been quite a ride," said Pinnacle.

Charlie nodded. "It's not over yet, Mark."

Evelyn was slow to let go. He smiled at her and she squeezed his arm. "You've been outstanding, Mr. President," she said.

Minutes later they were gone, and Morley retreated to prepare for his next telecast. Saber had stayed on because she had some technical background and might be able to help in an emergency.

"Mr. President?" Rachel's voice from the flight deck.

"Go ahead, Rachel."

"Mr. Kerr is trying to reach you. And the Russian plane is on the scopes. We're all here."

"Good," said Charlie. "Put Al through."

There were more questions, problems dealing with the UN, issues related to terrorist acts in the Midwest, a general breakdown of the whole structure of civilized life along the frontiers of the catastrophe. Law enforcement agencies, where they still existed, were too busy coping with the general emergency to confront organized military groups. Several small towns in the Northwest and in West Virginia had even been seized by individuals who were trying to install themselves as local dictators.

"We're not going to let it happen," Charlie told Kerr. "But right now we're looking at first things first. Tell the governors to concede nothing. You can reassure them we'll give whatever support is needed to put down insurrection. Issue a statement to that effect in my name. I'll be home tonight and we can start looking at options. Meantime, make the calls, Al. You know what I want."

"Okay, Charlie. I'll tell them."

"Just hang on, okay? Are we still running the government from Camp David?"

"Yes."

"What kind of shape's the White House in?"

"The water's gone down. But the place is wrecked."

"You mean, what—carpets, furniture, that sort of thing?"

"Yeah. We've had OSHA people in. They've declared it unsafe. It'll be months before it's usable."

"Al," said Charlie, "the whole world's unsafe right now. I want the White House reopened by tonight. When I come back, that's where I'm headed."

"But Charlie—"

"I don't care about the furniture. Just see that it's got telephones and lights. Get a situation room up and running. Prop up the walls if you have to. And make sure there's a flag flying over the place."

Kerr sighed.

Charlie listened politely to a series of questions about political appointments, requests from foreign governments, a policy statement on relocation camps, and other issues. He responded as best he could, and finally cut off his chief of staff. "I've got to go, Al. You know what we need. Get it done. Meantime, I'll try to move this rock off the road."

SSTO *Moscow* Flight Deck. 4:04 A.M.

"*O Gospodi!*" Dmitri Petrovik, *Moscow*'s copilot, did not look optimistic.

Conversation on the flight deck had all but died as they approached the Possum. It might have been that seeing it through a window was different from watching it on the screens, or that it was just too massive when measured against the tiny lights scattered around its surface and blinking immediately overhead. Fireflies trying to move a broken chunk of sidewalk.

"*Moscow,*" came the American voice, "this is Mission Control. Good to see you. Directional beacon is on Channel Four."

"*Privet*, Mission Control." Gregor Gregorovich Ilyanik picked up the beam, locked on, and turned control over to the autopilot. "We have it."

"*Moscow*, as soon as you're anchored down we'll start to rock and roll. The sooner the better."

"*Roger*. We'll be ready in a few minutes."

Gregor tugged at his pressure suit. He was unhappy; it was bulky and warm and he'd developed an itch he couldn't reach. But they'd been instructed to wear the gear throughout the operation.

His helmet lay off to one side.

The black rockscape filled their windows. They glided slowly across its midnight mounds and valleys.

Kolya Romanovna, his flight engineer, was watching a map of the Possum scroll across the navigational display. A green triangle designated their assigned site out on the Plain adjacent to *Arlington*.

"*Moscow*," said the voice from Mission Control, "we will initiate as soon as you are down."

"They're in a hurry," said Kolya.

Gregor looked ahead at the cloud-shrouded Earth. "*Ya tak i dumal*," he said. "I'm not surprised."

Moscow slowed. To their port side, at about two hundred meters, he could see *Arlington*'s lights. His thrusters fired gently, brief bursts, forcing them down. The landing gear was *up*, safely out of the way of the device that the workmen at Hartsfield had attached to his undercarriage.

"Ready?" asked Kolya.

"*Da*."

She touched the black button on the newly installed box on the right-hand side of her console. The landing-gear wells opened but the wheels didn't move. Instead, two self-seating pitons exploded from their sheaths and bit deep into the rock. Toward the rear of the undercarriage, another panel slid back and a third unit repeated the process.

The spacecraft shuddered with the jolts.

Kolya looked at her display. "We should be locked," she said.

Gregor sensed that they had indeed become a fixture on the rockscape. "How do you release it?" he asked.

Kolya opened the lid of the yellow control box and showed him the switch.

"Very good." He fingered his mike. "Mission Control, this is *Moscow*. We are ready to rock and roll."

Kolya looked at him, startled at his use of the American phrase. He grinned back. "Soon we shall see, no?"

Antonia Mabry, Mission Control. 4:10 A.M.

"All vessels, this is Mission Control. I'll remind you that as a precaution, all personnel in the SSTOs and the *Lowell* should now be in pressure suits. We will initiate program in four minutes. Gentlemen, and ladies, start your engines."

> *TRANSGLOBAL SPECIAL REPORT. 4:10 A.M.*
> "This is Keith Morley on board the *Percival Lowell*. We are riding with the Possum, which is now entering the exosphere. The exosphere extends out about ten thousand kilometers from Earth. A fleet of six space planes and three ferries are with us. The six planes and the *Lowell* have literally chained themselves to the Possum and are about to begin a complicated firing procedure which they hope, which we all hope, will lift this planet-killer into a higher and more stable orbit. The countdown has begun. We're going to stay right here and we hope you'll stay with us."

3.

Antonia Mabry, Mission Control. 4:11 A.M.

Unlike the moonbuses and ferries, whose power plants were either on or off, and operated with a constant power flow, the space planes and the *Lowell* were capable of modulating thrust. Feinberg, during the crush of the previous thirty-six hours, had sat with NASA engineers, reducing the mission objectives to a set of operational requirements. The requirements had been incorporated into a plan and passed on to a team of specialists to write a set of instructions. The instructions had been loaded into computers on board both the *Mabry* and the *Kordeshev*, to provide a backup against the possibility of an accident decapitating the project.

The program would be self-correcting, would monitor results from the seven drive ships through an array of sensors mounted on all three ferries, and would make adjustments as conditions warranted. One of the uncertainties that the planners faced, perhaps the one they perceived as most hazardous, was the possibility of a glitch in the software, which there had been no time to test.

It was this bug factor that was uppermost in Feinberg's thoughts. He was watching *Mabry*'s radio operator, who'd set up shop in the passenger cabin (which had been appropriated for Mission Control) to expedite communications. He was talking not only with the other ships, but with the Orbital Lab, which was monitoring the operation for the rest of the scientific community.

Wes Feinberg had never doubted his own abilities. He'd left Massachusetts for Atlanta with his usual cool demeanor. His colleagues had wished him luck and openly admired his composure under what they perceived as enormous pressure. He'd reassured them everything was under control. But he'd no sooner lifted into the cool skies of New England before he'd begun to feel his first doubts. His teeth had been literally chattering during the conference at Hartsfield. He should have brought something to calm himself, but he didn't use tranquilizers, hadn't taken one since his father's funeral thirty years before. So he never thought of resorting to medication, and if using medication occurred to him now, he shrugged it away as an open display of weakness.

He tried to keep focused on the operation, to remember

who he was, and why people had so much confidence in him. He'd gone over his own numbers time and again, like a man who keeps going back to make sure he's locked his front door. The problem was that, despite the surveys and analyses, he couldn't be sure of *everything*. He'd estimated, for example, the object's mass. He'd gauged the distribution of that mass. The tumble introduced a factor that, if not chaotic, could nevertheless only have been pinned down precisely by a reasonably extensive series of observations rather than the brief period for imaging they'd had. All in all, his calculations involved too many assumptions to allow any real degree of comfort.

Mabry was a hundred kilometers from the Possum, where it could more easily measure the movement of the object against marker stars. If they did not get the desired results, if the rock didn't accelerate according to plan, or did not change its attitude as required, Feinberg would have to make seat-of-the-pants adjustments. And that, he realized somberly, would be beyond almost anyone's capabilities. Maybe even his.

Percival Lowell Flight Deck. 4:12 A.M.

Unlike the SSTO pilots, who had to conserve fuel, Rachel had seen no reason to shut down her power plant. She sat at the controls, with the president of the United States in the right-hand seat, looking straight ahead at the foreshortened landscape, the landscape that ran a hundred meters or so and curled up into a ridge that resembled an approaching wave. She was not comfortable. All her training, all her instincts, honed over a lifetime with high-performance vehicles, told her that when the computer in Orly Carpenter's ferry put the pedal to the floor, the *Lowell* was going to roar out of Jonathan Porter's cables, rip her belly apart on the rocks, and slam into the ridge.

"*Two minutes,*" said the voice from *Mabry*.

Lee Cochran was seated behind the president, trying to look relaxed. Keith Morley was in back somewhere. They were all wearing p-suits.

"Rachel, you okay?" asked Charlie.

That was an embarrassment. Here she was, sitting beside a *politician*, for God's sake, and he was cooler than she was. She wondered if he was aware what would happen if Jonathan's collection of pegs and wires didn't work. "Sure," she said.

He tugged at his harness, trying to get comfortable in the p-suit, which was simply too bulky. That he was a big man himself did not help conditions. "Answer a question for me," he said. "If this whole operation's being handled by computer from the ferry, why are we even here? The pilots, I mean?"

"We're backups," she said. "In case something goes wrong. Anyhow, I doubt they had time to write the programs for a completely automated operation. This is a little bit rushed."

"One minute."

"Okay," she said. "Get ready. Here we go."

SSTO *Arlington* Flight Deck. 4:13 A.M.

The engines rumbled reassuringly.

A week ago George had been looking forward to an evening with Annie Blink, a bright, magnetic blond, a lady with an absurd name who said yes her name was a problem and she had every intention of changing it eventually but she was being careful because she didn't want to go through the rest of her life with another funny name and people trying to hold back grins when she introduced herself. And to tell the truth, George, *Culver* sounds suspect.

He'd broken through that evening and taken her to bed, the first time. The *only* time. The night had been full of laughter and passion and he'd decided Annie was the one for him. The future had looked pretty good last Tuesday.

"Thirty seconds."

He looked back at Mary and Curt. They were checking each other's suits.

He listened to his own breathing. Inside the helmet, he felt isolated, alone. Lights were moving above; it was one of the ferries; and there was another set of lights, on the surface, to starboard. That was the Russian-based unit. *Moscow.* A third spacecraft, *Tokyo,* was far forward on the Plain. *Atlanta, London, Berlin,* and the *Lowell,* were in the Back Country.

Mary, who wasn't much given to emotional displays, reached over unexpectedly and squeezed his wrist. He could barely feel the gesture through the suit. He glanced at her and saw that her lips were moving.

Yeah. If there'd ever been a moment for divine intervention, this was it.

Antonia Mabry, Mission Control. 4:14 A.M.

"Zero."

Feinberg pushed the button. *London* and *Tokyo,* the forward vessels on the Plain and in the Back Country, went to full thrust.

Simultaneously Carpenter activated the simulation. The main screen acquired an image of how the Possum should react; and an overlay in red depicted what was actually happening. So long as there was no divergence between white and red graphics, they would be okay.

The tension in the compartment was so great that Feinberg actually felt faint. The space had become claustrophobic, and he would have done almost anything to get normal gravity. His stomach pressed on his heart.

He'd found it difficult to eat since leaving Atlanta. All his anatomical systems seemed to be in disarray. He wished he'd insisted on staying at the AstroLab, where he'd have been more effective because he wouldn't have been constantly ill.

The program brought in the other engines, went to full

thrust here, quarter thrust there. It played the seven power plants like a symphony.

At zero plus one minute the tumble began to slow. The Possum edged toward stability.

Feinberg had placed *Lowell* at the rear of the Possum to take full advantage of its nuclear capability. There it would run throughout the operation at full power, acting as a kind of outboard motor.

The phone, surprisingly, did not ring. Carpenter had thought Haskell would be on it constantly, demanding updates throughout the operation, wasting his time. But it remained silent.

TRANSGLOBAL SPECIAL REPORT. 4:15 A.M.

"This is Angela Shepard outside Union Station in Chicago. Despite the late hour, you can see that enormous crowds have gathered here along Jackson Boulevard. The flight from the city goes on, but many of those who remain are coming together in the downtown area. We're getting reports that the same phenomenon is occurring throughout the Midwest, people gathering to await the outcome of the Rainbow mission. Here, the streets are filled, bells are tolling, traffic's at a standstill. But it's almost a festive atmosphere, unlike the terrifying scenes we witnessed over the weekend from the coastal cities, and even earlier today in parts of the Midwest.

"It's as if some vast herd instinct has taken over. People we've talked to seem to be optimistic. By ten to one, in our informal poll, they say they think the rock will be stopped. Some have brought pots and cowbells, and they're ready to celebrate.

"There've been some arrests for disorderly behavior, but police are telling us it's not what you might expect, not people looting stores, but just folks partying a little too hard. I have to say, it's one of the strangest things I've ever seen. We came here tonight expecting to see panic, and instead we get this." (*Camera pans the street filled with people laughing and singing.*)

"They've been told that, if the Possum comes, they'll be able to see it from here, looking toward the southwest. It's a warm night. The Moon-cloud is down, and the sky is absolutely clear.

"Almost everybody has a TV. They're slung over shoulders, or slipped into back pockets. The stores all seem to be open and televisions are on everywhere. I'm looking now at an image of this broadcast in the window of a furniture store. These folks started arriving in the early evening and they've been here all night. Whatever happens this morning, you have to admire the courage of these people." (*Off-camera applause.*)

"Back to you, Don. This is Angela Shepard in Chicago."

4.

**Minot, North Dakota. 3:16 A.M. Central Daylight Time
(4:16 A.M. EDT).**

Minot might have had a little more steel in its blood than the average North Dakota town. Its citizenry was reinforced by a large population of air force dependents, who'd decided they couldn't do anything about the danger in the sky, but who'd gathered at two elementary schools and kept them open for the hundreds of lost and stranded people who were coming in from the south. Now, with some bacon and scrambled eggs in her stomach, Marilyn Keep felt much better. She stood with her husband in a small crowd outside the Dwight Eisenhower Elementary School auditorium, drinking coffee and half watching a battery-powered TV somebody had put on a chair.

Most of the USAF operational personnel were gone, hauling supplies to stricken areas, carrying out sick and injured, trying to get through the emergency as best they could. But the support people, and the dependents, were still in Minot.

Marilyn was asked about New York, and she described the flooded streets, the sense of being isolated on the rooftop, the child against whom she'd closed the door. ("*It's okay,*" someone said, "*you couldn't help it.*")

The television carried a close-up of one of the space planes, the long fiery lances from its twin engines illuminating the dark rock. They were two minutes into the operation now, and the reporter said that everything was going well. So far. Even if it didn't, she thought, even if the situation broke down, surely they were far enough north to be safe.

Surely.

Percival Lowell Utility Deck. 4:20 A.M. Zero plus six.

The reality was that Keith Morley had no idea how things were going. He was in effect doing play-by-play, and he'd assumed that he'd somehow be able to *see* the operation. But he had only the images being transmitted from the monitoring vessels, flashes of light in the darkness, recognizable on close-up as flames boiling out of rockets. But there was no way to know what, if anything, was happening with the Possum. He had no background against which to measure movement. For that matter, he couldn't be sure that any *apparent* movement wasn't a result of changes in the position of the sensors on the circling ferries.

He'd tried to stay close to the president, but Haskell was up front in the copilot's chair and Lee Cochran was up there too, so there was no room for Morley.

But this president seemed to be unusually aware of the influence of the media. He called to tell Morley they were on schedule, and that was good, but Morley still had no real details. Nevertheless, he knew approximately what was supposed to happen throughout the operation, so he began simply to fabricate an account, assuming everything was happening as it should, and that they'd tell him if something went wrong. And there was this: If he was wrong, if he was caught hanging out, the world was going to have bigger problems than to simply come after an unfortunate journalist.

"The Possum's tumble has slowed by about thirty percent," he told a global audience.

SSTO *Berlin* Flight Deck. 4:21 A.M. Zero plus seven.

It may have been there were just too many things that could go wrong, too many moving parts, too much guesswork, too much improvisation.

The radio operator from the *Mabry* was reporting that the Possum was accelerating precisely along predicted lines. Gruder had never doubted it would be so. Assume success, adhere to the math, prepare for breakdowns, and keep focused on the task at hand. It was the formula around which he'd built his professional life. Unlike the bureaucrats, who were fond of saying "Win some, lose some."

So far there'd been little for him to do. He sat inside his p-suit, savoring the experience and contemplating a future filled with people pointing him out and saying, *Yes, that's Gruder Müller; he was with the fleet when they turned the Possum aside.* If he never did anything else it wouldn't matter. He could die tomorrow and his life would have been a success.

It was a glorious feeling. He'd always wanted to be a hero, and it was actually happening.

"Zero plus eight," said the *Mabry.* "Vector still looks good."

The *Berlin* crew had been on the Possum for almost three hours, and Gruder had detected a pattern in the way the Sun and Earth crisscrossed the skies of the microworld. It had been impossible to predict, except in very general terms, *where* a celestial body would rise. But he'd gotten the timing down. And now everything was running late. A good sign.

The view ahead was obstructed by a low mound, not much higher than the top of the spacecraft and flowing off into embracing ridges on either side. As he watched, the rim of Earth appeared over its left-hand incline.

Willem Stephan glanced at the fuel-use indicator. They had a ten-minute supply left at full burn. The program had nine minutes to run. Perfect. Stephan opened a channel to his crew. "I think we all deserve a good dinner when we get back," he said.

Kathleen, sitting beside him, raised her left hand to caution against premature celebration. Gruder, however, was of the same mind as the pilot, and had begun to think that sauerbraten and beer would fit the occasion well.

One of the imponderables had been the cohesiveness and stability of the rock. Feinberg had been forced to make estimates based on sensor readings and samples, which would not necessarily reveal, say, fissures or stress fractures. The rock in the area of the *Berlin*, which had melted during the collision with Tomiko, had not sufficiently rehardened before enduring a pair of subsequent collisions. As a result, it had developed a series of microscopic cracks. The twin rocket engines, operating at full thrust, were putting extreme pressure on the cracks. Now, while Gruder contemplated sauerbraten, one of them broke under the strain.

The port-side piton tore loose from the rock. The spacecraft twisted violently to starboard. Willem went immediately to manual, intending to shut off the engines. But it was too late. The rear piton broke apart within seconds, and the starboard side crumpled immediately thereafter. The SSTO roared across the rockscape and blasted into the mound at full throttle. Both fuel tanks exploded, and a fireball rose into the sky.

5.

TRANSGLOBAL SPECIAL REPORT. 4:23 A.M.
    "... just moments ago. Authorities haven't yet said what effect the loss of the plane will have on the mission. We can hope, Don, that the process was far enough along that the remaining six spacecraft will

be enough to finish the job. As of this moment there's just no word. We're trying to get through now to get a statement. Meanwhile, let's break away to Kitt Peak where the astronomers have been watching developments closely.

"This is Keith Morley on the *Percival Lowell,* anchored on the Possum."

Antonia Mabry, Mission Control. 4:24 A.M.

"Are you sure?"

"Yes, dammit!" Feinberg, who'd always prided himself on his aplomb, heard his voice going shrill. He was close to tears. The silhouettes on the display had separated and were growing steadily farther apart.

"If we keep pushing—" insisted Carpenter.

"It won't be enough. All we've done so far is move the impact point to the southeast."

"Where?"

"My God, I don't know. Do we *care*?"

"Yes, we *care*."

"Okay. Try eastern Florida. Jacksonville, maybe. Cape Canaveral. The ocean. Who knows?"

The phone sounded. "That'll be Haskell," said Carpenter. He looked panicked. "What do we tell him?"

"The truth," said Feinberg. "Tell him the truth. Meantime, I suggest we shut down."

Percival Lowell Flight Deck. 4:25 A.M.

"So we just give up?" Charlie's blood pounded in his temples.

The steady thrum of *Lowell's* engine died as it went to its equivalent of idle. "We don't have any option, Mr. President."

"Why not? What do we lose by trying?"

There was a click and Feinberg was on the line. "You must accept the situation, sir," he said. "It cannot be done, and we are only pushing the impact point east. Toward the Atlantic. If this thing falls into the ocean, which is already a distinct possibility, you'll be looking at an even greater catastrophe."

Charlie sagged. "My God in heaven."

"There's simply nothing we can do," said Feinberg.

Carpenter came back: "We've directed the *Kordeshev* to stand by to pick you up, and the *Talley* is on its way to get the crewmembers off *Arlington*. Please be ready to go. We've only got thirty minutes to effect the rescues. We're going to direct the other spacecraft to release the pitons and get the hell off the rock."

"No," said Charlie. "Isn't there any kind of fallback plan at all?"

"No, sir. I'm sorry. We've done what we could. We've done *everything* we could." Feinberg again, sounding annoyed, defensive.

The flight deck swam. Charlie had conceived an animosity for the Possum, a personal loathing. He still had an option, he could still nuke the son of a bitch. He took a deep breath and reminded himself to keep his head. "We still have some time. Let's think about it. There must be *something . . .*"

"If you can come up with an idea, Mr. President, you're a better man than I am. Meanwhile, the *Arlington* and your own vessel are chained to the rock. If we don't get the crews out quickly, including yourself, you'll all go down with it."

"We'll stay put for now," said Charlie. "Nobody leaves until I give the order. You understand?"

"Mr. President—" Carpenter's voice. "Please—"

"Be ready to move if you have to. But not till I tell you." *But physics is not politics. You can't make something work just by trying harder.*

He broke the connection and stared into a red haze.

"You all right, sir?" Rachel's voice.

"I'm fine," he said. "*We're* not doing so good, but *I'm* fine."

"What was it with the *Berlin*? A blown piton?"

"I guess. I don't know."

She nodded. The flight deck was silent. "I've got all kinds of calls for you, Mr. President."

"Not now," he said.

TRANSGLOBAL SPECIAL REPORT. 4:26 A.M.

". . . they've shut down the rockets. Right now the entire fleet, five SSTOs and the *Percival Lowell*, are still on the Possum, but nothing's happening. Bruce, I've been trying to get through to the command ship, which as you know is the *Antonia Mabry*, but they're not responding. I've also got a call in to President Haskell. I have to be honest, at the moment the situation here looks bleak."

Skyport Orbital Lab. 4:27 A.M.

"They've given up." Windy Cross braced his elbows on his work table, and buried his face in his hands. "It's over."

Tory sat paralyzed, listening to the electronic burble of the equipment. Images of the Possum played across a dozen screens, including the main display from Rainbow Mission Control, on which the twin representations of the object, red and white, had drawn hopelessly far apart.

Andrea Bellwether was signaling for her attention. "I have Keith Morley on the circuit," she said. "He's trying to find out what's happening."

"Hell, we don't know anything," Windy said. "Tell him to call Carpenter."

"He says Carpenter isn't taking calls."

"Goddam right. I wouldn't either." His voice dropped an octave. "Tell him they've thrown in the towel, and you'll start a panic."

"You think there isn't going to be one anyhow?"

"That's okay. Let somebody else take the heat. We're out of it."

•   •   •

Percival Lowell Flight Deck. 4:28 A.M.

"They're telling me it's not possible, Al."

"For God's sake, Charlie, what are we going to do?"

"I don't know." Rachel was watching Charlie as if she thought he might be on the verge of a stroke. "I don't know, Al. If you have any ideas, this'd be a good time."

"Listen, we're still doing a dance out there with the press. What do you want to tell them?"

So in the end it came down to that. As if it were somehow Charlie Haskell's fault that the world is about to end. *What do you want to tell them?*

A message light blinked on. "Carpenter," said Rachel's voice. "He says it's urgent."

"Hold a second, Al." He switched channels. "Haskell."

"Mr. President. We've got to evacuate. Do it now or forget it."

Charlie stared at the polished black handset. At that moment he'd have preferred to put a knife into his heart.

SSTO Arlington Flight Deck. 4:29 A.M.

"*Arlington*, stand by for evacuation."

George listened to his own breathing, magnified inside the p-suit. Beside him, Mary released her harness.

No one said anything. They got slowly out of their seats. It almost looked as if they were laboring under heavy gravity.

FRANK CRANDALL'S ALL-NIGHTER. 4:30 A.M.

"As you know, we've been devoting the show tonight to coverage of the attempt to deflect the Possum. We have a bulletin here, and I want you to listen closely. Scientists at the AstroLab have been quoted as saying that the loss of a space plane a few minutes ago means that the Possum cannot now be stopped. They estimate that the impact site, however, has moved farther east. No one is yet willing to say on the record where it is likely to fall, but unofficially they are suggesting the southeastern United States or the Caribbean. Bill Plant is at the AstroLab now, and we'll be going over there in just a moment.

"I want to add that we're going to be cutting this edition of the show short. As you know, we're based in Miami, and we want to let our people get home to their families. So after our report from the AstroLab, we'll be returning you to the network. We'll look for you tomorrow night at our regular time. I hope.

"This is the Old Trooper signing off."

6.

Skyport Orbital Lab. 4:31 A.M.

Tory Clark was never sure precisely when she had the idea. It seemed as if it had been flickering just beyond the limits of perception since dinner, since she'd heard about the three ferries that would accompany the SSTOs out to the Possum. The *Kordeshev*. The *Mabry*. The *Talley*. All named for crewmembers on Frank Bellwether's lost *Ranger*. And Andrea Bellwether, Frank's daughter, sat just a few paces away.

Bellwether.

Maybe the problem was that Feinberg and the rest of them were thinking in a box.

There might *still* be a way.

Antonia Mabry, Mission Control. 4:32 A.M.

"No, Tory," said Feinberg. "It wouldn't work. It's too massive."

"Are you *sure*?"

Of course he was sure.

"What else have you got?" she persisted.

Feinberg had never liked Tory Clark. She was a little too pushy for his tastes, and what was her background anyhow? She was just one more camp follower. "I don't really have time to argue about this."

"What *do* you have time for, Professor? Why not *try* it? What's to lose?"

"*What's to lose?* I'll tell you what's to lose. We've already driven it too far. It's probably going to go down in the ocean. That's not the best possible outcome. Moreover, to even try your idea, we'd have to sacrifice the people in the ships. Is that what you *want?*"

"If it works, they'll be okay."

"It *won't* work, Tory. What part of that can't you figure out?" His eyes were damp again. "We've already done enough damage. Let it be." He broke the connection.

Orly Carpenter stared at him. "What did she want?"

"Nothing." Feinberg bitterly regretted having offered his services for the project. It had failed, it wasn't his fault, and there was no way anyone could ever say *he* was responsible. But it didn't matter. His fingerprints were all over it. And somehow he knew he should have prevented this.

Skyport Orbital Lab. 4:33 A.M.

"What did he say?" asked Windy.

"He said *no.*"

"That's all?"

Andrea's eyes darkened with anger. "How could he do that? Does he have a better idea?"

"He says it would only make things worse."

"Well," said Windy, "we tried. Nobody can say we didn't try."

"*Dammit,*" snapped Andrea, "he's giving up. But it's not *his* decision to make."

On one of the TV screens, they watched people gathering outside a church in Boston. They were holding candles, and someone was leading a prayer.

"You're right," Tory said. "It's *not* his decision."

Windy was shaking his head. "So whose decision is it?"

"Hell," Tory continued, "the president's out there."

"Wonderful," said Windy. "You going to call him?"

"Why not? We know where he is." She reached for the phone.

"No," said Windy. "You have any idea what kind of trouble we'll get into?"

Tory punched buttons. Colonel Quinn's voice answered: "*Lowell*."

"*Lowell*, this is the Orbital Lab. I'd like to get through to the president."

"Get in line," Quinn said.

"Colonel, it's urgent."

"Everything's urgent right now. I'll put you in the queue."

"I need—" And she was talking into a dead circuit.

Andrea's small fists clenched. "There isn't time for this. I might know somebody who can get through to him." She leaned over her mike and stabbed the keyboard. "*Kordeshev*, this is the Orbital Lab. I need to talk to Chaplain Pinnacle. Right away, please."

Percival Lowell Flight Deck. 4:34 A.M.

Charlie was on the line with Al Kerr, who was on the brink of panic. And Charlie had nothing to tell him.

Rachel looked at him and tapped her earphone. Another call. He'd instructed her he didn't want to talk to anyone except Carpenter and Feinberg. "Hold on, Al," he said. Then he glanced over at her, irritated. "Who is it?"

"Dr. Hampton wants to talk with you, sir."

My God. "Tell her, later."

"She says it's urgent. Says you need to talk to her."

Charlie nodded. "Put her on."

Antonia Mabry, Mission Control. 4:37 A.M.
Nineteen minutes to impact.

"Yes," Feinberg admitted. "It *is* possible. But it's a long shot. God knows what—"

"Do it."

"Mr. President—

"*Do it, God damn you.*"

"We're not prepared. We're going to have to guess the firing sequence. If we get it wrong, and we probably will, we may lose *everybody* on the planet. Do you really want to take on that kind of responsibility?"

Images flashed through Charlie's terrified psyche: sun-drenched slaves hauling blocks through Egyptian deserts; men inventing religions to give meaning to disease-ridden, violent, pointless lives, and then becoming subjugated by the religions; women trying without much luck to civilize their hunter-husbands; everyone trying to control rulers. All the battles, the plagues, the rise and fall of the rivers, the inquisitions, the futility. . . . Sacrifices had been made by millions of individuals, most of whom never understood where the race was headed. Now, finally, the common effort was bearing fruit. To let the rock fall was to see it snatched away, to put everyone back in caves, to refight all the battles against war and disease and superstition, to do everything again.

"I understand," Haskell said. "The responsibility is mine."

SSTO *Arlington* Passenger Cabin. 4:38 A.M.
Eighteen minutes to impact.

George Culver opened the airlock hatch and Mary stepped inside. She looked weary and frightened. On the screen they could see the *Christopher Talley*, which was moving in to take them off. Curt leaned his helmet against the bulkhead, reluctant to leave. George put a hand on Curt's shoulder and eased him toward the lock.

"Look," said Mary. Her eyes were fixed on the monitor. The *Talley* had begun to move away.

"They're adjusting attitude," said George.

Curt shook his head. "I don't think so."

"*Talley*," said George, "We are ready to leave."

"Roger, *Arlington*. Change in plans."

Another voice, quiet, intense, the president's voice, broke in on the common channel. "Ladies and gentlemen," he said, "this is Charles Haskell. I need your help.

"You've seen the size of this thing, you know its velocity, and you know what will happen if it goes down." He paused, and they could hear his breathing. "We still have a chance to stop it. But it requires us, all of us, to stay out for a while longer. I'm sorry to ask you to do this, but I've no choice. *We* have no choice. Everything we've ever cared about, everyone we've ever loved, is at terrible risk. And there simply *is nobody else to step in and do what has to be done.*"

Antonia Mabry, Mission Control. 4:39 A.M.
Seventeen minutes to impact.

Feinberg opened the common channel. "Everybody go to manual," he said.

The Possum continued to rotate around its own axis, once every fifty-three minutes and eleven seconds. The strategy required that the Plain be on the downside as the object hit the ionosphere.

Unfortunately, as things stood now, that wasn't going to happen. In eleven minutes the Plain would be in perfect position. Then it would begin to turn away. He needed to accomplish two objectives: to accelerate the Possum, so that it would arrive on the outskirts of the atmosphere as quickly as possible; and to slow the rotation.

"Everybody," he said, "go to full thrust and maintain. All vehicles adjust port-side attitude jets to perpendicular along the rotational axis, and fire." That was going to achieve very little, but it *would* create a rotational drag, and he'd take whatever he could get.

He'd thought there were other things he might try:

manipulate thrust among the three vehicles—*Lowell*, *Moscow*, and *Arlington*—which had been sited directly parallel to the axis, and the others, which had been placed at offsetting angles. But there was simply not time for sophisticated maneuvers.

Carpenter read his mind and glanced at the fuel displays. He shook his head. "It's not going to be enough," he said. "Does it matter whether we burn the fuel now or later?"

"Now," said Feinberg. "Keep it simple." The Plain was sliding down toward the blue seas and distant shimmering clouds. But it continued to turn.

"We have to slow it down," Carpenter said.

Feinberg scanned the numbers and images on the screens, saw nothing, looked out the window, saw the lights of the *Talley*, saw Solitary Ridge just coming into view. "There *might* be something we can do."

The *Mabry*, the *Kordeshev*, and the *Talley* were designed to operate exclusively between L1 and Skyport. They never landed on a planetary surface, and they never had to climb from the bottom of a gravity well. Consequently, they produced nothing like the thrust of an SSTO, or of the *Lowell*. But they did generate a reasonable amount of power.

"Enough to slow the rotation down?" asked Carpenter, who grasped the idea immediately.

"We only need to buy a couple of minutes," said Feinberg. "Let's find out."

He opened channels to the pilots of the three ferries. He explained what they hoped to achieve. "The ferries will take up station along Solitary Ridge, *Kordeshev* on the left, *Talley* to the right. Find a good spot, but spread out, try to keep a half-k distance between ships. Set up posthaste. Nose in. Go to full thrust on my signal."

Jay Bannister, pilot of the *Kordeshev*, acknowledged, and then told him the idea was crazy. "We'll use up too much fuel," he said. "None of us'll get home. I've got four passengers on board."

"They'll have to take their chances along with the rest of us, Jay," said Carpenter. "Unless we turn this thing aside, there won't be any home to go back to."

And they heard from Rita, in their own ship: "I'm not sure the hull will stand up to this."

The big drawback was that the ferries, like the buses, had no throttle. Thrust was either on or off. So it now fell on the pilots to ease the vessels in against the ridge using their thrusters. "Snuggle in as best you can," Carpenter advised them. "Look for as flat a piece of wall as you can find."

The Possum was picking up speed.

A light winked on and the radioman pointed at it. "The president, sir," he said to Carpenter.

Feinberg sighed.

Carpenter listened to his earphones and nodded. "So far, okay, sir," he said. "I'll let you know."

They were looking out the window at the Back Country now, dropping to ground level. Rocks, mounds, and gulleys drifted past. Ahead, Feinberg could see Solitary Ridge, stretching away to the horizon on both sides. Off to port, the Sun was setting. It had become their job to hold it in the sky, to see that it didn't rise again. Like Joshua.

A radio voice crackled over static: "*Kordeshev* is in position."

"Stand by," said Carpenter.

Feinberg watched the clock.

Rita scanned the cliff wall for the flattest section she could find and glided toward it. If they were to have a reasonable chance to survive, the line of thrust had to be perpendicular to the face of the ridge. An imbalance, even a very slight one, could be fatal. She moved in carefully, cut all forward motion, and allowed the ridge to come to her.

In Mission Control, they felt the slight jar.

"Ready to go," she said. "But God help us."

"Are we ready to fire yet?" demanded *Kordeshev*.

"Not yet," said Feinberg. "We'll do this together."

Seconds later, *Talley* called in. They were having trouble finding a site. "The cliff face is rough over here," the pilot said. *Talley* was to their starboard side.

"We don't have time for a hunt," said Carpenter.

7.

Talley Flight Deck. 4:41 A.M.
Fifteen minutes to impact.

"There," said Ahmad.

"You call that *flat*?" Pilot Oscar "Hawk" Adams was a part-owner of Mo's Restaurant on Skyport. He was the only millionaire among the flight crews.

"I don't think there's anything else here," said Skip Wilkowski, the flight engineer. They needed a relatively smooth piece of rock face, something against which to place the prow. But this part of Solitary Ridge was severely gouged. "We're going to have to make do."

"Son of a bitch," said Adams. He steered toward it.

Antonia Mabry, Mission Control. 4:43 A.M.
Thirteen minutes to impact.

The ferries fired in unison. *Mabry* groaned and popped, but did not break open as Rita had feared. Carpenter and Feinberg hadn't taken time to get into p-suits, not that it would have mattered had things gone amiss. After a few uneasy moments, Carpenter returned his attention to the data coming in from the other vehicles. "All three running hot," he said. "I wouldn't have thought these units would stand up under this."

Feinberg watched the screens and thought how good it was to be alive. He'd always feared death, feared the final annihilation of light and the long plunge into oblivion. He saw his own mortality as a kind of personal black hole, dragging him inexorably through his days to suck him down at last. And he wondered now, with the ferry's rocket engine hurling itself against the vehicle's frail frame, using that frame to hold back the enormous mass of the Possum, whether he hadn't already slipped inside a Schwarzschild radius.

He had neither a religious faith to console him nor a functional philosophy to fight off the demons. For the first time in his life, he was behaving in a manner that could suitably be defined as heroic. And he suspected that eventually he'd be recognized for this day's deeds. If they succeeded. But if he was dead, if he wasn't on the platform to accept whatever medal might be offered, then of what use was any of it?

In the darkness stirred up by his fears, he searched for a presence, for a God who might intervene. *If you're there,* he murmured, *please get me through this.* He didn't try to close a deal, didn't promise to amend his life. He asked only for help. It was as close as Feinberg had come to a prayer in more than twenty-five years.

Percival Lowell Utility Deck. 4:46 A.M.
Ten minutes to impact.

The most frustrating aspect of the entire problem for Charlie was his sense that he could not actively participate in the effort, other than to sit helplessly in *Lowell*, as he had earlier sat helplessly in the Micro, and watch events unfold. He remained on a direct link with Mission Control, but he wished now that he'd been able to take Feinberg's suggestion—or had it been Carpenter's?—to monitor events from the *Mabry*.

He had retired from the flight deck, relinquishing his seat

to Saber. It was almost as if, knowing he could not help, he did not wish to watch.

The only other person with him was Keith Morley. Morley was talking into his mike, and looked up when Charlie came in. He signaled, silently requesting permission to ask the president a few questions on camera. But Charlie shook his head no and collapsed into a seat.

Up front, calls kept coming in for him. Rachel had a waiting list a couple of hundred deep. He'd accepted a few. Twenty minutes ago, when things had begun to go wrong, Charlie had taken a call from the pope. Were they going to be successful? the pontiff asked. And Charlie responded, not entirely diplomatically, that it was anybody's guess, and that if the pope had any influence this was a good time to use it.

His cell phone chimed. The *Mabry* tone. "Haskell," he said. His heart pounded.

Carpenter's voice: "We got two planes with dry tanks. But we've got a chance. We've slowed it down a little. Feinberg's a genius."

"Yeah," said Charlie. "He's pretty good." But thank God for the woman at the Orbital Lab. And Evelyn. (And, though he did not know it, Chaplain Pinnacle.)

Talley **Flight Deck. 4:50 A.M.**
Six minutes to impact.

Hawk Adams had maintained the delicate balance between the ferry's prow and the rugged cliff wall. It was essential to keep the plane of the cliff precisely at a ninety-degree angle to the central axis of the ship. Should that angle go even slightly out of balance, *Talley*'s engine would demolish the ferry, break her spine, in effect drive the rear of the ship through the forward compartments and crush the flight deck and the people in it. That scenario never left Hawk's mind.

In fact, he held the ferry steady longer than he would have

thought possible. But something—a hiccup in the fuel lines, a computer blip, a distraction, something—momentarily tipped the flow of power. The end came so quickly that Hawk never knew there was a problem.

Antonia Mabry, Mission Control. 4:51 A.M.
Five minutes to impact.

"We've lost *Talley*."

Feinberg nodded.

Carpenter looked at the displays. "What do you think?"

"Not yet."

Percival Lowell Flight Deck. 4:52 A.M.
Four minutes to impact.

The fans had come on in her suit and cool air bathed her face. "Getting warm," said Saber.

Rachel nodded. "Going to get warmer." They were into the ionosphere now. The ship wasn't designed for atmospheric travel. It was going to heat up very quickly.

Streaks of light, charged solar particles, were raining down on the surrounding rockscape. The sky was turning pink and the stars had winked out.

Among the SSTOs, only *Arlington* was still firing. And, of course, so was the *Lowell*.

"Hang on," said Rachel, and she switched to the PA. "Brace yourselves, gentlemen. It's about to get rough."

SSTO Arlington Flight Deck. 4:53 A.M.
Three minutes to impact.

The last of the fuel ran out and the engines shut down.

"That's it," said George. There was something terribly final about the silence that now engulfed them. They were indeed bound to the rock, headed presumably for Florida.

A low ridge to starboard exploded, and the pieces flew backward, whipped from sight.

"Atmosphere," said George. Crunch time.

Antonia Mabry, Mission Control. 4:54 A.M.

Feinberg watched the numbers spin across his display. His mind had gone numb and he could do nothing now but wait. Not that it mattered: Events were moving far too fast for analysis, blurring, flowing into a jumbled stream of scattered images and physical forces and sheer terror. Everything depended on whether they'd got enough of the angle and whether the Possum's underbelly was sufficiently flat.

Carpenter sat strapped in his seat. Now that there was no more to be done, he'd withdrawn into some interior space to await the outcome.

Questions, demands for information, crackled over the intercom. The Brits, the Russians, the Japanese, even that impossible woman, what's her name, Tory Clark, sitting safe and secure at Skyport: "Did we do it?" "What's our status?"

"Rainbow, are you still there?"

What's our status?

A low murmur began. Gusts of wind blew up out of nowhere and rocked the *Mabry*. The bulkheads creaked and the storm exploded into a hurricane. Feinberg was thrown violently against his restraints. The cabin tumbled and rolled. Already he could feel the temperature rising.

It went on for almost a full minute before their pilot got the ship under a condition that might pass for control. "We've been blown clear of the rock," she announced over the P.A. As if it weren't obvious.

He waited for his stomach to settle and opened the general channel. "This is Rainbow," he said. "We are evaluating the situation." And he laughed. Roared at his own joke. *Yes, give me two minutes and I will tell you precisely how we are doing.*

The storm continued to hammer at them. Something, a piece of rock, maybe a piece of the ship, rang against the hull.

Skyport, Orbital Lab. 4:55 A.M.

No one dared speak. But Tory watched the Possum descend through sunlight, sinking toward the Atlantic. The ocean was dark and eternal beyond the pools of light that marked the southeastern coast of the U.S.

The rock passed gradually into the night.

She saw one of the ferries, both of the remaining ferries, tumble clear. The rock was still turning on its axis, enveloped in flames. A plume tracked behind it.

The plume glittered in the red light. But its downward curve was leveling off!

An ocean of air had gathered beneath the Possum. Forming a barrier.

The rock was beginning to skid.

Like a pebble skipping across the surface of a pond.

Fiery particles blew away. Some fell down the sky; others soared back into sunlight.

Like the Ranger.

Percival Lowell Utility Deck. 4:56 A.M.

Charlie Haskell couldn't bring himself to watch the images any longer. The *Lowell* was trying to shake itself to pieces and the roar of the engines seemed to have become louder. Rachel was still trying, he thought, still pitting the nuclear fire against the vast dead weight of the Possum, trying to lift it out of the atmosphere, to haul it away from the fragile terrestrial surface.

The glut of voices asking mission control for a status report had faded into background noise. If Feinberg didn't respond in any meaningful way, it could only be because he had no news to give. They had done everything they could, thrown the full weight of the world's fleet into the effort. And it hadn't been enough.

POSIM–38 rumbled across the sky, and Charlie rode with it, he and thirty-odd others, like Slim Pickens in the old movie riding the H-bomb to its target.

Dead.

They were all dead and the world with them.

Charlie was usually inclined to take an optimistic view of events. If on this occasion he'd given up and concluded all was lost, it was easy enough to understand: the *Percival Lowell* was engulfed in flames and shaking itself to pieces, Feinberg was cackling on the command channel, and he was suddenly beginning to feel the tug of gravity after a long period of zero-g.

That the latter fact was a good sign, that it indicated the rock was changing course, never occurred to him. He waited for the killing blow, consoled only by the knowledge he had given his best effort.

At forty-eight hours, his would be the shortest presidency on record, easily eclipsing William Henry Harrison's thirty-one days. He wondered whether he might not also be the last U.S. president. He was considering that doleful possibility when his cell phone trilled. It was a remarkably prosaic sound, cool and mundane amid the chaos. He pulled the instrument out of his pocket. "Haskell," he said, impressed at how good his voice sounded.

"Mr. President." It was Feinberg. "Congratulations. We've done it. It's headed back out."

Charlie felt his pulse throbbing. "You're sure?"

"Yes. I'm sure."

"Thank God," he said.

"It'll take a while to analyze the new orbit. We need to determine whether, and to what degree, the Possum will remain a threat."

"But it's not coming down *today*?"

"No, Mr. President. I can assure you it's not coming down *today*."

Charlie clicked off, closed his eyes, and allowed himself to luxuriate in the moment. He was drenched, and was deliriously happy. And he suddenly realized he was starved.

Rachel's voice broke in. "Good show, Mr. President," she said.

Within minutes Charlie was talking to a global audience, giving them the news. The world began to celebrate in its time-honored fashion: church bells rang, drums beat, fireworks exploded, politicians made speeches. At that moment, Charles L. Haskell could have been elected planetary chief executive, had such a position existed. He knew that his popularity could not fail to carry him to the White House. He also understood that the acclaim would last only until the first recession.

But it was a thought unworthy of the hero of the hour.

Up front, Rachel's comm board had lit up. The entire population of the Earth wanted to talk with him.

The first call he took was from Evelyn.

EPILOGUE

The New White House, Presidential Dining Room.

The dinner had included notables from around the globe, celebrating the first anniversary of what many were now calling the birth of the Space Age, but what President Haskell liked to think of as the long-delayed birth of the Human Family. They'd watched year-old videos of crowds cheering in Paris and Shanghai, Jerusalem and Kansas City, as the Possum sailed across the skies over Florida, trailing fire, and faded at last from human sight.

Not forever, of course. They had a six-year reprieve. Which meant that the nations of the world had no choice but to see Project Skybolt to its conclusion.

The first lady had made it her special responsibility to coordinate the construction of a memorial museum to be dedicated to those who gave their lives in the common effort, to the flight crews of *Copenhagen, Rome, Berlin,* the *Christopher Talley,* to Bigfoot Caparatti and Tony Casaway.

A new world had emerged from the catastrophe. Los Angeles was gone, apparently forever. The lake that formed in the desert regions of central California between the coastal ranges and the eastern peaks was being described by geologists as "temporary," but they were talking in millennial terms. A group of towns was already springing up along its shores.

No one was left unscarred. The drain on national treasuries caused by the destruction forced world leaders into a cooperative effort unlike anything history had seen before. Military forces seemed to have lost, at least for the time being, their ancient function. No one, in the days after the coming of the

Possum, seemed willing to take up arms against a neighbor. The peoples of the world had stood together against a common misfortune, and a new bond may consequently have formed among them, a bond that transcended national and religious identities, that recognized a common vulnerability. Even in Jerusalem, at long last, an accommodation seemed to have been reached.

In its own dark way, the comet may have been a blessing.

The special guests at the White House dinner had been Andrea Bellwether and Tory Clark. The architects of survival, the president had called them, knowing that Rick Hailey would have approved of the phrase. Tory had said the usual things, spread the credit around, looked embarrassed, and sat down to waves of applause. Andrea said only that her father would have been proud.

Feinberg remarked later that history would remember the technique as the Bellwether Maneuver.

Later the president invited both women to a private party in the Kolladner Room, where they passed the evening with Saber, Keith Morley, Chaplain Pinnacle (who with quick thinking had selected Evelyn Hampton to carry the crucial message to the president), Wes Feinberg, Orly Carpenter, Jonathan Porter, and the flight crews of the various vehicles of Project Rainbow. And of course, with the first lady, Evelyn Haskell.

There are plans to make the celebration an annual event. Unfortunately, however, Rachel Quinn and Lee Cochran will be unable to attend next year. They'll be on their way to Mars.